"Frankly, there isn't much Ashley Herring Blake can't write. . . . *Iris Kelly Doesn't Date* is the best book in the Bright Falls series."
—Culturess

"Another immensely satisfying and heartwarming installment in the Bright Falls series. I highly recommend it to anyone who enjoys sapphic romance, fake dating, and stories that feature fabulous friend groups / found families." —The Bookish Libra

BERKLEY TITLES BY ASHLEY HERRING BLAKE

Delilah Green Doesn't Care
Astrid Parker Doesn't Fail
Iris Kelly Doesn't Date
Make the Season Bright

MAKE
the
SEASON
BRIGHT

ASHLEY HERRING BLAKE

Berkley Romance
NEW YORK

BERKLEY ROMANCE
Published by Berkley
An imprint of Penguin Random House LLC
penguinrandomhouse.com

Book design by Daniel Brount

Library of Congress Cataloging-in-Publication Data

Names: Blake, Ashley Herring, author.
Title: Make the season bright / Ashley Herring Blake.
Description: First Edition. | New York: Berkley Romance, 2024.
Identifiers: LCCN 2024010443 (print) | LCCN 2024010444 (ebook) |
ISBN 9780593550595 (trade paperback) | ISBN 9780593637630 (ebook)
Subjects: LCSH: Christmas—Fiction. | LCGFT: Romance fiction. | Novels.
Classification: LCC PS3602.L3413 M35 2024 (print) |
LCC PS3602.L3413 (ebook) | DDC 813/.6—dc23/eng/20240314
LC record available at https://lccn.loc.gov/2024010443
LC ebook record available at https://lccn.loc.gov/2024010444

First Edition: October 2024

Printed in the United States of America
1st Printing

For Meryl, Zabe, Emma, Mary, Christina, and Crash—
the best feral crew a demigirl could ask for

author's note

While *Make the Season Bright* is a joyful romance, please be aware that the story contains alcohol use, mentions of parental neglect, abandonment, and one claustrophobic scene. There are also consensual and explicit sex scenes. Please take care of yourself while reading this story, and always.

MAKE
the
SEASON
BRIGHT

chapter 1

Charlotte Donovan was cursed.

She'd been trying to ignore the signs all day long, but now, three weeks before Christmas, she found herself stuck in a vintage cage elevator between floors four and five having a panic attack, and denial was no longer an option.

Granted, she'd known the truth since she was a kid—December was the month the universe conspired against Charlotte and rained down an amalgam of mishaps, everything from a mundane red wine spill on a white blouse to the disaster five years ago she wouldn't even let herself think about anymore.

Except here she was, clawing at the latticed elevator door of Elle's Upper West Side building, *thinking* about it.

"We'll get you out of there, sweetie. Just stay calm."

This was from Sloane, her colleague at the Manhattan School of Music and cofounder of the Rosalind Quartet, which they'd started together two years ago. Charlotte couldn't see her—well, she could see Sloane's booted feet standing on the fifth floor,

cuffed jeans just above her ankles—but her friend gave off a decidedly relaxed air that made Charlotte want to scream.

"Easy for you to say," Charlotte said, bouncing a little in hopes
the elevator would take the hint and do its goddamn job.

"I don't understand it," Elle said from next to Sloane. Charlotte could also only see their feet, which were covered in socks
featuring tiny cellos and Christmas trees.

How wonderfully festive.

Charlotte's lip curled as she turned her gaze away, looking up
at the elevator's ceiling as if it held a clue to escaping this hell.

"This has never happened before," Elle said.

"Of course it hasn't," Charlotte said through her teeth.

"What do you mean by that?" Sloane asked.

Charlotte exhaled, closed her eyes, tried to breathe through
her frantically pounding heart. For all intents and purposes,
Sloane was her best friend, though Charlotte never thought about
her in those terms exactly. Sloane was definitely a friend. A *good*
friend. They drank nice wine together. Arranged music for their
ensemble, for their students. They'd even cowritten a few original
pieces that had ended up on the quartet's debut album, *Evergreen*,
just released this past October. Charlotte also knew that Sloane's
parents had divorced amicably, and she had an older sister who
lived in Nashville, who, according to Sloane, was the butch lesbian complement to Sloane's femme bisexual style.

Best friends, though?

Charlotte balked at the term, even though she was pretty sure
it was the one Sloane would use. Still, *best* came with expectations, a ride-or-die sort of commitment, and Charlotte hadn't felt
that for anyone in a long time.

Five years to be exact.

Not that she missed that kind of closeness. If anything, its absence was a relief, which was probably why Sloane knew nothing about Charlotte's December curse. Last Christmas was their first in each other's lives, and Charlotte had managed to avoid any and all disasters in Sloane's presence. Clearly, this year, the universe was upping its game.

"Holy shit, *that's* why the elevator isn't working?"

This London accent belonged to Manish Sahni, the fourth member of their quartet—he played viola—who had obviously just arrived on the fifth floor safe and sound via the marble staircase Charlotte had been too tired to take.

Oh, December, you fickle little bitch.

"It's fine, Manish," Sloane said in that tone she used when she was trying to keep Charlotte calm during rehearsals. Charlotte hated that tone, like she had to be managed. *She* was the manager, not the managee, goddammit.

The elevator's walls seemed to close in on her then, as if to say, *Oh, really?* Charlotte hugged her violin case to her chest and whimpered.

"Sweetie, it's okay," Sloane said softly, which only made Charlotte's panic rise like lava inside a brewing volcano. She hadn't meant for that whimper to be audible, but in her defense, she'd been stuck in this cage for a good fifteen minutes, and she was about to lose her shit.

Maybe she should give in, let December win, because it was only the seventh, and the jammed elevator was already the third mishap of the day.

The first misfortune was easy to chalk up to coincidence. It was New York City in December, after all, so when Charlotte had stepped off the curb at the crowded street corner by her apartment early this morning and been promptly jostled so vigorously she'd ended up ankle-deep in a slushy puddle, her tea upturned and mixing with the snow and ice, she'd tried to shake it off. Sure, her brand-new leather boots didn't appreciate the dip, but maybe that was just what she got for wearing them the day after the season's first snowfall, light as it had been.

The second calamity happened hours later, while she was grading finals for her Arranging for Strings class in her office at the Manhattan School of Music. It was the last day of the semester before break, and grades were due by four o'clock that afternoon. Her vision had started to blur, and she realized she hadn't yet had a single drop of caffeine. She got up, calm as could be, exited her office for the small faculty kitchenette down the hall, turned the corner, and was very soon wearing what seemed to be a giant smear of jam all over her black cashmere turtleneck.

"Oh my god, Ms. Donovan, I'm so sorry." Tansy, the String Department's secretary, who changed her hair color weekly and always looked at Charlotte as though Charlotte might unhinge her jaw and devour her at any second, stood there red-faced and purple-haired. "I'm so, so sorry."

"It's fine," Charlotte said tightly, the *right* thing to say, her arms held out to avoid spreading the mess.

Tansy looked like she might cry, and Charlotte fought a long-suffering sigh. Instead, she forced a smile and chose to focus on the pleasant aroma of what smelled like raspberry-pepper jam currently mottling her sweater.

The secretary handed Charlotte her napkin, then retrieved her toasted bagel from the floor, and that was that. It was just a sweater, and Charlotte moved on with her day. She changed into a spare black blouse she kept in her office and surged forward, marked finals, went over her arrangements for the quartet's rehearsal that evening. A normal Thursday if ever there was one.

At least that's what she told herself.

At five o'clock, she turned off her computer, packed up her violin, put on her black peacoat, and tugged a black knit hat over her long salt-and-pepper hair. She headed out into the cold evening, the Upper West Side already bustling with holiday energy—lights framed shop windows, garland curled around lampposts, and there was a group of young carolers just outside Sakura Park—all of which she tried to ignore. She walked with her head down, her violin tucked like a treasure under her arm. She watched her feet, making sure she avoided anything that could potentially trip her, cover her in something sticky, or damage her person in any way.

When she made it to Elle's building on Central Park West, she smiled to herself as she rang the bell, a silly kind of triumph swelling in her chest.

"Come on up!" Elle's voice trilled from the box.

Elle lived alone on the top floor of a historic Upper West Side building called the Elora. Their grandmother, Mimi, the only family member Elle still had a relationship with and who was an actual actress in LA during the latter years of the Golden Age of Hollywood, had owned the large, sparsely furnished apartment since the 1960s but lived in LA full-time, as she hated the cold eastern winters in New York. In her absence, Elle was more than happy to take care of the apartment, a corner of which made the perfect rehearsal space for the Rosalind Quartet.

A buzzer sounded, and Charlotte stepped into the marble-floored foyer, a vast space that sported an ornate chandelier, a set of marble stairs, and one of those vintage cage elevators with a gate you had to pull shut yourself.

It was beautiful and glamorous, and Charlotte always felt like she was stepping into another era when she was inside. And now here she was, trapped—not in some glitzy age of stardom but in purgatory.

"Okay, my super is calling the fire department," Elle said now.

"Seriously?" Sloane said. "He can't fix it?"

"I don't think he's all that handy."

"He's the *super*."

"Not so super at fixing shit, apparently," Manish said.

Their feet shifted around at Charlotte's eye level, but she tuned them out. She was going to be here forever. She lived here now. Just send down some bread and water and she'd make it through somehow. Christmas in the Elora's elevator—not all that much worse than her actual plans, which consisted of DoorDash and triple-checking the itinerary for the quartet's European tour their manager, Mirian, had just sent over that morning. One whole month starting in London on December 29, complete with guest lecturer events at the Royal College of Music and the Conservatoire de Paris. It was everything Charlotte had been working toward her entire life—international reach for her edgy interpretations of classics, her original compositions, a chance to prove that Charlotte Donovan was a force in the music world, that everything she'd given up had been worth it.

Every*one* she'd given up.

A flash of white in her mind.

White everywhere—an intimate space with white twinkle lights lining every crease and curve, white flowers garnished with red winter berries, the crispness of her white suit as she waited . . . and waited . . . and waited . . .

Fuck. She pressed her fingers to her temples before yelling, "Get me the hell out of here!" Desperation clung to her voice, and she hated it, but she couldn't change it either. She pressed her back against the far wall, closed her eyes, and waited . . . and waited . . . and waited . . .

Two hours later, Charlotte spilled out of the elevator and into Sloane's arms. She tried to hold it together. She really did, but she clung to her friend like a kid, pushed to the absolute brink with zero ways to manage herself.

Still, she didn't cry. She wasn't a crier. Hadn't even cried when she'd been left at the altar five years ago. Not right away, at least, and certainly not in front of anyone. No, that lovely response waited until two days later, when the manager at the hotel in Paris had called to see why she and her wife had not yet checked in to their honeymoon suite. Even then, she hadn't let the tears spill over, but had squeezed them back where they belonged. In the years since, she'd learned coping mechanisms for when her moods went dark or stress tugged her edges a bit too taut. But December was always a tricky month to navigate, and the elevator . . . well, it was hard to hold everything in check when stuck in a four-by-four square of wood and metal.

"Sweetie, it's okay," Sloane said, freezing for a second but then pulling Charlotte close. "It's over. You're out." She held Charlotte tightly, and Charlotte allowed herself to be comforted.

Just for a second.

Finally, she pulled back, rolled her shoulders straight, and took a breath. "I'm fine. It was fine."

"Fine?" Manish said, holding a glass of red wine, his black hair messy, as though he'd run his hands through it over and over. "I nearly had a nervous breakdown."

Elle patted him on the shoulder, their short, pale-pink locks swooping over one eye. "Yeah, Manny, real tough for you, buddy, what with the couch you sat on for the last ninety minutes and the whole bottle of wine you went through."

Manish sent a brown hand through his hair again, then took another sip. "Half, at most."

"*Bottle* of wine?" Charlotte said, her limbs still trembling a little. "Manish, we have rehearsal."

"I said half!"

Sloane ignored him and folded her light-brown arms. "Honey, I think we can skip that for tonight."

"What?" Charlotte said. "Absolutely not."

"Char," said Elle, who loved to shorten everyone's name, whether they liked it or not, "how about a glass of wine?"

"If Manish left you any," Sloane said. Manish flipped her off.

"I don't drink when we're playing," Charlotte said tightly. She was out of the elevator, but the panic remained, this feeling that she was slipping, losing control. She never let herself get to this state. Usually, she just spent the month of December hibernating in her apartment and trying not to regret turning down the invitations she'd received back in September to join a symphony's holiday concert lineup.

She didn't play Christmas music.

Hardly played in December at all, lest disaster strike. Her violin alone was nearly irreplaceable, and if anything were to ever befall her hands, wrists, or fingers . . . well, needless to say, very little was worth that risk. But this year, with the tour coming up and their album just released, she'd had no choice. The quartet had completed a small New England tour over fall break in October and played a number of smaller venues here in New York, all to packed houses. So far, she'd managed to avoid major performances in December, but that didn't negate the need to rehearse.

"I know," Elle said, "but maybe a few sips will take the edge off?"

Charlotte shook her head and brushed past her colleagues toward Elle's apartment. Inside, she went straight for the northwest corner, where four mismatched chairs sat facing one another, a rainbow of color, and promptly set her violin case down on her usual lilac-hued seat.

She opened her case, taking out Rosalind, her violin, so named for Rosalind in Shakespeare's *As You Like It*. A woman who adapted, who did whatever she had to do to get what she wanted, what she needed. She'd always been Charlotte's favorite Shakespearean heroine, thus the inspiration for her violin's name. She'd had this violin for seven years, since *before*, and it had seen her through some very low and dark times, her one constant. When she and Sloane met two years ago and started throwing ideas around for a quartet, Rosalind seemed like the perfect name for an all-queer group that took classic string pieces and twisted them just so, creating something new and powerful, something unexpected.

Now she breathed easier just setting her hands on Rosalind's neck, feeling the strings under her fingers. Granted, her fingers still trembled a bit, but that would stop as soon as she started playing.

"Charlotte," Sloane said firmly, coming up next to her and eyeing her shaking hands. "Just sit down for a sec."

Charlotte shook her head. "I can beat this."

Sloane frowned, glanced at Manish, who shrugged. "Beat what?"

"December," Charlotte said. "This whole season. I've done it all my life and—" She cut herself off, pressing her eyes closed for a beat before lifting her violin to her shoulder, more to keep her own mouth shut than anything. She didn't talk about the curse. Never had . . .

Except with one person.

She zipped her bow over the strings, then adjusted the fine tuners until all four strings sounded perfect.

"What are you talking about?" Sloane asked.

"Nothing," Charlotte said, forcing a smile. "Let's just play, yeah?" She turned around to beam her commanding smile at Manish and Elle as well, only to find the other two members sitting on Elle's giant turquoise sectional, glasses of wine in their hands. "What are you doing?"

Sloane tilted her head, curls bouncing into her face. "Protesting."

"Protest—what?" Charlotte let down her violin and met Sloane's eyes. "Seriously?"

"Seriously," Elle said, crisscrossing their jean-clad legs and patting the spot next to them on the couch. "What Slo said."

"We're not playing a note, love," Manish said, "until you sit down and take a bloody breath."

Charlotte felt her shoulders drop in defeat. It wasn't often that her group rebelled against her—after all, her single-minded ambition had gotten them pretty far—but on the rare occasion they bucked her orders, she knew there was no moving them.

The only way out was through.

"Fine," she said, all but stomping over to the couch and sitting on the edge next to Elle, violin propped primly on her knee. "Fine, see? I'm breathing." She made a show of taking several deep breaths, all of which resulted in a sense of dizziness rather than calmness.

"Oh, yes, very convincing," Sloane said, sitting down on Charlotte's other side and pouring them both a glass of wine from the open bottle on the tufted lavender ottoman. Elle, agender and pansexual, was very into pastels. There was even a pink

Christmas tree in the corner, complete with colorful lights and sparkly silver garland.

Charlotte took a single sip of wine. It was the only way she'd get out of this intervention and back to work.

"Okay," Sloane said, tucking her legs underneath her, "no shop talk for a full fifteen minutes."

"What?" Charlotte said. "Preposterous."

Sloane just lifted a brow.

Charlotte sighed. "Ten."

"Twelve."

"Fine," Charlotte said, knowing Sloane was just as stubborn as she was.

Sloane lifted her glass as if in a toast, then held it there until Charlotte set her violin next to her and clinked her own glass against Sloane's.

"Great," Sloane said after taking a deal-sealing sip. "So. What's everyone doing for Christmas?"

Charlotte resisted a groan but was pleasantly surprised when Manish and Elle both released their own disgruntled noises.

"Don't ask," Manish said, gulping back more wine.

"You and Nate aren't—" Charlotte started, then stopped. She couldn't remember if Manish and Nate—his on-again, off-again boyfriend for the last year—were currently together. She didn't usually try very hard to keep up. As long as Manish did his job with the quartet, she didn't pry.

"We are not," Manish said, clicking his teeth together hard on the final *t*. "He's going home to Maine."

"I didn't think people actually lived in Maine," Elle said.

"He didn't invite you to join him?" Sloane asked.

"Nope," Manish said, popping the *p* this time.

"Ouch," Sloane said.

"Yeah," Manish said. "So I'll be spending Christmas on my parents' couch in Ithaca eating chocolate-covered pretzels while my brother and his perfect English wife coo and sing to her pregnant belly, and my mum most likely invites every South Asian gay man with whom she's ever crossed paths over for dinner."

"At least you have a place to go," Elle said. "Mimi is taking a cruise with her new boyfriend, which leaves me here singing Christmas carols with my DoorDasher."

"Oh, honey," Sloane said, sitting up and frowning at Elle. "You can't do that."

"It's fine," Elle said, but Charlotte got a familiar lump in her throat. Elle's parents lived in Illinois and were extremely conservative. They'd never quite accepted Elle's queerness, and Elle had left home at the age of seventeen, moving to LA to live with Mimi, their liberal grandmother. They still spoke to their parents, but rarely, and they'd never spent a major holiday with them, at least as far as Charlotte knew.

"No one should spend Christmas alone," Sloane said, still looking at Elle like someone had just run over their cat.

Elle laughed. "Slo, it's fine. I'm used to it."

"Same here," Charlotte said.

Three pairs of eyes swung toward her. She hadn't meant to say it. She'd never really shared the intricacies of her family life with the quartet, and she certainly hadn't shared why she hated December so much.

"What do you mean?" Sloane said, her eyes wide.

Charlotte took another sip of wine to steady herself. "Nothing. Just . . . Christmas is no big deal to me. Just another day."

Yet even as she said it, her throat thickened. Her body did that sometimes, rebelling and forcing her to feel something she'd really rather not.

"What do you usually do?" Sloane asked.

Charlotte shook her head. "Nothing."

"Wait, wait, wait," Elle said, turning on the couch so they were facing Charlotte. "Nothing?"

Charlotte sighed, looked down at her lap. While Charlotte didn't have a bigot for a mother, she, too, spent most holidays alone. Anna Donovan was a successful thriller novelist who liked to keep to herself and had never wanted kids. When she ended up pregnant at the age of thirty-five—the result of a one-night stand during a book tour—she thought raising a human might be a fun adventure. Something new. Needless to say, the ways in which baby Charlotte fucked up Anna's life were unexpected and unwelcome. Anna took care of Charlotte, provided for her and paid for violin lessons and music camps, but she was never really *there*. From a young age, Charlotte had always had the sense she was in the way. Her mother was constantly writing, churning out two to three books a year, had had a couple of movies made from her bestsellers, and involved Charlotte in very little of any of it.

Christmases were cold and lonely affairs, usually highlighted by a wad of cash from her mother and watching *Meet Me in St. Louis* by herself in the dark, trying her best not to think too hard about the fact that December always brought with it an irremovable stain on her favorite shirt, a couple of failing grades among her usual straight As, a few slips into muddy puddles during her walk to school. She hated December, hated that it was filled with joy and lights and love for everyone, it seemed, but her.

And then, when she was twelve years old, the Fairbrook family moved to Charlotte's Grand Haven neighborhood on Lake Michigan, right next door. They were a close crew—mother, father, and daughter Brighton, who was exactly Charlotte's age—and Charlotte felt seen for the first time in her life.

Seen and heard and loved.

From then on, almost every holiday—every Christmas, every birthday—was spent with the Fairbrooks. The Fairbrooks loved Christmas, went all out in every possible way, their house bedazzled with lights, their kitchen always filled with something sweet and warm. And for ten years, Charlotte thought she'd finally beaten the December curse.

It made complete sense that Brighton had wanted a Christmas wedding. And Charlotte had wanted to give Bright anything she wanted.

Forever.

Except forever had turned into never, and now here Charlotte sat, five years later, more Christmas cursed than ever and trying to avoid confessing just how sad her life actually was to her fellow musicians.

"I'm just not a fan of Christmas," she said. "I never really . . . for the past several years, I just . . ."

"What about your family?" Manish asked, and Sloane and Elle leaned forward a little, their curiosity piqued.

"I don't really have a family," Charlotte said firmly, trying to keep any and all emotion out of her voice. It was more or less true. Anna had emailed last week, sure, but just as part of her monthly "check-in," something Charlotte felt her mother did to avoid being a completely horrible human being. The emails were usually filled with news of her latest book, a benign question or two about Charlotte's music.

"You . . . you what?" Sloane said, pressing her hand to her chest.

Clearly, Charlotte was going about this all wrong, digging herself deeper and deeper into Sloane's sympathies.

"No, I do have one," Charlotte said. "But Anna—my mom—and I don't really . . ."

Really what? Get along? They didn't interact enough for even that to be true, particularly after everything with Brighton went to hell. Charlotte hadn't been back to Michigan since.

"Hold up," Elle said, holding out a hand. "Anna . . . Donovan? The author?"

"Yeah," Charlotte said slowly. "You've heard of her?"

"Heard of her?" Elle said. "Fuck, I love her books."

"Wait, she's that thriller writer, right?" Manish said. "Her book *The Wives* was just made into a movie, yeah? Came out last year?"

Charlotte nodded.

"Your mother wrote *The Wives*?" Sloane asked, her eyes a little glassy with hurt. "How . . . how did I not know this?"

Charlotte opened her mouth, then closed it again. She had no clue what to say. *Because I never tell anyone anything* didn't really feel appropriate, though that was, essentially, the reason. Charlotte was painfully aware that her story—her past, her mother, her engagement to her childhood best friend that ended in the worst way imaginable—wasn't exactly happy. She'd rather not dwell on it. She was a successful violinist. She was known because of her talent. Her mind. Her skill. Why couldn't everyone simply focus on the now and move the hell on?

"I'm sorry," Charlotte finally said. She didn't want to hurt Sloane, didn't want to hurt any of them. She just wanted to live her sad little life, thanks very much.

Sloane shook her head, eyes on her lap. Awkward silence reigned for a few seconds, Manish and Elle widening their eyes at each other meaningfully, Charlotte's fingertips going white on her glass.

Finally, Sloane sat up straight, knocked back the rest of her wine, and all but slammed the stemless glass onto the ottoman. "You know what? No. This is not how you three are spending Christmas. I fucking refuse."

She stood up and dug her phone out of her back pocket. "You're all coming home with me."

A shocked quiet hung in the air while Sloane tapped on her phone's screen with enough vehemence to crack the glass.

"Wait, what?" Elle finally asked.

"Um, seconded," Manish said.

Charlotte just sipped her wine, because surely "all" did not include her.

"You heard me," Sloane said, still tapping away.

"To Colorado?" Elle said.

"Clarification: to Bumfuck Nowhere, Colorado," Manish said.

Sloane finally glanced up, a slight smile breaking through her determined expression. "Winter River."

"Same thing," Manish said, pouring more wine.

"It's actually really lovely at Christmastime," Sloane said, her voice taking on a dreamy quality. "Our town square has this huge tree—the biggest one west of the Mississippi—and there's music and skiing and lights and food. Plus, my mom owns a bakery, been in our family for generations, so there's always something buttery and sugary around. There's even this horrific event they have every year called Two Turtledoves, which is basically a series of holidates for single people to get drunk and hook up. Everything culminates the day after Christmas with an open mic at a bar for people to declare their love . . . or lust, as the case may be."

"I mean," Manish said, "that doesn't sound awful."

"Shut your mouth," Sloane said. She leaned forward and whispered, "My mother will hear you."

"Come on, Two Turtledoves?" Elle said. "That's fucking cute."

Sloane shook her head. "Forget I mentioned it. My point is that Winter River is Christmassy and homey and my mom is the best cook in the entire world. Plus, my dad and his wife just renovated her family's ski lodge in the next town over. My sister and I always spend a night or two over there—ski all day, cozy up by the fire at night. It's magical."

"Sounds fake. Like a Hallmark movie," Elle said.

Sounds like a Fairbrook Christmas, Charlotte thought. She swallowed, looked out the window at the twilit city.

Sloane laughed. "Exactly. Except with more queer people and extremely liberal politics."

Manish pressed a hand to his chest. "Such a winter wonderland does not exist."

Sloane lifted one brow. "I dare you to prove that."

Manish twisted up his mouth, eyes narrowed. Manish loved dares—reveled in them, concocted them all the time for the quartet. One night this past April, they'd ended up playing in the middle of the Brooklyn Bridge at ten o'clock, the result of a bet between him and Elle as to how much money they could make busking. Charlotte had tried to squash this tendency in Manish when he first joined their quartet, but she'd learned it was best to just ride the wave—they got back to work quicker that way.

"Oh, challenge accepted," he said. "I've got the miles for a plane ticket and a fierce need for a cheery, queery Christmas."

Even Charlotte had to crack a smile at that one.

"A cheery, queery Berry Christmas," Elle said, adding Sloane's last name. "But, Slo, is there room for all of us?"

"Totally. We might have to share rooms, but my mom says the more, the merrier," Sloane said, tapping away at her phone. "So we're all set. Elle?"

Elle ran a pale hand through their hair. "Yeah. Sure. Not like I've got anything better to do."

"Yes!" Sloane said, pumping her fist into the air. "Plus, with you all there, the less my mother will harass me about my perpetually single status."

"No, but I might," Manish said. Elle elbowed him in the ribs.

"Wonderful," Charlotte said, standing up. "It's settled. You all will have a lovely time, I'm sure. Now can we please get back to rehearsal?"

Sloane's smile vanished, quickly replaced with that take-no-shit look she got on her face whenever Charlotte got really grouchy. "Oh no. There is no *you all*. There is only *we*." She circled her finger around to include all four of them.

Charlotte blinked. "I'm not—"

"Yes, you fucking are," Sloane said.

"Sloane, I don't do Christmas. You saw what happened in that elevator. And we've still got three weeks to go."

"What the hell are you talking about?" Sloane said.

Charlotte pressed her eyes closed. She couldn't say she was *cursed*. They'd think she'd gone truly bananas. "Nothing. I just . . . I'm fine here. I promise."

"You are not. You're coming home with me, or I'm not playing another note until our first concert in London."

Charlotte's stomach plummeted. "You're seriously going to manipulate me into spending Christmas with you?"

Sloane just folded her arms. "It's for your own good."

"Agreed," Manish said, then waved a hand around Charlotte's form. "You're like Elizabeth Scrooge over here."

"Ebenezer," Charlotte said.

"Exactly," Manish said, sipping on his wine.

Charlotte looked to Elle for help, always the sweet one of the group, the peacemaker.

Elle just winced. "Sorry, Char, but they're right. I really think you should come."

"This is ridiculously unfair," Charlotte said.

"Think of it this way," Sloane said, standing and setting her hands on Charlotte's shoulders. "The two weeks off I was taking so I could go home for Christmas? Well . . . now you get it all back."

And that did it. Sloane knew it, they all knew it. If Charlotte went to Colorado, they'd all be together. Sure, maybe she'd have to engage in some Christmas cookie baking and sing a few carols, and she'd definitely have to avoid accident-prone situations— skiing? Absolutely not. But she'd get to rehearse for the tour. She'd get to work, and her work had always saved her in the past.

"Fine," she said. "Now can we please play a fucking concerto?"

chapter 2

Brighton Fairbrook wiped down the lacquered bar, glaring as that night's live musician crooned a twangy version of "Silver Bells" into the tiny stage's microphone. The singer wore a jean skirt and cowboy boots and had long strawberry-blond hair, her pale fingers plucking deftly at her Taylor guitar—a three-hundred series by the looks of it—while she sang about city sidewalks.

"She's not bad, huh?" Adele said, nudging Brighton's shoulder. Adele folded her brown arms, the sleeves of her button-up rolled to the elbow, a deep-green vest cutting the perfect fit, just like always. Her dark braids fell over her shoulders, black glasses perched on her nose as she listened to the act she herself had booked. Adele was Brighton's boss, owner of Ampersand—the bar where Brighton worked—and her only friend in this godforsaken city.

"Mesmerizing," Brighton said flatly, nodding at a customer lifting their empty gin-and-tonic glass for another.

"Oh, come on," Adele said. "She's good."

"And hot," Brighton said, grabbing a new bottle of Beefeater gin from the amber-lit shelves behind the bar.

Adele smirked. "Aren't they all?"

Brighton had to laugh. Adele, a passionate lesbian, had yet to meet a woman she didn't appreciate. Although, wisely, she never "slept with the talent," as she put it—the myriad singer-songwriters who came through here each month, searching for any stage that would have them and a willing audience. This was Nashville—stages abounded, as did audiences, but finding listeners who actually gave two shits . . . well, that was the real challenge. Everyone was a musician here, which meant everyone was good, everyone was competition, and no one was ever, ever impressed.

Brighton placed a fresh gin and tonic in front of her customer, telling herself she was glad to be free of Nashville's hamster wheel. She was glad to have steady work and decent tips at Ampersand. She was glad she didn't have to constantly restring her guitar, worry about humidity and the wood of her own Taylor getting warped. Didn't have to chase gigs, email bookers who would never email her back, and spend hours every night pouring out her heart and soul and blood into her songwriting notebook, only to be told she wasn't good enough, didn't have what it took, and face betrayal by the very fuckers she'd brought together as a band in the first place.

"You've got that look on your face again," Adele said. She was now sitting on a stool at the corner of the bar, the light from her iPad a blue glow reflecting on her glasses.

"What look?" Brighton said, slapping down a towel and wiping at a spot that wasn't even dirty.

"That look that means you don't give a shit about tips."

Brighton lifted a brow. "Are you telling me to *smile*?"

"I would never. But maybe, you know, try to at least look like you're not out for blood."

Adele had a point. Brighton was just barely making ends meet with her tips as it was—she couldn't afford to be grumpy. Her roommate, Leah, had been pretty flexible on the rent lately, but it came with caveats. Last week, Brighton had found herself at an ornament exchange party for the singles group at Leah's church. After being late with the rent three months in a row, Brighton hadn't felt like she could say no to the invite, so she'd ended up with a plastic Christmas pickle ornament and fake smiling for an hour at a guy in khakis and boat shoes while he talked about the album he had just released, a folked-up version of sacred Christmas music, because of-fucking-course he was a musician too.

Leah had asked her about Boat Shoes for the next three days, but Brighton couldn't even remember his face, to be honest. Brighton liked cis men sometimes, but it took a lot to catch her attention, and Boat Shoes had done nothing but bore her, despite Leah's insistence he was *the greatest guy*. Leah was twenty-four and a conservative Christian, a tiny detail she'd neglected to include in her Craigslist ad for a roommate six months ago. The resulting partnership had made for an interesting living situation, considering Brighton was not only agnostic but also very, very queer.

Suffice it to say, Brighton was desperate to make the rent on time this month. Leah was perfectly nice, but whenever Brighton got roped into some church event, she ended up stuck in a conversation that was, essentially, some version of "hate the sin, love the sinner," and Brighton preferred to leave the word *sin* out of her identity altogether.

So she put on a smile and fluffed her dark bangs until they fell over her forehead just so. At least she'd get out of this town in a few days, heading home to Michigan for Christmas. Brighton couldn't wait. She wanted her mom's cinnamon hot chocolate and her family's traditional lineup of Christmas movies playing every night, always starting with *Home Alone*. She wanted to walk along Lake Michigan's snowy shore, icy waves locked in midcrest so that the whole world looked like another planet.

She and Lola used to—

She froze midstir of a dirty martini, shook her head to clear it. She and Lola . . . there was no she and Lola. Not anymore. Not for five years now, but Lola still crept into so many of her memories, like a habit, especially at Christmastime. Five years was nothing compared with the ten before that. Still, Lola might as well be a ghost, might as well not even exist at all, and Brighton didn't care to think too deeply about why.

About how it was all her fault.

She plopped an olive into the drink and handed it over to a girl with brown curls and green eyes. Their fingers brushed, just for a second. The girl smiled, her gaze slipping down from Brighton's own dark eyes and pale face to the black-and-gray tattoo of the Moon tarot card surrounded by peonies on her upper right arm.

"I love that," the girl said, eyes back on Brighton's.

"Thank you," Brighton said, feeling her cheeks warm, and rested her forearms on the bar. She rightly sucked at dating, but hookups she could do. She looked at the girl through her lashes, smiled with one corner of her mouth. "It's—"

But she froze as the musician onstage shifted from "Silver Bells" to a song that most definitely was *not* a Christmas tune, the familiar, catchy melody like a splash of ice water in Brighton's face.

Rain is gone and I'm feeling light
Your ripped jeans like silk and wine
Cherry lipstick still on my mind
Can't blame me, darling, I'm back in line

Brighton closed her eyes, tried to block out the lyrics she'd heard on *Saturday Night Live* a month ago and now couldn't seem to escape, even sitting in her own bar. The song, "Cherry Lipstick," was everywhere—Instagram, TikTok, YouTube, Spotify, covered at least twice a week in Ampersand. In the last six months, the band, a trio of queer women called the Katies, had rocketed from near nothingness to the hottest thing to hit millennial and Gen Z ears since Halsey.

To most people, "Cherry Lipstick" was just a song—a damn good indie pop song that many a gal would probably attach to their queer awakening, but a song nonetheless—and the Katies were just a band finding some success. Good on them. So this ubiquitous song playing in all corners of the world was fine and dandy . . . except for the fact that a mere nine months ago, Brighton had been the Katies' lead singer.

And now she most definitely was not.

The singer arrived at the chorus, belting out the lyrics with such gusto, Brighton was positive the woman was in the middle of her own awakening.

"Oh, I love this song." The girl was still standing in front of Brighton, martini in hand. "Don't you?"

"Ah, Christ," Adele said under her breath. "Here we go."

Brighton glared at her friend, then turned a saccharine smile on the girl. "It's a fucking masterpiece."

At Brighton's tone, the girl's smile dimmed, and she drifted away toward her friends. Just as well. Brighton was clearly in no mood to be accommodating, and anyone who loved "Cherry Lipstick" was bound to be horrible in bed. Granted, Brighton knew her logic there made absolutely zero sense, but it made her feel better in the moment, so she went with it.

"Isn't it time for your break?" Adele asked.

Brighton sighed, pressed her fingers into her eyes. "Yeah."

"Then by all means." Adele waved her hand toward the back room, but her expression was soft. Adele knew all about the Katies and Brighton, knew the whole affair was still an open wound. Knew Brighton hadn't touched her guitar or sung a single note since Alice and Emily's betrayal nine months ago.

Adele reached over and squeezed Brighton's hand, then gave her shoulder a little shove. "Go. Jake's got this."

Brighton obeyed, nodding to Jake, the other evening bartender, before pouring herself a large glass of water. She disappeared into the back, passing through the bustling kitchen, fry cooks dipping Monte Cristos into vats of oil, until she reached Adele's office. The song followed after her like a ghost.

I can't, I can't forget the taste
Your cherry lips, your swaying hips . . .

She gulped her water, then set the empty glass on Adele's desk and kept moving, passing by the big leather couch on her way to the back door. She burst outside into the cold December air, breathing it into her lungs like a new form of oxygen. She leaned against the building's red brick and closed her eyes, which were starting to feel tight and watery. On Demonbreun Street, she could hear the bustle of the Saturday night crowd—laughter, more live music, all the sounds she used to love.

The sounds she used to be a part of.

Because she clearly loved being miserable, Brighton took out her phone and opened up the Katies' Instagram page. Three hundred and ninety-three thousand followers. And counting, no doubt. Emily's dark curls haloed around her lovely face, falling nearly to her shoulders. She favored crop tops and plaid pants, and Brighton even spotted the pink-and-green pair Brighton herself had found at that thrift store in the Gulch last winter. Alice was brooding, as always. A tiny, dark-haired pixie with huge butch energy.

Brighton and Emily had first met at a restaurant in Green Hills where Brighton had gotten a job as a server when she first moved to Nashville five years ago. They bonded quickly over music, melancholy queers like Phoebe Bridgers and Brandi Carlile. They started playing together on their days off, messing around on Brighton's guitar and Emily's keyboard in Emily's tiny East Nashville apartment that she shared with three roommates, but they soon began writing. Lyrics turned into whole songs, which turned into small gigs at coffee shops, just to try it out.

That was how they met Alice.

They'd just finished playing a late-afternoon set at J&J's, a quirky coffee shop–slash–convenience store on Broadway that also hosted live music, and Alice walked up to them afterward, declaring they needed a drummer.

"And you're just such a drummer?" Emily had asked.

Alice had grinned. "I sure as hell am."

And she was—brilliant and passionate and driven. Soon the three of them were sharing an apartment in Germantown, and when they discovered they all shared the same middle name, same spelling and everything—Katherine—the Katies were born.

That was four years ago. Four years of struggle, gigs that paid nothing, tiny regional tours to audiences of ten or less. Still, it was everything Brighton had ever wanted. Being in this band, part of something that she'd made, something that felt like *her*, had been worth it all. Emily and Alice had been a lifeline during a time when she was sure she'd ruined her life, ruined every good thing she'd ever had. They'd reminded her that she still had *herself*. Still had what it took to create and perform. At least she'd thought so at the time, when those dreams were still possible. Still alive.

Now Brighton couldn't help but smile at a photo of Alice smirking at a topless Emily, Emily's bare back to the viewer. The two of them had always had chemistry, though they'd never officially gotten together. Brighton wondered if they were now, this silly photo evidence that they might have taken the leap.

Then she read the post's caption—a shoot for *NME* magazine.

And on Emily's other side, there she was.

Sylvie.

Even her name sounded musical. Red hair like a Siren, feathery bangs like a rock star. Emily and Alice had discovered her in some bar in East Nashville nearly a year ago, when Brighton had been home for Christmas. Emily had wanted to bring her into the group as another singer and songwriter, a suggestion Brighton did not take very well. The three of them had been clashing on their sound at the time—Emily and Alice wanted to go more King Princess–style pop, while Brighton clung to angsty folk-rock as her inspiration.

Sylvie, of course, was pop all the way, funky and fresh and sexy as hell. Even Brighton could admit that. Then, this past March, it had all come to a head when Emily invited Sylvie to a Katies practice without even running it by Brighton first. Sylvie played one of her own songs on her guitar—"Cherry Lipstick"—and

Brighton hated it. Said as much, which Sylvie took with an annoying amount of grace.

"This is the direction we're going, Brighton," Emily had said. "If you don't like it, maybe this isn't the best fit for you anymore."

Brighton had left rehearsal before she really started crying, then went home to Michigan for a week, figuring everyone would calm down with some time off. But the day before she flew back, Emily had called her, told her she was out.

And that was it.

Nearly four years of friendship and struggle and creative work finished in a single phone call, all for a redhead with a talent for writing bops.

Brighton knew she should swipe out of Instagram—her own account was currently set to private with all of 120 followers, so there were no notifications for her to check. For Brighton, social media was now nothing more than a catalog of her failures, everything she was missing out on. Still, she couldn't help but type another name into the search bar, another account she didn't dare follow but couldn't seem to leave alone either.

@ROSALINDQUARTET

The grid was much different than the Katies'—muted colors and the deep wood of stringed instruments, four beautiful, very clearly queer musicians in the throes of their art in various auditoriums and theaters.

One woman in particular drew Brighton's eye, always did. Salt-and-pepper hair and gorgeous, quintessential red lipstick, black attire. Lola's style never changed, not that Brighton ever expected it to. Lola had started going gray at twenty-one, and Brighton was glad to see she'd just let her hair silver, never once dyeing it, as far as Brighton could tell. It looked beautiful—regal and ethereal, just like Lola.

"What the hell are you doing out here?" Adele's voice piped up from behind her. Brighton clicked her phone dark. Adele knew about Lola . . . Well, she knew that Brighton had been engaged and it hadn't worked out, but that was about it. Brighton left out the smaller story points, including Lola's name and the fact that she was pretty much a world-famous violinist now. She was simply known to Adele as *the fiancée*, like some mythical creature who only existed in legend. Brighton left all the finer details—as well as the particulars surrounding her and Lola's disastrous wedding day—to her own torturous musings.

"Just getting some air," she said to Adele now.

"It's freezing," Adele said, rubbing her arms.

Brighton nodded, goose bumps texturing her own bare arms. She hadn't even noticed, honestly. Too busy being a sad sack.

"Hey," Adele said, nudging her shoulder, "do you need to go home?"

"Do you want me to?" Brighton asked. God, she really was a sad sack—her own boss was pretty much begging her not to work.

Adele pressed her mouth flat. "You've got to move on at some point, baby girl."

She said it so softly, so gently, Brighton nearly started crying right there. Trouble was, she felt like she'd been *moving on* for the last five years, and she hadn't gotten anywhere.

Before she could say anything else, her phone vibrated in her hand with a call. Only one person ever called her, so her heart already felt ten times lighter when she saw *Mom* flashing across the screen.

"Mama, hey," she said, her throat thickening as she pressed

the phone to her ear. *Mama* only slipped out when she was feeling really sorry for herself.

Adele gestured to the door, but Brighton shook her head, grabbed onto Adele's arm. She didn't want to stand out here alone anymore, even with her mom on the phone.

"Hi, darling," her mother said. "I've got Dad on the line here too. You're on speaker!"

"Hey, Rainbow," her dad said, employing the name he had used for her ever since she was four and latched on to a Rainbow Brite doll. The nickname became even more fitting when she came out as bisexual when she was thirteen. "How are you?"

"I'm good," she said, her voice nearly fluorescent. Adele rolled her eyes. "Can't wait to be home in a few days." She stuck her tongue out at Adele.

"Oh, honey," her mom said. "I know. That's actually why we're calling."

Brighton's back snapped straight, all her senses on alert. Her mom's tone had gone a bit too sweet, almost songlike, the way it always did when she had to deliver bad news.

"What's wrong?" Brighton asked. "Are you both okay? Is Grandma all right?"

"Fine, Rainbow," her dad said. "Everyone's fine. Fit as fiddles."

Brighton exhaled. "Okay. Then . . . ?"

Her parents were quiet for a second before her mom said it all in one rushed breath. "The magazine is sending me to Provence to review a new winery, so your dad and I are going to be in France for the rest of the year. I'm so sorry, baby."

It took Brighton a second to register her mother's words. But when they hit, they hit hard. "What?" was all she could get out, her voice a pathetic squeak.

"I know," her mom said. "The timing is so horrible, but the

magazine just landed a spot at the winery's opening, and we're the only American publication invited, so it's a pretty huge deal."

Brighton felt dizzy and slid down the wall a bit more. The rough brick scratched her back, and Adele grabbed her arm.

"You okay?" Adele mouthed.

Brighton couldn't answer. Didn't *know* the answer. Her mom had been the head chef at Simone's, a fancy restaurant in Grand Haven, for all of Brighton's childhood. Four years ago, she retired—arthritis making it too hard for her to continue working in a kitchen—and started writing for *Food & Wine* magazine, traveling the country and reviewing restaurants and bistros. She loved it, and Brighton knew going to France to do nothing but eat and drink wine and write about all the eating and drinking was a dream come true for her.

"That's great," she managed to say.

"I wish we could bring you with us, honey," her mom said. "I asked the magazine, but—"

"No, it's okay," Brighton said carefully. "It's fine. I'll be fine." Her brain whirled, trying to think just how she'd be *fine*. Her only grandmother lived in Florida, near her mom's oldest sister, Brighton's aunt Rebecca. She supposed she could go there, but the idea of spending Christmas in swampy Tampa, her uncle Jim drinking Bud Light Lime in his pleather La-Z-Boy and watching Fox News twenty-four hours a day, made Brighton literally nauseous.

"You sure?" her mom said. "We don't have to go."

That sobered Brighton up a little. "Mom. Of course you have to go."

"That's my Rainbow," her dad said, and Brighton could tell he was smiling. "I told her you'd be fine. You're a grown woman."

"A grown woman," Brighton repeated, as though saying it out loud would make it true. She felt anything but her two years shy of thirty right now. Still, a lie rolled off her tongue, easy as pie. "Yeah. I . . . I have some friends here who are getting together on Christmas Day. Adele and . . . some others."

Adele's brow lifted.

Brighton ignored her.

"I'll spend the day with them," she continued. "It'll be fun."

"Oh, good," her mom said, exhaling so loudly her breath buzzed into the phone. "I'm so glad to hear that, baby. Tell Adele we said hi."

Brighton nodded, even though her mother couldn't see her, and proceeded to ask all the right questions about her parents' trip—when they were leaving, the name of the winery, etcetera and so forth.

By the time she hung up ten minutes later, her chest felt tight enough to burst.

"Aren't you a smooth liar," Adele said, facing Brighton with her arms folded.

Brighton leaned her head against the building, looked up at the inky-black sky. "My parents are going to France for the holidays. I had to say something."

Just like she'd said so many somethings to her parents since the Katies had booted her out—*I'm doing awesome! Things are going great! Of course I'm still playing! I've got a gig this weekend! And the next! I'm a star!*

Okay, she hadn't exactly said that last one, but the spirit was the same. Her parents believed she was a fully functioning adult in Nashville, paying her rent dutifully and living her musical dream as a solo artist. They didn't even know how to access Instagram or TikTok, much less search for their own daughter among the accounts. The lies were easy, harmless, and made

Brighton feel like someday they might actually cease to be lies if she just kept at it.

Kept at what, exactly, she wasn't sure. All she'd done for the last nine months was sling martinis and draft beer and grind her teeth at every musician who stepped onto Ampersand's stage.

"Fuck," she said, dropping her head into her hands. She just wanted to go home. Maybe she still could. She had a plane ticket. She loved Grand Haven more than any other place in the world. She'd be fine spending Christmas . . . all alone.

But without her parents, she'd have no buffer. No traditions to fall back on. Every shop and restaurant, every bike path and snow-covered sand dune, every rise and fall of the lake already reminded her of Lola every time she went home, but she always had her parents to distract her. Her mom, only twenty-one years old when she'd had Brighton, was pretty much her best friend, and without her . . .

Brighton would drown under all the memories. She'd absolutely drown by herself. She knew she would.

Before she could stop them, tears streamed down her cheeks. She tried to wipe them away, but Adele saw them anyway.

"Baby girl," Adele said, pulling Brighton into her arms, which really set Brighton's tears loose. Adele patted her back and let her cry, which Brighton took full advantage of. She couldn't even remember the last time someone had hugged her—probably her mother, back in March, right before her entire life blew up.

Again.

"All right," Adele said, rubbing Brighton's cold arms. "Okay, here's what we're going to do." She pulled back and looked Brighton in the eyes. "You're coming home with me for Christmas."

Brighton blinked. Sniffed some snot back up her nose. "What?"

"You heard me," Adele said. "You're not going home by yourself, and I know I'm your only fucking friend in the world, so you're coming to Colorado with me. You can tell all your woes to my mom over a nice cup of cocoa. She'll love it—my sister and I never tell her anything."

Brighton prepared herself to refuse, but who the hell was she kidding? Adele *was* her only friend, and she was desperate enough right now that the idea of crying into a strange woman's lap actually sounded pretty nice. She knew Adele's parents were divorced and her mom owned a bakery and liked to meddle, which Adele and her sister—whose name Brighton couldn't remember at this very moment—took it all with a grain of salt. Honestly, a little motherly meddling sounded pretty damn great right now.

So she nodded, dried her eyes with her shirt, and then she and Adele went back to work. The next day, she got on her airline's website and spent all her rent money on the exorbitant fee to change her plane ticket from Grand Rapids to Colorado Springs. She dreaded telling Leah and hoped, at the very least, someone brought homemade peach pie to the next potluck dinner.

chapter 3

harlotte stared at the house nestled on the outskirts of Winter River, the frosted Rockies rising up behind it, and knew she was in trouble.

The Berry home was a complete nightmare.

Oh, it was lovely—large and warm and inviting, its exterior all mountain logs and stone, with a wraparound porch and snow-covered roof. Christmas lights were everywhere—a soft golden glow draping from the eaves, lining the huge windows, and curling around banisters. There were wreaths and electric candles and evergreens in the yard coated in lights, luminarias sparkling along the snowy walk.

It was the picture of a perfect mountain Christmas.

Which was going to be a problem.

For the past two weeks, Charlotte had done her level best to avoid catastrophe, mostly staying in her apartment and working on arrangements for their tour, or taking a Lyft to Elle's place for rehearsal. No subways. No walks down obstacle-laden Manhattan sidewalks. Whenever her colleagues had chatted about their impending trip to Colorado, Charlotte had just smiled and zipped her bow over her strings to get them all back on track. Last night, she'd packed methodically in her largest suitcase, choosing all of her warmest black sweaters and tops, her highest-quality jeans, as well as her concert wear for Europe—all black, of course. She knew where she was going. She knew the trip was occurring over Christmas, and she knew Sloane's family was very into the holiday.

And yet.

Nothing could've quite prepared her for the scene in front of her—a home, complete with a loving mother standing on the porch in welcome, a dog at her side. Charlotte stood frozen with what felt like one of those Christmas wreaths tightening around her throat, the door to their Lyft XL still hanging open behind her.

"Hi, my loves!" Sloane's mother—Nina—called out from the porch.

Loves.

Like they were all her children. Of course, Charlotte had met Nina and Raymond Berry before. Though divorced, they were still close and had come to New York together several times over the last few years, so Charlotte already knew Nina was a very involved mom who cried at nearly every Rosalind Quartet performance—so did Raymond, for that matter—but this was different than a dinner out after a concert.

This was the Berry house. A *home.* A place Charlotte didn't belong and didn't even know how to look at without feeling like she was twelve years old again—fourteen, seventeen, twenty—running over the sandy path from her place to the Fairbrook house, breathing a sigh of relief as soon as she walked through the back door without knocking.

Home.

"Welcome!" Nina said as she started down the snow-cleared steps.

Charlotte shook her head, clearing out the sticky memories, and focused on what was right in front of her. She could do this. She was excellent at focus, at homing in on what really mattered.

The tour.

Music.

Her colleagues.

"You okay?" Sloane said softly, appearing next to her.

Charlotte blinked, then smiled as she closed the car door and adjusted her black hat over her ears to block out the cold. "Of course."

And she was. There had been no major mishaps on the flight or on the twisty ride to Winter River from the Colorado Springs Airport, despite her history of motion sickness. Her luggage hadn't been lost, her violin had survived its own journey in the plane's overhead compartment, and she hadn't even spilled her tiny plastic cup of tomato juice during the flight's turbulence.

Yes, she was just fine, kicking December's ass more than halfway through the month.

"Snickerdoodle, no!" Nina shouted when she was about ten feet away from the group. Her dog—a lovely black labradoodle with short curly hair and a sweet face—broke away from his owner and lumbered toward . . .

Charlotte.

Before she could even react, a pair of paws loomed in her vision and planted themselves on her chest. She let out a surprised "Oof!" as her back hit the car's cold metal side.

Snow and mud from Snickerdoodle's paws coated her black wool peacoat.

"Oh my god, Snick!" Sloane said, tugging at the monster's collar. "Get off, you idiot."

"I'm so sorry," Nina said, hurrying toward them. She had short silver hair that framed her pale face and wore a Christmas sweater with so many sparkly bits and bobs, Charlotte wasn't sure where to focus. "He never does that."

"It's okay," Charlotte managed to say between Snickerdoodle's licks. She laughed, cupping the dog's face between her hands.

"You've got a new best friend," Nina said, laughing as she joined in tugging at Snickerdoodle's collar.

It took both Berrys to get the dog off Charlotte, but he finally relented, settling at her feet and staring up at her with, well, puppy-dog eyes, like he expected her to give him a treat for the minor assault he'd just inflicted on her.

Charlotte brushed off her coat, but that only made a bigger mess of the snow-and-mud mixture.

Score one point for December.

"We'll get that dry-cleaned, dear," Nina said, gathering Charlotte in her arms despite the mess. "I've got plenty of winter gear you can borrow in the meantime."

"Thanks," Charlotte said, going a little stiff, but trying not to show it. Nina smelled like cinnamon and butter.

Nina patted Charlotte's cheek and moved on to Manish, who picked Nina up in a bear hug and twirled her around. Charlotte watched him, Elle too, both of them so easy with parents not their own. So easy with everyone.

"Is Deli here yet?" Sloane asked once her mom had finally greeted everyone.

Nina shook her head. "About twenty minutes behind you, give or take. She's bringing a friend too, so we'll have a full house."

Sloane lifted a brow. "Like a *friend* or a friend?"

Nina laughed. "A friend. She assures me. Though I do need to talk to you about—"

"Mom, god, no. At least let us get in the door and get a drink before Operation Marry Off My Daughters commences, will you?"

Nina's mouth snapped shut.

Charlotte tilted her head at Sloane. "Your sister's name is Deli?"

Nina brightened at that, cackling like it was some sort of joke, but Sloane's mirthful expression fell. Charlotte realized right then that she should know the answer to her own question, that Sloane had most certainly mentioned her older sister's name to Charlotte in the past, probably more than once, and Deli was some sort of nickname. In this moment, though, Charlotte couldn't remember for what.

"They've called each other silly nicknames their whole lives," Nina said. "Adele calls Sloane here Noni. When her sister was born, Adele was only eighteen months old, and she couldn't say Sloane's name correctly until she was around four. By then, Noni had stuck."

"Adele," Charlotte said, closing her eyes. That was right, she remembered now, though too little, too late. Sloane had turned and busied herself emptying out the back of the SUV so they could release their poor Lyft driver.

Soon, suitcases and instruments littered the front walk, and Charlotte was eager to get inside, get a moment to herself in her room, but as soon as their car made it down the drive, another one appeared, this one a silver sedan.

"Oh, that'll be Adele," Nina said, lifting her arm and waving. The driver honked the horn. "God, what was her friend's name again?"

"I can't keep her girlfriends straight," Sloane said.

"No, no, this isn't a girlfriend," Nina said. "I told you. A friend only. Just like Adele, always taking care of people down on their luck."

"Oh?" Manish said.

"Yes, this one's a musician like you all, though Nashville-style, you know? Guitars and moody lyrics, I believe." Nina laughed. "Her name's unusual too." She folded her arms against the icy air as the car came to a stop. "Something like Leighton or Crighton . . . No, that's not it . . ."

Snickerdoodle leaned heavily against Charlotte, and she found she didn't mind. His weight was nice—grounding—and her hand smoothed over his head as she watched Sloane hurry around to the car's driver's side and open the door. A woman stepped out, and she and Sloane hugged. They were nearly the same height, but didn't look much alike beyond that. Adele's skin was a shade darker, and she wore her hair in braids, while Sloane's was all natural curls. Adele had glasses on and wore a navy pea-coat unbuttoned over a collared shirt and jeans with brown boots.

A flurry of Berry hugs started again, such a cacophony of laughing and questions that, at first, Charlotte didn't notice the second woman who had stepped out of the car's passenger seat. Long dark hair, a red-and-white plaid coat, a leather satchel across her body. She stood oddly, with one booted foot half-propped on the inside of her other ankle. Charlotte narrowed her eyes, her heart stuttering to a near stop.

Only one person she knew had ever stood like that.

And that person was staring straight at her, eyes wide, mouth open in a tiny pink circle.

"Brighton!" Nina announced in triumph as she released Adele

and pointed at the woman over the car's hood. "That's it—that's your name."

Adele's friend shook her head, her throat moving in a hard swallow. Then she laughed. "It . . . it is. How are you, Ms. Berry?"

"Oh my goodness, call me Nina."

Charlotte stood frozen, her fingers curling into Snicker-doodle's fur, staring as Nina pulled the woman into her arms. Charlotte blinked, waiting for the scene to change, to wake up, anything.

But no. A pair of dark eyes met hers over Nina's shoulder. Eyes she hadn't seen in five years and never, ever wanted to see again.

chapter 4

Adele maneuvered their rental car onto a snowy lane nestled in the mountains, revealing her childhood home, and Brighton had never seen anything so beautiful.

Well, aside from her own home on Lake Michigan, icy waves and frosty sand in the backyard instead of grass, her playground as a kid, and Christmas lights on every possible surface of her sage-green house. Every year, her parents' goal was to make their exterior decorations as over-the-top as possible, full *National Lampoon's Christmas Vacation*–style. The holiday wasn't the holiday without a call from the power company.

Brighton smiled to herself, letting her mind drift over the memories, aching to hear her mom yelling at her dad from the back porch, warning him to try to avoid falling into the bushes this year. Lola had always loved decorating, and she'd even climbed a ladder the year she turned seventeen to help secure icicle lights to the eaves.

Brighton cleared her throat, blinked Winter River, Colorado, back into focus, and checked her phone again.

No notifications.

Her parents had been in France for three days now, and she'd only talked to her mother once. She felt slightly ridiculous, like a little kid missing her mother even though she was nearly thirty years old, but it was Christmas, and she *did* miss her mother.

"What do you think?" Adele asked as she honked the horn.

Brighton looked up as the house loomed closer, all warm and glowing, the twilit clouds pink and orange and swirling across the Rockies behind it.

It was idyllic.

It was perfect.

It wasn't her home.

"It's lovely," she said, which was true. She did her best to swallow the lump in her throat, but she couldn't help the emotions swirling in her chest. Still, Adele had invited her here, and she was determined to be grateful.

She leaned forward, squinting through the slightly fogged windshield at all the people standing in the Berry family driveway. "Is your mom having a party?"

Adele laughed. "Not yet, god help us. That's my sister and her music group. I didn't tell you she was bringing the whole crew?"

Brighton shook her head, craning her neck to see better. She saw Adele's mom and a man in an olive-green bomber jacket, a person with short pink hair who wore a bright-yellow scarf, and a third person in a dark peacoat and a black beanie hat, a huge dog leaning against her legs. Brighton knew Adele's younger sister was a musician, some classically trained type who lived and worked in New York City.

"What does your sister play again?" she asked.

"Sloane plays violin."

Brighton nodded, but as they got closer, coming to a stop in front of the porch, Sloane and her friends came into clearer focus.

Crystal-clear, high-definition, familiar focus.

"Adele," she said, her heart creeping into her throat as her friend put the car in park. "Is . . . is Sloane in a string quartet?"

"Yeah," Adele said, turning off the car. "They're actually kind of a big deal, but god, don't tell her I said so. I don't get any of it, really."

Brighton didn't respond, her mouth suddenly dry. The woman who had to be Sloane—the woman Brighton had seen dozens of times on Instagram, warm-brown skin and soft curls around her face—ran around the car to Adele's side, all but hauling Adele out of the car and hugging her. Soon Adele was surrounded by her mom and sister, laughter and exclamations about new glasses and longer braids echoing in Brighton's ears.

She had to move.

She knew she did.

Or did she? She could simply stay in the car all season. Sounded plausible. Adele could bring her food and water and blankets. She'd just keep the engine running for heat, refill the gas tank in town every few days. It would be fine.

Totally possible.

She peeked out the window again, gauging where the person in the black hat had ended up. She spotted her by the front porch steps, quietly standing apart from the others with the dog still by her side.

Lola had always wanted a dog. Brighton's family had had cats—still did, Luna and Hazel—but as a kid, Lola had stopped to pet every dog they met on the sidewalks or on the beach. Her mom had never let her get one—too loud and needy and extroverted—and Brighton had always suspected Lola really wanted one for those very reasons.

A companion for when the nights got too long living with her mother, the days too quiet in her pristine lake house.

Lola.

Her Lola.

It couldn't be . . .

But it was. She was here, and Brighton had no clue what to do. It didn't seem like she'd noticed Brighton quite yet, but that would change the moment Brighton moved. The earth would tip on its axis, reverse orbit.

Adele shut the driver's-side door, then rapped on the window with her knuckle, urging Brighton out of the car. Brighton's fingers curled into the worn leather of her bag as she breathed . . .

And breathed . . .

And breathed . . .

Finally, she managed to move her fingers to the handle . . . pull it—the soft release of the door opening was a bomb exploding. She froze, glancing up at the woman in the black hat, still hoping she'd hallucinated the whole thing. But no, she—*Lola*—was watching Nina Berry flock around Adele and Sloane with a sort of wonder spilling across her expression.

Brighton stayed still, giving herself this moment to take in her former best friend.

Former girlfriend, former fiancée.

Former everything.

God, she was gorgeous. Always had been—that dark-and-silver hair, that full red mouth, eyes light-brown and always so perceptive, noticing things no one else ever did. Brighton felt her own eyes start to fill, the *missing* she hadn't let herself feel in years flooding back in like a river into a dry valley.

She shook her head. Had to get it together. Had to. It was either that or live in this rental, possibly becoming a headline in Winter River's local paper, and she'd rather not sully Nina Berry's good name.

One leg . . . then the next. She looped her bag around her body, clicked the car door shut as quietly as possible. Maybe she could make a run for it, duck her head and yell about a bathroom emergency, one that would keep her in her room for the next . . . week.

She was fucked.

She stood still, a statue—just wrap some Christmas lights around her and call it a day—and waited for the apocalypse. Seconds passed, whole lifetimes it felt like, until—

"Brighton!"

She squeezed her eyes shut, wincing.

"That's it—that's your name!" Ms. Berry called from over the car's roof.

Brighton opened her eyes to see Adele's mom beaming at her, heading around the front of the car with her arms held open.

"It . . . it is," Brighton said on a laugh. "How are you, Ms. Berry?"

"Oh my goodness, call me Nina."

Ms. Berry—Nina—drew Brighton into a hug so tight, Brighton was pretty sure she emitted a tiny squeak. And then it was like muscle memory took over, Brighton's gaze finding the person she'd spent ten years finding over and over again in every crowd, every Grand Haven middle and high school classroom, every busy Boston sidewalk when they were in college at Berklee, even across the kitchen in their small Manhattan apartment.

Their eyes locked.

Brighton stopped breathing.

The world stopped spinning, she was sure of it.

Nina released her, and Brighton still couldn't look away. Lola couldn't either, it seemed, and suddenly, they were twenty-three again, the day of their wedding, the last time Brighton had seen Lola in person.

"You ready for this?" Lola had asked. They were lying in Lola's bed, blankets soft and warm around them. The whole world ready for them, a million possibilities. Lola tangled their fingers together. "Ready for forever?"

And Brighton had said yes.

She'd said yes when she should've said . . .

Brighton's shoulders tensed, her throat aching. She took another step forward, slow and steady, like she was approaching a feral animal. Lola's eyes followed her, her face expressionless. Lola had always been good at that too—masking any and all emotion. Her chin lifted just slightly, her gaze going steely and vacant.

Brighton stopped in front of her. Took one more steadying breath, though she felt anything but solid right now. "Hi, Lo—"

"Hi," Lola said curtly, sticking out her gloved hand. "I'm Charlotte."

Brighton froze, her mouth still forming an *o*. Lola didn't budge. Didn't blink. Wasn't even breathing, as far as Brighton could tell. After a second, Brighton slid her hand against Lola's palm, and Lola gave her fingers a tight pump before releasing them like they were on fire.

Brighton managed to say her own name, though the two-syllable word sounded strange in her ears, which were roaring with blood and a rapid heartbeat.

"Nice to meet you," Lola said, then looked away and cleared

her throat loudly. This seemed to grab Sloane's attention, who pulled Adele over for more introductions. Soon Brighton had met the entire Rosalind Quartet, faces she'd been staring at on Instagram for the better part of two years. She liked Manish and Elle immediately, though her head still swam with Lola's strange behavior.

"Okay, everyone, let's get inside!" Nina called. "It's freezing, and we're having chili and my homemade cornbread."

"Hell yes," Adele said. "God, I love coming home."

"Yeah, because you automatically forget how to clean a dish when we're here," Sloane said.

"Okay, Little Miss 'Mom, Make Me Some Hot Chocolate with a Thousand Marshmallows While I Sit on the Couch and Watch *The Holiday* for the Billionth Time.'"

"I can't help it if I know how to relax," Sloane said.

Nina just laughed and climbed up the porch steps, dragging Charlotte's rolling suitcase behind her. "Come on, Snickerdoodle."

The Berry sisters followed their dog up the stairs with their own bags. Manish and Elle went along as well, giant luggage and instrument cases in tow.

The noise faded, quiet closing around Brighton and Lola as they stood in the snowy drive. Lola wasn't looking at Brighton, her gaze on the front door.

"Lola," Brighton said quietly. Almost reverently.

Still no reaction. Lola simply bent down to pick up the same vintage leather violin case she'd had since she was twenty-one, turned on her heel, and walked up the porch steps without another word.

chapter 5

Charlotte was about to lose her shit. And that was the thing about Charlotte Donovan. She did *not* lose her shit.

Ever.

She walked into the Berry house, warmth curling around her. She tried to focus on keeping her expression placid, which was proving difficult because Christmas decorations were everywhere, so many she couldn't even process them all—garland twining up the staircase banister, a giant winter village spread out on the console table in the hallway, bells hanging from doorknobs, and the biggest Christmas tree she'd ever seen in the living room right in front of her, sparkling with white lights and homemade ornaments, right next to a large stone fireplace, complete with a crackling fire. The air smelled like some kind of savory spice, with a breath of sugar underneath.

It smelled like the Fairbrook house.

She stopped beside the large leather couch, full of Christmas-themed pillows, a red-and-green plaid blanket folded neatly over the back. Breathe in for four . . . out for four. She'd learned about mindfulness through her meditation app, but right now, *feeling* her feet on the floor and her fingers on the cool dark-brown leather wasn't really doing the trick. She needed . . . hell, she wasn't even sure. The last thing she'd expected to encounter on this holiday was her former fiancée, who literally left her at the altar and never looked back.

She squeezed her eyes closed, breathed. Voices filtered in from around the corner, Sloane's being one of them. Charlotte needed her room, and she needed it now, just a moment alone. Or maybe many moments. Her chest felt tight, her eyes ached, and she swore to god, she would *not* cry in front of these people.

"Can we talk about your latest Facebook post?" Sloane was saying.

"Oh, this should be good," Manish said as Charlotte stepped farther into the living room to see a large, open-space, kitchen-dining-living combination. At the far end of the house, the kitchen area was cozy, despite its size, with teal cabinets and butcher-block countertops, and a large center island covered in all manner of chopped veggies and crackers and cheese. Christmas decorations covered every available surface here as well, everything from fresh garland curled around the window over the farmhouse sink to red-and-green ceramic canisters labeled *Sugar* and *Coffee*. Nina stood at the stove stirring something steaming in a large silver pot.

Sloane was already pouring glasses of red wine, while Elle and Manish munched on gherkins and cubes of pepper jack cheese from a charcuterie board. Adele got a brown bottle of beer from the large stainless-steel fridge and cracked it open.

"What Facebook post?" Adele asked.

"Excuse me, Sloane?" Charlotte said.

"Hey, come join," Sloane said, waving Charlotte closer. Snicker-doodle, who'd been lying at Nina's feet, got up and trotted over to Charlotte. "We've got snacks and chili coming up."

"Actually," Charlotte said, petting Snickerdoodle's head, "I was—"

"You want to tell Deli, Mom?" Sloane said, looking at her mother.

Nina frowned as she opened a cabinet and took down a stack of white ceramic bowls dotted with red and green snowflakes. "Tell her what?"

"Sloane," Charlotte said again, but Sloane's attention was fixed on her mother. Elle placed a glass of wine in Charlotte's hand, then nudged it toward her mouth with a wink.

Charlotte looked down at the deep-red liquid, her stomach churning too much to take a single sip.

"Mom, you're still using Facebook?" Adele asked. "It's where souls go to die."

"Oh, it is not," Nina said, laying a handful of large spoons next to the bowls.

"And I quote," Sloane said, taking her phone out of her back pocket, then tapping at the screen, "'If anyone knows any single queer darlings, ages twenty-five to thirty-five, please do let me know.' End quote."

"I mean, I'm a fan of queer darlings," Manish said.

"Same," Elle said.

"Exactly," Nina said. "I'm just putting out some friendly social feelers for you all while you're here. Want you to feel, you know, *seen*."

"Seen," Adele said, her voice deadpan. "Mom, you're the only cishet person in this house. I think we're good."

"Sloane," Charlotte said, setting down her glass of wine, "could I—"

"I'll have you know, I kissed a girl or two in my day," Nina said, moving to the stove and stirring the chili.

"Mother, oh my god," Sloane said, her jaw slack.

"Wait, wait," Adele said. "What day? You married Dad when you were, like, nineteen."

Nina went to the fridge to retrieve a stick of butter. "Twenty. And I was in college for two whole years before that."

"Sloane?" Charlotte tried again.

"Okay, fine, your bi-curiosity notwithstanding, you're up to something," Sloane said to her mother.

"Super shady," Adele said.

Nina blew a silver strand of hair off her forehead. Her cheeks were rosy from the stove's heat, her eyes bright behind her tortoiseshell glasses. "You're both ridiculous."

"Are we?" Adele said. "I'm still trying to decide if my fifty-four-year-old mom just came out to me."

"We need a rainbow cake," Sloane said.

"Streamers," Elle said.

"A sign in the yard," Manish added.

"I see, we're all jokesters now," Nina said, but she was smiling.

"Some confetti at the very least," Sloane said, "and I—"

"Sloane!"

It took Charlotte a split second to realize she'd yelled, her throat buzzing a little with the effort. Five pairs of eyes settled on her—six if you counted the dog's—wide and worried. Which was the last thing she needed, to be honest—*concern* from the people she was supposed to be leading.

"I'm sorry," she said. "I just . . ." She pressed her fingertips into her collarbone. "I'm not feeling great. Could you show me where I'm staying?"

"Yeah, of course," Sloane said. She came closer, placed her hands on Charlotte's shoulders. "You okay? You need some ibuprofen or anything? Water?"

Charlotte shook her head. "Just my room."

Sloane nodded, then glanced at Manish and Elle. "Yeah. Sorry, I should've done that first. We're all upstairs." She looked back at her mother, who was now scooping chili into bowls. "We're not done, Nina Berry."

Nina just laughed and shook her head.

Charlotte didn't waste any time, turning and hurrying toward the staircase near the front door. She just needed to be alone for five damn minutes to get herself together, without wine and cheese and mothers confessing queer inclinations.

Then she'd be fine.

Then she'd be ready.

"Snick, stay!" Nina called out, and Charlotte heard the jingle of the dog's collar at the same moment the front door opened, revealing Brighton, her cheeks red from the cold. Her eyes met Charlotte's.

"Lola."

Brighton's voice echoed through her entire body, that name she hadn't heard out loud in five years. The name no one else called her, ever.

"Charlotte's a pretty name," twelve-year-old Brighton had said the day they met on the beach, the warm July sun shimmering over the clear water.

"Thanks. So is Brighton."

A moving van was parked in the next-door neighbor's driveway, and Charlotte had already been on the beach, alone, her mother writing in the house and tired of Charlotte's bored wandering, when a girl around Charlotte's age had ambled onto the sand.

Charlotte had never seen anyone as pretty as Brighton Fairbrook. Long dark hair tangled by the wind, lashes a mile long, eyes so deep brown they looked nearly black. She seemed almost magical in her white sundress and bare feet, like some sort of fairy or sorceress.

"You can call me Bright," she'd said. "I like that better."

"Bright. That's even prettier."

Brighton nodded, kicking at the water and then bending down to pick up a smooth stone.

"What should we call you?" she asked.

Charlotte frowned, confused. Her mother had named her Charlotte, and that's what everyone called her.

"Um . . . Charlotte?" she said.

Brighton laughed. "No, silly, you need a special name. A secret name." She squatted down to dig into a wet patch of sand. "A name just for us."

Us.

The word reverberated in Charlotte's chest. She'd never really had an *us*. She and her mom were a sort of *us*, she guessed, but that was by default. A forced relationship, an obligation. She had friends in school, but no one who ever lasted past the school year. No one who called her and invited her to sleepovers or Skoops for afternoon ice cream.

"It's got to be a good one," Brighton said. "Lottie?"

Charlotte made a face, and Brighton laughed, the sound like the wind chimes already hanging from the Fairbrooks' back porch.

"I've got it," Brighton said, standing up with a smooth piece of beach glass. It was turquoise and, if you turned it just so, shaped like a heart. She placed it in Charlotte's hand. "Lola."

Charlotte closed her fingers around the glass, bits of sand gritting into her palm, and smiled.

Lola.

And that's who she was for the next ten years.

Who *they* were.

Lola and Bright.

Now, fifteen years later in Colorado, she tore her eyes from Brighton, hurrying up the steps, her violin case clutched to her chest, doing her best not to care why Brighton was walking into the house ten minutes after everyone else, her eyes slightly watery. She was no longer Charlotte's problem or concern. Hadn't been for five years.

At the top of the stairs, she paused, then pressed herself against a wall so Sloane could pass and lead them down a hallway filled with framed family photos and mountainesque art.

"Manish and Elle, you're at the end of the hall in the guest room. Brighton is in Adele's room just there on the left, and Charlotte, I put you in here with me." She motioned to the first door on the right.

Sloane just stared at her, the reality sinking in. Of course. The Berrys didn't live in a mansion—she saw now how absurd she was to assume she'd have her own room, but in her defense, she hadn't been thinking clearly for the last half hour or so.

"Right," Charlotte said, more to herself than anyone else. Manish and Elle bumbled past, already arguing about who got the left side of the bed, which they both wanted for some unknown reason.

Sloane tilted her head at Charlotte, then nodded toward the door. Charlotte followed her inside to find a lovely room with a queen bed covered in what looked like a handmade quilt crafted out of T-shirts, fluffy pillows wrapped in crisp lavender sheets. There were posters of famous violin players all over the walls and shelves packed with trophies and ribbons from music competitions and festivals. Both Sloane's and Charlotte's suitcases were tucked into a corner by the bed.

"My mom hasn't changed much in here," Sloane said, laughing as she sat on the cushioned window seat at the far side of the room. "Which I kind of love, honestly. It's sort of nice, coming home, remembering how things—"

"Where's the bathroom?" Charlotte asked.

Sloane blinked, her smile dipping. "Right. Sorry, you're not feeling well. It's just across the hall."

Charlotte mumbled a thanks, ignoring the way guilt bubbled up in her chest—she suspected she was being a bit of an asshole—and all but threw herself into the bathroom. She pressed her back against the door, her violin case still in her arms.

She waited for the tears to come, almost wanted them, wanted the relief. But her body was in full fight-or-flight mode, and they wouldn't release, like water held back by a dam.

She set her violin case on the toilet lid, draped her soiled coat over the clawfoot tub and set her hat on top, then ran the water in the sink. It came out freezing cold, but she left it like that, cupping it into her hands and splashing her face, hoping the temperature would shock her into . . .

What?

She had no idea what to do here. Pretending like she and Brighton didn't know each other had just happened, an instinct, her hand flying out in a stoic greeting before she'd really thought it through.

But it was the right instinct.

She couldn't possibly get through this trip with Brighton if they actually acknowledged their history. And their specific history? Completely untenable. Acting like they'd never met before was the only way to go.

It was either that or leaving.

Charlotte grabbed a forest-green towel covered in embroidered candy canes from a brushed-nickel ring and dried her face. She stared at herself in the mirror, her mascara now a bit smudged but her red lipstick still perfectly in place.

No.

She couldn't leave, couldn't do that to Sloane, not after traveling all the way here. Plus, with her December luck, a blizzard would blow in right before she boarded her flight, effectively stranding her in a Colorado airport with no way to escape. Here, at least, she could practice some good old-fashioned avoidance.

Leave the room when Brighton entered.

Hole up in her and Sloane's room and work on arrangements. There was a desk in there, room to practice.

Smile politely when she and Brighton were forced together.

Yes. There was no reason whatsoever she'd need to actually speak to Brighton. Not with so many people in the house.

She could do this.

She *would* do this.

Charlotte rolled her shoulders back and smoothed her hair into a fresh ponytail, then cleaned up the black shadows under her eyes.

She took one deep, fortifying breath.

She and Brighton Fairbrook didn't matter. They weren't anything. Not anymore. Brighton was just another person, a stranger.

She nodded to herself, then turned to get her violin case. She paused, only for a second, before her fingers were flipping the case's buckles and lifting out Rosalind, but not to play her. She held her instrument carefully, then opened the tiny velvet compartment right under the neck rest. She kept her rosin in here, extra strings.

And there, at the very bottom, wrapped in a dustcloth she never used, was a perfectly smooth, heart-shaped piece of beach glass. She didn't touch it. Simply stared at it, still hidden by the cloth, and wondered—not for the first time, not even for the thousandth time—why she couldn't seem to make herself throw it away.

chapter 6

Brighton knew Lola hated chili.

And yet here Brighton was, sitting across from Lola at Nina's large farmhouse dining table, watching her ex-fiancée scoop beans and beef delicately into her mouth.

Granted, five years was a long time. Maybe Lola had tried different kinds of chili in Manhattan and learned to like cumin, which was what Lola always said she couldn't stand.

"So you hate tacos too?" Brighton had said when she first discovered this information years ago when they were in ninth grade, sitting in their school cafeteria on chili day. "How can you hate tacos? No reasonable human hates tacos."

"You don't like cake," Lola had said back, smiling as she popped a chip into her mouth. "Who's the unreasonable human now?"

But she was right—Brighton didn't like cake. It was too spongy, the icing too sweet. She much preferred denser desserts, like brownies or even cake pops, the icing already baked in and creating a rich, buttery sponge. For her birthday, Lola would always—

Brighton shoved a spoonful of chili-soaked cornbread into her mouth to get her brain focused on something else. Memory Lane was a dangerous road, which she always knew, but it was nearly atomic while Lola sat there acting like they were complete strangers.

Brighton couldn't stop the hurt from billowing through her like smoke. She knew she had no right, that of the two of them, *she* was the asshole here, but still.

They were Lola and Bright.

Despite what she'd done to them five years ago, Brighton couldn't stop the swell of happiness at seeing Lola, the way her heart strained for her friend, reaching, reaching, reaching like it had since the day they met.

And it crushed her that Lola wasn't reaching back.

Lola had always reached back. Always reached for Brighton, reached for *them*. Brighton's thoughts flew back to their final year at Berklee and the last Christmas they'd spent together in an apartment they had off-campus, a year before their wedding. A huge snowstorm was headed for the Northeast, and Michigan had just been pummeled, completely cutting off any transportation into and out of the state and most of the Midwest.

Which meant Brighton couldn't get home for the holidays. She'd been looking forward to it so much—to getting out of Boston, away from constant talks with Lola about moving to New York that spring—that when the airports shut down, she'd spent an entire half hour sobbing in the shower, which she'd hidden from Lola at the time. She'd felt so silly crying for her mommy when the love of her life was on the couch by the roaring fire in their living room—a gas fire, but still. It was warm, and Lola was lovely, and she was already talking about what they could do on Christmas Eve instead of Bonnie's usual feast of roast duck and fresh green beans and parmesan mashed potatoes and sour cream and sweet potato pie.

But Brighton hadn't wanted anything else.

By Christmas Eve, the storm had angled north, but Boston was still covered in white, just not enough for the restaurants to close. Brighton hauled herself to work to pick up a lunch shift, since she was in town and needed the money. She served glazed turkey and mulled wine and eggnog that cost more than her rent to patrons who kept oohing and aahing over the snow and how *beautiful* it was. How *picturesque*. How *perfect for Christmas*.

By the time five o'clock rolled around and her boss insisted she leave early to *enjoy her Christmas*, she was in the foulest mood she'd ever experienced. On the walk home, she nearly ran into a lamppost that had burned out, which caused her to side-step into a darkened puddle of slush.

When she finally trudged through her apartment's door, boots wet and coat too warm, she was so lost in her own misery that she didn't notice it at first.

The lights.

The smells.

The music.

"What . . . ?" she said, but couldn't get out anything else, because her apartment had been completely transformed into a winter wonderland.

No, into a *home* wonderland.

"Hey, you're early!" Lola said, scooting out of their small kitchen with an apron tied around her waist.

"I'm early," Brighton said dreamily, taking off her scarf, her mouth still hanging open. "Lola, what is all this?"

Lola grinned, spread her hands, which were both covered in bright green oven mitts with holly berries printed all over them. "I'm taking you home for Christmas."

Brighton felt her eyes fill, her throat close up. She looked around at their apartment, which was completely covered in all manner of Christmas lights and paraphernalia. They'd only decorated moderately after Thanksgiving, since they'd be going back to Michigan for Christmas. They hadn't even gotten a tree, as getting a real tree into a Boston apartment was quite a feat and Brighton couldn't stomach a fake one that came in a box.

Still, now, there was a tree in the corner of their living room. Real, going by the piney scent, and it was covered in a mix of white and colored lights, just like Brighton's family tree at home. There were also stockings—red with white trim—hanging over their little gas fireplace and lights draped over the mantel, the window frame, the entertainment center. Little knickknacks were set up on the coffee table and bookshelves, dotting nearly every free space throughout the apartment. Nothing was familiar, so Lola must have gone out and bought every single piece, but they still made the space feel homey and cozy, like Brighton had always had that green glass Christmas tree that lit up in different colors on the end table.

There was music on too, even though Lola hated most Christmas music. Ella Fitzgerald's *Ella Wishes You a Swinging Christmas* by the sound of it, an album that pretty much played on repeat in the Fairbrook house from December first onward.

"Is that . . . ?" Brighton asked, stepping toward the kitchen. "Do I smell duck?"

Lola grinned. "You do."

"With cranberry curry sauce?"

Lola just smiled even bigger.

"Babe," Brighton said, "what did you do?"

"I got your mom's recipes," Lola said, shrugging. "And I cooked."

"You cooked."

"I cooked."

Bright just blinked, still processing.

"Okay, with your mom's help," Lola said. "I've been on the phone with her pretty much all afternoon." A timer sounded, and Lola gasped, turning around and dashing back into the kitchen. "My pie!"

"Your . . . your pie?" Brighton followed her into the kitchen, which was warm, the air muzzy with spices and sugar.

And a total disaster.

Every inch of the countertops was covered, every bowl they owned utilized and dirty and piled in the sink. And there was duck. Right there in a pan sitting on the stove. It was a little more well done than Bonnie's ducks, but it was *there*. It existed, along with Bonnie's famous cranberry curry glaze. And there were green beans—a bit soggy looking—and sour cream and sweet potato pie, fresh out of the oven, the top a little charred.

It was flawed and messy, and it was for her.

It was perfect.

"Lola," she said.

"Oh, shoot, I cooked it too long," Lola said, setting the pie on the cooling rack. "But I did it for thirty minutes, just like your mom . . . Oh, shit, the oven was on four hundred! It was supposed to be on three-fifty."

"Lola."

Lola flipped the oven off just as the music switched over to Sinatra singing "I'll Be Home for Christmas."

"Lola, it's perfect," Brighton said.

Lola snorted. "Not quite." She took off her oven mitts and set them on the counter, glaring at the duck. "I followed her directions to a T."

Brighton smiled, took her fiancée's hand. "It's perfect."

Lola smiled at her. "Yeah?"

"Yeah. Thank you."

"You really like it?"

"I love it." Brighton glanced around the apartment, the lights, the decorations. "But you . . . you hate Christmas."

"Not with you," Lola said, then wrapped her arms around Brighton's waist. Pulled her close. "I love you. Anything with you. Everything. And I just want you to have the Christmas you've dreamed about all year."

"Done," Brighton said, then kissed her.

And Lola kissed her back, and it really was perfect—everything was perfect—for that moment, for that night.

Now, six Christmases later, Brighton could hardly believe she was with Lola again, yet a very different Lola than the one who had spent a small fortune on Christmas tchotchkes for her once upon a time.

Reached that far for her.

Lola wasn't reaching toward Brighton at all now. Wasn't even thinking about extending a single finger, judging from her placid expression. Conversation swirled around them—a tour the quartet was leaving for right after Christmas, how Ampersand was doing in Nashville, a story about Elle's grandmother Mimi and how she'd once poured a full pitcher of water on a director back in 1968 when he copped a feel of her ass on set.

Lola nodded and smiled, offered some details about the tour.

And she kept eating that fucking chili.

"Do you *like* chili, Charlotte?" Brighton asked.

She was pretty sure she'd interrupted Elle saying something about Europe, but she couldn't hold it back any longer. It was like fire in her mouth, this knowledge that Charlotte Donovan *hated* chili.

Lola lifted a cool eyebrow. "I do."

"Because you look like you're having a hard time swallowing," Brighton said. Actually, Lola looked perfect, but that was half the fucking problem, wasn't it?

"Not at all," Lola said. "It's delicious, Nina."

"Thank you, dear," Nina said. "I—"

"Has a lot of cumin, doesn't it?" Brighton said, taking another bite herself. "I love cumin. Don't you, Charlotte?"

"Yes," Lola said tightly. "I love it."

"Do you need a nap, Brighton?" Adele asked. "Or another drink?"

"No," Brighton said cheerily. "I'm fine. Just fine."

"Maybe we'll have *cake* for dessert," Lola said.

Brighton just laughed. "Oh, wouldn't that be perfect."

"Am I missing something?" Sloane asked.

"I think Brighton is, at least," Manish said, then tipped his wineglass at her. "Sorry, no offense."

"None taken," Brighton said. She couldn't possibly be offended. She was too damn busy trying to get this mime sitting across from her to break character.

"So, Lola," she said, changing tactics. "How do you like New York? Dream come true?"

It was a dick move, she knew. They'd only lived in Manhattan together for a short time before everything fell apart—New York had always been Lola's dream and one of the main reasons why Brighton had done what she did on their wedding day. New York had never been her own dream, and they both knew it. Still, she just needed Lola to look at her. Say something. Do anything other than remain so infuriatingly composed.

But Lola just tilted her head at Brighton, her expression completely blank.

"Lola?" Sloane said. "Who—"

"My name is Charlotte," Lola said evenly.

"My apologies," Brighton said, scraping her spoon across the bottom of her bowl. "You look a little like someone I used to know."

Lola lifted her glass of wine, sipped it primly. "No worries. And yes, I love New York. My life there is everything I ever wanted."

"Oh, I bet it is."

"And yours?" Lola asked. "You're a *musician*, right?"

She said the word *musician* as she might say *herpes*, and Brighton felt her spine stiffen. She opened her mouth to assert that her life was exactly what she wanted, what she had dreamed of, goddammit.

But that wasn't exactly true, was it?

Still, Lola—*Charlotte*—didn't need to know that.

And Brighton never, ever wanted her to.

"Yes," she said. "I am. And it's great. It's just really, really great."

"Great," Lola said. "You have an album, then? I mean, I assume so."

Brighton's jaw tightened, her throat suddenly aching. Was she really here, in fucking Colorado, trying to one-up her ex?

Not just her ex. *Lola.*

"Hey, Mom," Adele said, clearing her throat and squeezing Brighton's leg under the table. "Did you know Noni hasn't been on a date in three years?"

Sloane's mouth dropped open. "You rat fink!"

"Three years? Really, Sloane?" Nina asked.

"Well, Deli eats women out *on top of her bar* after hours," Sloane said. "Talk about a health code violation."

"That was once!" Adele said. "Told to you in confidence! And I cleaned it . . . you know . . . after."

"I think this conversation is the definition of TMI," Nina said, sipping her wine.

Manish and Elle burst out laughing, while the weight of her interaction with Lola—or, rather, their soft-spoken pissing match—felt like a mountain on Brighton's chest. They watched each other for a split second—not long enough for anyone to notice but long enough for Lola to raise a single brow, then look away as though Brighton were nothing more than a nuisance, an annoying fly buzzing around her personal space. She even swiped her hand through the air in front of her face, as though batting Brighton away, followed by a tuck of hair behind her ear.

Perfectly natural.

Brighton looked away too, refused to look down, and took a large gulp of the red wine Nina had poured them all for dinner. She absolutely had not noticed that Lola was on her second glass since they'd all sat down to eat, and she certainly didn't recall that red wine always, always gave Lola a headache if she had more than a few sips, or that Lola's beverage of choice was a Manhattan with top-shelf bourbon, a product of Anna Donovan's taste and lack of care when Lola had sneaked sips as a teenager.

Nope, Brighton didn't think about any of that at all.

"So," Nina said, lifting her wine, "moving on from the topic of cunnilingus—"

"Oh my god, Mom," Sloane said.

"You brought it up," Adele said.

"What do you all plan to do while you're here?" Nina asked.

"Girls, I'm sure you have some Winter River attractions you want to share with your friends. Ice-skating at Bailey's Pond, perhaps?"

"If we want to break an ankle," Adele said.

"Maybe horseback riding," Nina said.

"Oh god, I'm scared of horses," Brighton said, the admission just popping out of her mouth. She hadn't quite found solid ground since arriving in Winter River, very clearly evident by her immature behavior and loose lips.

Nina frowned. "Are you really, dear?"

Brighton glanced at Lola—couldn't fucking help it, could she?—and Lola was looking right back. Except . . . she wasn't. Her gaze was cold, impersonal, full of the politeness of simply paying attention to the speaker at a gathering like this.

"I am," Brighton said. "Had a scary encounter with one when I was thirteen. Never got over it, I guess."

"Hmm." Nina tilted her head at Brighton. Then, more quietly, she said, "Could be a problem."

Sloane lifted a brow. "Mother. What do you mean?"

Nina waved a hand. "I know! What about some cooking while you're in town? I heard Wes Reynolds is giving some holiday cooking lessons down at his restaurant next week."

"I actually really need to learn how to do more than heat up leftover takeaway," Manish said.

"Perfect," Nina said. "I'll sign you up."

"Mom," Adele said. "Slow down."

"We are not taking cooking lessons from Wes," Sloane said.

"He's still single," Nina said casually, taking a sip of her wine. "And very handsome, if I may say. This chili is his recipe."

Sloane frowned, stared down at her spoonful of chili.

"It's delicious," Brighton said, wanting to fill the space somehow, and maybe make up for Chiligate a few minutes ago.

"It is," Nina said. "My best friend, Marisol, suggested adding cocoa powder to this batch." She beamed at them for a second, then clapped her hands together once. "So, you're going to Greenbriar Ridge this week to see your father, yes?"

"Of course, Mom," Adele said. "Dad has us booked in the cabins with unlimited skiing."

"I'd love to do some skiing," Elle said.

"Excellent, Elle," Nina said. "And what else do you like to do, my dear? Hiking? Crafts? What's your favorite color?"

"Okay," Sloane said, taking her napkin out of her lap and placing it on the table. "I said it before, and I'll say it again—you're up to something."

Nina pressed a hand to her chest. "I'm just trying to make sure everyone has a great time."

"We will," Sloane said.

"We have a lot of rehearsing to do as well," Lola said evenly.

Manish groaned.

"She's not wrong, though," Sloane said. "We all agreed. It was the only way I could get Charlotte on a plane, remember?"

Brighton glanced at Lola, who just smiled.

"A deal's a deal," she said, lifting her glass toward Manish.

Manish groaned again. "Can't we do that Two Turtledoves thing instead?"

"Manish!" Adele and Sloane exclaimed together, causing him to startle and slosh his wine a bit.

"We do not speak those two words in this house," Sloane said through gritted teeth.

"Actually," Nina said calmly, taking a sip of her wine, "I wanted to talk to you all about—"

"No, nope, not happening," Sloane said, shaking her head vigorously. "It's time for Yahtzee and more wine."

"Yahtzee!" Adele yelled, turning in her chair toward the rustic sideboard behind her and opening the door to reveal an amalgam of board games and cards. She took out a bright-red box and set it in the middle of the table.

"What are we wagering?" Sloane asked, an eyebrow quirked at her sister.

"Loser does the dishes," Adele said.

"I'm not making Manish do our dishes," Sloane said.

"Hey," Manish said, looking hurt, "I happen to be quite adept at Yahtzee, thank you very much."

"Sure, buddy, sure," Elle said, patting his shoulder.

"Just because I needed remedial maths in college does not mean I can't count dots on a pair of dice," he said. "And music is mathematical in nature."

"Gay and math don't mix," Elle said, and Brighton laughed. They weren't wrong—Brighton, for her part, was awful at numbers.

"I'll get the wine," Lola said, standing up, an amused smile on her face. Snickerdoodle, who'd been banned from the dining area during dinner, perked his head up from his spot in the living space, big brown eyes fixed on Lola. "Red is still fine with everyone?"

"Thank you, dear, yes," Nina said. "There's a bottle in the wine rack."

Lola nodded and headed toward the kitchen. Brighton twisted her fingers into her napkin, then shot up so quickly her thigh banged against the table, rattling everyone's glasses.

"Whoa, baby girl," Adele said, steadying her own wine. "You good?"

Brighton smiled. "Sorry. I'll take everyone's plates." She started stacking chili-smeared bowls before anyone could protest.

"Don't wash them, though," Elle said as they passed out tiny squares of paper to use as scorecards. "That'll be Manish's job."

"I hate you," he said, his voice deadpan, but he was smiling.

Brighton gathered as many bowls and pieces of cutlery as she dared, balancing the ceramic tower while she walked into the kitchen area.

Lola was there, uncorking another bottle of syrah.

Brighton set the bowls next to the sink, then turned.

Took a breath.

Cleared her throat.

Cleared it again.

Still, Lola said nothing. Didn't even look at her.

"That'll give you a headache," Brighton finally said, motioning toward the wine.

Not even an annoyed pursing of Lola's mouth.

"Are we really doing this?" Brighton asked. "We're really just going to—"

"As opposed to relying on passive-aggressive questions about each other's spice preferences?" Lola said. "Yes, I think we're doing this." She finally met Brighton's eyes, and they stayed like that for a second, just staring. Looking. Lola's gaze didn't budge, but Brighton felt exposed anyway.

Seen.

"Lola. Please. Just—"

Lola turned away then, her heeled black boots clicking against the hardwood as she went back to the table, topped off her own glass, and knocked back the contents.

Brighton just watched, her heart aching against her ribs, and hoped like hell Nina had some strong coffee and a lot of ibuprofen on hand in the morning.

chapter 7

Good morning!"

Light splintered through Charlotte's eyelids as someone—a horrible person, surely—threw the curtains open.

"Mom, Jesus Christ!" Sloane said, her voice raspy with sleep.

Charlotte threw a hand over her eyes to block out the light, which literally felt like a thousand knives prying under her lashes.

Her head ached.

No, not ached—pulsed like a bomb about to explode, counting down to some catastrophic event. She wasn't hungover, exactly—she never got drunk enough for that diagnosis—but her skull despised red wine, despite her taste for it. She hated that Brighton was right, but syrah was all Nina had been serving last night, and Charlotte hadn't felt like she could swan into dinner demanding a Manhattan.

And abstaining, sipping calmly on water, wouldn't have cut it.

Not with Brighton and beach glass and *Lola* whispered like a plea in the kitchen.

So red wine it had been, and lots of it throughout the evening, which also included the cacophony of dice clattering in the cup, then hitting the wooden table, yells, and laughter. Charlotte had even rolled a Yahtzee and managed not to lose horribly. Manish, however, hadn't been so lucky.

The thought made her nearly laugh, which was a mistake, because any motion in her face hurt, everything aching right down to her teeth.

"Oh my god," she mumbled as Nina not only opened the curtains but twisted the blinds wide too, letting in every bit of the winter Colorado sun. She pressed her face into her pillow. Sloane's sheets smelled like clean linen, though her mouth tasted like the streets of New York on a ninety-degree day.

"Mother," Sloane said, her eyes still closed. "I love you, but please get out."

"I'm sorry, I'm going," Nina said, turning away and heading toward the door. "But neither of you heard me knocking."

"Because we're sleeping!" Sloane said.

Charlotte heard a jingling sound, then felt something wet on her face. She cracked an eye open to see Snickerdoodle panting next to her side of the bed, his face eager and sweet. She would laugh but knew the motion would make her want to die, so she settled for tangling her fingers into his soft fur.

"Well, I had to get you up," Nina said, halfway out the door now. "It's almost nine, and you need to be at Hazelthorne Farms at ten."

"What?" Sloane said, sitting up. Her curls were wrapped in a silk scarf, her eyes still a bit bleary. "Why the hell do we need to be there?"

Nina waved a hand as she walked out the door. "Horseback riding. Wear something warm!"

And with that proclamation, she disappeared down the hall. Snickerdoodle remained, sitting down now and submitting himself obediently to Charlotte's pets, which were actually helping to soothe her pounding head.

"Mom, what are you talk—" Sloane started but cut herself off, though her mouth remained hanging wide open. "No," she said quietly. "Oh my god, please tell me she did not."

"What is happening?" Charlotte asked. She hadn't even tried to sit up yet, terrified if she moved, her skull would shatter. "Did she say horseback riding?"

Sloane dropped her face into her hands and groaned. "Two Turtledoves."

"I'm sorry?"

Sloane let her hands slap back onto her lap. "Two Turtledoves. The first date for Two Turtledoves is always horseback riding at the Hazelthornes' farm. I think my mom signed us up."

Charlotte blinked at the ceiling, trying to make sense of horses and farms and turtledoves.

"I knew it!" Adele's voice screeched from down the hall, startling Snickerdoodle. The dog barked once—Charlotte was positive her head exploded—and took off down the hall. "I knew you were up to something! Sloane!"

"I know!" Sloane called back, so loudly that Charlotte pressed her hands to her ears.

"Oh, don't be so dramatic—it's just horseback riding," Nina called.

Footsteps pounded on the carpeted hallway, then Sloane's door flew open again to reveal Adele in a white tank top and a pair of dark-green boxers with little Rudolphs all over them.

"Our mother is a monster," she said.

"That's lovely, dear," Nina said calmly, appearing next to her eldest, Snickerdoodle at her side, tail wagging. "I tried to tell you last night, but you wouldn't hear it. Then you all drank far too much, by the way, so I couldn't possibly tell you then."

"Mom," Sloane said. "No one wants to do this."

"Correction!" Manish yelled from somewhere down the hall. "I'm totally up for some holiday snogging, thanks very much."

"What about Nate?" Sloane yelled back.

"Oh my god, please stop screaming," Charlotte said, but Sloane only patted her on the arm.

"Nate's a dick!" Manish called back.

"See?" Nina said, waving her arm. "Nate's a dick."

Adele cracked a smile at that but shook her head.

"I'm in too," Elle called. "Nina said there was cookie decorating!"

"And cooking lessons!" Manish said.

"And don't forget the sure-to-be-so-awful-it's-amazing open-mic finale," Elle said.

"I dare you!" Manish called. "I triple-dog dare you to Turtledove your love life, Sloane Berry!"

"Oh, *Turtledove* your love life," Nina said. "I like that."

"Dear god," Sloane said, then groaned at the ceiling.

"Mom, Two Turtledoves costs a fortune," Adele said.

"Like three hundred bucks a person," Sloane said. "We can't ask everyone to—"

"Already taken care of," Nina said.

"What?" Adele asked.

"Consider it your Christmas present."

"I'd rather have some new AirPods," Sloane said.

"Nonrefundable, I'm afraid," Nina said, shrugging casually. "And it's a fundraiser for the public schools, so don't be a grinch."

"Extortion," Sloane said. "That's what this is."

"What about Brighton?" Adele asked, lowering her voice to a whisper. "She's scared of horses."

Charlotte's stomach fluttered. Damn traitor. Last evening, she'd kept herself in check—all night, in fact, even after three glasses of wine—but now she couldn't stop her brain from going places she'd rather it not.

Like to Brighton on their eighth-grade field trip to Ashcroft Farms, a huge smile on her face as she sat astride Gertrude, one of the farm's sleek brown horses. Their whole class was lined up for a ride, and Charlotte waved at Brighton, who was the first to take her turn.

"She's so pretty," Brighton had said a split second before Gertrude lurched into a quick canter.

A canter that quickly turned into a gallop.

"Gertrude!" Hattie, one of the workers at the farm, had yelled, but Gertrude wasn't listening. She continued her run, heading right for the opening in the fence like a prisoner set loose.

Brighton didn't scream. Didn't make a sound, in fact, but Charlotte could see her expression—terrified—and how tightly she held on to Gertrude's saddle horn while the reins flapped near the ground.

Charlotte's heart was in her throat as Gertrude took off through the fence. Hattie was running after them, but there was no way she'd catch a horse on foot. She yelled at someone ahead of her, an older woman who turned out to be one of the farm's owners. The woman stepped in front of Gertrude like it was nothing, her hands on her overalled hips, a chastisement on her tongue. Gertrude immediately dug her heels into the dirt, coming to such an abrupt stop, Charlotte thought Brighton was going to fly over Gertrude's head to her death.

"Gertrude, you big idiot," the woman had said, gathering the reins and giving Gertrude a pat on her flank. Gertrude, shamed, simply bent down and nosed at some scattered blueberries on the ground, chomping at them lazily, as though nothing had even gone awry.

After the woman helped Brighton down, called her a brave girl, it had still taken an hour for Brighton's breathing to go back to normal. Charlotte sat with her on a bench by the old mill, water turning the creaky wheel, now as part of a history lesson rather than practicality. She rubbed Brighton's back as her friend sipped on some water and told her it was okay. Brighton rested her head on Charlotte's shoulder. She smelled like a meadow, like fresh air and ripe blueberries. And that was the first time Charlotte felt it.

That flutter.

That tiny spark in her heart that she'd never really felt with anyone else since.

Now Charlotte sat up too quickly, cutting off the memory with a swell of pain in her head. Just as well. Preferable, in fact, as she had no room to be sentimental here. This was survival, plain and simple.

"She'll be fine," Nina said. "Just keep an eye on her."

"Mom," Sloane said, "I really don't—"

"Let's do it," Charlotte said.

"Et tu?" Sloane said, glaring at Charlotte.

"I'm afraid you girls are outnumbered," Nina said. "Bagels and coffee in the kitchen in fifteen! Come on, Snick." And with that, she flounced down the hall, humming what sounded like "Santa Baby," Snick trotting behind her.

"You have betrayed me," Sloane said.

"Your mother's right," Charlotte said. "You *are* dramatic."

Adele cackled at that, clapping her hands together once before turning to go back to her room.

Sloane just groaned and fell back on the bed. "I would've thought you, of all people, would be on my side. Don't you want to argue for a six-hour rehearsal sesh?"

"We've got time for that," Charlotte said. "It's not like you actually have to *date* anyone. Just ride a horse. You don't even have to smile."

"Easy for you to say. Small-town singles are feral. You'll see."

"I'm from a small town."

Sloane turned to look at her. "Michigan, right?"

Charlotte nodded. "Right by the lake."

"And how many singles events did you go to there, hmm?"

"None. I was a coldhearted hermit without a social life, remember?" Charlotte forced a laugh, even though it made her head feel like it was swelling in size. She felt she was playing off her childhood pretty well, particularly with this precarious topic of singleness and hometowns.

But Sloane didn't laugh. She just sat up and looked at Charlotte, eyes softly narrowed. "Were you really?"

Charlotte frowned. "I . . ." She trailed off, not sure what to say here. No, things weren't exactly the way Charlotte had described them, but she had no clue how to talk about living in Grand Haven without mentioning Brighton, which was why she never, ever talked about Grand Haven.

Sloane crossed her legs, turned toward her like they were two girls at a sleepover. "Just tell me one detail. Anything you want."

"Why?" Charlotte asked.

Sloane rolled her eyes. "Because I'm your best friend."

Something bloomed inside Charlotte's chest, an emotion she

couldn't name, and it pushed at her and shoved and pinched. She pressed her hand to her chest, trying to keep it in, but then she started talking.

"There was a girl . . ." Charlotte said.

"Oh, here we go," Sloane said, grinning. "Now we're getting to it."

Charlotte paused, the whole story *right there*, swirling and brimming like a river in a downpour. She inhaled, exhaled, imagined herself saying everything, the weight of it all leaving her lungs, her bones.

She imagined Sloane's reaction.

Sloane *knowing*.

And then Charlotte felt it happening—the dam's doors closing—and she let them, because even now, the humiliation of being left by the one person who had promised to love her no matter what was so visceral. Charlotte could still smell the wood sage and sea salt perfume she'd bought especially for that day, perfume she'd never worn since. She could still see her mother sitting at the first table at Simone's, Bonnie Fairbrook's restaurant, which they'd rented out for the wedding. Anna had chosen a blush-colored suit for the event. She looked perfect and refined, but all Charlotte remembered was the bored expression on Anna's face as it became clear Brighton wasn't going to show.

Charlotte could still hear the music too.

Their song.

She hadn't played her violin part since, but the melody, the whimsical notes Brighton had woven together the day they'd gotten engaged played in her dreams sometimes. She'd wake up with the song in her head like a ghost stalking her through sleep.

No, Charlotte couldn't possibly tell this story. Couldn't admit it all to Sloane, who would undoubtedly try to comfort her, join her in hating Brighton, even. But underneath all that, Sloane would *know*.

She'd know Charlotte. Really know her. And letting someone in like that had never worked out very well for her.

"She just . . . she was my best friend," Charlotte said, schooling her expression into something unaffected. "We grew apart, that's all. But I guess I wasn't a complete hermit." She laughed, smiling in a way she thought was convincing.

Sloane frowned, clearly disappointed. "Did this girl help you figure out you were bi?"

Charlotte blinked.

"For me, it was Gemma Villanueva." Sloane's eyes took on a dreamy quality. "Tenth grade. I'd known her forever, but one day, it was like a lightning strike. I noticed her butt in this certain pair of jeans, and god, I can't even tell you. I thought I just, you know, wanted my butt to look like that, but then, one day, we were in the orchestra room together after school, and—"

"It wasn't her," Charlotte said.

Sloane snapped her mouth shut.

"It wasn't my friend," Charlotte said again, the denial coming too quickly, some lie about who actually did bring about her bi awakening coming too slowly, so she said nothing else. Just fiddled with the edge of the lavender sheet.

Sloane looked away, then sighed. "Right."

"I'm sorry. I didn't mean to interrupt you," Charlotte said, which she knew wasn't exactly true. She'd panicked. She hadn't realized how close she'd come to sharing her saddest story. Sloane's own story had simply felt like too much.

Too much like the kind of closeness she'd promised herself she'd never fall into again.

Sloane only nodded in response, her eyes distant on the

dresser in front of her, a jewelry holder still full of friendship bracelets taking center stage. "Well, we should probably get ready for this horror show you've all agreed to." She flung off her covers, grabbed a pair of jeans and a sweater from her closet, and left the room without another word. Charlotte heard the bathroom door click shut, and she flopped back onto the bed, her head still screaming at her, a horrible mix of guilt and relief humming just under her ribs.

chapter 8

The horses were monsters.

Beasts.

Veritable behemoths.

"You okay?" Adele asked for the third time since they'd pulled into a field next to a red barn. The Hazelthorne house, according to the Berry sisters, was another mile up the road, but the Two Turtledoves event started in this grassy area near a paddock, where what seemed like a wild pack of horses waited with plaid flannel blankets draped over their backs.

"I'm fine," Brighton said robotically. And she was. She could do this. It was just a horse, and one used to having people on its back. Granted, Gertrude, the Demon Horse of Western Michigan, had been the same. Then again, Brighton had been thirteen. Everything was scary at thirteen, and she wasn't thirteen anymore.

She was a grown-up, dammit, complete with a dead-end dream and a lackluster love life.

She suppressed a groan and focused on the atmosphere around her, which she had to admit was idyllic. Snow covered the ground, an expanse of fields that seemed to go on forever to the east. Just ahead was the drive that curled through tall oaks and led to the house, and to her left, an evergreen forest rose up before her, snowy and verdant all at once, a tiny path carved through the middle. The air was crisp and cold, perfect for her blush-colored infinity scarf, hat, and mittened fingers, which warmed around a cup of hot apple cider.

Then there was the company, at least twenty people of different genders, races, and ethnicities gathered for the event, all of them ranging in age from midtwenties to midthirties, if Brighton had to guess.

And some of them very, very cute.

Her attention caught on a woman with brown skin and short dark hair, her hands in the pockets of her navy puffer coat, clunky Doc Martens on her feet. Their eyes met, and the woman smiled. Brighton smiled back, but then her gaze immediately slid to Lola, who was standing by Sloane, her posture ramrod straight in her tailored peacoat, somehow marred by what looked like a mud stain. Brighton shook herself inwardly, forced her eyes back to the woman in the Docs, whose wide and confident stance sent just the right kind of pheromones in Brighton's direction.

"Hey," Brighton said to Adele. "Do you know all of these people?"

"Most of them, yeah. Why my mother thinks Sloane and I are gonna find true love amid the people who used to make fun of our hair behind our backs and ask us *what we were*, I'm not sure."

"God," Brighton said. "They actually asked you that?"

Adele gave her a look. "Oh, my sweet summer child."

Brighton winced. "I'm sorry. That's awful."

Adele took a sip of her cider. "That's having a white mom and a Black dad in a small town. It wasn't everyone, though. In fact, there are a lot of pretty decent people here. Queer people too." She motioned toward a Black guy talking to Sloane. He had short hair with a fade and a neatly trimmed beard, a jawline that could cut glass. "That's Wes, Sloane's boyfriend her junior and senior years of high school and all through college. Good dude. One of the only pan kids at our school. Owns a restaurant downtown."

"He's cute," Brighton said.

"He is." Adele smiled. "Looks like he thinks the same of Charlotte."

"What?" Brighton said, eyes snapping to Lola once again, who was now offering a smile to Wes's outstretched hand. Lola hated shaking hands, said it was the equivalent of licking a subway turnstile in New York City, but she caved after a shoulder nudge from Sloane, showing all of her teeth as she slid her palm into Wes's.

His smile widened.

Brighton's stomach tightened, something that was absolutely not jealousy pulling at her insides. "What about her?" she asked Adele, nodding toward the woman in Docs.

"That's Gemma Villanueva, Sloane's first queer crush. She's also my mom's best friend's kid, so we all sort of figured out our queerness together."

"Sweet."

"And swapped spit around, you know, *experimenting*."

"Gross."

Adele laughed, then nudged Brighton's arm. "We're all very platonic now. She's good people. You should go for it."

Brighton just frowned, watching Gemma laugh at something

a person next to her said. She glanced back at Lola, who was still talking to Wes and Sloane. His body was definitely angled toward her, and she was still smiling, smiling, smiling. Fake smiling—Brighton would know Lola's grin-and-bear-it look anywhere—but she was still interacting, never glancing in Brighton's direction. They weren't even twenty-four hours into their stay in Winter River, but Brighton was already exhausted from all the wondering and caring and looking she was doing.

She needed to stop.

Needed to focus on something else.

Go for it, Adele had said. There was nothing stopping her. Granted, she lived in Nashville, and Gemma—all of these people, for that matter—either lived here or was only home for the holidays, but still. Why shouldn't she have a little fun? Why shouldn't she spend time with someone who was hot and thought she was hot too and, you know, actually *spoke* to her? If they ended up making out and Lola just happened to hear about it, well, all the better.

Because Lola was clearly fine without Brighton Fairbrook in her life. Clearly, Brighton's betrayal five years ago had been the best decision for both of them. Clearly, Brighton just needed to let it the hell go.

Let Lola go.

"Yeah," Brighton said, taking in a deep gulp of cold winter air. "Maybe I will."

"That's the spirit," Adele said, then lifted her hand in a wave. "Hey, Gemma!"

"Oh god, *now*?" Brighton said.

"Now, baby girl."

"Fuck. Do I look okay?" She adjusted her hat so her bangs peeked out just so, made sure her coat was buttoned correctly.

Adele gave her a once-over. "Totally hot if I was into you like that."

Brighton laughed, but Adele's joke did help her relax. "Gee, thanks."

"Think nothing of it," Adele said, then chin-nodded at the woman approaching them. "Gemma, hey." They clasped hands in a sort of high five–slash–handshake, the kind of greeting beloved by butch lesbians everywhere.

"It's been too long," Gemma said. "How's Nashville?"

"Can't complain," Adele said. "Business is good. You still in LA?"

Gemma nodded, her gaze flicking to Brighton, then back to Adele. "Had to buy a new coat just for this trip."

Adele laughed, then said to Brighton, "Gemma is a landscape architect. Designs, like, botanical gardens for movie stars and shit."

Gemma shook her head. "More like koi ponds for C-list actors, but let's go with what you said."

Adele grinned. "Gemma, this is Brighton. She's a musician."

"Hey," Gemma said, tilting her head at Brighton. "Nice to—"

"Oh, no, I'm not a musician," Brighton said. It took her a second to realize she'd just blurted it out mid-introduction, but it felt important to start off on the right foot here. "Not really. I used to be. Guitar, songwriting, singing. You know. But I stopped. Because, well . . . I just did."

Gemma blinked at her, mouth slightly parted. "Okay. Um, cool."

"I bartend at Ampersand," Brighton said, motioning toward Adele, who was staring at her with a horrified expression on her face. Still, Brighton couldn't seem to shut up. "So that's my calling, I guess. Liquor and other people's sad music." She laughed awkwardly, could already feel her face heating up several degrees.

"That's . . . nice," Gemma said, then turned to talk to someone who had just come up on her left.

"Wow," Adele said after a few seconds of shocked silence.

"I know," Brighton said.

"You are supremely bad at this."

Brighton pressed her hands to her crimson cheeks. "Was it as awful as I think it was?"

"Worse. Were you always this bad? Like, you've had hookups in the past few years, right?"

Brighton closed her eyes, took a deep breath. "Yeah, I just . . . I'm just a bit . . ."

Do not look at Lola, she told herself. *Don't you fucking dare.*

"I'm jet-lagged," Brighton said. "Off my game."

"*Off* your game?" Adele said. "More like your game fell out of the airplane somewhere over the Midwest."

Brighton didn't reply, just filled her cheeks with air before blowing a raspberry. She glanced at Gemma. She could fix this. She'd done it before, goddammit—she'd had plenty of hookups since she'd moved to Nashville. She could be cute and alluring and even suave. Not as suave as Adele, but that's the kind of shit one was born with. She needed to work with what she had here.

She was just about to step closer to Gemma when a blond woman in her fifties stepped up onto a crate in front of the paddock and clapped her gloved hands.

"Okay, everyone!" she said. She was wearing a puffy vest over a plaid flannel shirt, and her boots were caked in mud. Definite farmer vibe. "Most of you know me, but I do see a few new faces. I'm Jenny Hazelthorne, and we're very excited to be sponsoring this event for Two Turtledoves. As you know, it's for a good cause, so take advantage of all the cash you've already dropped and step up your romantic game!"

Chuckles rippled through the crowd. Adele side-eyed Brighton, and Brighton stuck out her tongue.

"Before we get started," Jenny said, "I just want to give you a few tips about our wonderful animal friends." She waved toward the horses that the Hazelthorne employees were now leading out of the paddock. Jenny went on to talk about mounting, how to work the reins, and how all of these horses had been chosen for their gentle temperaments.

Regardless, Brighton's stomach clenched as a guy in a flannel shirt and puffy vest brought a brown horse to a stop next to her.

She gulped.

"This here is Cupcake," the guy said, smiling a wide cowboy-like smile, all swagger and ease. His name tag read Scott. "She's sweet as sugar."

Cupcake's eyes were doelike, long lashes surrounding a soft brown in which Brighton could see her reflection, but still, she was gigantic and muscular, and Brighton couldn't believe people actually straddled these things willingly.

"Take a second to get to know your horse," Jenny said. "Pet them. Let them sniff your hand so they can get to know you."

Brighton held out a hand to Cupcake, determined to conquer her fear, but when Cupcake's nostrils flared and she let out a loud huff, Brighton yelped and yanked her hand back.

"Good, everyone, good," Jenny said, then motioned to a woman next to her with short red curls sticking out from under her hat. "This is my wife, Shannon, and she and I will both be leading the tour through the woods in case anything goes awry."

Brighton relaxed a little at the word *wife*, just like she always did when in the company of other queer people. She could be undergoing a root canal, and as long as the dentist was queer, she was bound to be at least 50 percent calmer, the feeling of safety and camaraderie like a mild muscle relaxer.

Still, Cupcake's nostrils were the size of whole human fists, and she wasn't sure how she felt about that. She wasn't sure how she felt about anything right now.

"Okay, everyone, mount up!" Jenny announced, and Brighton's stomach flipped. *Mount up? Just like that? Just . . . mount up?*

Everyone around her did exactly that. She watched as Elle got onto a black-and-brown horse, and Manish let out a triumphant whoop as he settled into the saddle of his black horse. Adele and Sloane slipped onto their horses like selkies into water, and Lola . . .

Lola was looking right at her.

She already sat astride a brown horse, her posture perfect as she nodded at something Wes was saying atop his own horse next to her, but her eyes were on Brighton.

Brighton looked back, her hands on the saddle as Scott held on to the horse's reins. Brighton waited for Lola to . . . what? Smile? Nod in encouragement?

Anything, really. Brighton just wanted Lola to do anything but gaze at her with that dead-eyed expression, as though her ex-fiancée were nothing more than a photograph on a wall.

"Just grab hold of the horn there, ma'am," Scott said when Brighton didn't move.

She blinked, and Lola's gaze was gone, turned toward Wes. Brighton focused on Cupcake, but everything Jenny had said about getting on the damn thing flew right out of her head.

"Ma'am?" Scott said, but Brighton couldn't stop watching as Lola laughed at something Wes said. It actually took quite a lot to get Lola to laugh genuinely. She didn't let everyone in like that, didn't—

"Can I help you with something?" Lola asked.

Brighton blinked. She'd been so lost in thought about how Lola used to be, she hadn't realized Lola was staring right at her again.

And Brighton was staring back.

"Help me?" Brighton asked.

Lola looked her up and down. "You have to get on the horse in order to ride it."

"Oh, is that how it works?" Brighton asked. "How about common courtesy?"

"Do you really want to talk about courtesy right now?" Lola said, her hands tightening on her reins.

No, in fact, Brighton did not. But goddammit, Lola's *who the fuck are you* attitude was making her skin feel too tight for her body.

"Do you two know each other?" Wes asked, his eyes darting between them.

"No," Lola said before Brighton had even opened her mouth. "Not at all. Just not hitting it off."

"Oh, I don't know," Brighton said, because she was an asshole. "I rather like a little verbal sparring as foreplay."

A few laughs fluttered through the group, and Lola's face flooded red.

"I prefer mutual respect and, as you said, *courtesy*," she said. "For example, when someone is going to be late for an appointment or, I don't know, not show up at all, a little heads-up is nice. You know"—here she smiled widely, showing all her teeth—"being a decent human being and all. Don't you think so, Wes?"

He blinked. "Um, punctuality is . . . a trait I admire. I'm sorry, *are* we talking about punctuality?"

Lola just laughed. "Something like that."

Brighton opened her mouth, a real zinger on the tip of her tongue, something really mature, like where certain moles were located on Lola's body, but she stopped herself just in time, turning away and biting her tongue.

"Fuck," she said instead, because she had to say *something*, then realized far too late that she'd all but yelled the curse. Eyes latched on to her from all around, including Adele's and Gemma's. Brighton laughed it off, shrugging like the himbo Gemma undoubtedly thought she was. Still, the awkwardness was strong enough to motivate Brighton to get on her horse. She turned to face Cupcake, put her left hand on the saddle horn and her left foot in the stirrup, then hoisted herself on top of the beast.

Cupcake swerved a bit, but Brighton managed to stay on her back. Brighton's entire body was shaking, and she was sure she was about to puke, but she'd done it. She was so high up, the world taking on an entirely different quality from this perspective. She couldn't imagine moving through the snowy woods like this, but it was happening regardless.

Jenny, now astride her own magnificent beast, applauded everyone's success and started modeling how to flick the reins and use one's legs to get a horse going.

"Squeeze your thighs, lovebirds!" she called, which made everyone laugh.

Somehow, Brighton managed to direct Cupcake into a walk without falling off or throwing up. Two farm employees on huge black horses corralled the group on either side, keeping everyone together, with Jenny and Shannon in the lead.

The path was narrow enough that the Turtledovers, as Brighton had chosen to think of them, had to merge into pairs. Somehow—call it fate or karma or whatever the hell—Brighton ended up riding alongside Gemma, with Lola and Wes right in front of them. Adele was next to Elle just ahead, and Brighton could hear Manish talking with Sloane behind her, saying something about how Nate kept calling him and the queer gods must hate him.

"At least I won't break your heart," Sloane said.

"I'd rather a little heartbreak if it gets me laid," Manish said, and Sloane laughed.

"Look at our girl, though," Manish said. "His name is Wes?"

Sloane must've nodded, then said, "He'll be good for her."

"He'd be good for anyone," Manish said. "He's hot."

Sloane said something else but so softly Brighton couldn't hear the words.

"Really now?" Manish said in response. "Interesting."

"Oh, shut up," Sloane said, louder this time, and Brighton felt herself straining backward a little to get a better listen.

"So," Gemma said loudly, startling Brighton forward into her saddle. Cupcake gave a little jolt as well, and Brighton tightened her grip on the reins. She smiled, focused on the pretty dimple pressing into Gemma's left cheek.

"Hi," Brighton said.

"Hi," Gemma said.

They fell into silence for a few seconds, which was honestly better than Brighton's unhinged babbling about the sad state of her life. She thought about the dating apps she sometimes logged into, how most of the time, when you got a match, it was best to start off the conversation with some interesting question rather than the standard fare. She was just about to ask Gemma about her favorite board game when Gemma beat her to it.

"So what sort of music did you used to play?"

Brighton blinked, her thighs tightening around Cupcake. The horse sped up for a second, then slowed when Brighton yanked on the reins, finally settling next to Gemma's horse again.

"Sorry," Brighton said. "Um . . . just . . . you know, singer-songwriter stuff."

"You played guitar?"

Brighton nodded.

"Why'd you quit?"

She opened her mouth, then snapped it shut. She hadn't really done this yet—explained her fallout with the Katies to anyone other than her parents and Adele. Hadn't needed to. She hadn't had a hookup since the band's breakup, and she certainly didn't make a habit of offering the information freely. Still, she didn't want to mess this up. Gemma was sweet and sexy and was giving her a second chance here.

"I just . . . needed a break," Brighton said. There. Perfectly reasonable. "It's difficult, trying to keep up with the pace in Nashville."

Gemma nodded. "I can't imagine. Was it hard to book shows?"

Brighton exhaled, her breath puffing in front of her in the cold. Cupcake huffed too, shaking her mane a little as they headed deeper into the forest.

"It was," Brighton said, and left it at that. "So what kind of board—"

"I love a live concert," Gemma said. "I was just at the Katies' show in Anaheim last month. They were amazing. You've heard of them, right? I mean, of course you have—every queer person has heard of them."

Cupcake reared up for a second, her front legs leaving the

ground altogether before stomping back down onto the snowy forest floor.

"Whoa," Brighton said, gripping the reins. "Whoa, girl."

"She okay?" Gemma asked.

Brighton didn't answer, her fingers going numb on the reins. Her heart had doubled its pace. She remembered hearing something about how horses could sense fear—or was that dogs? Either way, Cupcake was antsy, and Brighton tried her best to stay calm. The scenery was beautiful, after all—towering pines, a clear blue winter sky, a white blanket of snow as far as the eye could see. But no matter how gorgeous and serene her surroundings, she couldn't seem to settle down. That name—*the Katies*—was like a starter pistol. She couldn't hear it, couldn't even think it, without her thoughts leaping into a race of self-loathing and bitterness.

And, apparently, Cupcake was a mind reader, because the beast grew more agitated by the second. She started to stomp a little as she walked, whinnying softly and shaking her mane. Then she jerked to one side and straightened out, only to jerk to the other.

"Um," Brighton said, desperately pulsing her thighs in the saddle and pulling on the reins as gently as she could. "Good girl."

Cupcake, it seemed, was having none of it. She whinnied some more, then sped up before slowing down again.

"Brighton, you all right?" Manish asked from behind her.

"Yeah, yeah, I'm fine," Brighton said, more to herself than to Manish. She *was* fine. She was not about to die atop this horse.

"Maybe we should stop for a second," Gemma said.

"No, I'm good," Brighton said, trying to keep her voice steady, but she could hear it—the wobble in her throat, accompanied by a stinging behind her eyes she couldn't blame on the cold air.

And Cupcake felt it all.

She neighed—or whatever the hell one calls it when a horse essentially lets out a battle cry—and took off galloping.

"Whoa, girl!" Brighton yelled, but Cupcake had made up her mind, and she bolted down the snowy path, passing all the other couples in a blur of colors and shouts of alarm.

Brighton doubled over, the saddle horn jabbing into her chest as she hunched down to try to stay as low as possible. Tears streamed down her cheeks, and she had no idea if she'd actually started crying or if the winter air was simply yanking all the moisture from her eyes. Her ass slammed onto the saddle over and over again, and she was positive her tailbone—along with all of her other bones, to be honest—was in the process of shattering.

She squeezed her eyes closed, awaiting her grisly end. Just when she'd nearly made peace with the fact that she was probably going to die here in Winter River while her poor mother was drinking Château Lafite in France, another rider pulled up beside her.

"Whoa, girl, it's all right," a serene voice said, and bit by bit, Cupcake slowed to a trot, whinnying a little until she stopped altogether.

Brighton stayed hunched, eyes clenched shut, knuckles gnarled into Cupcake's mane.

"Jesus, are you both okay?" another voice called from behind her. Brighton thought it was Jenny Hazelthorne.

"We're fine," the first voice said.

Familiar.

So fucking familiar.

"That was some fast thinking," Jenny said.

Lola didn't answer—because it *was* Lola, that voice, calm and confident.

Brighton tried to uncurl her spine, tried to simply open her eyes, but she couldn't. Her whole body was locked up. A pulsing hush surrounded her, and it took her a second to realize the sound was her own breathing, fast and nearly out of control. She was dizzy, her mouth watering in warning, and—

A hand on her back.

"You're okay."

The hand moved up . . . then down, unsure at first, but then settling into a rhythmic circle.

"You're fine," Lola said. "Everything's fine."

"Shit, Brighton, are you all right?" Adele asked as she came up behind them.

"She's fine," Lola said. "Just give her a second."

Her hand kept moving, soothing, and second by second, Brighton felt her mind slow down, then her heart, her lungs. Her fingers released Cupcake's mane, and her shoulders loosened. Finally, finally, she opened her eyes.

Found Lola's.

Lola was still calm, no smile or even the slightest curve to her mouth, but she was looking at Brighton with . . . *something*. Something more than the cool disdain with which she'd talked to Brighton just a few minutes ago.

Brighton reached out and grabbed Lola's other hand, which held not only her own horse's reins but also Cupcake's, and Lola let her. Their fingers tangled together, Lola's free hand still on her back, and Brighton felt as though she'd just fallen into a feather bed after a week without sleep.

"You're okay," Lola said again, and Brighton nodded, their gazes still locked.

"My god, Charlotte, where'd you learn to ride like that?" Sloane said.

And the spell broke.

Lola untangled their fingers, removed her hand from Brighton's back. She straightened her posture and cleared her throat.

"I wasn't going that fast," she said. "Just instinct, I guess." Her eyes flicked to Brighton's one more time, then away.

"Well, it was quite the rescue," Jenny said. Shannon, who had come up on Cupcake's other side and dismounted, smoothed a hand over the mare's neck and whispered to her. "Some might say the stuff meet-cutes are made of." Jenny was smiling, her gaze going back and forth between Lola and Brighton.

"Okay, now we're getting down to it," Manish said. "The magic of Two Turtledoves at work, I see."

"Char and the damsel-in-distress trope," Elle said. "I love it."

"Right?" Manish said. "All we need is a clinch cover for the book."

"You two are ridiculous," Lola said, then laughed. She *laughed*, the sound so genuine that Brighton felt anger surge through her veins. Granted, her heart rate was still working to slow down after her adventure, but she was getting damn tired of this roller-coaster ride with Lola. She either ignored Brighton or insulted her, then quite literally saved her life, only to laugh at the mere idea of the two of them together.

As though they hadn't very nearly promised to love each other forever.

"Are we ridiculous?" Elle asked.

"We are not," Manish said. "You two could at least ride together for the rest of the morning, see if there's a spark."

"There's definitely something," Elle said.

"There isn't," Lola said. "And I'd rather—"

"I think there might be," Brighton said, lifting her chin when Lola slowly turned to meet her gaze. She hadn't planned it, but canting along with Lola right now seemed to be the only way she was going to get her ex to talk to her. *Really* talk to her. "Remember how I said I enjoy verbal sparring?"

Lola pressed her mouth flat. "I'm not sure you're up for continuing on horseback."

"I'm fine," Brighton said, forcing more steadiness into her voice than she felt. But then she smiled. Lowered her lashes a little, flicked them back up. And, hell yes, she absolutely did coat her next words with every ounce of flirt she possessed. "Especially if you're by my side to help me."

"Damn," Manish said.

Lola's jaw tightened.

"All right, looks like we have the first match of Two Turtledoves!" Jenny announced, clapping her gloved hands together. The rest of the group joined in, and Brighton heard Adele's signature whistle over the crowd.

Lola still continued to stare at her.

Brighton didn't look away. Didn't dare. Lola wanted to play games with her? She'd play them right the fuck back.

chapter 9

Charlotte wanted to scream.

She wanted to kick at Cinnamon's sides again and take off through the woods, her middle finger raised in farewell as she went.

Really, she wanted to go back in time and simply observe Brighton fly by her on the path, dark hair flapping in the frosty air, doing nothing whatsoever about her ex-fiancée's brush with death.

Oh, wow, poor thing. I hope she's okay.

But no, of course she had to play the hero, had to swoop in and clean up Brighton Fairbrook's mess, just like she'd always done—holding Brighton's hair back so she could puke up all the Jägerbombs she drank at their first party their freshman year at Berklee, pretty much dragging her across the finish line of their music theory class because Brighton had always relied on her ear far too much, covering for her when she skipped AP English their senior year of high school to stand in line for tickets to see Florence + the Machine.

The list went on and on, ten years of half-baked plans and impulsivity that Charlotte had tried her best to hold together, make cohesive.

Make last.

Let's get married.

That had been Brighton's biggest impulse of all.

Let's get married.

Whispered on the lakeshore when they were twenty-two years old. They'd just arrived home from Berklee for Christmas break of their junior year. The Fairbrook house was glowing and alive with soft lights and wreaths, with candles and hot toddies and presents under the Christmas tree—some of them with Charlotte's name on them—while Charlotte's house was dark.

Closed up, even.

When Charlotte had slid her key into the front door, a blast of cold, stale air had rushed out to meet her, nothing but the single Tiffany lamp on the front hall's console table to light her way, casting watery blue and red shadows on the wall.

The lamp Charlotte's mother only left on during the day if she was out of town.

Charlotte had called Anna then, pressing her phone to her ear, her heart thrumming under her ribs, but she already knew, even before her mother picked up, voice casual and crackling over the distance, that Anna Donovan was not at home to greet her daughter with Christmas cheer.

"I'm in London," Anna had said. "I didn't tell you?"

"I'm sure you did," Charlotte had said, even though she knew her mother hadn't said a word to her about a trip to London over the holidays.

"It's a research trip for that Jack the Ripper copycat book I'm working on," Anna said. "I'll be back New Year's Day. See you then?"

"See you then." Charlotte had ended the call before her voice split, tears clouding into her chest and up her throat. She allowed herself to break, overwhelmed by the stress of the fall semester and her upcoming spring show, by this constant desperation for Brighton to do well too, even as she felt Brighton's interest in classical training waning more and more. It was too much, December closing in on her, reminding her she was nothing, no one. She sat on the bottom of the stairs, the Tiffany lamplight pooling at her feet, and cried.

Brighton had found her like that. Charlotte hadn't meant for her to see. While Brighton was the safest place, Charlotte's *person*, she didn't like losing her shit quite that much in front of anyone, even her one true love, who she knew would take her in her arms and whisper in her ear how much she loved her, how beautiful she was, how perfect.

And that's exactly what Brighton did.

She held Charlotte and whispered and kissed her tears away and then led her out to the snowy beach where the sun was setting over the frigid water, icy waves frozen in time.

"So Anna's a narcissistic bitch," Brighton had said, her fingers laced with Charlotte's as they walked. "This we know."

Charlotte nodded, but the tears started flowing again anyway, evidence that Charlotte still cared a little too much, still wanted Anna to *not* be the way she was.

"Hey," Brighton said, stopping them and turning to face Charlotte. "Fuck her. It's not you, it's her, okay? Remember that."

Charlotte nodded again, her forehead pressed to Brighton's, her heart finally slowing down, settling into this familiar rhythm.

Brighton kissed her then, softly, sweetly, gloved fingers on her face. "I'm your family. You're mine. Forever, right?"

"Forever," Charlotte said.

"Let's get married," Brighton said then, barely even taking a breath before the words tumbled from her cool mouth.

Charlotte leaned back to see her more clearly. "What?"

"You heard me," Brighton said, smiling. "Marry me."

Charlotte shook her head but couldn't keep the smile off her face. "When?"

"Today?" Brighton had said, and they both laughed. "Tomorrow, next month, next year, I don't even care when. Just say yes. Just say it'll happen."

Charlotte didn't have to think much more past that. Brighton was her best friend, her love, her everything. There was no other answer to give, no other words that even existed.

"Yes. Of course, yes."

Brighton had curled her arms around Charlotte's waist then, twirling her in a circle on the snowy shore, their kisses sweet at first but then turning wild, warm breaths clouding between them in the cold. They'd run into Charlotte's house after that, not even bothering with lights, throwing clothes off as they stumbled to Charlotte's bedroom and fell onto her bed in the growing dark, limbs slotting together like puzzle pieces. Brighton parted Charlotte's legs, her fingers slipping inside, palm pressing down right where Charlotte needed it, so perfect, and Charlotte came so fast, Brighton's name a cry into the chilly air. Then she'd flipped her fiancée onto her back, Brighton laughing, a laugh that turned into the softest gasp as Charlotte's mouth—

"So what's your favorite board game?"

Now, Charlotte startled at Brighton's deadpan voice, blinked the Winter River woods back into focus. They were riding again, slower this time, Brighton and Charlotte positioned right behind Jenny and Shannon for safety's sake. Charlotte glanced behind her at Sloane, now riding next to Wes, who offered her a wave. Sloane shot her a thumbs-up, mouthed "Good luck," and then actually waggled her eyebrows.

This was a disaster.

This whole group would have her and Brighton engaged by the time they reached the hot chocolate and doughnuts awaiting them at the end of the trail.

"Mine is Balderdash," Brighton said, a sarcastic lilt to her voice.

"What?" Charlotte asked, adjusting in her saddle. She was flustered, uncomfortable, memories from the day Brighton became her fiancée making everything feel blurry and unreal. She didn't often reminisce about her sex life with Brighton, but when she made that mistake . . .

She sighed, rubbed her forehead, and thought of broken E strings, notes just a hair off-key, the squeak of her rosin across her bow.

"Making up vocabulary and definitions," Brighton said, unbelievably still rambling. "It's a good game."

"Yes," Charlotte said, rolling her shoulders back. "I'm sure you're wonderful at nonsense words and meanings."

"Lola—"

"Stop calling me that," Charlotte said through clenched teeth, her voice low and almost dangerous. After everything Brighton had done, Brighton's name for her should be like a cold shower, but no. The low, nearly whispered way Brighton said it, like a prayer almost—the sound thrummed between her legs, instant and overwhelming, and her position in this damn saddle made getting her mind back on track decidedly more difficult.

"You want everyone here to know our history?" Charlotte

said, focusing on the hum of irritation just below her skin. "Is that it?"

"You're the one acting like a spoiled child around me."

"I'm acting like someone who doesn't *like* you. I think that's allowed."

"I don't want everyone to know," Brighton said. "I just want you to act like it happened at all."

Charlotte laughed. "Oh, I'm well aware of what happened."

Brighton released a grunt of frustration. Her horse whinnied a little, swerving to the right and nearly colliding with Cinnamon.

"Shit," Brighton said, pulling on the reins.

"Would you hold it together?" Charlotte said.

"I'm trying," Brighton said, patting her horse's flank awkwardly. "You could help by not being such a coldhearted bitch."

This time Cinnamon huffed and sped up a bit.

"I think I'm entitled," Charlotte said when she'd calmed her horse.

"Okay, so I'm the bad guy here, I get it, but—"

"I don't think you're the bad guy, Brighton," Charlotte said. Her mind cleared, a stoic calm settling into her bones, any and all arousal vanishing like a puff of smoke. She knew she should shut up, just swallow what she was going to say next, but it was necessary. She had to let Brighton know, in no uncertain terms, that any kind of camaraderie between them during this trip wasn't going to happen. They weren't going to kiss and make up. They weren't going to fake a cutesy little romance for these ridiculous Two Turtledoves events.

They weren't going to do anything.

Up ahead, the trees broke and the path widened, spilling out into the backyard of a green two-story farmhouse with a wraparound porch and twinkle lights in the bushes. Tables were set up with hot chocolate and pastries, a fire crackled in a stone firepit, and a Bluetooth speaker played "I'll Be Home for Christmas."

"I don't think you're the bad guy," Charlotte said again as she turned Cinnamon to the right and kicked at his sides with her heels to speed him up. "I don't think about you at all."

And with that, she moved Cinnamon into a faster canter away from Brighton. She waited for a wash of triumph, her parting words delivered perfectly—indifferent, quiet, calm. Surely, that would be it. Surely, Brighton would take the hint.

She pulled Cinnamon to a stop and slid out of the saddle, boots crunching on the snowy ground, then took a second to get herself together, brushing her gloved hand over Cinnamon's neck. He huffed, angled his head to nuzzle her hand, and she leaned against him.

The feeling of triumph didn't come.

She waited, heard the rest of the group dismounting and chatting, exclaiming at the picturesque winter scene, but the only thing she felt was a knot in her throat, the desire to press her face to Cinnamon's flank and cry.

A few deep breaths helped, and she rolled her shoulders back, ready to get the rest of this shit show over with. As she turned, though, she found herself face-to-face with Brighton again, her face a storm of emotion.

Brighton had never been good at holding back, holding it all in.

"You want to blame me for what happened?" she said quietly. "Fine. I get it."

"Brighton, don't—"

"No." Brighton held up a hand. "You don't get to deliver your Anna Donovan one-liners and walk away. You don't get to do that."

"I get to do whatever I want," Charlotte said, her jaw tense.

"Why? Because I made a mistake when we were twenty-three?"

"A mistake?"

"Yes, I fucked up," Brighton said, lifting her arms and letting them fall back down to her sides. "I panicked and fucked up, and I should've done every single thing differently on that day five years ago. I should've done a lot of things differently."

Charlotte flattened her mouth into a straight line. If she spoke, she'd scream, calling attention to them. But leaving your best friend—your fiancée, your everything—alone at the altar in a white suit, everyone watching, waiting, wondering, was not some simple mistake. It was not something to reflect on and wish for a do-over.

It was catastrophic.

A world-ender.

And Brighton was kidding herself if she thought it was anything different.

Brighton stepped closer, her dark eyes a little shiny. "But I was right."

Charlotte scoffed. "You were *right*?"

"I handled it badly. Really, *really* badly. But we should not have been getting married that day, Lola, and you know it. You just didn't want to see it. You didn't want to see *me*."

Charlotte's mouth fell open. She knew she should let it go, but defensiveness swelled. The absolute fucking nerve of this woman. "How in the hell did I not—"

"How are the lovebirds doing?" Jenny appeared next to them, slapping them both on their backs so hard they lurched forward a bit.

"Not compatible, I'm afraid," Brighton said calmly, her eyes never leaving Charlotte's. Then she turned and walked off toward the refreshments table and grabbed a foam cup of hot chocolate before joining Adele and Elle in conversation without another glance in Charlotte's direction.

The rest of the morning was nothing short of torture. Charlotte could barely stomach the too-sweet hot chocolate, no doubt made from a packet of powder and water, and Brighton didn't look her way again.

She didn't sneak a glance.

Didn't so much as get within twenty feet of Charlotte as those in the group milled around the fire and chatted about their interests and jobs and just how drunk their uncles would get at the traditional Christmas Eve dinner.

Charlotte should feel relieved.

She should not be sitting on a rough-hewn log around the firepit right now, feeling even more aware of Brighton than she had an hour ago, sneaking her own glances every ten seconds, and using peripheral vision to track her. This was what she'd wanted, after all—for Brighton to leave her alone, to become nothing more than a stranger in a crowd.

So why Charlotte couldn't seem to focus on anything but Brighton's exact location, she wasn't sure.

You just didn't want to see it. You didn't want to see me.

"Fucking ridiculous."

"What's ridiculous?" Sloane asked, sitting down on the log next to Charlotte.

"Did I say that out loud?" Charlotte asked.

Sloane nodded.

Charlotte just shook her head, then lifted her foam cup. "Just . . . this hot chocolate."

Sloane laughed. "I mean, it's bad, but I'm not sure if *fucking ridiculous* is quite accurate."

Charlotte let herself laugh too, took a few seconds to breathe through the tightness in her chest.

"What happened with Brighton?" Sloane asked. "Didn't hit it off?"

Charlotte snorted. "You could say that."

"Why not? I was starting to wonder if all that tension last night at dinner was purely sexual."

Charlotte nearly choked on her sugar water. "No. Absolutely not. She's . . . she's just not my type, I guess."

Sloane hummed. "Still, she's lovely."

Charlotte snapped her gaze to Sloane, who was watching Brighton—now sitting on the back porch, talking to a woman with short dark hair and wearing Docs—with curiosity. Something foreign and unwelcome rose up in Charlotte's chest, closing tight fingers around her throat. Suddenly, flashes of Sloane and Brighton together played in high definition behind her eyelids.

Another ridiculous thing.

She should want Brighton with someone else right now. It would get her out of Charlotte's hair for the rest of this trip, and it wasn't like Sloane was looking for anything serious anyway. She never was. In all the time Charlotte had known Sloane, she'd never gone beyond a few dates, mostly for the sex. Her words, not Charlotte's. It'd be the perfect distraction for all of them.

You should go for it formed on Charlotte's tongue, but she couldn't quite get the phrase out of her mouth.

"Did you know she was in the Katies?" Sloane asked.

Charlotte blinked as Sloane's words jumbled into her head, then slowly snapped into the right order. "Wait, what?"

"Founded the band or something like that. Years ago."

Charlotte didn't particularly like the Katies, but she'd certainly heard of them. Elle loved them, had even arranged a string piece of their hit song, "Cherry Lipstick," for the quartet that they had performed at live shows as a crowd-pleaser.

And a crowd-pleaser it was, especially with Elle's pop-driven style combined with the fluidity of their strings. Even Charlotte enjoyed playing the song, the quick slash of her bow during the chorus.

Still, the Katies' percussion-driven style wasn't her favorite for daily listening.

And they didn't sound anything like Brighton Fairbrook. Charlotte would certainly have noticed. She and Brighton had spent years playing together, watching each other perform at concerts and recitals—Brighton's melancholic folk style and Charlotte's elegance and knack for arranging and interpretation. The Katies were nothing like that. They were the bright summer sun to Brighton's cloudy autumn sky.

"So what happened?" Charlotte asked.

Sloane blew out a breath, leaned closer. "Well, apparently, according to Adele, the other two members kicked her out to make room for a new lead singer. Then, like, they went viral right after that. Totally blew up."

"My god," Charlotte said, her gaze instinctively going to Brighton on the back porch.

"I know, right? Worst luck in the world. Adele said she hasn't touched her guitar since it all went down back in March. I wonder if she's actually any good."

"She's good," Charlotte said, a defensive instinct.

Sloane frowned. "How do you know?"

Charlotte swallowed, looked down at the swill in her cup. "Just a guess. She's got . . . I don't know, a vibe."

"A *vibe*?" Sloane laughed. "Charlotte Donovan is talking about *vibes*. You sure you two didn't hit it off?"

Charlotte's mouth parted, her breath catching in her throat. She watched Brighton laugh at something, tuck her hair behind her ear. She couldn't imagine Brighton Fairbrook without her guitar, without that notebook with the cartoon cats on the cover she used to scribble in all the time, forgoing homework and meals, showing up late to appointments or outings she and Charlotte had planned because she'd gotten lost in some song she was writing. She couldn't imagine Brighton Fairbrook ever giving up her dream.

But she didn't really know Brighton Fairbrook anymore, did she?

"Like I said, she's not my type." Charlotte cleared her throat, tipped a bit more lukewarm chocolate sugar into her mouth.

Sloane narrowed her eyes. "What *is* your type?"

Charlotte ignored the question, forced her eyes in front of her—she definitely did *not* look at the long-haired bohemian in the red plaid coat.

"Ah," Sloane said. "I see."

"See what?"

Sloane lifted her cup toward someone across the fire, someone Charlotte's eyes had apparently landed on when she was trying very pointedly *not* to look at Brighton.

Wes Reynolds.

He was talking with someone Charlotte hadn't yet met, a woman with long blond hair and heeled boots.

"Oh, no, I—" Charlotte started to say but then froze.

Wes was a nice guy. Sloane had dated him for years in high school, so he had to be. It wouldn't hurt to spend a little time with him, would it? She had absolutely zero interest in anything romantic or sexual happening, but conversation and some pottery-making or whatever fresh hell was in store for them at the next event—that would keep her distracted, at least.

Keep her safe from Brighton's unwelcome and fundamentally wrong opinions about their relationship's implosion.

"He is . . . cute," Charlotte heard herself say.

Sloane laughed. "He is."

"You're okay if I talk to him more?" Charlotte asked.

Sloane's smile dipped but was back in place so fast—and so genuinely—that Charlotte didn't have time to ponder it.

"Yeah," Sloane said, rubbing her hands on her jeans. "Absolutely. Wes!" Her abrupt call echoed across the fire, and Wes immediately turned toward her, his mouth open in midsentence. Sloane waved her hand. "Come over here."

He said something to the blond woman, then rose, circling around the firepit until he was standing in front of Charlotte and Sloane. "What's up?"

"Here, take my seat," Sloane said, standing. "Charlotte wants to know more about your restaurant."

"I do?" Charlotte said, then mentally slapped herself. "I do."

Wes laughed. "Happy to talk about it."

"Great," Sloane said. "Catch you both later." And before Wes even fully sat down, she was already halfway across the pit, taking his spot next to the blond and immediately launching into some conversation that had the woman laughing.

"How does she do that?" Charlotte asked.

Wes stretched out his long legs, clad in slim dark jeans, a bottle of water between his gloved hands. "Do what?"

"Just . . . talk. To everyone."

He laughed. "That's Sloane. Always has been."

Charlotte tilted her head at him. "Really?"

He nodded. "Did she ever tell you how we got together in high school?"

Charlotte shook her head, completely sure Sloane had never even mentioned Wes Reynolds before this trip. Not that she'd say that to Wes.

"I joined the orchestra fall semester of our junior year," he said. "Had never touched a stringed instrument in my life."

"Oh my god."

"Yeah. Our teacher, Dr. Stone, wasn't amused, but our school had a policy that students could try any elective they wanted. It was just the basic orchestra class, not the advanced one Sloane was in, but"—here he held up a finger and grinned—"Sloane was so damn good that Dr. Stone convinced the administration to let her TA for the beginner's class."

Charlotte felt a slow smile spread over her mouth. "You took the class because of Sloane."

He laughed, spread his hands out in front of him. "She helped everyone, constantly talking them through what they were doing right, doing wrong, how they could improve. Made her a good teacher. I was a horrible student, but she decided I was pretty cute, I guess. Finally agreed to a date in October if I promised to drop orchestra after the semester and stop torturing everyone with my scales."

"How long?" Charlotte asked.

"How long what?"

"How long had you been in love with Sloane before you signed up for the class?"

He laughed, a lovely booming sound. "Oh, I've been in love with Sloane Berry for forever." His eyes found her across the fire-pit, a soft smile still on his face.

"Forever?" Charlotte said, a teasing lilt to her voice as the puzzle pieces of Sloane and Wes fell into place, along with a possible reason why Sloane had never mentioned him.

Just like Charlotte had never mentioned Brighton.

She shook her head, dispelling that preposterous thought as Wes's smile vanished. He looked at her, squirming on his log.

"I mean . . . when we were kids," he said.

"Right," Charlotte said, lifting her brows at him.

He ran a hand over his short hair but said nothing.

"Forever?" she said again.

He sighed. "Shit, I'm really bad at this."

Charlotte laughed. "You're in good company, trust me."

"Look, I'd rather not be . . . you know." He waved a hand toward Sloane, his meaning clear. "If that counts for anything. My mom signed me up for Two Turtledoves—she does every year, and I do it as a kind of Christmas present to her, go on a date or two that are usually excruciating—but Sloane's never been here. She . . . well, it's hard to concentrate on other people when I'm around her."

"Makes sense," Charlotte said softly. She would *not* look at Brighton, she fucking would *not*.

"Pathetic, huh?" he said.

"Not at all," she said, smiling at him.

"What about you?" he asked, taking a sip of his water. "No sparks after your daring rescue? What's her name? Brighton?"

Charlotte pressed her lips together, an instinct, keeping it all inside, but suddenly, her whole history with Brighton felt impossibly heavy, weighing down her limbs, her bones, even her blood. She looked at Wes, his expression open. He was easy to talk to—he was sweet and genuine and just *kind*. Not that others in her life weren't, but he didn't know her, and she didn't know him, and they'd likely never see each other again after Two Turtledoves was over. There was a sort of safety in that.

She didn't think too hard about it—knew she'd talk herself out of it if she did. She just let herself say what she wanted, what she needed to say to someone.

"It's hard to reignite sparks between two people when one of them left the other at the altar five years ago," she said quietly.

The confession landed like a single snowflake in the wind—fluttering and delicate before settling peacefully on the ground. Charlotte exhaled, felt her facial muscles relax. All her muscles, really.

"Holy shit," Wes said softly.

"Yeah," Charlotte said.

"And you, wait . . ."

"Haven't seen her since. Not until we both showed up with a Berry sister for a Cheery, Queery Christmas."

Wes let out a shocked laugh, then slapped his hand over his mouth. "Shit, I'm sorry," he said through his fingers.

"Don't be," Charlotte said, then let herself laugh a little too. It *was* fucking funny when she really thought about it. The pure cosmic twist of it all. Then, suddenly, her gentle laugh turned into a longer one—louder, harder—and soon she and Wes were rightly guffawing, bent over on their logs, their shoulders pressed together, tears running down Charlotte's cheeks in the cold. At one point, she wasn't sure if she was laughing or crying.

Probably a little bit of both.

Charlotte noticed Sloane smiling at them, a question on her brow—in fact, everyone was looking their way, including Brighton, though Charlotte didn't even care at that moment. It just felt so damn good to let it all out.

"Do we have another match at Two Turtledoves?" Jenny yelled over the crowd. Charlotte ignored her and was relieved when Wes did too.

"No one knows about it," Charlotte said when they'd recovered. She wiped her eyes with the tiny napkin that once held her doughnut, printed fir trees dotting the rough paper.

"Wait, no one?" Wes said. "Not even Sloane?"

Charlotte shook her head. "She doesn't even know I had a fiancée, much less that she's sleeping down the hall. From the way Adele has acted so far, I don't think she knows either." She looked Wes in the eyes, said softly, "I'd like to keep it that way."

Wes frowned, then was quiet for a bit, staring out in front of him. Finally, he blew out a long breath. "My first instinct is that you should tell someone."

"I just did," she said.

He smiled at her. "Fair. But someone who loves you."

"Okay, now I'm offended."

He laughed, shook his head. "I'm serious."

She fiddled with her napkin, tracing the tiny green trees over and over. "It's not that easy."

"Yeah, I know that too. My best friend, Dorian? No clue I'm still ass over heels for Sloane. And he's my business partner at the restaurant. I see him more often than I see my own shadow."

Charlotte peered up at him and smiled. "Ah, so you're a hypocrite."

He presented his palms in surrender. "Hey, I said my first instinct was that you should tell someone. I didn't say it was my last."

"Fair enough."

They went silent for a bit after that, but it was a nice silence. Friendly, easy. Charlotte was shocked by how much lighter she felt, though there was still an entire holiday to get through, and she wasn't sure how many more of these Two Turtledoves events she could handle emotionally. She'd be spilling all her secrets to Jenny next time.

"So what do we do now?" Wes asked.

Charlotte exhaled. "Well, you're officially my Secret Keeper."

"And you're mine."

"I say we stick together." She turned to look at him. "What do you say? Partners?"

His mouth dropped open. "Why, Charlotte . . ." He trailed off, his brows pushing together.

"Donovan," she said.

"Charlotte Donovan, are you asking me to be your fake Turtle-dove?"

"It's not fake," she said, laughing too. "Look, neither of us is looking to actually date someone here, right?"

He shook his head, then pointed to a white guy with a red beard standing by the doughnuts. "I've known that dude since preschool. Jameson. He ate glue. And crayons, now that I think about it."

Charlotte grinned. "So we hang out during these events. We . . . look out for each other. You can tell your mother and Do-rian and whoever else that you met a mesmerizing violinist named Charlotte—"

"My, we are confident."

"—and you can help me keep my distance from Brighton. We don't even have to use the word *dating*. We just let our proximity speak for itself."

He pursed his mouth in thought. "And we both stay safe from Jenny's mating calls."

"Is she going to be at other events?"

"Oh, she comes to every single one. Loves matching up all the sad and lonely queers in town."

Charlotte winced. "All the more reason."

He paused again, his gaze going to where Sloane was now standing with Manish and Brighton. Charlotte felt everything that had gone loose inside her in the past half hour tighten up again. But no . . . Brighton wouldn't tell anyone about them. The truth only made her look like an asshole.

Still, Charlotte had the sudden urge to hold Wes's hand, just for some human connection, something alive and warm other than her own frantic heartbeat.

"Please," she said, her voice bordering on begging. She cleared her throat. "I promise not to fall in love with you."

He scoffed. "That's what everyone in a romantic comedy says before they promptly fall in love."

"Yeah, but I actually mean it," Charlotte said. "I don't even think I can . . ." She trailed off, her gaze drifting and landing on Brighton without her even realizing it. She yanked her attention back to Wes, smiled broadly. He was looking at her with narrowed eyes, an expression that called bullshit.

"And we both know you won't fall in love with me," she said.

He sighed dramatically. "As much as I might want to . . . probably not."

She nudged his shoulder with hers. "So?"

"So. You've got a deal, partner."

She held out her gloved hand, and he took it, kissing her knuckles softly, winking as he did so.

"Oh, you are good," she said.

He grinned. "Was there ever any doubt?"

chapter 10

Late that afternoon, Brighton closed herself in Adele's room and called her mother.

Hi, this is Bonnie! Leave a message, and I'll get back to you—

Brighton grunted in frustration and tapped the red button on her phone's screen a little more vehemently than necessary. Called again.

Hi, this is Bonnie! Leave—

"Fuck!" Brighton whisper-screamed, then flung herself onto Adele's bed and promptly burst into tears. She'd been holding them in for long enough—since Lola had so eloquently declared Brighton wasn't even worth her passing thoughts—a feat that only became more difficult when Lola and Wes spent the rest of the morning giggling and smiling at each other.

After all of this, their group spent the afternoon driving around Winter River, with Brighton stuck in the third row of Nina's Ford Expedition next to Adele. Her thighs were killing her, which apparently was normal after a day of horseback riding and, of course, made worse by her rogue adventure with Cupcake. So she not only endured her friend's constant worried glances but also had to hold back grunts of pain as she kept digging herself out of the car so they could tour Winter Berry Bakery, a general store called Matilda's Market, and a bookstore that sold only romances and thrillers and was cleverly dubbed Kiss-Marry-Kill.

By the time they arrived back at the Berry house for a late lunch, she was exhausted and just wanted some time alone, but then the quartet had disappeared into the finished basement for a rehearsal—led by Lola, whose cheeks were flushed with cold and whose smile and banter had seemed to come so easily all morning—which left Adele and Brighton to help Nina with the meal. Of course, Brighton didn't want to be rude, didn't want to call attention to her near nervous breakdown at all. So she'd pasted on a smile and stirred tomato soup on the stove, humming along to the steady stream of Christmas music playing from Nina's Bluetooth speaker.

But all of that only made her miss her mother even more, which was how she now found herself creating a puddle of saltwater tears on Adele's navy comforter, clutching her phone and willing her mother to call back, all while trying to keep her sobbing at a low volume.

This proved challenging. When Brighton cried, she rarely did so with any sort of grace—flowing snot, heaving gulps of air, whimpers that sounded like a dying animal rolling out of her throat. She really gave it all she had.

Her phone vibrated in her hand, and she shot upright, wiping her eyes with the back of her hand so she could see the screen.

You good?

A text from Adele.

Very much *not* her mother, a disappointment that pulled forth a fresh wave of tears.

All she wanted right now was her mother's calm voice, her soothing tone, simple words like *It'll be okay*, which always seemed to mean much more when they came out of Bonnie Fairbrook's mouth, as though she twisted some magic through usually useless phrases.

That was all Brighton needed, really.

To know it'd be okay.

That *everything* would be okay.

She sat there hiccupping as more tears came. She was determined to get them all out now—wring herself dry before she left this room again.

And she knew exactly what would do the trick: a good pour of salt over her open wounds. She flopped back onto the bed and rolled onto her stomach, a pillow tucked under her chin and her phone in her hands.

Then she opened up her Photos app.

She had to scroll back a bit, the tiny squares of color blurring past old Katies rehearsals, pics of her and Emily and Alice sticking their tongues out at the camera after a show, images of her parents and their cats, the lake at the height of summer, random shots of Nashville streets when she'd first moved there.

And then it was like clouds parting, revealing a different world underneath. A different time, a different dimension, even.

Lola and Bright.

It had been years since Brighton had let herself scroll this far back in her photos, and the images in front of her felt like a splash of cold water. She tapped on one photo they'd taken at their rehearsal dinner at Simone's restaurant, a selfie, Brighton holding the camera up and looking at it head-on as Charlotte's nose pressed against Brighton's cheek, a real smile on her perfect mouth. Brighton searched her own face, looking for signs of the doubt she'd been feeling for months by then, but all she saw was a girl in love.

Because with her and Lola, it had never been about a lack of love.

Her throat tightened, and she moved her thumb over the screen, found a photo she knew her mother had taken of Brighton and Lola playing together at Java Blues, a coffee shop in Grand Haven. It was one of the last times they'd played together before their wedding, performing a song Brighton had written back when she was fifteen called "Warm When I'm Cold." She'd written it out of love for Lola before she even realized it *was* love.

She zoomed in on their faces, both of them at a microphone. Lola had never considered herself a singer, but she had a lovely tone perfect for harmonies. She knew how to blend, how to cut off consonants at the end of phrases when needed, how to match Brighton breath for breath. The tune played in Brighton's head— a simple song and certainly not the best thing she'd ever written, but it was true.

It was *them*.

She kept scrolling, not even bothering to stop the tears now as she took in the entirety of her and Lola's life together—first days of school and the black-and-white dresses they'd worn to senior prom, days at the lake and fireworks in the sky and cold autumn nights around a bonfire in the Fairbrooks' backyard.

The day they left for Berklee.

The day they left for New York.

The morning of their wedding.

A photographic map of their relationship, every image leading them further along, closer and closer to the day Brighton finally broke.

Brighton stared at a selfie she'd taken of them that morning in Lola's room, and she could see it then. She could see the dark circles under her eyes from a sleepless night, could see the panic brewing behind her eyes. She could—

"I knew it."

She yelped at the voice behind her, the shock making her flop like a fish. She rolled over, covering her phone's screen with her hand, and saw Adele standing at the end of the bed with a glass of what looked like straight bourbon in her hand.

"Adele, what the hell?"

Adele smirked. "You know, I've always loved how that phrase rhymes with my name, but right now, you are not the one who should be using it."

Brighton just stared at her, hoping Adele hadn't seen . . .

"You know her," Adele said, and hope vanished like a wisp of smoke in the wind. "You know Charlotte. I knew you two had a weird vibe going on."

"Adele."

"But I figured there was no way, you know? Because surely, *surely*, I would know if you and my sister's best friend used to fuck."

Brighton flinched at the word.

Adele's brows went up. "So it was more than fucking."

Brighton just groaned and let herself collapse on the bed again like a starfish, limbs spread in defeat.

"Oh my god," Adele said, the mattress dipping a bit as she sat down. "She's not . . . no. No fucking way."

Brighton lay like a slug, waiting for Adele's sharp mind to come to the correct and awful conclusion.

"She's the fiancée," Adele said, awe curling around her voice. "The one you won't talk about. I honestly thought you'd made her up."

Brighton pushed herself up on her elbows. "What? For real?"

Adele shrugged. "Seemed sketchy."

"Your confidence in me is astounding."

"You're the one keeping secrets, baby girl."

Brighton sighed and sat up, tapping on the picture of her and Lola at their rehearsal dinner and handing the phone to Adele.

Adele took in the details, a slight crinkle to her brow, the image reflected in her glasses. "May I?" she asked, her finger hovering over the screen, ready to scroll.

Brighton waved her onward, because what difference did it make now? Adele had caught her mooning over Lola like a homesick kid, and honestly, it was a relief.

"Wow, this goes back . . . far," Adele said after a couple minutes.

"We met when we were twelve," Brighton said, her gaze going unfocused, their history playing like a montage behind her eyes. "Fell in love. Went to college together. Moved to New York after we graduated. Came home to get married that December."

"So what happened?" Adele asked. "Why didn't you get married?"

Brighton opened her mouth. Closed it. Adele let her sit in silence, sipped her bourbon like she had all the time in the world. Finally, Brighton lay down and curled onto her side, took Adele's hand, and started talking.

chapter 11

Brighton stared at the ceiling fan in her childhood bedroom, a thin layer of dust dotting the white blades. Outside her window, the morning had just started to break through the night, a blue-purple glow slowly unfurling into pink.

She sat up and rubbed her face, sent a hand through her tangled hair. She didn't think she'd gotten even two hours of sleep, nerves keeping her thoughts and stomach roiling all night long.

That was all it was.

Nerves.

Proverbial cold feet.

Still, when she thought about spending her life with Lola, it wasn't the *forever* part that scared her.

She thought about their apartment in Chelsea, how much Lola loved it. It was tiny—barely bigger than the bedroom Brighton grew up in—but it was theirs. That's what Lola kept saying.

It's ours.

And yet, six months into their life there, Brighton still had no idea how she was going to make her share of the rent every month. She worked at a restaurant, for god's sake, and while waiting tables in Greenwich Village was decent money, it wasn't nearly enough to cover her expenses, especially if she was keeping a few nights a week free for gigs.

Gigs she hadn't booked.

Gigs she honestly couldn't even stir up the courage to look for in earnest. She'd sent some emails to no avail, gone to a couple of places to talk to the booking manager with her demo, but she was no one, a twenty-two-year-old Michigander who was scared of the subway and had graduated from Berklee with a C average. Her biggest claim to fame so far was that she'd once held the door open for Sufjan Stevens as he'd come out of a coffee shop in Grand Haven one summer, his arms laden with cold brew and his sunglasses firmly over his eyes, hair a mess.

He'd said thanks.

So unless her old pal Sufjan could call in a favor, New York City would mostly likely keep its back to Brighton Fairbrook.

And yet . . .

Lola loved it so much.

Brighton had never seen Lola more alive—she'd unfurled at Berklee, sure, finally studying music properly, flourishing, excelling, winning every director's award and landing spots in orchestras all over New England every summer. But Lola in Manhattan . . . it was everything Lola had ever wanted. She'd been offered a spot in the Chelsea Symphony right after graduation, had been invited to play on several more established musicians' studio albums, and had been a guest soloist with the Chamber Orchestra of New York and the New York Philharmonic.

Lola was thriving, just as Brighton knew she would, just as everyone knew she would.

The only problem was, Brighton felt like she was drowning.

She groaned, dropped her head into her hands.

No. She wasn't drowning. She was *adjusting*, that was all. That's what she'd been telling herself for months, what she'd told her parents when they'd expressed concern, when she'd called her mother a few weeks ago at two in the morning, quietly sobbing in the bathroom while Lola slept, and her mother had whispered, so quietly that Brighton had barely heard it.

Come home, honey.

But she couldn't.

Lola was her home now.

Lola had always been her home.

And she'd been Lola's.

Now the morning of their wedding was here, an event they'd been planning for a year, an event Brighton had convinced herself would change everything, make her life click into place with Lola's.

Brighton kicked her covers back, the cold December morning biting at her bare legs. She walked to the window, pulled back the sheer curtain to let in the winter sun. The sky was clear blue, perfect, Lake Michigan all icy waves curling frozen onto the frosty sand beyond the backyard. She loved the lake in winter, loved everything about December and Christmas and the cold. Always had. It was why they were getting married in December, why they'd rented out Simone's restaurant downtown for the day, covering the dining room in white lights and dozens and dozens of white candles in glasses of all sizes, white manzanita branches arching over the makeshift aisle and forming the centerpiece at each table.

It would be a small wedding, only fifty people or so, but it would be beautiful. A winter wonderland, the kind of wedding Brighton had dreamed of. As they'd planned it, Lola definitely had her opinions, but she'd always deferred to what Brighton liked the best, the things that made Brighton's eyes widen, made her heart beat a little faster.

Just thinking of walking down that beautiful aisle they'd created toward Lola . . . it was a dream. Breathtaking.

"It's what I want," she whispered to the window, her breath fogging the glass. She turned to look at her dress hanging from her closet door. Sleek and white. Long sleeves and a high neck, lace covering the entire thing, fanning out at the thigh like a trumpet.

It was perfect.

Everything was perfect.

It *was*.

She just needed to see Lola. This feeling in her stomach was simple nerves, and if she saw Lola, held her, kissed her, maybe even confessed some of her anxieties and let Lola's calm surety soothe her, she'd be fine.

She'd be ready.

She pulled on a pair of sweatpants and a blue Grand Haven High sweatshirt, found her coat hanging over a chair in the kitchen. Her boots were harder to locate, but she finally found them just outside the back door, so they were freezing when she slipped her feet inside.

The winter wind whipped her hair into her face, and a hat certainly would've been helpful, but it was a short walk to Lola's, and she nearly ran, kicking up the snow that had fallen three days ago as she went.

Lola's back door was locked, but Brighton had a key and let

herself in quietly. As she sloughed off her boots and tiptoed through the all-beige-and-white living room toward the stairs, she hoped to god that Anna was still tucked away in her room with her sound machine on full blast.

A single Tiffany lamp lit her way, the only splash of color in the whole Donovan house.

Upstairs, she paused by Lola's door. It was early, barely seven o'clock, but Lola had always been an early riser. Brighton pressed her ear to the white wood, listening.

It was quiet, and when she eased the door open, she found Lola still in bed, curled underneath her white duvet, her long salt-and-pepper hair in a ponytail on top of her head, the ends fanning over the mint-green sheets. Brighton stood there for a second, just watching her fiancée, letting her heart settle around Lola.

This was right.

This was *them*, Lola and Bright.

And yet . . .

Even as Brighton took in Lola—her beauty and secret softness, Brighton's heart swelling at the sight—her stomach wouldn't relax. Her chest. Everything from her navel up felt tight, coiled, her heart working too hard to get everything else inside her in line.

She slipped fully into the room, closed the door behind her. She shucked off her sweatshirt and pants, then pulled back Lola's covers and slid into bed beside her, wrapping her arms around Lola's waist, pulling Lola's back against her chest. Lola murmured a little, and Brighton pressed her nose to the back of Lola's neck, breathing in her clean linen scent. She could stay like this forever.

Why *couldn't* they just stay like this forever?

Brighton drew Lola even tighter against her, as though she were afraid Lola might slip away if she loosened her grip.

Or that Brighton herself might slip away.

"What . . . ?" Lola said, her voice muzzy with sleep. She stirred, lifted her head, then arched her neck to see Brighton behind her. "Baby, what are you doing?"

"Hi to you too," Brighton said softly, resting her chin on Lola's shoulder.

"Hi," Lola said, pressing her knuckles into her eyes. She always did that—rubbed her eyes with full fists like a little kid. It was adorable. "And also, what are you doing? It's bad luck to see me before the wedding."

Brighton made a face. "I think we're a little bit past traditional conventions, don't you?"

"It's December," Lola said. "I'm not taking any chances."

Still, she turned in Brighton's arms and placed her hands on Brighton's face.

"Hi," Lola said more softly.

"Hi," Brighton said. "Will you kiss me good morning?" She just needed *closer*, the space between them getting smaller and smaller.

Their mouths touched, that familiar press so perfect. Brighton took Lola's bottom lip between hers and tugged a little, the way she knew Lola liked.

Lola whimpered, opened for her. Their tongues touched, softly at first, but then things grew heated fast. Brighton slipped a hand under Lola's thin tank top, her breast perfect and warm. She rolled Lola's nipple between her fingers, and Lola let out a moan.

"We can't," Lola panted, but she spread her legs as soon as Brighton slid a hand down her thigh. "It's our wedding day."

"All the more reason," Brighton said, finding that inviting

warmth between Lola's legs. She needed this. Needed Lola, her body, the sounds she made, the way she kissed like Brighton was a cup of cold water, the way Lola always came so fast for her, like she'd already been dreaming about Brighton's fingers inside her before they even touched.

Lola tilted her head back, a sigh escaping her throat, and laughed. "Well, I do want my bride to have everything she wants."

"You," Brighton said, shoving off the covers to reveal Lola's perfect body—curvy and soft and *hers*. "I want you."

She slid down between Lola's legs, looked at her for a second. God, she was gorgeous. Her underwear wasn't anything special—pale-yellow cotton—but Brighton could see that Lola was already wet for her, and she couldn't resist pressing her mouth to that wet spot, sucking at Lola through the cotton.

"Oh my god, Bright," Lola said, and fuck yes, this was what Brighton needed, Lola's hands in her hair and her name on Lola's lips.

Brighton kissed her, lapped at her perfect pussy through her underwear, but it wasn't enough. She needed more, needed to taste Lola, feel her fully. She pulled her underwear off—it got stuck on her ankle, and they laughed, but soon Brighton was back in position, and Jesus Christ, that first touch. First taste. It never got old, never got so familiar that Brighton wasn't in awe of Lola every time she buried her face between her legs like this, reveled in her smell and taste and feel.

She slid her tongue inside, just like she knew Lola liked, closed her mouth over her clit.

"Fuck," Lola said, opening even wider for her. "God yeah."

Brighton increased the pressure, felt her own arousal building. She wrapped her arms around Lola's thighs, swirled her tongue, and then tilted her chin upward, sucking on Lola's clit as she went.

Lola tensed, her hands pulling at Brighton's hair, a whispered *yeah, yeah, yeah* falling from her mouth. Brighton didn't let up until Lola did, kept her mouth in place even after Lola softened onto the mattress, then giggled when Brighton's touch became too much for how sensitive she now was.

"God," Lola said, laughing as Brighton crawled back up her body. "You're trouble."

"You love it," Brighton said, her own need at a crisis point now. She was in no hurry, though. She wanted this moment to last forever.

"I do," Lola said, then tugged at Brighton's underwear until Brighton removed them, leaving her bare with only a T-shirt on. Lola smirked and dragged a thumb up Brighton's center, causing Brighton to hiss a breath. Then Lola pulled one of Brighton's legs over her so that she was straddling Lola's stomach. The feel of Lola's skin on Brighton's was almost too much. She arched her head back and nearly came right there, just from the initial touch.

"That's right, baby," Lola said, her hands on Brighton's hips, urging them to move over her stomach. Brighton knew Lola loved this just as much as she did, loved Brighton on top, loved the feel of Brighton's own wetness on her skin.

Lola slid a hand up Brighton's torso, underneath her T-shirt to cup her breasts. She tugged on Brighton's nipples.

"Harder," Brighton said, and Lola complied, twisting so that Brighton nearly had to cover her mouth to keep quiet.

"Shh," Lola said, a teasing lilt to her voice, knowing that telling Brighton to be quiet only made her more desperate to be loud. Brighton leaned forward, forearms on either side of Lola's head, and kissed Lola feverishly as she moved her body, pumping her hips for more friction.

"That's my good girl," Lola said, kissing her, because fuck, Brighton did have a praise kink. "That's my perfect girl."

Brighton moaned, burying her face in Lola's neck, her orgasm building. She was so wet, Lola's stomach no doubt soaked as well, and the thought made her even more desperate to come.

"Let me see," Lola said, kissing Brighton's neck before pushing her upright. Brighton knew what Lola wanted, so she leaned back even more, bracing her hands on Lola's thighs behind her, baring her pussy for Lola. Lola's eyes were fixed on Brighton's center, watching as she dragged it over Lola's skin, over and over.

"You're so good," Lola said, her hands on Brighton's thighs. "You gonna come for me?"

Brighton nodded, her hips moving faster. Lola's hands slid up Brighton's thighs, closer and closer to her cunt, callused fingertips pressing harder and harder the closer she got.

"Fuck," Brighton said. "Please."

"Please what?"

"Please, god, make me come. Lola."

"Yeah? You're ready?"

Brighton could only nod.

"I don't know if you're ready," Lola said, the top energy in her surging.

Brighton whined. "Please, baby, please."

Lola tilted her head, then slid one hand closer and closer until it touched Brighton's cunt, her thumb dragging up her lips teasingly until settling on her clit.

Brighton imploded. She clapped a hand over her mouth, her

body still undulating over Lola, the pressure of Lola's thumb paired with the slide of her pussy over Lola's skin so fucking perfect that Brighton felt tears spring to her eyes. She came, and then when Lola pushed her back even more and got two fingers inside her, she came again, Lola's name a ragged gasp on her tongue.

"Jesus," she said, untangling herself and collapsing next to Lola.

Lola laughed and pulled her close. "Good, huh?"

"God yeah."

Lola pressed her mouth to Brighton's neck. "We get a whole lifetime of that, baby. Starting today."

Brighton froze. She wanted everything Lola just said. All of it. Except her brain kept getting caught on one word.

Today.

"You and me," Lola said, exhaling. "New York. Music. Everything we've always wanted."

Brighton nodded, but even as Lola said it, she felt herself shrinking. It wasn't everything *she'd* always wanted. Yes, she wanted Lola, wanted a life with her, but she needed her own life too, and that still evaded her. She couldn't catch her breath in New York, couldn't seem to make her feet fit on those sidewalks the way Lola's did.

She'd told Lola more than once about how much she liked Nashville, how after she'd taken a trip there with her mother for a chef's convention when she was fifteen, she'd felt that spark for the city, knew it was a great place to be for singer-songwriters. And Lola had listened whenever Brighton spoke of it, had nodded and said they'd make it happen. But as the years passed, New York loomed as the only option for Lola, Nashville receding into the background.

And Brighton didn't know how to stop it or change it. The last thing she wanted was to keep Lola from anything she wanted—Lola had grown up with a cold mother, a quiet house in a town that afforded few opportunities for someone of Lola's talent. All Lola had ever wanted since the day they'd met on the beach was Brighton—a family of her own—and a career as a musician in New York City.

Brighton couldn't take that away from her. Didn't want to.

And yet . . .

She inhaled, closed her eyes, let out her breath slowly. Maybe if she just told Lola the truth. She'd always been able to tell Lola everything, anything.

Everything except this.

"I . . . I think I'm a little nervous," she said.

She felt Lola freeze up, her arm going stiff around Brighton's middle.

"Not about us," Brighton said quickly. "Just . . . I don't know."

Lola propped herself up on her elbow, her ponytail now halfway falling over her bare shoulder. "About the wedding?"

Brighton swallowed, searched Lola's brown eyes. She just wanted Lola to *know*, to see the fear she couldn't give voice to, the unhappiness she felt in New York that she couldn't put into words.

"Maybe," she said.

"It's going to be beautiful. Your mom has been such a help, putting all of this together and planning everything. And with her food at Simone's? Immaculate."

"No, I know, I just . . ."

Brighton exhaled, took a tress of Lola's hair and wrapped it around her finger, smoothing the silvery strands. Took a second to get her thoughts together.

"I think," she finally said, releasing her words slowly, carefully, "I'm just not as settled in New York as I want to be."

As soon as the words were out of her mouth, everything in her felt lighter. Just to finally *say* it. She'd wanted everything about their transition to New York to be so perfect for Lola that she hadn't really realized just how small she'd become. How much she hadn't said.

Surely now that she'd finally admitted it—even with that mild statement—she and Lola could talk about it. Figure out what kind of life was really *them* instead of just *her*.

"What do you mean?" Lola said.

"I just . . ." Brighton looked Lola right in the eyes, pulled on her hair a little to get her closer . . . closer. "I think I feel a bit lost."

Lola's brows pushed together, her lovely mouth turning down a little. She smoothed a hand over Brighton's hair, drifted her fingers down Brighton's cheek. Brighton felt her eyes close, felt herself loosen.

"I think that's normal with a big move," Lola said.

Brighton opened her eyes.

Lola cleared her throat. "I mean, New York is a lot. I get that."

"Yeah."

"But, baby, it's only been six months," Lola went on. "That's not nearly long enough to get used to a place, especially Manhattan. You just need some time. It'll be amazing, just give it some time. You'll find your place, and it'll be everything we always dreamed of. You and me."

Brighton felt herself nodding, even as tears swelled behind her lids. She looked away, because right then, she felt like she was showing as much of herself as she could, and Lola wasn't seeing what Brighton needed her to see.

Either that or Lola didn't want to see it.

"Yeah," Brighton said. "You're right." There was a quiver to her voice she couldn't have hidden even if she'd tried, and she turned back to look at Lola, because maybe that little quiver, just maybe—

"That's my girl," Lola said, her expression relaxing. "You and me, right?"

Brighton could only nod. Lola kissed her neck, then blew a raspberry into her skin, and Brighton laughed. Twenty minutes later, after they'd taken a selfie of themselves curled up in bed together and kissed a bit more, Lola kicked Brighton out so they could both start their morning and get ready for their five o'clock wedding. Brighton sneaked back through the Donovan living room and out the back door, taking deep breath after deep breath, telling herself over and over again that Lola was right.

She just needed time.

Brighton stood in front of the full-length mirror on the back of the fancy gender-neutral bathroom door at Simone's.

She looked perfect.

Her dress fit like a dream, sliding down her body to skim the floor, the lace covering every inch except the open back. Her hair was coiled into a loose bun at the nape of her neck, tendrils framing her face, her bangs freshly trimmed and falling to her brows. Her makeup was subtle, just a little mascara and eye shadow paired with a bold red lip to accent the white-and-red winter wedding theme.

Yes, she looked perfect. Everything was perfect—the winter-blue sky, the snow on the ground outside, the hum of wedding guests in the beautiful, softly lit dining room, stringed music playing as they all took their seats.

Everything was perfect.

"You're shaking, love," her mom said as she fastened a pair of pearl dewdrop earrings to Brighton's ears, smoothing her hair back.

"Am I?" Brighton asked, but even her voice trembled. She gritted her teeth, twisted her fingers together in an attempt to get herself under control, but that only made everything worse, her body tensing until it felt ready to break apart.

"Hey, Rainbow, just breathe," her mom said, coming to stand in front of her.

But that didn't help at all. If anything, her mother's gentle voice and concerned brown eyes only made Brighton's tears swell, made her throat ache with the effort of holding them back.

"Honey," her mom said gently. Bonnie Fairbrook looked beautiful too, her curly brown hair pinned back, her ice-blue dress long and elegant. Brighton hadn't even told her how lovely she looked, hadn't even thought to yet because she couldn't stop her pulse from thrumming, her bones from feeling like they were about to crumble to dust.

Her mom took her hands, tucked her hair behind her ear. "Sweetheart, I think you need to talk to Charlotte."

There was no *What's wrong?* No *Let's just slow down for a sec.* No probing of any kind. Because Bonnie Fairbrook already knew. She had never been a huge fan of their getting married so young, even though she adored Lola and never questioned that they loved each other.

She had just questioned the timing.

More than once.

Gently and in a way that told Brighton her mother trusted her to do what was right for herself. And so Brighton had always smiled and rolled her eyes and said she and Lola knew what they were doing, knew what they wanted. But now, lately, god, Brighton didn't know.

She didn't know anything except that she loved Lola, but if this were enough, if timing didn't matter, then why was she shaking right now? Why was she struggling not to cry? Why could she not convince herself that this was right, right, right?

"I'll go get her," her mom said. "It's okay if we start late. You two are the stars—everyone else will wait, all right? They'll wait as long as you need."

Brighton nodded and watched her mother slip out the thick wooden door, then turned back to the mirror, staring at the bride before her.

She just needed Lola.

Just needed to talk.

And that's what broke the dam, stripped away whatever barrier she'd put up that was holding the tears back. Because they'd already talked.

And talked and talked and talked.

And every time, Lola had convinced her. Every time, Lola said *You and me*, and Brighton believed it was enough, for a month, a week, a day.

A few hours.

That was what had happened earlier this morning, and that's exactly what would happen now. Lola would come into the bathroom, looking gorgeous in her white suit, her lips full and red. She would take Brighton's face in her hands, whisper, kiss, do all the right things, and Brighton would nod and say, again, that it was enough.

And they'd get married.

And they'd go back to New York.

And Brighton would . . .

Brighton dropped her head into her hands. She'd what? Because everything after that was fuzzy, a smeared watercolor portrait of her possible future. There was Lola, and Lola was perfect and beautiful, and god, Brighton loved her so much, but she couldn't find *herself* in the image.

Outside, the music shifted, the musicians they'd hired starting a song that Brighton knew all too well. But instead of excitement, of happiness, she felt only dread. Pure panic knowing that Lola was walking down the aisle, as they'd planned for her to go first, then turn and wait for Brighton.

Suddenly, before she could think, talk herself out of it, or into it, again and again, Brighton was moving. Tears clouded her vision as she gathered her toiletries and makeup from the counter, then stuffed it all into the suitcase she was supposed to take to Paris on their honeymoon. Later, she didn't even remember stepping into the dimly lit hallway and heading for the back door in the kitchen, Bonnie's staff preparing the reception meal. She didn't slow down until she flung herself into her old Toyota Corolla, which she'd left in her parents' care when she moved to Manhattan. She only remembered motion, cold winter air biting through the lace of her dress, snow soaking her delicate off-white shoes, the purr of the engine starting, and the relief she felt when the gas gauge needle soared up to three-fourths of a tank.

She'd forgotten her coat, her scarf, her snow boots. Forgotten a lot of shit, most of which she wouldn't even realize until a couple of days later, when she finally got out of bed at the roadside hotel just outside Indianapolis where she'd eventually stopped driving. The frizzy-haired receptionist who'd checked her in had eyed her wedding dress with a thousand questions.

On her wedding day, though, in that exact moment, none of it mattered. Logic, the repercussions, a different path—none of it existed. The only thing that existed was the wide road in front of her, Grand Haven shrinking in her rearview mirror.

chapter 12

When Brighton finished her tale, Adele didn't say anything for a long while. When she finally spoke, "Well, shit" was the only thing that came out of her mouth.

Brighton laughed, though the sound was bitter, brittle. "You can say that again."

"I *will* say that again. I mean, good goddamn, Brighton."

"I know." Brighton rolled onto her back and stared at the ceiling. She felt empty, the husk of a runaway bride. She hadn't told that story to anyone, not even her mother, who had just intuited what Brighton had been feeling. It had been so much easier that way. The *telling* of the whole ordeal was fucking exhausting. Granted, Brighton had kept the finer details about the last time she and Lola had had sex from Adele, only mentioning that it had happened. But this hadn't stopped every moment of that last morning from blooming in Brighton's own memory, leaving her now with a confusing swirl of guilt and longing and lust.

"You haven't seen her since then?" Adele asked. "Not even a glimpse at Christmas?"

"Not a single silver hair," Brighton said. "I don't think she's been home since then. I called her after everything settled down. Called her a lot. Texted. God, I texted so much, it's embarrassing."

"And let me guess."

Brighton blew out a breath. "Yep. A big silent *fuck you*."

"And now she wants to pretend like she doesn't even know you."

Brighton shot finger guns Adele's way, clicking her tongue. "Bingo."

"Maybe that's what you need to do too," Adele said.

"How am I supposed to do that? I just want to . . ." But she trailed off, because *make it right* was never going to happen. She knew that much, at least. But it was *Lola*. She could never act like Lola didn't exist. That she wasn't who she was—or used to be—to Brighton.

"You might have to, just for your sanity," Adele said. "You can't make her talk to you. You can't make her forgive you either."

"I know that."

"You need a distraction."

"I tried that with Gemma."

Adele pulled a *yikes* face. "Okay, fair, but a date might help. You know, make her a little jealous. Maybe it'll make her want to talk to you more."

"The only way I'm getting a date with this"—she motioned around the mess of her mascara-smeared face and tangled hair—"is if it's fake."

Adele's eyes brightened. "Fake date me. Then maybe my mom will let me out of Two Turtledoves."

Brighton rolled her eyes. "Okay, sure. We walk into your bedroom platonic friends and walk out an hour later all moony-eyed for each other? No one would buy it."

Adele laughed, but Brighton sat up, tilted her head.

"You don't want to actually try and find someone?" she asked Adele.

"In this town? Nah."

"Why not?"

Adele took a sip of her bourbon, then handed it to Brighton, who tipped the drink into her mouth. It burned all the way down but in a good way. Like a cleansing.

"I'm not interested in hookups with people I went to middle school with," Adele said, taking back the glass.

"What about more than a hookup?" Brighton asked, releasing her words carefully. She didn't want Adele to think she was shaming her love life. But she was curious about her friend's lack of girlfriends. Adele was a damn catch. Charming, sexy, funny, smart. Brighton and Adele had even kissed once, way back when they first met a few years ago, at a Katies show at Ampersand.

It was like kissing a sister.

They'd both laughed but exchanged numbers because they liked each other's company anyway, and then Adele had promptly taken another girl home.

Now Adele sighed, looked down at her hands. "I don't know. I've been thinking about it a lot lately. And I think I might be . . . I think I might be aro?"

She said it like a question, peered at Brighton with her nose scrunched up.

"Yeah?" Brighton said, and Adele shrugged. Brighton reached out and took Adele's hand. "You know that's okay, right?"

"No, I know, I just . . ." She shrugged again. "Romance is a hell of a drug, you know? It's hard to get out from under it sometimes.

That feeling that I *should* be a certain way, want a certain kind of life. And, like, I get it. I like rom-coms, and I like seeing my friends in love, want everyone I love to have that if they want it. I just don't think *I* want it. I never really did. Never got all moony-eyed, as you say, over a girl, even in middle and high school. I knew I was gay because I liked the way Vivian Manzoli filled out her tank top in ninth grade."

Brighton laughed.

"But I never wanted to hold her hand in a romantic way," Adele said. "I want friends, close ones. I want intimate relationships. I want sex and lots of it. And I think maybe, someday, I *do* want a partner. But I'm not sure what kind of partner I want or what that looks like exactly. The *how* of it all, I guess."

"I think that's great, Adele," Brighton said, squeezing her hand tighter. "You get to want whatever you want."

Adele nodded. "Just takes a while to figure that out sometimes, you know? I'm still working on that. The figuring it out part."

"Yeah. Wait"—Brighton leaned closer to Adele—"am I the first person you've told this to?"

Adele blew out a breath and laughed. "Shit, you are."

"I'm honored," Brighton said. "Really. And god, congrats. How do you feel?"

Adele took another sip of bourbon. "Good. Feels good. Feels right."

"Good. You deserve that."

"Thanks, baby girl."

They sat there like that for a while, holding hands, their secrets not so secret anymore, a tether pulling them closer together. Brighton let herself feel it, even as a tiny part of her bristled at it all, at letting someone so close again.

Still, Adele was right—it did feel good. To trust someone again. Not even Alice and Emily had known about Lola. And she was glad she could give that to Adele too, that beauty of being known.

And not only known . . . but loved.

"A fake girlfriend," Adele said abruptly, pulling her hand out of Brighton's and snapping.

"What?" Brighton asked.

"You can't fake date me, so make up some hot piece back in Nashville. A daddy. Swoopy hair. Wears ties. Excellent with their fingers." Adele waggled her eyebrows and made a gesture with her hands that was so Adele—sexy and completely unassuming all at once.

Brighton laughed, but then her throat went unexpectedly tight at the thought of actually inventing someone to love her. "I can't . . ." She swallowed, tried to get ahead of the surge of feelings in her chest. "I can't lie to her again."

Fuck, she was going to cry.

Adele set her glass on her nightstand, then took both of Brighton's hands in hers. "Baby girl. When did you lie to her the first time?"

Brighton just stared down at their entwined fingers, let the tears drip down her nose. "Every day. For months. When I didn't . . . when I didn't tell her the truth about what I was feeling, about New York, the wedding. Everything."

"When you didn't know *how*. There's a difference."

Brighton could only shake her head.

"You know what I think?" Adele said. "You need to forgive yourself, that's what the fuck I think."

Brighton didn't say anything. And maybe Adele was right, but Brighton didn't know how to even begin untangling the knots of guilt inside her. They were easy enough to ignore with a thousand miles between her and Lola, but here, with Lola mere feet away—

"You still love her."

Brighton snapped her head up at Adele's question—no, it wasn't a question. Adele's intonation was flat and even.

"I don't," Brighton said.

Adele pursed her mouth, narrowed her eyes. Didn't push the matter. Still, Brighton didn't think she'd convinced her.

But she didn't still love Lola.

She was just . . .

It was *Lola.*

Tears swelled again, but she pushed them back, reached over and downed the rest of Adele's bourbon to keep herself in check.

"Okay," Adele said after Brighton had slammed the glass down on the nightstand, empty. "If you're not going to go about this the romantic or sexual way, let's try another tactic."

"What do you mean?" Brighton asked.

Adele got up and opened her closet door, stickers all over the white wood—cats, rainbows for various queer identities, women of different races and ethnicities surrounded by flowers and stars with their fists held up, and a Tracy Chapman poster, just in case anyone doubted Adele was a lesbian. She disappeared inside for a few seconds, and when she emerged, she held Brighton's worst nightmare in her hands.

"Hell no," Brighton said.

"Come on," Adele said, holding out the guitar. The wood was pale-colored and cheap-looking, and it was probably horrifically out of tune.

"Why do you have that?" Brighton asked. "You can't even hum on key."

Adele flipped her off. "Like every queer teen hoping to woo their way under a girl's bra, I wanted to learn."

Brighton laughed.

"I sucked, as you already guessed," Adele said. "Plus, part of my motivation might have been to keep up with my insanely talented little sister, which didn't work out in my favor."

"It's not going to work out in your favor now either."

"It's not kryptonite."

"Might as well be."

"Goddammit, Brighton, this isn't *you*."

Brighton's spine straightened at Adele's suddenly sharp tone, but Adele didn't apologize. She rarely did. And it wasn't like Adele was wrong. Brighton Fairbrook without a guitar—she barely recognized herself.

But Adele didn't get it.

Brighton had left everything she loved, the person she loved most in the world, for herself. For a future that featured *her* dreams, *her* songs, *her* talent.

And she hadn't been good enough.

She looked at the guitar, wanting to give her best friend what she wanted, wanting to let Adele help her. She just wasn't ready.

She wasn't sure she'd ever be ready.

"Okay," she said, backing up on the bed, away from the guitar, until her back hit the headboard. She got out her phone and opened up Spotify. "A compromise."

Adele lifted a brow, listening.

"Put that thing away," Brighton said, waving at the guitar, "and I'll listen to some Katies songs. Exposure therapy. Maybe it'll dull the sting a little so that I can"—she flicked her eyes down to the guitar and back up to Adele's face—"you know."

"You're so full of shit," Adele said, but she put the guitar back into the closet, then settled onto the bed next to Brighton, their shoulders pressing together. "Play 'Cherry Lipstick.'"

"God, not you too."

"It's a bop, and I'm a simple queer."

Brighton laughed, typing *the Katies* into the search bar. She took a surreptitious deep breath as she did so. Yes, she'd suggested this little listening party to appease her friend, but honestly, this probably *was* the first step toward getting back to herself. She needed to figure out who she was apart from the Katies, who she was on her own. If she was ever going to be anything in the music world, she was solo now. That was the whole reason why she'd broken Lola's heart in the first place, wasn't it?

To be a major player in that world.

Not just a side character in someone else's.

And right now she was a bartender who scared patrons when they expressed appreciation for certain songs and couldn't even talk to a cute person without tripping all over herself.

Eventually, she had to get over it.

The Katies popped up—Brighton did her best not to flinch— a verified artist with nearly two million monthly listeners. She scrolled down to their songs, ready to hit play on "Cherry Lipstick," when another song caught her eye.

"What is it?" Adele asked, leaning closer to peer at the screen.

"They just released a new single." Brighton's thumb hovered over the title, its letters blurring in her vision and rearranging. "What does that say?" she asked, not trusting what she was actually seeing. She held the phone out toward Adele.

"One sip of bourbon and you're already seeing double?"

"Just tell me," she said.

Adele sighed, then read the title. "'December Light.'"

Brighton said nothing, and then her thumb seemed to move on its own, tapping those two little words.

Soft piano music filtered out of her phone's speaker. Mellow, but it had movement to it, a guitar in the background and something else deeper. A cello, maybe. Then Sylvie's buttery voice.

Winter lake, December light,
tears on your face, but I'll make it right.
That Tiffany lamp, a rainbow on the floor,
pieces of glass holding your whole world.

December light, those colorful shards,
you think it's all broken, but that's not your heart.
December light, snow mixing with sand,
it's you and it's me at the edge of the land.

"A love song," Adele said, nodding her head. "Different for them, but I like it."

But Brighton couldn't respond. Couldn't nod, shake her head, breathe, anything. She tapped on the song in the play window, the full lyrics popping up. She scrolled through them fast, hoping for something different, but no. That melody, the chorus, the verses, the bridge—it all speared through her chest, pushing her back, back, back five years . . . no.

Seven years.

She clapped a hand over her mouth to keep in a sob, emotions she'd just resolved to get a grip on swirling like a windswept sea. Only music could really do that—bring everything to the surface, make the memories *alive*, sharpen the time-dulled pain to a point.

"Baby girl, it's just a song," Adele said softly. "Tell yourself that—it's just a song. It's got nothing to do with you."

But Adele didn't understand, and Brighton couldn't form the words, not with this song in her ears, her fingertips, her heart.

She jammed her thumb at the screen to stop the tune, but the notes continued somehow, now muffled but louder, filling the entire house. Brighton dropped her phone on the mattress, scooted off the bed, and flung open the bedroom door, "December Light" swelling in symphony now. She rushed down the stairs to find Elle and Manish slow dancing in the living room, but in a cheesy way, Manish laughing as Elle attempted to dip him. Wes was there too—he must have shown up while Brighton was sobbing upstairs.

"New Katies song!" Manish said when he straightened and saw her on the stairs, Adele behind her.

The song played through the house via Nina's Bluetooth speaker.

December light, snow mixing with sand . . .

Nina herself was on the couch with Sloane, both of them smiling and listening intently, each with a glass of wine in their hands.

Only Lola stood apart from everyone.

She was leaning against the wall next to the fireplace, her arms folded over her chest, Snickerdoodle lying at her feet. A muscle ticked in her jaw, her eyes fixed on Brighton as the song Brighton had written the day they'd gotten engaged, a song meant to be played at their wedding, echoed through the house.

chapter 13

Charlotte couldn't believe what she was hearing.

It was their song.

The one Brighton had written while lying in bed with Charlotte the day they got engaged seven years ago, tucked away just for them. The one she and Brighton had never played anywhere publicly other than the recording studio session Charlotte had booked, Brighton on guitar and lead vocals, Charlotte on violin and harmonies, laying down the version that was supposed to play as they walked down the aisle.

The version that *did* play as Charlotte walked down the aisle, then turned to face her mother and the smiling faces of Brighton's family, waiting for her bride to appear.

And waited and waited until—

She squeezed her eyes shut, her throat aching, and yet this goddamn song played on, someone's voice she didn't even know singing her own story.

This winter love, this December dream.
This winter love, you don't have to be
alone anymore . . . alone anymore . . . alone anymore . . .

She had to get out. Had to get away.

"I'm going for a walk," she said to no one, anyone, didn't care if they heard or not. She headed for the mudroom, then shoved her feet into her boots. She found her still-soiled coat on a hook, grabbed a hat—it wasn't even hers, but she didn't care—and all but flung herself outside.

The sun had just set, coating the world in a purplish twilight glow. The cold bit through her black sweater, wrapped a hand around her neck. It was snowing lightly, giving the lavender air an ethereal quality. She buttoned her coat as she walked, no clue where she was going. The Berry property was pretty expansive—she could see another house to the right, but it was at least two hundred yards away. To the left, there was nothing but snowy woods.

She turned left, her boots crunching through the snow, moving her quickly away from the house. She didn't slow down until she was deep into the shelter of the trees, the pines closing like a curtain around her. She stopped and put her hands on her hips, her heavy breaths curling into white wisps in front of her. Tipping her head to the sky, she blinked at the snow-covered canopy above her, then closed her eyes.

There.

Quiet.

Sweet, blessed quiet.

Too quiet.

Her mind wandered, nothing to grab on to but thoughts of Brighton, the way they used to play together at coffee shops in high school and when home from Berklee, sitting on stools while the patrons glanced at them skeptically, unsure anything decent would come out of these two girls holding their instruments.

And then . . . that first note. The first word Brighton sang into the mic. The first moment Charlotte joined her in harmony. Eyes would widen, brows lifted as a delighted shock settled on people's faces, an experience that usually pissed Charlotte off and made her feel proud all at once. The kind of music they'd made together had always been good. Even before it was *great*, it was theirs— new and real and theirs.

"December Light" was theirs.

As she watched the sky grow darker, her throat thickened with memory, with music. Tiny snowflakes fell on her face, and she closed her eyes and breathed in the frigid air, let it numb her lungs, her heart. Let it push out the song, Brighton, everything that—

"Lola."

She flipped her eyes open. "Are you fucking kidding me?" she said without turning around.

"You shouldn't be out here alone," Brighton said.

Charlotte laughed, a bitter sound. "So you're not fucking kidding me."

"Lola."

She whirled around, her anger finally reaching its limit and spilling over. "Don't you dare call me that. Stop fucking calling me that!"

Her yell echoed through the trees, reverberating like a warning.

Brighton's mouth dropped open, that ridiculous red plaid coat hanging unbuttoned around her frame. She didn't have a hat on, no scarf or gloves. Typical Brighton. She stepped forward slowly, as though trying not to spook a wounded animal, and pressed her hands together. "Just let me explain."

Charlotte shook her head and turned around, then took off through the trees without another thought, walking fast enough that she hoped Brighton would give up. She walked and walked and walked, but she heard her ex behind her, footsteps keeping up, tracking her like a hunter.

"Goddammit," she said, finally slowing to catch her breath. She didn't turn around, but she knew Brighton was there, a damn leech sucking at her blood.

"Lo—Charlotte," Brighton said through her own gasps for air. "Please. Just let me—"

"You gave them our song," Charlotte said. "You gave it away like it was nothing."

She kept her back to Brighton. Couldn't turn around. Couldn't let Brighton see how her eyes were filling, her cheeks trembling with the effort of holding everything in, keeping everything together. But she couldn't stop the words, the accusation. It flowed out of her mouth on its own, needing freedom.

"I . . . I didn't," Brighton said, her voice small, thick with tears. "I promise, I didn't."

Charlotte didn't respond. She didn't care how the song got to the Katies—at least, she told herself she didn't care. Couldn't right at that moment, because it was all rushing back.

The day they got engaged.

Their wedding day.

All the times in between when Brighton had played that song for her, just for her, whenever she was stressed or feeling lonely.

"Do you have any idea," Charlotte said after a few moments, "what it felt like to stand there by myself, waiting for you?" Tears crawled up her throat. She tried to swallow them down, but goddammit, they were relentless, five years of words she'd never said finally tired of being held inside. "What it felt like to stand there and smile and *wait* for the love of my life to come and join me, and seeing your mother instead? Your *mother*, with pity in her eyes as she walked toward me, a fake smile on her face for all the guests."

"Charlotte," Brighton said, and Charlotte knew she was crying. Well, good.

"And then," Charlotte went on, "she took my hand and she said . . . Do you know what she said?"

Brighton didn't say anything.

"She said, 'Honey.' That was it. Just one word, a little press of my hand, and I knew. I knew it, but I didn't, you know? I couldn't believe you'd actually leave me, but deep down, I knew you had. If you hadn't, Bonnie wouldn't have been standing in front of me. You would have. But you weren't, and I . . . I just . . ."

She couldn't finish. It was all too much, reliving that day, "December Light" playing while Charlotte's whole world fell apart. The musicians kept going, unsure of what to do when it was clear that Brighton, the other bride, wasn't coming. So Charlotte had not only walked down the aisle to that song, she recessed to it too, Bonnie leading her back up the white tree-lined aisle, candles flickering warmly, her own mother just sitting there in the front row with her lips pursed, as though she'd suspected this might happen all along.

Somehow, Charlotte had ended up in the Fairbrooks' kitchen, a cup of tea in her hands, Bonnie sitting in front of her with a concerned look on her face.

I'm so sorry, honey.

And Charlotte hadn't even cried.

She hadn't cried then, and she hadn't cried when she got up, tea untouched, and went back to her house and locked herself in her bedroom, the very room she and Brighton had just had sex in, cuddled in, whispered in not ten hours before. She hadn't cried when Brighton texted, called, left voicemails a few days later. She hadn't cried as she deleted them all without even listening to them.

She hadn't cried when she packed up Brighton's stuff in their New York apartment. She hadn't cried when she slipped the engagement ring Brighton had picked out for her—gold with a geo-cut blue-green sapphire in the middle—off her finger for the last time and tossed it into a box full of Brighton's sweaters before shipping everything back to Grand Haven. She hadn't cried when Brighton stopped calling, stopped texting.

She hadn't cried through any of that. She'd moved on, lived the life she meant to. And she loved her life. She *loved* it, didn't miss this woman standing behind her, this woman who'd betrayed every single piece of her heart, this woman who'd left her like she was nothing.

She'd never cried over her.

Never needed to.

But now she couldn't seem to stop the flow—it was like a dam breaking, a river set loose. Her face flooded, eyes spilling over. She pressed her hands to her face, cold fingers trying, trying, trying to push everything back inside, but it didn't work, and her sobs echoed through the sleeping forest.

Then . . . hands on her wrists.

Soft. Familiar.

"Lola."

A whisper, gentle, her own name curling around her in a way that pulled more tears from deep inside her, dissolving her anger. She was tired, so tired, after five years of holding herself up, and it suddenly felt like she hadn't gotten a full night's sleep in all that time, rest only coming in fits and starts.

Brighton pulled Charlotte's fingers free, replacing them with her own hands. They were freezing but somehow still felt warm as her thumbs swiped the tears from Charlotte's cheeks, her palms cradling Charlotte's face. Then her forehead was against Charlotte's, whose hands somehow circled Brighton's wrists, holding her there instead of pushing her away.

Their breaths mingled, Brighton whispering "I'm sorry, I'm so sorry" over and over, but Charlotte barely heard the words. They would never make it right anyway, and they both knew it, but still, Charlotte couldn't seem to put space between them. Brighton was so close, so familiar—she smelled the same, like summer, like warm breezes and mint, even in the middle of winter.

The snow fell a little harder, as though the weather were reacting to the pull between them. Charlotte felt herself curl closer, their noses bumping. They were nearly the same height, Charlotte only about half an inch taller, and she remembered now how perfect that was, how perfectly they fit together, like they were made to be close, to kiss, to melt into one.

And, god, it had been so long.

Five years, nearly to the day, since Charlotte had been kissed. Been held like this. She'd planned to move on sexually, romantically, but she never had time, never wanted it badly enough to go through the effort of meeting someone, feeling comfortable. And she'd been fine. She could take care of herself in the pleasure department, and she had her music, her work, her quartet.

But now Brighton was here, *here*, holding her, and everything in her wanted to shove Brighton away and at the same time swallow her whole. She wanted to disappear into her, the desire so strong that she couldn't fight it, didn't want to, and then their mouths brushed, the gentlest whisper of a touch, and Charlotte fell.

Into.

Under.

Against.

Brighton's mouth closed around her bottom lip, and god, it felt so good, so right, like nothing had gone wrong between them, like it had only been five minutes since they'd last kissed instead of five years. Charlotte pulled Brighton closer, hands going from Brighton's wrists to wrap around her waist, under her coat, while Brighton threaded her hands into Charlotte's hair, pushing off whoever's knit hat she was wearing. Brighton's teeth tugged at Charlotte's bottom lip, so gently, right before their tongues met, sending a swell of warmth between Charlotte's legs. She opened to Brighton, and Brighton opened to her, a letting in or a letting go, she didn't know—because all that mattered was that moment, that second, Brighton's breath and tongue and teeth and the little sounds rolling from her throat, tiny whimpers Charlotte had always loved.

Charlotte found the hem of Brighton's green sweater, slipping her hands underneath, discovering Brighton's warm skin as if for the first time, the shock of softness and goose bumps. She pulled her closer, licked at Brighton's top lip, making her gasp.

"Lola," Brighton said, then tilted her head so Charlotte could trail her mouth down her neck.

But in that moment, that breaking of contact, the woods came rushing back in. Colorado. December. *Five years later.* Charlotte froze, her nose pressed to Brighton's lovely throat, reality a cold splash of water.

She let go.

She let go so suddenly that Brighton stumbled backward, the arms once holding her close no longer there.

Charlotte backed up, her breathing coming even faster than when they were entwined, panic replacing all arousal.

"I'm sorry," Brighton said. Her cheeks were flushed, her lips swollen and pink. "I . . . I don't know what happened."

Charlotte said nothing. Couldn't. Didn't want to talk about it, knowing Brighton *would* want to talk about it. She always wanted to talk about everything, every single feeling she ever had.

Well.

Every single feeling except one—whatever secret emotion had sent her fleeing from their wedding five years ago.

The bitterness swelled back to full strength. Charlotte wiped her mouth with the back of her hand, made sure Brighton saw her do it. She watched Brighton flinch, then flatten her lips into a thin line to hide it. Charlotte scooped the hat from the ground, dusted off the snow, and slipped it on her head, smoothing over the tangles Brighton's fingers had left in her hair. She was methodical, calm, using these movements to slow down her heart, to get her brain back in control.

"I'm heading back," she finally said, and turned away from Brighton without another word.

Except when she turned, there were only trees. She turned again—more trees, more fallen snow covering any tracks they'd left on the forest floor. She had no idea which way they'd come from. She glanced at Brighton, who was only looking at her, then closed her eyes and sighed.

She was lost in the Colorado woods with her ex-fiancée, because of fucking course she was.

chapter 14

Brighton's mouth buzzed with that post-kiss feeling, her limbs liquid, her brain jumbled and still slotting the pieces of what had just happened into place.

They'd kissed.

Lola and Bright.

Bright and Lola.

They . . . Hadn't they?

She blinked the scene back into focus, the woods and the snow, Lola ten feet away from her now, turning in a circle with her hands on her hips.

Like nothing had happened at all.

The snow fell harder around them, a curtain between her and her ex.

"Lola," she said.

"Do you remember which way we came from?" Lola asked, not looking at her.

Brighton blinked again, then finally registered what was happening—no tracks in the snow, trees all around, no clear path or trail.

"Well, do you?" Lola asked, finally stopping her circling to glare at Brighton. To most people, she would've sounded calm, but Brighton heard the tinge of panic in her voice, the slightest tremble.

"Um, well," Brighton said, glancing around too.

"Helpful," Lola said, huffing a sigh.

Brighton gritted her teeth. Lola got bitchy when she was stressed—always had. Granted, it wasn't like she'd been anything *but* since they'd arrived in Colorado, except for the last few minutes, when she'd felt like the old Lola, soft and sweet, that impenetrable armor she wore for the world dropping away for Brighton, just like it always had.

The kiss . . . she now understood the phrase *It just happened*, because that's what kissing Lola just now had felt like—an inevitability, a tug of magnets finally close enough to snap together. One second Lola was reliving that awful day, revealing details Brighton had never known, had been too ashamed to even ask her mother about, and the next, Brighton's hands were on Lola's face, pulling her closer, closer, closer.

And, god, it felt good.

Lola felt good.

But now *Charlotte* was back in control, Jekyll or Hyde, Brighton wasn't sure which, and all Brighton wanted to do was flip that switch again, have her Lola back in her arms and—

You still love her.

Adele's voice echoed in her ears.

No. Brighton *didn't*.

She couldn't.

She squeezed her eyes closed, felt the chill in her bones, the snow on her cheeks, let winter shock her back into reality.

Because Lola was gone. Or else she was so hidden, so covered in that armor again, that even Brighton—who could always make Lola laugh or cry or whatever she needed to do—didn't know how to break through. At least not in any lasting way. The woman in front of her was cold, unaffected by what had just happened between them. *Charlotte* was calling the shots—she'd made that very clear.

It was time Brighton accepted it.

She took a deep breath, buttoned up her coat, ignored the ghost of Lola's fingers skating up her bare back. Then she looked around, studied her surroundings for clues. She'd always been observant, good with tiny details and elements in a scene. Her mother said it was the artist in her, looking at the world closely, creating an interpretation wholly new and unique.

You're a storyteller.

That's what her mother had told her when she was young, when she'd first started playing guitar at eleven years old, teaching herself from the internet and taking to it like a baby bird to the spring air on their first flight. Guitar just made sense to her, the rhythm and strings, the progression from one chord to the next, and songwriting paired perfectly, the poems she'd scribbled down since she could write sliding effortlessly into a medium that fit, that made her words sound like *something.*

Like a story.

Now, in the middle of the woods in Colorado, her stomach swooped with memory, with seventeen years of music and writing and performing.

Dammit, Brighton, this isn't you.

She shoved Adele's voice out of her head for the second time and focused. Because she could do *this* at least. She could get Lola—*Charlotte*—out of the fucking forest.

"Okay," she said, shoving her freezing hands into her coat pockets, then looking at the sky. "Where's the sun?"

Charlotte huffed again. "It's already set. And it's cloudy."

Brighton said nothing, breathing in patience as she scanned the sky through the trees for any hint. Charlotte was right—the sun had set before they'd even embarked on this little adventure, and it was nearly dark.

"This is how horror movies start," Charlotte said, clutching her stomach. "Or end. The girl in the woods. Everyone knows she's a goner."

"She's only a goner because the writers make her out to be an idiot. We're not idiots."

"Okay, thrillers, then. Women just vanish, disappear, and they're not idiots. Women's bodies are *not* okay in thrillers."

"Lo—Charlotte."

"Bad things happen all the time to non-idiots, and this is the setting. This is where it all goes down." She spun in a circle, her breathing coming even faster now. "Then again, I did take off into the woods without my phone, and then I ki—"

Charlotte cut herself off, shaking her head. She couldn't even say it, but she wiped at her face, as though a tear had dared to escape.

Brighton fought the urge to comfort her again. Charlotte would never accept it now anyway, so Brighton kept scanning the trees, ignoring the fact that she'd displayed plenty of idiocy in the last hour, including leaving her phone on Adele's bed. The sky that had been a white-purple when she ran out the door after Charlotte was now more of an inky eggplant, which made finding any sort of glow from the western-setting sun impossible.

She walked forward a little, then back, then to the side, spanning the perimeter of the area they were in, searching for something, anything. Her chest felt tight, panic rising, but not from being lost. She felt oddly calm about that detail—she just wanted to *do* this. Wanted to do something right.

Tears were clouding into her throat, a sense of complete hopelessness and loneliness washing over her when she saw it.

A knot on a tree, right at her eye level, that looked a bit like a star, gnarled and swirling like something in a van Gogh painting. It was unique enough that her eye had snagged on it before as she chased her ex deeper into the woods, her brain registering it but then immediately forgetting it when Charlotte stopped and cursed at her.

"Here," she said, putting her hand on the trunk and feeling the knot, which had an odd, five-pointed shape. "I remember this."

Charlotte all but stomped over, glared at the knot in the thickening dark. "Remember what?"

"This knot. I faced it like this"—she moved her body so she was angled straight toward it—"when we were walking into the woods. So if we—"

"Charlotte!"

Brighton turned a perfect one-eighty toward the voice, toward the way she now knew they needed to go. Shapes coalesced in the gloom, moving closer.

"Brighton!"

"Here!" Charlotte yelled, moving toward them. "We're here!"

There were three of them—Adele, Sloane, and . . . Wes.

Because of course he was here too.

"There you two are," he said, looking overly relieved. He had just *met* Charlotte, for god's sake. "It's dangerous to be in the woods this close to dark."

"This is how horror movies start," Adele said.

Charlotte didn't even look at Brighton. "I just needed some air. We both did." A graceful inclusion, no glance to the side, no faltering. Charlotte Donovan at her full strength.

"Next time, get some air on our back porch," Sloane said. "There's a mountain view and everything. And take your phone. You scared me to death."

"I'm sorry," Charlotte said. "Thank you for coming to find us. We were totally lost."

Brighton pursed her mouth, said nothing. She just watched as Wes put an arm around her ex and started walking, Sloane on Charlotte's other side.

"You okay, baby girl?" Adele asked. She regarded Brighton carefully, a black knit hat pulled over her braids.

Brighton swallowed. Made sure her voice was steady. Adele knew everything, yes. Brighton was safe with her, no doubt, but if she said anything but yes right now, in the middle of these woods after everything, she'd fall completely apart.

And she wasn't sure she'd get herself back together this time.

So she just nodded, touched the star knot once more before looping her arm with Adele's and walking straight out of the woods.

chapter 15

"Okay, so what do we do now?" Wes asked.

He and Charlotte stood together in a corner of Winter Berry Bakery, pressed closer together than she'd normally stand next to a near stranger, but desperate times and all that.

It had been two days since the Forest Incident, as she'd come to refer to it in her head, refusing to attach the word *kiss* even in her own ruminations. For the most part, she'd managed to avoid Brighton at the Berry house, dragging her quartet into the basement for rehearsals anytime they all agreed. When they weren't practicing, most everyone else lay around watching *Love Actually* and *The Muppet Christmas Carol* while drinking spiked hot chocolate.

But Charlotte worked.

She checked arrangements, reordered set lists, sent emails to their manager checking on venues and equipment, even though she'd already verified all of those details weeks ago. She knew she was driving Mirian crazy, but she had to do something. Sitting around watching Kevin McCallister's improbable defeat of two buffoons wasn't in the cards, especially since she knew *Home Alone* was Brighton's favorite Christmas movie. When she ran out of emails to deal with and her quartet rebelled against her work ethic, she practiced on her own, sitting on a chair in the Berrys' finished basement between the comically large flat-screen and the leather sectional, unfurling song after song after song.

No one bothered her.

No one asked her to take a break. Her quartet knew better, and Brighton . . . well.

Brighton hadn't spoken to her since the Forest Incident.

And that was exactly how Charlotte wanted it.

Except now she found herself at Winter Berry Bakery in a waking nightmare called Speed Date and Decorate. It was the second Two Turtledoves event, with Nina and her friend Marisol at the helm, during which half of the group stayed at tables and started decorating a giant sugar cookie, and the other half moved around the room whenever Nina struck a singing bowl, shifting to a new table and a new partner.

"Then we'll change up who stays put after about forty-five minutes," Nina had said at the start. "That way, everyone will get to talk to everyone, no matter your sexual orientation!"

"Good god, Mother," Adele had said under her breath, causing Manish to start snickering.

"And," Nina had gone on with a glare at her eldest, "you can decorate the cookie any way you'd like while you're at that table." She gestured to the pastry bags and ceramic bowls full of icing in various colors, sprinkles, edible glitter, M&M's, and Red Hots. "Once we're all done, we'll have a set of cookies as unique as all of you!"

"And we'll see if we have any lovely love matches!" Jenny

Hazelthorne had chirped from the back, a mug of coffee in her hands and a plaid shirt on her back.

"That's right," Nina had said, winking at one of her daughters. Charlotte hadn't been able to tell which one. "For now, enjoy the cheeseburger sliders—vegetarian options are on the second tray—and we'll get started in about half an hour!"

That was five minutes ago, the clock ticking down to when Charlotte would have to decorate a communal cookie—god, that couldn't be sanitary—with strangers. All the food was set up on a table at the other end of the bakery, with smaller tables set up in the middle for eating and the speed dating event. The shop's atmosphere was cheery, to say the least—Christmas music filtered out of a speaker somewhere, garland and lights hung everywhere, and in one corner there was a tree decorated with ornaments in the shape of muffins and slices of pie. Despite the holiday decor, Charlotte had to admit the bakery's vibe was lovely, with its white vintage counter and pastel-colored stools, and white shelves filled with mugs and tumblers made from milk glass in various colors.

"I have no idea what to do," she said to Wes's question.

"Drastic measures, seems to me," he said.

He was dressed smartly in dark-gray jeans and a checkered button-up under a navy sweater, and his beard looked freshly trimmed. He was handsome, there was no doubt, and Charlotte found herself really wishing they *would* find themselves in a romantic comedy and fall for each other.

It'd be so much easier.

She spotted Brighton moving through the line with Adele, piling tiny cheeseburgers on her plate. She was dressed in jeans and a cream-colored vintage blouse with mesh sleeves covered in velvet polka dots. Her hair was long, her bangs sleek and shiny.

Beautiful.

Except she wasn't, because Charlotte didn't notice her at all.

Of course, at that moment, Brighton glanced up, catching Charlotte's eyes on her.

"Dammit," Charlotte said, looking away quickly.

"Deer in the headlights," Wes said.

"Shut up," she said, and he just laughed. "Okay, what sort of drastic plan do you propose?"

He grinned. "It's big."

"Hit me with it."

"It requires some physical contact."

She narrowed her eyes. "How much?"

"Don't look so horrified."

She laughed. "I'm just not a very touchy-feely person."

Wes's smile only widened. "Nothing sordid, I promise." He pressed his hand to his chest. "But maybe I'm the one who's changed your life. Turned you. You just can't keep your hands off me."

"That seems like a stretch."

He laughed. "Fair. But do you trust me?"

"I don't know you."

"I won't corrupt you, I promise." Then he held out his hand, his eyes glittering. "Just a little—how do I say this?—harmless fun."

"Harmless fun?" Charlotte said. "What does that even mean?"

Wes rolled his eyes. "I gather subtlety is not your strong suit."

"You gather right."

He lifted her hand and placed it in his, then tangled their fingers together.

Charlotte sucked in a breath.

"It means," he said, kissing the back of her hand, "let's make 'em a little jealous."

"Oh god," she said, but he kept hold of her hand and pulled her toward the food table, getting in line. "You know we're going to have to let go of each other to actually get the food."

"We've got a few people to go yet," he said. "Milk it."

He let his shoulder brush hers, spoke to her in a low voice, his mouth close to her ear. Her palm was sweating against his, her heart pounding.

She hadn't held someone's hand in a long time.

"How do you know Sloane will be jealous?" she asked, turning her head to meet his eyes. He looked at her so intently, so adoringly.

Oh, he was good.

"I don't," he said. "But you're fun to hang out with, so it's worth a shot."

"Fun?"

"Fun," he said, then tilted his head. "Not used to that adjective?"

"To describe me? Not at all."

"All the more reason to loosen up a little here. We're just having fun, Charlotte. That's it. Serving the true purpose of Two Turtledoves, as the founding romantics intended."

Charlotte laughed, let herself lean against him. He *was* fun, she knew that. And kind and safe. But then she made the mistake—or was it actually a great decision?—of resting her cheek against his shoulder and looking out at the dining room.

Brighton was staring at them from where she sat with Manish, Elle, and Adele, her eyes wide, her mouth open a little. She looked down as soon as Charlotte caught her.

Charlotte turned back to the food, the line moving up. Her heart was pounding and felt three times its normal size. But she also felt . . . she wasn't sure.

Vindicated.

No, that sounded too petty.

Maybe . . . satisfied?

That was it. She felt satisfied. Relieved, even. Because for that split second when she and Brighton watched each other, Brighton looking ever so slightly shocked, and Charlotte didn't feel like the unlovable, leavable person she'd felt like for the last five years.

She smiled at Wes, then lifted their joined hands and kissed the back of *his* fingers before separating so they could get their dinner.

Forty minutes later, Charlotte was holding a tiny pastry bag full of icing while "Jingle Bell Rock" played in the background. She sat across from a very attractive man with auburn hair and freckles who was sneezing so often that she worried about the sanitary state of the large cookie they were supposed to be decorating.

"So what do you do for work?" the man—Jack—asked as he blew his nose into a handkerchief covered in tiny Christmas trees.

She pressed her lips together and sighed through her nose, catching Wes's eye at the table where he was stationed. He looked completely panicked. Not only did Charlotte hate small talk with strangers more than anything else in the world, but the euphoria she'd felt earlier with Wes had totally worn off. Moreover, she'd failed to realize until this moment that this horrid event would eventually pair her with Brighton. In this first round, she was fixed at a table, people moving around her, and it looked like Brighton was currently two people away.

"I'm a violinist," Charlotte said, wincing as Jack folded his handkerchief to reveal a clean side. She'd always abhorred the idea of handkerchiefs, despite their benefits to the environment.

"Oh, well done," he said. "You any good?"

"I am good, yes," she said right before he sneezed again. "Are you okay?"

He dabbed at the corners of his eyes. "Fine, fine, sorry. I'm not sick, I promise. I sneeze when I'm nervous. Makes going to the dentist a real adventure."

Charlotte offered a sympathetic smile, glad her own nerves didn't manifest themselves in a similar manner—she'd be a sneezing mess half the day. Instead, her anxiety held her posture so tight and straight she usually gave herself a headache.

Mercifully, Nina gonged a wooden mallet against the singing bowl just then, the warm and brassy sound reverberating throughout the room.

"Nice to meet you, Jack," Charlotte said politely, moving her hands to her lap to avoid shaking hands. He smiled and moved on, and Wes crashed into the seat in front of her.

"Jesus H. Christ," he said, dropping his head into his hands.

She exhaled, flopped back against her seat. "Yeah."

"I mean, Nina is truly evil."

She laughed, glancing at the undecorated cookie in the shape of a snowman in front of her. "Quick, help me get started on this."

He dipped a knife into a tub of white frosting and started spreading it over the naked sugar cookie.

"Looks like Brighton's up next," he said quietly, keeping his eyes on his work.

Charlotte glanced to the right, where Brighton was currently chatting up a lovely woman with gray and black tattoos all over her arms. Brighton rolled up her blouse's sleeve to reveal something inked on her upper arm, and Charlotte felt her stomach plunge to her feet.

She'd had no idea that Brighton had gotten a tattoo.

They'd talked about it before, how Brighton wanted one and had even wanted to get matching ones, but Charlotte had always been hesitant, worried it would diminish her professionalism. Now she knew that was silly, but as a fledgling in the music world, she'd been high-strung about missed opportunities.

She forced her gaze away, forced her brain not to care.

"Yeah" was all she said back to Wes. "Have you seen Sloane yet?"

He nodded, his expression going a bit dreamy. For a second, Charlotte envied him—at least he knew what he wanted, even if he didn't think it was possible. She found Sloane across the room, now talking to Gemma and laughing about something. Sloane's gaze slid to Charlotte. Charlotte smiled, but Sloane didn't react, so Charlotte offered a little wave. Still nothing. Charlotte frowned . . . until she realized Sloane wasn't looking at her—she was looking at Charlotte's current Speed Date and Decorate partner.

"Did she mention our hand-holding?" Charlotte asked him.

"Um . . . she did, actually," he said, still spreading icing.

Charlotte tilted her head. "And?"

"And . . ." He blew out a breath and shoved the knife back into the tub of icing as though committing a murder. "She told me to go for it."

"Go for it?"

"Go for it." He waved his hands between the two of them, looking like someone had just run over his puppy.

"Hmm," she said as she watched Sloane's eye flit to his back over and over again.

"Hmm? That's it? That's all the sympathy I get?" he asked.

She just shrugged. "Obviously, you're not going to go for it. Nor am I."

"I feel like I should be offended."

"Wes, come on," she said, taking the knife and filling in some thin spots of icing Wes had left behind.

He narrowed his eyes. "Okay, that's it."

"What's it?"

"What happened?" he asked.

She tilted her head. "When?"

A lifted brow. "You know when. Your little trip into the forest with Brighton the other day. Doesn't seem like you."

"Oh, because you know me so well now?"

"I know that you're not the type to take off into the woods in the dark. Or put up with any bullshit from your ex."

"It wasn't dark." She finished her icing work and gently set the knife back inside the tub.

"Twilight. Close enough in the winter."

Charlotte sighed, then grabbed the pastry bag full of red icing and started to make a sugar scarf as the Forest Incident replayed in her mind. The song, the ridiculous tears she couldn't seem to control, Brighton's hands on her face, then—

"No," she said out loud, her grip on the pastry bag a bit too tight. A blob of red puddled onto the snowman's neck, like something out of a holiday horror movie.

Wes frowned. "It *was* dark. I was there."

Charlotte shook her head, the word *kiss* teasing the edges of her mind. She couldn't seem to vanquish those four tiny letters, the action, the memory of Brighton's mouth and tongue and—

She squeezed her thighs together under the table, as though she could strangle any and all emotion or lust relating to Brighton Fairbrook.

And goddammit, she could. She'd been doing it for five years and had been just fine. No, better than fine—she'd *thrived*.

"We kissed," she forced herself to say quietly. Speak it, take away its power. Simple as that.

Wes's eyes widened. "You and Brighton?"

"No, me and Jack," she said, waving a hand at her former conversation partner the next table over.

He laughed. "Shit."

"Yeah."

"And?"

"And what?"

He smirked. "And how was it?"

Incredible.

Another damned word she couldn't seem to get any control over, ten letters popping into her brain like a randy jack-in-the-box, a gateway adjective that only led to others—*mind-blowing, stunning, perfect.*

"Speaking of, I think you should tell Sloane the truth," she said.

Wes blinked. "Nice diversion."

"Thanks, I'm an expert. So?"

He laughed, shook his head. "What about us? I distinctly saw Brighton eyeing us while we ate dinner. I should've put you in my lap, dropped grapes into your mouth."

"There were no grapes," Charlotte said, refusing to look over at Brighton again. "And besides, this charade is short-lived. Eventually, this will all end, and we'll leave for Europe, and you'll still be here sad and in love."

"Don't sugarcoat it or anything."

"Oh, I won't."

Wes laughed. "How would I even tell her? At the open-mic event? Woo her with a Pablo Neruda poem?"

Charlotte smiled. "I mean . . . maybe?"

Wes's own smile vanished. "I'm kidding. I'm not setting myself up for another heartbreak where Sloane is concerned."

Charlotte glanced again at Sloane, whose gaze definitely kept drifting to Wes.

"I don't think heartbreak is in your future," she said.

He tilted his head, eyebrows raised. "Has she said something?"

Charlotte opened her mouth before realizing that the answer was no, but not for the reasons Wes would assume. She searched her memory, trying to remember the last time she'd actually asked Sloane about her love life, her past, her desires for anything romantic. She knew Sloane didn't want anything serious, but had she ever actually asked *why*? Charlotte had just assumed they shared the same ambitions—career first and above all else.

But deep down, Charlotte knew those weren't even her own reasons for staying single, though she didn't like to think too hard about it. Career was the easy excuse, something no one could fault her for.

She looked again at Sloane, her oldest friend other than Brighton, something pulling tight in her chest.

"Wes, I—"

But then the singing bowl sounded, and Wes groaned, cast a wary eye at the next table.

"It's Jameson," he whispered.

"The glue eater?"

"The very one."

"Well, at least you know what to prepare as an appetizer if you ever cook him dinner."

Wes flipped her off, and she couldn't help but laugh. They both wished each other good luck, and Charlotte's stomach clenched even tighter. She felt rather than saw Brighton approaching, and she busied herself with fixing the bloodied scarf on her snowman. Brighton's hand came into view, taking the pastry bag full of chocolate icing. She went to work on a top hat for Frosty, but she didn't say anything.

Neither of them did for what felt like an hour, even though it couldn't have been more than a minute or two. In the silence, Charlotte thought she'd have to fight to keep her thoughts off the k-i-s-s, but she didn't. Instead, another thought nudged at her mind, crescendoing to a push, a shove, something she'd thought of several times over the past couple of days and hoped she'd just forget about.

Stop caring about.

But with Brighton sitting right here, they were trapped in each other's company for at least another five minutes, and she couldn't seem to think about anything else.

"How did the Katies get that song?" she asked. She didn't look up. Didn't stop her scarf mending.

Brighton's hand stilled.

"In the woods, you said you didn't give it away," Charlotte said. "So how'd they get it?"

Brighton was quiet for long enough that Charlotte dared a glance. Brighton was staring down at the top hat she'd started, brushing the pastry bag's nozzle through the icing mindlessly, her eyes a little hazy in thought.

"Brighton," she said sharply.

"Are you and Wes dating?" Brighton asked without looking up.

Charlotte opened her mouth. Closed it. Waited for the satisfaction of knowing that *that* was the question on Brighton's mind right now, but it didn't come. Instead, she felt almost embarrassed playing these games with Brighton.

Charlotte closed her eyes, counted to four. Opened them again. "Answer my question."

Brighton finally lifted her head.

Their gazes snapped together like lightning crackling through a stormy sky. Charlotte felt nearly breathless. Her fingertips started to tingle, and her stomach fluttered like they were sixteen again.

Like they were *anything* again.

"I played it for Emily," Brighton finally said, looking back down. "When we first met."

"Who's Emily?"

"The Katies' keyboardist," Brighton said. "I was . . . we were . . ."

"You were in the Katies, I know," Charlotte said, and Brighton flinched. Charlotte softened her tone, an instinct. "Sloane told me."

Brighton sighed. "Anyway, that's how they got the song."

Charlotte frowned. "So you did give it away."

"No, I . . ." Brighton shook her head. "I played it for Emily when we were getting to know each other's style, and once we formed the Katies, we put the lyrics and guitar tab into our drive on the cloud, like our song database. I never wanted to play it live, really, and both Emily and Alice said it was too . . ."

Charlotte leaned forward. "Too what?"

Brighton shrugged. "Too emotional? Too . . . I don't know. *Lovey-dovey* was the term Alice used. And I was fine with that, because it was *our* song, and I just—" She cut herself off, sat back in her chair. "Can we talk about something else?"

"No."

"Fine. Then we won't talk at all." Brighton picked up a tiny canister of green glitter and started shaking it over the snowman's body.

"Brighton."

Nothing.

"Brighton, for Christ's sake. How did that song end up as a Katies single?"

"I don't know. It doesn't matter," Brighton said.

"The hell it does. That's *your* song. Did you sign away the rights? Did you give them permission? Did they give you writing credit? You're owed royalties. They can't just—"

"Drop it, Charlotte."

Charlotte flinched. She'd asked Brighton to stop using her nickname, true, but the reality of it—hearing Brighton call her anything but Lola—was like hearing a symphony played just a hair off-key.

"Just like that, huh?" she said as Brighton continued to sprinkle green all over the snowman.

"Just like that what?"

"You're giving up just like that? Guess I shouldn't be surprised."

Brighton's hand stilled, her jaw tight. "I'm not giving up. There's nothing to give up on." She started her glittering again, shaking way too much over the snowman's belly.

"Oh, I see," Charlotte said. "You're just a coward, is that it?"

"I'm not a coward. I just know when something is futile."

Charlotte's jaw dropped of its own accord, hurt zigzagging through her like electricity. "You're a piece of work, you know that?"

Brighton laughed, a bitter sound. "Me? I'm the piece of work?" *Shake, shake, shake.* The glitter was now more of a blanket than a detail. "When *you're* the one who couldn't see what was right in front of you?"

"What the hell are you talking about?" Charlotte said, her voice rising. "And what the hell are you *doing*? You're making my snowman look like a swamp creature."

She reached out to grab the glitter from Brighton's hand, but Brighton held on tight, yanking it back toward her. Charlotte wouldn't give in, though, and she tugged it in her direction.

Hard.

Brighton let go. Charlotte saw a puff of green sparkles before she squeezed her eyes shut as the glitter went everywhere—her face, her neck, her hair. It coated her like a second skin. She sat still for a second, willing herself somewhere else as silence settled around her—a silence she knew meant everyone in the bakery was staring at her while "Have Yourself a Merry Little Christmas" played like a lullaby from hell.

December had struck again.

"Oh, honey, it's okay," she heard Nina say. "We'll get you cleaned up in no time."

Charlotte cracked an eye open but yelped as pain seared across her cornea and she slammed her lid shut again.

"I've got it, Nina," she heard Brighton say. "It's my fault."

Then she felt someone take her hand—Brighton, she knew, from those callused fingertips, though they were a little softer than Charlotte remembered—and pull her out of her chair.

"The restroom is just through there," Nina said, and Charlotte let herself be led to wherever *there* was, as she really didn't have a choice here. She even had glitter in her mouth, the taste too sweet with a plastic undertone.

A true delicacy.

"Here are some towels," Nina said, and Brighton said thanks. Soon Charlotte heard a door click shut, the conversation that had started back up at the event now muffled.

"Over here," Brighton said softly, guiding her forward. Charlotte heard the squeak of a faucet followed by the sound of water, the soothing *whoosh* of it slowing her pulse a little.

Then the warm glide of a damp towel over her closed eyes. Brighton held Charlotte's face with her other hand and wiped gently. Charlotte could hear Brighton's breathing, slow and steady, as though she were making an effort to keep it that way. The breadth of her touch changed, a towel-covered fingertip carefully working the glitter from the corners of her eyes, her lashes.

Charlotte held perfectly still, worked on her own breathing. The air between them was charged, like lightning about to strike at any second. Her chest felt tight, packed with emotions she didn't know what to do with.

You're the one who couldn't see what was right in front of you.

She curled her fingers into her palms, breathed in slowly. Defensively, she wanted to ask Brighton again what she'd meant by that . . . but deep down, Charlotte knew.

Maybe she'd always known.

"Do you remember Senior Day?" Brighton asked softly as she moved the cloth up to Charlotte's eyebrows.

Charlotte smiled without meaning to. "Of course I do," she said softly, a whisper. She didn't open her eyes, even though Brighton had moved on to her hairline, her temples. Somehow, shutting off her sight—the vision of Brighton in front of her, taking care of her like this—felt like the only thing keeping her from falling to pieces.

"I think this is worse," Brighton said, scrubbing at what

seemed to be a particularly stubborn piece of glitter near Charlotte's ear.

"Worse than paint in my hair?" Charlotte asked.

"At least that was washable."

Charlotte laughed, keeping her eyes closed as her memory drifted back to Senior Day at Grand Haven High, an event every spring where the school rented out the local fairgrounds and hosted a small carnival for the seniors, including rickety roller coasters, games with giant polyester stuffed animals as prizes, and a labyrinthine paintball course constructed from old rubber tires and shapeless inflatables. Charlotte and Brighton had banded together with some other orchestra kids, trying fruitlessly to take down the school's championship-winning baseball team.

Not that they'd ever expected to win against a group of athletes, but they'd given it their best shot. The battle itself wasn't what was memorable, even though both Charlotte and Brighton had gotten so much paint in their hair that it had taken days for all of it to wash out completely.

No, what Charlotte remembered most was the final showdown. Only Brighton and Charlotte had been left standing, and when Brighton had gotten caught at the end of Kyle Peterson's paint gun, Charlotte had flung herself in front of Brighton, taking all of his fire, red and purple and blue splatters to the chest.

Of course, he nabbed Brighton in the shoulder as soon as Charlotte fell, but it was the gesture that mattered. The sacrifice. They both crumbled into a heap on the paint-stained grass, Brighton flailing dramatically.

"I'm hit, I'm hit!" she yelled as she went down next to Charlotte's already prone form. Laughing, she leaned over Charlotte, slapping her cheeks gently. "Lola! Lola, talk to me! Don't tell me this is the end!"

Charlotte tried her best to lie still, even stuck out her tongue and let it hang limply from her mouth.

"No! Lola!" Brighton screamed, wailing at the sky and clinging to Charlotte's shoulders. "It can't end like this! I won't let you die for me. You can't die, you hear me?"

Charlotte released a giggle then but managed to stifle a full-blown laugh.

"The horror!" Brighton continued to lament. "The indignity! The unfairness of life! Why? Why, goddess, why?"

She shook Charlotte, then sobbed at the heavens until Charlotte finally lifted her head.

"Know that I loved you," Charlotte whispered, her voice strained from her dying breaths. She drifted her hand over Brighton's face.

Gently.

So gently that Brighton's dramatics stopped abruptly, her smile fading into something like wonder. Charlotte's hand felt electrified, and what started as a silly declaration, a touch of theatric flair, suddenly felt charged, the five years since they met culminating into this one moment.

"Yeah?" Brighton asked, leaning closer to Charlotte.

"Yeah," Charlotte said, such a simple answer to a simple question, but the effect was world-changing. Charlotte realized, right then, that they'd been dancing around this for years. She'd always thought Brighton was beautiful, talented, funny, smart. But she was her best friend.

And best friends didn't kiss.

They didn't dream of a romantic future together.

Or did they?

In that moment on the paintball course, while the baseball bros whooped around them in victory—she wasn't sure about anything except that her fingers ached to pull Brighton even closer.

To get rid of all the space between them.

So that's what she did.

She slid her hand from Brighton's cheek to the back of her neck and pulled, slowly, giving Brighton plenty of time to stop the whole thing, but Brighton didn't and soon they were kissing—their first kiss—covered in a rainbow of paint, not caring that the baseball guys had stopped hooting about their win and started whistling at two girls kissing in the grass.

None of it mattered.

Nothing mattered but smiles against each other's mouths and hands in paint-streaked hair.

Now, in the cold Winter Berry Bakery restroom, walls a pale blue and adorned with vintage black-and-white photographs of Winter River's small downtown, Charlotte opened her eyes. Brighton was looking right at her, though her eyes flicked to her work every now and then, still swiping glitter from Charlotte's neck. Her breathing sounded a bit shallow, her cheeks a bit flushed, as though she, too, had been reliving the same memory.

And goddammit, Charlotte missed her. Suddenly, after days of fighting it—no, five years of fighting it—she could admit it. And it was a relief just to let the feeling have its way.

She missed her best friend, her best everything.

She missed Brighton Fairbrook.

She felt dizzy, confused by the swirl of different emotions, because no matter how much she missed Brighton and what they'd shared, she was still angry.

So, so angry.

And hurt. Devastated, even, still, after all these years. But the last few days since they'd collided in the Berrys' driveway had felt like decades, a lifetime of wear and tear on Charlotte's heart. Ignoring Brighton's existence, who they *were*, wasn't working.

Not one bit.

She felt unhinged by the effort, exhausted in a way she hadn't felt since the first few days after their wedding. Still, she wasn't sure how to move forward. If she kept on going this way for the next week, she worried she'd be a complete mess for tour, but she couldn't risk opening herself up to Brighton like she had in the woods.

She could never let her guard down like that again. That's how she'd gotten here, adrift in a dizzying mix of lust and anger and longing and sadness. No, she had to get ahead of this. And one didn't get ahead of things by pretending they didn't exist.

One got ahead of them by planning.

By being the one in control.

For the past few days, things had just been *happening* to her, and she didn't like it. She felt small and helpless, like she had when Brighton had left her, incapable of changing anything.

But it didn't have to be like that now. *She* made things happen. That's who Charlotte Donovan was. Who she'd always been, how she'd always combatted the shitstorm of her mother, her childhood, her loneliness. She could do the same now—control her interactions with Brighton. Do them on purpose. If she planned a friendship of sorts—or at least a cordial coexistence—she would never again find herself in the middle of the woods stress-kissing her ex.

She stilled Brighton's hand on her neck, took the cloth from her. Brighton let go of it easily, but her eyes never left Charlotte's.

"I think we need to start over," Charlotte said. She made sure her voice was steady, her fingers deftly folding the cloth to hide the glittery mess on the cotton.

Brighton tilted her head. "Start . . . over?"

Charlotte nodded. "We're stuck with each other for the next week, and I think we should use it."

"Use it," Brighton said. "For . . . ?"

"For moving on." Charlotte's voice cracked a bit on the last word, a thickening in her throat she didn't expect, but that was the whole point here. Exposure therapy—spend enough time with Brighton so that the mere thought of her didn't feel like wood splintering under Charlotte's fingernails.

"What does that even look like?" Brighton asked, folding her arms. "Moving on."

Charlotte paused. Turned to look in the mirror. Despite Brighton's efforts, she still looked like a mess, glitter dotting her cheeks and hairline, her neck. She flipped on the water and rinsed out the cloth, green sparkles swirling down the drain. Then she handed the cloth back to Brighton.

"It looks like this," she said, closing her eyes and angling her chin forward a little in invitation.

Brighton hesitated but only for a second. Soon Charlotte felt the warm press of the cloth against her skin again, Brighton's touch gentle and sure.

chapter 16

*M*oving on.

Brighton couldn't get the words out of her head as she absorbed the friendly way Lola—*Charlotte*—was behaving toward her. The change was sudden, a shock, like a lamp switched on in a dark room. While Brighton continued to clean the glitter from Charlotte's skin, Charlotte talked.

Rather, she asked questions.

A lot of questions.

Do you like Nashville?

Where do you work?

What's your favorite cocktail to make?

Do you visit your parents often?

How are Bonnie and Hank?

Brighton answered them all, trying not to notice that Charlotte avoided any and all inquisitions into Brighton's dating life or their direct shared history. She asked her own questions as well: *How was the Rosalind Quartet formed? How is teaching going? What cities are you visiting on your European tour?*

She also sidestepped Charlotte's love life, but by the time Charlotte was mostly glitter-free, Brighton felt . . . lighter. Their interaction in the restroom was all small talk, to be sure, a clinical sharing of facts about each other's lives over the past five years, but it was better than Charlotte's cold shoulder and labored sighs, and better than the myriad knots that had formed in Brighton's stomach over the past few days every time she'd seen her ex.

"And your own music . . . how's that going?" Charlotte asked as Brighton rinsed out the washcloth.

Brighton kept her eyes on the rush of water. Charlotte had made her stance on the Katies' use of "December Light" very clear, and Brighton honestly couldn't bear to get into it right now, not with Charlotte Donovan, who'd achieved every dream her mind had ever conjured.

"One step at a time, okay?" Brighton said, shutting off the water and then folding the cloth into a square.

Charlotte's mouth twitched, but she said nothing else about it.

"Ready to go back out there?" Brighton asked.

Charlotte nodded, then hesitated at the door. "One more thing." Her hand stilled on the doorknob, and she took a deep breath. "I still don't want anyone to know."

Brighton frowned. "About us?"

Charlotte nodded. "I think it's just too much for the holidays. For everyone. And I've got this tour to get ready for. I don't want my quartet to . . ." She trailed off, sighed.

Hurt flashed through Brighton—a secret to be hidden—but she also got it. When she really thought about it, she didn't necessarily want the entire household to know she had left Charlotte at the altar either. Adele's reaction was hard enough, and she was Brighton's best friend.

"Okay," Brighton said. "A fresh start."

Charlotte lifted a brow but nodded. And when the two of them walked out of the restroom and joined the rest of the Two Turtledoves attendees, Brighton had nearly convinced herself that a friendship—*a fresh start*—with Charlotte was possible.

Nearly.

Watered Down was a rough-and-tumble pub in downtown Win- ter River—weathered wood exterior, roof in need of replacing, an old door that used to be red but had faded to resemble something like cat sick. "Rockin' Around the Christmas Tree" wafted against the poorly insulated windows, which were rimmed with vintage-style Christmas lights, a fourth of which had burned out.

It was messy and a little down on its luck, and Brighton had never seen anything so beautiful.

She sat at a round table in the corner with all the other guests from the Berry house—and *Wes*—the pleather of her chair cracked like a spiderweb, and smiled as the server set down a pitcher of something called Mistletoe Margaritas, which looked like plain old margaritas to Brighton, but that would also do just fine. She'd enjoyed all of Nina's wines since she'd arrived in Winter River but, Jesus, did she ever welcome something stronger.

"To kicking ass!" Manish called out, tipping the lime-green beverage into all of their glasses and then holding his up.

"Hear, hear," Adele said, and they all clinked glasses.

Charlotte sat next to Brighton, Wes on her other side, her posture erect as she inspected her tequila-heavy drink with some trepidation. Come to think of it, Brighton wasn't sure Charlotte had ever even had tequila.

"It's good," Brighton said, nudging her shoulder. "Try it."

"Be careful, though," Wes said, taking his own sip. "This thing'll strip your skin right off your bones."

"Sounds unpleasant," Charlotte said.

"Oddly enough, quite the opposite," he said.

Charlotte laughed and wrinkled her nose, then sipped daintily. Brighton most certainly did *not* notice the way her red mouth closed around the glass, the pink of her tongue licking at the salt.

She didn't notice that at all.

Nor did she notice how her stomach tightened at the way Charlotte laughed so lightly and easily with Wes. She had no idea what was going on between the two of them and tried not to think about it. *Fresh start* probably meant the opposite of losing her shit over her ex flirting with someone else.

Holding his hand.

Fresh start meant *friends*. *Fresh start* meant Charlotte could hold anyone's hand she wanted and Brighton would toast to their happiness.

She knocked back a large swallow of her beverage and focused on Charlotte's widening eyes as she drank too, the tiny smile that pulled at her lips.

"Told you," Brighton said.

"Careful, killer," Sloane said as Charlotte took another sip. "Wes is right—tequila is a fair-weather friend."

Elle waved their hand. "Charlotte deserves to let loose; leave her alone."

"Hear, hear," Adele said again, then winked at Brighton, because of course Brighton had updated her on what had gone on in the bakery's restroom earlier that day.

Now here they all were at Watered Down for Holiday Movie Trivia Night, and Brighton planned to dominate. She also planned to get a little tipsy, enough to dull the memory of the last few days, the Katies, and "December Light" in her mind.

For a night, at least.

Brighton tipped back more of her own drink, relishing the salty-sour-sweet in her mouth. Oh, this was good, and it would go down easy, that was certain.

"Hey, welcome, everyone!" A guy with tight jeans and a nearly obscene holiday sweater held a mic on the tiny stage at the front of the pub. He had sandy hair and eyeliner and the brightest white smile Brighton had ever seen.

"Okay, hello, now," Manish said, turning his chair to face the host.

"I'm Eli, and this is Holiday Movie Trivia!"

The crowd erupted into cheers and whistles.

"Now why isn't *he* part of Two Turtledoves?" Manish asked.

"Because he's married to the bartender," Sloane said.

Manish turned to look at the bearded and tatted fellow behind the bar, then sunk down in his chair. "Noted."

"Rules are simple," Eli said, pacing the stage. "Come up with a team name, and write it at the top of your form. For each round, record your answer, bring it to me, and we'll see who the true holiday movie royalty is."

"Oh, that'd be me," Brighton said loudly. The tequila was already buzzing through her blood, and she always got talkative under alcohol's influence.

"No, no," Sloane said just as loudly. "Queen, right here."

Charlotte laughed, her glass at her lips. "I don't know, Sloane. I'm pretty adept at Christmas movie quotes."

Sloane scoffed. "You? Elizabeth Scrooge?"

"I wasn't always such a scrooge."

She glanced at Brighton, barely, but enough that a wash of memories crested through Brighton's chest, all the Decembers they had spent in the Fairbrook living room with bowls of popcorn and hot chocolate, a constant stream of Christmas movies playing on the TV.

Eli explained some of the different genres they'd be covering, as well as the winner's prize—a lamp in the shape of a leg, reminiscent of the lamp from *A Christmas Story*.

"You'll have to share custody," Eli said, and everyone laughed.

"Okay, we *have* to win that for Mom's living-room window," Adele said.

"Agreed," Sloane said, and clinked her glass against her sister's.

"I want that for the restaurant," Wes said.

"No, wait, I need that for my apartment," Manish said.

Elle laughed. "It'll be your personal item on the plane."

"My lovey," Manish said.

"Okay, people, we need a name," Adele said, ripping off a square of trivia paper from the pad in the center of the table. "Thoughts?"

"The Elizabeth Scrooges," Sloane said, winking at Charlotte.

Charlotte took another gulp of her margarita, then lifted a single devastating brow. "I approve."

"What about the South Bend Shovel Slayers," Brighton said. "You know, from *Home Alone*?"

"Clever, clever," Adele said, her pen in her mouth.

"Um, the Cheery Queeries," Manish said, spreading his hands out. "How is that not obvious to everyone?"

"That's got my vote," Wes said.

"The Cheery Queeries!" Elle said.

"That's not movie-related," Brighton said.

"It's gay," Manish said. "It defies expectations and knocks down walls."

Brighton laughed. "Fair enough."

"The Cheery Queeries it is," Adele said, writing the name at the top of their paper.

"All right, trivia players, first round is coming up!" Eli said. He held up a large Santa hat, then dipped a hand inside and pulled out a red card. "First question: Name all of Kevin McCallister's siblings in *Home Alone*. Remember, Google is strictly forbidden!"

"Easy-peasy," Brighton said. "Buzz, Megan, Linnie, and Jeff."

"Damn, girl," Manish said.

"I've seen it at least twenty times," Brighton said. "I can name all the cousins too."

Adele wrote down the answer and took their paper up to Eli. Then the group exploded in victory when it turned out they were the only team to get all four names correct.

"Next question!" Eli said. "What was the name of the doll that Scott Calvin's company worked on in *The Santa Clause*?"

"What?" Elle said. "Who the hell would remember that?"

"Oh god, I know this one," Sloane said. "That scary little white-girl doll that wasn't even cute. Shit, what was her name?"

"Polly?" Brighton said, the name just outside her reach. "Holly?"

"But it was, like, a whole name, not just a first name," Adele said. "Wasn't it?"

"I've never even seen this movie," Wes said.

"It's awful," Manish said.

"If by *awful* you mean *fucking great*," Brighton said. "Dammit, the doll was, like . . . she was in a little dress and—"

"Do-It-All-for-You Dolly," Charlotte said casually, pouring herself another glassful of Mistletoe Margarita.

The group blinked at her.

"What?" she said, sipping. "I'm right."

"Oh my god, you are," Sloane said.

"Do-It-All-for-You Dolly?" Manish said, his brows raised. "What, *exactly*, does Dolly do for you?"

Elle nearly did a spit take.

"Sounds iffy, that's all I'm saying," Manish said.

Charlotte laughed, a real laugh, *her* laugh, and Brighton couldn't help but smile back, something swelling around her heart. It had been five years since she'd heard that laugh.

"You're brilliant," Brighton said to her while Elle took their answer up to Eli.

"Like you didn't already know this about me," Charlotte said quietly.

Brighton laughed then, her shoulder pressing into Charlotte's. "I did know."

They looked at each other for a second, the air between them growing thick with—

No.

Brighton didn't want to say it. Didn't want to even think it.

Charlotte's throat bobbed as she swallowed, her eyes bright and lovely. A strand of silvery hair fell over her cheek, and Brighton lifted a hand to tuck it behind her ear.

An instinct.

But she stopped herself just in time, instead changing course to pull her own hair over her shoulder.

Charlotte cleared her throat and looked away, then took another gulp of her margarita. Several gulps, in fact, then pulled the pitcher closer to her. "I need another drink."

♪

Brighton didn't realize Charlotte was completely plastered until they were leaving Watered Down with the leg lamp nestled in Manish's arms.

Charlotte grabbed Brighton's arm as they meandered through the tables toward the door, nearly pulling Brighton down with her.

"Whoa, are you okay?" Brighton asked, turning to steady Charlotte. Wes grabbed Charlotte's other arm.

"I'm fine," Charlotte said, but she blinked at the dim room, then pulled at her coat, which Brighton now noticed was buttoned crookedly. "I'm hot. Is it hot in here?"

"No," Brighton said slowly. Her own head was swimming a little, but she'd also had plenty of water and a generous helping of duck nachos. Now that she thought about it, she didn't recall seeing Charlotte eat much more than a few nibbles.

"It's definitely hot," Charlotte said, her voice slurring her consonants.

"Uh-oh," Brighton said.

"One too many," Wes said. "Or maybe five."

"Yeah," Brighton said.

"What?" Charlotte said as Brighton looped an arm through hers.

"I think you're drunk," Brighton said.

"I am not." Charlotte tilted to the side, then batted at her face. Brighton thought she might be trying to prove her sobriety by touching her nose.

It was kind of adorable.

"You most certainly are," Wes said.

"I don't *get* drunk," Charlotte said. "Never have, never will."

Except her words came out like "Ner-ha-ner-will," pretty much disproving her point.

Still, as Brighton laughed and she and Wes led Charlotte out of the bar and into the frosty night, she realized she'd never seen Charlotte Donovan actually drunk, or anything past buzzed. Not in high school, not in college. Their first night in Winter River, she'd definitely gotten tipsy but nowhere near drunk. Not like this. Charlotte had *tasted* any wine they'd sneaked from Bonnie's collection as teenagers, interested in blends and vintages, and at Berklee, she'd been far too focused to mess around with excess drinking. They'd gone to parties, but Charlotte had either sipped demurely or forgone alcohol altogether.

"If it's not *good*, why drink it?" she'd said one time at a Halloween party when they were sophomores. Brighton had been slurping happily on something green that admittedly tasted like a combination of bile and sour apple.

"I guess you liked those margaritas, huh?" Brighton said now, doing her level best to keep Charlotte from slipping all over the icy parking lot.

"I did," Charlotte said. "They were delibous . . . delimous . . ."

"Don't hurt yourself," Brighton said, laughing.

"Why can't I say the word?" Charlotte said.

"Tequila."

"Tequila!" Charlotte shouted into the night, pulling the attention of the rest of their group, who were already at the car. They turned as one, jaws dropping.

"Oh my god," Manish said. "Am I seeing what I think I'm seeing?"

"Charlotte," Sloane said, hurrying toward them. "Are you okay?"

"She's drunk," Brighton said. "Very."

"I'm *not*," Charlotte said, waving a finger at Brighton, then narrowing her eyes at her. "*You* are very, very pretty."

Brighton laughed, but her cheeks warmed nonetheless. She glanced at Wes, half wondering if maybe he'd be bothered by the comment, but he simply gazed between the two of them, a small smile on his face.

"Oh my god, I've never heard her compliment someone like that," Sloane said. "Let's get her in the car."

"Wait, Charlotte *complimented* someone?" Elle asked.

"She said Brighton was pretty," Sloane said as she took Charlotte's other arm and led her toward Nina's SUV.

"She *is* pretty," Charlotte said, then tipped her head back and looked at the sky. "Like the stars. The moon."

"Wow," Manish said. "We should keep some tequila on hand at rehearsals. I'd love more than a that-was-sufficient glare at the end of a concerto."

Sloane slapped Manish's chest as she passed him, then hauled Charlotte into the front seat.

"You're okay to drive?" Wes asked Sloane.

"Deli's driving," she said as she buckled Charlotte inside, then looked up at Wes. He stood by the passenger door, his hands in his pockets. "Are you okay?"

He nodded, but his eyes were all soft and gooey as he looked at Sloane. Brighton watched them stare at each other for a second, a million questions about their history spilling into her head before she scrambled into the first row, diagonal so she could keep an eye on Charlotte. Adele drove, Sloane slid in next to Brighton, and the rest of the quartet piled into the back row. Brighton watched Charlotte the entire drive back to Nina's house, Wes and Sloane's tender moment forgotten, concern and something else billowing in her chest.

Something soft but sore, like a day-old bruise.

Like the stars. The moon.

She shook off the happy swell she'd felt when Charlotte said she was pretty. She was just a bit romance starved, a bit discombobulated over this whole week and seeing Charlotte again.

And Charlotte was drunk.

She hadn't meant what she'd said . . . or, at least, she never would have said it if she were sober.

The drive felt like an eternity, winding along mountain roads. Once they arrived, Brighton all but leaped from the car, rounding the front to get to Charlotte. When Brighton opened the door, Charlotte nearly tumbled out and into her arms, laughing as she did so.

"I feel funny," she said.

Brighton held on to her shoulders. "I bet you do."

Once inside, Brighton headed for the stairs with Charlotte. "Can I take her to your room to lie down?" she asked Sloane.

"Yeah, of course," Sloane said. "I'll bring up some water and Tylenol."

"Perfect."

"Oh dear," Nina said, appearing from the kitchen and wiping her hands on a dish towel. Snickerdoodle rounded the corner as well, wagging his tail and sniffing at Charlotte. "Mistletoe Margaritas?"

"The one and only," Adele said. "But in happier news, we won you this incredibly tacky lamp!" She grabbed the fishnet-clad leg from Manish and plopped it into her mother's arms.

"Oh . . . wow," Nina said. "Thank you?"

Their laughter faded behind them as Brighton hauled Charlotte up the stairs toward Sloane's room. Snickerdoodle followed, but Brighton managed to keep him in the hall, even as she smiled at how much this dog seemed to adore Charlotte. As soon as she released Charlotte, just for a second to close Sloane's door and turn on the light, Charlotte fell face-first onto the bed.

"Jesus," Brighton said, hurrying toward her.

But Charlotte was laughing as she turned slowly onto her back. She blinked at the ceiling, and Brighton started unlacing her boots for her.

"That looks like a boob," Charlotte said, pointing at the light fixture, a glass sphere with a brass-plated nickel border and center lock.

Brighton glanced at it. "It does."

"Boobs," Charlotte said, drawing out the o's.

Brighton laughed. "Boobs."

"They're nice."

"That, they are."

Charlotte sighed. "I think I'm drunk."

"Oh, I don't know, seems to me like you're behaving pretty normally."

Charlotte smiled at that, her eyes now following Brighton's movements as she tugged off Charlotte's boots and unbuttoned her coat, then moved to the top of the bed and pulled down the covers.

"Get in," Brighton said after she worked off Charlotte's coat, then helped her under the duvet. It was quite a sight, Charlotte Donovan contorting her body into a complicated pretzel to achieve such a simple task, but Brighton let her figure it out. Soon she was situated in the bed, covers pulled up to her chin.

Brighton set a trash can next to the bed in case Charlotte got sick, then tucked in the sheets around Charlotte even tighter. "We've got to get some water and Tylenol in you before you can sleep, okay?"

Charlotte nodded like a little kid, her eyes wide and still glued on Brighton, as though she were working on a mental math problem. And then—Brighton couldn't help it—she crouched down and smoothed Charlotte's hair back from her forehead, the silver strands a little coarse yet so familiar under her fingers. Charlotte's eyes fluttered shut, then back open.

Brighton felt shaky, a little drunk herself, though she didn't think it was the tequila anymore. She forced her hand back to her side, forced herself to stand all the way up, forced herself to take a step back toward the door.

"Don't," Charlotte said, reaching out to take her hand. "Don't go."

And god, those two tiny words, spoken on a whisper with Charlotte's amber eyes fixed on Brighton's, they felt like a revelation. A nugget of truth, finally, after so many hours spent building up facades.

"Okay," Brighton said, sitting down on the bed, Charlotte's hand still curled into hers. "I'll stay as long as you need."

Charlotte smiled, blinked heavily. "You're so good to me."

Brighton laughed, shook her head. "I'm not."

"You are. You *were*. Always, every day. Until . . ."

Brighton looked down, shame warming her cheeks. Silence settled between them for a while, long enough that her shame receded as Charlotte squeezed her hand, a few deep breaths working into her lungs and blood.

"I miss you."

Charlotte said it so quietly that Brighton wondered for a second if she'd imagined it. But a ghost of the words swirled between them, Charlotte still looking at Brighton, still gripping her hand.

"You do?" Brighton asked, her eyes already stinging.

"Every day," Charlotte said. Her own eyes didn't fill, but her voice shook a bit, a rasp to the consonants revealing her emotion. "I've never loved anyone like I love you. Never will."

Tears spilled over Brighton's cheeks, and she leaned down, tucking Charlotte's hand to her chest, pressing their foreheads together.

"Lola," she said, and that was all she could get out, Charlotte's declarations taking up every other space in her brain.

"I miss that too," Charlotte said. "My name."

Brighton nodded against her. "I . . . I want to make it right. Make us right."

"You—"

"There are so many things I need to explain," Brighton went on, "if you'll just let me."

"Bright—"

"We can go slow. As slow as you want. Just please let me try."

Brighton knew she was starting to babble, her adrenaline pumping at Charlotte's words, Charlotte's *sweetness*, which Brighton hadn't realized she'd desperately wanted, needed, for years. She took a deep breath, trying to slow herself down. She didn't want to scare Charlotte off, didn't want to fuck up again. Charlotte trembled, and Brighton held her tighter, their mouths brushing.

"Lola," she whispered.

Then, suddenly, Charlotte shoved her away so violently that Brighton nearly slid off the edge of the bed. Brighton gasped, clinging to the duvet as Charlotte bent over the bed, grabbed the trash can, and proceeded to hurl up the contents of her stomach.

Brighton blinked, taking a second to realize what had happened, then scrambled up to hold back Charlotte's hair, which was falling precariously around her face while she puked.

"It's okay," Brighton said, securing Charlotte's hair with one hand and rubbing her back with the other.

Charlotte groaned.

"So we're at that stage," Sloane said, appearing in the doorway armed with a huge glass of water and a bottle of Tylenol. She set both on the nightstand.

"We are," Brighton said.

Sloane winced as Charlotte retched again. "She's gonna hate herself in the morning."

Brighton certainly didn't envy the headache and nausea Charlotte would probably endure. Still, even as she heard Charlotte's sick hit the plastic-lined wastebasket and wished she could magically make Charlotte feel better, she smiled.

Charlotte's confessions filtered through her brain, settling around her heart.

And Brighton knew. Right then, with the smell of vomit wafting around her. She knew Adele was right—she loved Charlotte Donovan.

Her Lola.

And Charlotte loved her too.

"Want me to take over?" Sloane asked.

Brighton shook her head. "I've got it."

Sloane nodded, tilted her head at Brighton. "You're pretty devoted for having just met her."

Brighton opened her mouth but then closed it. She simply smiled, shrugged. She didn't want to lie to Sloane, who'd been nothing but wonderful to her, but she knew their history was Charlotte's to tell.

"Okay, well, let me know if you need anything," Sloane said.

"I will. See you in a bit."

Then Sloane left, and Charlotte eventually emptied herself out, flopped back onto the bed with sweat on her brow. Brighton helped her drink some water and take the pills, then turned her on her side and rubbed her back, humming "December Light" as Charlotte fell asleep.

chapter 17

Charlotte opened her eyes and immediately regretted it.

The room was bright, painfully so, the sheer curtains doing very little to block out all the white. She could hear the gentle hum of voices coming from downstairs, but Sloane's bedroom was empty but for her. Her stomach roiled, and it felt like a tiny person with a jackhammer now lived inside her head.

She didn't dare sit up.

Instead, she closed her eyes again, took some steadying breaths, tried to piece together the events that had landed her in this state.

Trivia . . . she remembered trivia. She remembered winning and getting a lot of questions correct herself. She remembered margaritas—*tequila.* So much tequila. The drinks had gone down easily, and they'd tasted amazing. More blurry images floated through her sluggish brain—the parking lot, the ride home, Sloane's bedroom, Brighton, puking in the—

She bolted upright, immediately regretting it and pressing her fingers into her pulsing temples, but she stayed where she was.

Brighton.

Brighton had taken care of her. She was sure of it—Brighton's hand on her forehead, smoothing over her back as she got sick, the gentle hum of a song as she finally drifted off.

But there was something else, something that Charlotte—

I miss you.

Oh god.

I've never loved anyone like I love you.

Oh, holy shit.

Never will.

Oh, fucking hell.

Had she really . . . ? Did she . . . ?

"No, no, no," Charlotte said out loud—another mistake, her voice's vibrations rattling her skull. She dug her fingers into her scalp, massaging her aching head, hoping to press out the entirety of the last eighteen hours as well, but no luck there. She found a half-full glass of water on the nightstand and gulped, then popped two more Tylenols and tried to convince her mouth to stop watering in warning. Honestly, she wasn't sure if the nausea was from alcohol or what she'd said to Brighton.

Both. Definitely both.

She was supposed to be *moving on*. That's what she'd decided, what she'd declared to both of them in the Winter Berry restroom. She was supposed to be in control, for Christ's sake, but here she was, hungover and nursing the effects of what pretty much amounted to a declaration of love to her ex.

Jesus Christ, how did she get here?

She shook her head—mistake number 1,293—and shoved back the covers. She swayed on her feet, but she pushed through it and made it to the bathroom unnoticed, where she took the hottest shower possible. After that, she pulled on a pair of tight black jeans and a black turtleneck before smoothing her hair back into a perfect low ponytail. She put on mascara and her reddest red lipstick, then looked at herself in the mirror.

She could still do this.

She was still in control.

All she had to do was act like last night had never happened. Easy as knocking back a Mistletoe Margarita.

♪

Downstairs, everyone was gathered around the dining table, feasting on toasted bagels topped with over-easy eggs. Charlotte's stomach rumbled. Food sounded both divine and like a terrible idea, but she needed something to soak up all the booze still floating in her blood. She walked confidently to the table and sat down in an empty chair next to Manish, then grabbed a bagel and started spreading it with butter.

The group went silent, but she simply smiled, made sure her butter was touching all the edges of her bagel, and took a bite.

"Tequila!" Manish said, breaking the silence.

Everyone burst into laughter, and Charlotte felt her cheeks redden. But she just smiled brighter, took a surreptitious deep breath, and felt a calm settle over her bones.

She could do this.

She was *great* at this. When one had an indifferent mother as their only parent, self-soothing was a priceless skill, a matter of survival, even. She'd learned at a very young age how to take care of herself, control her emotions, and wear expressions that fit the situation so no one asked questions or suspected she wasn't okay.

Because she *was* okay.

She was goddamn thriving.

"Yes, yes, have your laugh," she said to the group as she took another bite of her bagel. Brighton sat across from her, putting her in the perfect position to look directly at her ex as she chewed.

She smiled.

Made sure it reached her eyes.

"You feeling okay?" Brighton asked.

"Great," Charlotte said, then shrugged. The best lies held some truth. She laughed. "Okay, not great, but I'll make it."

"I'm pretty sure the state of Colorado ran out of tequila after you descended on Watered Down," said Adele.

"All the better," Nina said. "Tequila never did anyone any favors."

"That's the truth," Charlotte said, smiling at her host. "I don't think I'll be partaking again anytime soon."

"Hang on," Sloane said. "Mom, do you have some tequila stories?"

Nina waved a hand and got up. "Not today, Satan."

Adele and Sloane looked at each other, then shot up from the table, both following their mother into the kitchen.

"Rehearsal in five!" Charlotte called after Sloane, her raised voice nearly splitting her head in two. Still, she smiled.

Smiled and smiled and smiled.

"Ugh, seriously?" Manish asked. "But we're going to Greenbriar Ridge this afternoon."

Charlotte took another bite of her bagel to hide her grimace, chewing slowly. She'd forgotten about the overnight trip they were taking to Briar Lodge in Greenbriar Ridge, a town about an hour away. Sloane and Adele's stepmother's family owned a ski lodge, which she and Raymond Berry had just renovated. Raymond had booked them all cabins, given them all access to the slopes and spa.

"It's supposed to snow a lot too," Elle said. "We should probably leave sooner than later."

Charlotte nodded, but they hadn't rehearsed yesterday either, and she needed the calm that only her violin provided before heading off into the snowy wilderness with this crew again.

"A quick one," she said.

"Three songs," Manish said.

Charlotte narrowed her eyes. "Six."

"Four."

"Deal."

Manish's eyes widened. "I won." He gripped Elle's arm and shook them. "I won."

"You didn't win," Elle said. "It's called compromise."

"That is a win where Charlotte is concerned."

"Actually, I like odd numbers," Charlotte said, smiling wryly at him.

"Nope, nope, you said deal on four. Four it is. Four is law," he said, then slid out of his chair. "I'm going to go tune my viola. Elle?"

"Good idea," Elle said.

"Don't think we've forgotten about Compliment Charlotte," Manish said as he ambled out of the room, and Charlotte frowned at him.

"Who?" she asked.

"Brighton knows," he said, winking at Brighton before he and Elle scurried down to the basement, laughing and whispering something about someone being pretty and—

Oh, for fuck's sake.

You are very, very pretty.

The parking lot memory hit Charlotte like a slap. She stuffed the rest of her bagel into her mouth.

Smiled at Brighton, who, she realized, was now the only other person in the room. And Brighton was looking right at Charlotte, a tiny smile on her lips. Her eyes . . . god, they were lovely. Dark and surrounded by thick lashes that used to brush her thighs when—

No, no, that wasn't the point. The *point* was that Brighton's eyes were shining. They were what one might call *starry*. Brighton released a little laugh and looked away, ran a hand over the back of her neck.

She was nervous.

She was . . . flushed, her cheeks pink. And she was blinking a lot, those damn lashes fluttering like butterfly wings.

Oh, dear devil in hell, what had Charlotte done?

"So . . . ," Brighton said, lifting those moon-soaked eyes to Charlotte's once again. "Last night—"

"I can't remember a single thing that happened," Charlotte said. She knew her posture was too straight, too tight. She forced her shoulders to drop a little. Forced a tiny, shy laugh of her own.

Brighton's expression froze, her mouth open in a small circle. "You . . . you don't?"

Charlotte shook her head. "Not one thing. I hope I wasn't too obnoxious."

Brighton swallowed, looked down at her plate, and pressed her forefinger into some errant poppy seeds. "No. Not at all."

Charlotte nodded. "Good." She wondered briefly if she should offer up some thanks for Brighton's care last night, but then that would indicate she remembered the care, and that would lead nowhere good.

Complete oblivion was best.

For both of them.

She popped her last bite of bagel into her mouth—the food actually was doing wonders for her stomach—and dabbed the crumbs away with her napkin. She was feeling good—decent, at least.

In control.

She cleared her throat and stood up, knowing that she needed to say one more thing to Brighton to wrap up the conversation, something casual and breezy.

Except when she moved her confident gaze to Brighton's, Brighton was already looking at her with her eyes slightly narrowed. Had Charlotte been less in control of herself, she would have startled at Brighton's piercing expression.

The kind of expression she used to use on Charlotte all the time, usually followed by a bevy of questions about Charlotte's *feelings*.

Well, that sure as hell wasn't going to happen right now. Or ever, for that matter.

"What do you have planned this morning before we leave?" Charlotte asked, keeping her tone light.

Brighton pursed her mouth. "Oh, I don't know. But I had an idea to run by you."

"Oh?"

Brighton nodded, leaned forward with her elbows on the table. "If you're open to it, I was thinking we could room together at Briar Lodge. The cabins are small—made for two people, Adele said—and I think it might be good for us. You know, for *moving on*." She stretched out the words like taffy.

Charlotte smiled without showing her teeth, perfectly controlled, but her mind was whirling, panicking, imagining being in a tiny cabin in the snowy woods with Brighton overnight.

Still, *no* wasn't an option here. *No* meant she remembered last night. *No* meant she was affected. *No* meant she couldn't handle Brighton Fairbrook so close.

"Of course," she said. "That'll be . . . fun."

"Fun," Brighton said, her eyes still fixed on Charlotte.

Fuck, she needed a minute—many minutes, a whole week to prepare for this one night. "Yes, fun." She picked up her plate and escaped to the kitchen.

"You okay?" Sloane asked. She was scrubbing the egg pan while Adele loaded the dishwasher. Nina sat on a barstool smiling down at her phone. "Need more Tylenol?"

"I'm okay," Charlotte said, pausing to squeeze Sloane's shoulder. She wanted to slow down, talk to her friend, ask her all the questions about Wes she'd thought of yesterday at Speed Date and Decorate, but her hands were shaking, her brain so overstimulated that she couldn't get the words in the right order. "I'll be right back."

She made her way upstairs and closed herself in the bathroom. She pressed her back against the door, let her breath go shaky, let tears swell into her eyes.

Just for a few seconds.

One . . . two . . . three . . .

I miss you.

She squeezed her eyes closed, wiped her face clean. She could do this. She could do anything. She'd survived neglect and abandonment and made herself a fucking star in the classical-music world. She could spend one night in a little cabin with Brighton Fairbrook.

She smoothed her hair back, stepped up to the mirror. She reapplied her lipstick like armor, then rolled her shoulders back and lifted her chin, preparing for battle.

chapter 18

Charlotte Donovan was full of shit.

Brighton had known it from the second Charlotte walked into the dining room with that immovable smile on her face—Anna Donovan's daughter was in control. Not Charlotte, and certainly not Lola.

She glanced at Charlotte as Nina's SUV, which the group had borrowed for the trip to Greenbriar Ridge, came to a stop in front of a huge log cabin–style lodge. They all piled out of the car, ooh-ing and aahing at the beautiful building. Snow fell steadily from the sky, blending with the silver strands in Charlotte's hair. She had been drunk last night. *Plastered*, in fact. It was naive for Brighton to take her confessions as truths—or, at least, as truths that would be discussed easily in the sober light of morning. Still, Charlotte was lying her poised ass off when she said she didn't remember the night at all.

Charlotte remembered everything, every detail, and Brighton was sure of it. She was sure of it, *and* it pissed her off, this roller-coaster ride she'd been on since arriving in Winter River. Charlotte ignoring her. Charlotte kissing her back in the woods. Charlotte declaring them friends. Charlotte saying things like *I miss you* and then pretty much taking them back.

Brighton was tired, and tender, and goddammit, she was angry.

"Welcome, welcome!" a voice boomed as they entered the lodge. The space was open and warm, all whiskey-colored logs and bronzed-nickel light fixtures, a wide concierge desk to the right and a lobby area with dark leather couches covered in red-and-black buffalo-print throws, a fire roaring in the giant fireplace. A huge Christmas tree sat in the back corner, white lights gleaming, windows all around sparkling with fairy lights.

It was a true winter wonderland.

"Daddy, hey," Sloane said, wrapping her arms around a man with dark skin and salt-and-pepper hair. He wore black-framed glasses and a green sweater covered in embroidered snowflakes.

"My girls," he said, scooping Adele into his embrace as well, hugging both of them close. "Merry Christmas."

Brighton's throat suddenly felt achy. She still hadn't talked to her mom, though she'd had a few emails. She missed her parents so much she couldn't breathe sometimes, a state that only contributed to her irritability.

"This place is beautiful, Mr. Berry," Elle said after introductions were made.

"Call me Ray, please. And thank you. We like it," he said. "Nicole is teaching a ski class, so you'll meet her later, but right now, let's get you settled into your cabins before this snowstorm locks us all in!"

He laughed, but Brighton saw Charlotte freeze.

"Locks us all in?" Charlotte asked. "Is . . . is it going to do that?"

Raymond waved a hand. "Supposed to get around six to ten inches. Perfect for the slopes."

After Ray put on his coat and boots, he nodded them toward the back of the building, waving at a few guests lounging by the fire with books as he went, and led them back outside. The snowfall had lessened, though the sky was a thick white and gray, packed clouds swirling above them.

They followed a stone path, overnight bags in hand, toward a set of tiny cabins so quaint and perfect that Brighton couldn't help but smile. Each structure had a green tin roof and was about the size of a large room, complete with a holiday wreath on the front door and white lights bordering the windows.

"Heat's pumping, and room service is on me," Ray said as he dropped three sets of keys into Adele's gloved hand. "And these will get you on any slope you choose." He handed out passes to each of them, and the group offered a chorus of thank-yous.

"Just glad to have you," he said. "We'll see you for dinner in the big house at seven."

And with that, he kissed Adele and Sloane on their cheeks and tromped off through the snow.

"Okay, come and get 'em," Adele said, holding up the keys, their fobs numbered one through three.

Brighton grabbed number one before anyone else could say anything. "Charlotte and I will take this one."

Adele lifted her brow at Brighton. "Oh, really?"

"Really," she said.

"I hope you know what you're doing, baby girl," Adele said, quieter this time.

"I do," Brighton said, though at that moment, she didn't at all. She just knew she was done feeling small, ignored, forgotten. Done feeling like the whole disaster of her relationship with Charlotte was all her fault. They both shared some blame, and she needed Charlotte to understand that. Clearly, the only way to get her ex to slow down for one damn second and be real was to semi-trap her in a luxury cabin in the middle of Colorado. Brighton would have felt slightly guilty if she weren't so frustrated.

"Okay," Adele said, "though you realize this means you're making me room with my sister." Manish plucked a key from her palm and winked before he and Elle, two peas in a snowy pod, hurried off toward cabin number three.

"You'll survive." Brighton jiggled the key, then turned to where Charlotte was looking like a fox caught in a trap, her eyes wide, her mouth held tight. "Ready?" Brighton said to her.

"Sure," Charlotte said, rotating her shoulders back, a classic Charlotte move when she was bracing herself for something.

"I won't bite," Brighton said.

Charlotte said nothing, just looked at Sloane with a sort of "save me" expression, but Sloane simply looked back, a tiny crinkle to her brow.

"Hey, everyone," a deeper voice said just as Brighton slipped the key into the lock. She looked up to see Wes walking up to them all bundled up, a duffel bag over his shoulders. A tall Black man with shoulder-length braids stood next to him.

"Wes," Charlotte said on an exhale.

Brighton's jaw clenched so hard her teeth ached. She liked Wes. She really did. He was nice and smart and funny, but she swore to god, if Charlotte so much as slipped a pinkie finger into his palm, she'd lose her shit.

"What are you doing here?" Sloane asked, frowning. "Hey, Dorian," she said to the other man.

"Ray invited us for this shindig," he said. "Dorian, this is Charlotte, the woman I told you about. And that's Brighton."

"What's up?" Dorian said, smiling. "I've heard a lot about you, Charlotte."

"You have?" Sloane asked.

Adele coughed.

"I have," Dorian said, subtly nudging Wes in the side.

Brighton felt like she might scream, right there on the side of that mountain.

"All good things, I hope," Charlotte said, her tone suddenly light and flirty.

Brighton was definitely going to scream. She was going to yell at the top of her lungs like that little spoiled brat in *Willy Wonka & the Chocolate Factory* any second now.

"Great things," Dorian said.

"Like what?" Sloane asked, her voice casual, but Brighton heard an edge there, the same edge she felt sharpening her own mood.

Dorian glanced at Wes. "Like . . . the quartet. You, uh, live in New York."

"Quite the biography," Sloane said flatly. "Adele, can I have our key?"

Adele handed it over wordlessly, watching as Sloane tromped through the snow to the next cabin. Wes watched her go too. So did Charlotte, for that matter, and then they locked eyes with each other, a wordless conversation passing between them.

"You're all a bunch of idiots," Adele said lightly before following after Sloane.

"Is it just me, or was that weird?" Dorian asked.

Wes just cleared his throat. "See you out there?" he said to Charlotte.

"Oh, I don't ski," she said, "but I'll come watch as you wipe out at the bottom."

Wes laughed. "Sounds cheery."

"Cheery and queery," Charlotte said brightly.

Brighton shoved the key in the lock and flung the door open, then hooked her arm around Charlotte's and pulled her gently. "See you later," she said to the guys. "Nice to meet you, Dorian."

"You too," he said. Brighton saw him say something to Wes she couldn't hear before she tugged Charlotte inside and closed the door. She pressed her back to the thick wood, watching as Charlotte took in the tiny living room—slash—kitchen, the warm log walls, the leather couch, the fire already crackling in the stone fireplace.

"This is nice," Charlotte said, setting her duffel down on the hardwoods.

"What the actual fuck?" Brighton said.

Charlotte whirled around. "Excuse me?"

"Who the hell even are you?"

Charlotte pressed her mouth flat. "What are you talking about?"

"The flirting? The breathless *Oh, Wes.*"

"I did not *Oh, Wes* him."

"Yeah, you kinda did."

"Well, maybe I like him."

"Yeah, maybe," Brighton said, then her next words flew out of her mouth before she could stop them. "Or maybe you're using him as a crutch so you don't have to deal with anything real."

The accusation hung between them. Charlotte paled, her jaw

tightening. Still, Brighton didn't regret saying it. Not one damn bit. They stared at each other, both of their chests heaving. Brighton waited for Charlotte to respond, to swear at her, to yell— Brighton would take anything at this point.

But Charlotte just picked up her duffel and headed toward one of the two bedrooms on either end of the cabin, calling out "I'm going fucking skiing!" as she went.

chapter 19

Charlotte stood at the top of what felt like the tallest mountain in the world and contemplated her death.

Rather, she thought about the choices that had led her to this point, about how December had really fucked her over good and proper this year, and she wondered just how sore her rear end would be if she slid all the way down this slope on her ass. But as she registered Brighton's presence next to her—the infernal woman had insisted on skiing with her, and Charlotte had quite pointedly not looked directly at her since they'd left their cabin—she felt determined to conquer December once and for all.

December, Brighton Fairbrook's relentless hold on her, their history, everything.

And it started with this mountain—Sloane insisted it was just a hill, a "green" slope, as the ski world called it, and perfect for beginners, but still. It felt big to Charlotte. Felt like a risk she'd never have taken in Decembers past. Granted, she never would've climbed onto that ski lift had Brighton not thoroughly pissed her off with her assumptions about Wes, but did it really matter what had gotten her here?

She was here. She was ready. She was Charlotte fucking Donovan. Never mind that the snow was now falling in what could only be described as torrents, creating a thick sheet of white over the whole world. Charlotte would prevail.

Just as soon as she could get her body to slide forward.

Then she would prevail, no doubt.

"I thought you hated skiing," Brighton said. Of course, Charlotte had skied before—she grew up in Michigan, and the Fairbrooks loved the slopes in the winter. She had gone with them once when she and Brighton were fourteen, in January so as not to risk a December disaster, but it wasn't Charlotte's favorite activity. The aching ankles, the cold wind slapping you in the face, the risk of broken bones, no matter the month.

Charlotte clenched her jaw. "You don't know me."

"Sure, Lola, you keep telling yourself that."

"No, *you* tell yourself that," Charlotte spat back, fully realizing it was a paltry comeback, but her patience was less than thin at this point, a gossamer line between control and losing her shit.

Brighton sighed, pursing her mouth. Charlotte risked a glance, then directed her gaze back to the slope in front of her. She refused to admit how damn cute Brighton looked in her ski pants and coat, her thick gloves and yellow-tinted goggles, which she'd rented from the ski shop. Her fleece hat was pulled down to her eyebrows, her brown hair flicking in the snowy wind.

"Ready for this, Char?" Elle called from where they stood next to Manish, because of course their entire group was there to witness her ineptitude on the slopes. Meanwhile, Sloane, Adele,

Wes, and Dorian slid around the flat area where the ski lift had dropped them off with ease, having practically grown up with skis attached to their feet.

"Race you to the bottom?" Wes asked Sloane as they came to a stop at the precipice of the mountain.

"On a green?" Sloane asked. "I'll slaughter you."

"Oh, like in ninth grade, when I finished a full minute before you?"

"Like junior year, when *I* won the Valentine's Day Cupid Sprint and left you in my dust," Sloane said.

Wes grinned. "Best Valentine's Day yet."

Sloane's eyes widened a fraction. "Really?"

"You know it was," Wes said softly.

"Jesus Christ," Charlotte said.

Loudly.

Seven pairs of eyes landed on her, which she could feel even with the wind whipping her ponytail into her face. She shook her head, unable to explain her outburst, how she suddenly couldn't stomach two people so obviously in love with each other but ignoring it, ignoring being happy, belonging to someone, and—

I miss you.

I've never loved anyone like I love you.

"Oh, for fuck's sake," she said, stabbing her poles into the ground and launching herself forward. She released a tiny yelp as she flew over the edge of the mountain, her skis sliding easily over the fresh snow.

"Lola!" she heard Brighton call behind her, but it was too late. She was already gone, plummeting to her untimely demise. The hill wasn't steep, she realized this, but it felt like a ninety-degree angle as she started going faster and faster. She snowplowed her skis, a move she remembered seeing others do as they came down the slope—granted, mostly kids—but all that did was send up a flurry of frost and snow into her face. People whizzed by—Sloane and Wes, laughing as they raced; Manish screaming and yelling "Shit, shit, shit!" the entire way down with Dorian on his tail, cracking up as he zigzagged like an expert; Elle flying down with ease because Mimi had taken them to Vail at least once a year throughout their childhood.

And Brighton.

Brighton sliding up next to her, of course.

"You okay?" Brighton shouted over the wind.

"I'm fine!" Charlotte shouted back. "I don't need your help!"

"I never said you did!"

Charlotte swerved to the right and nearly lost her balance but managed to hold it together.

"Just go!" she yelled at Brighton.

"I am going!"

"I mean without me!"

"You call this *with* you?" Brighton yelled, dodging a slow-moving kid in a permanent snowplow position. "Charlotte, nothing is *with* you."

"What's that supposed to mean?"

"You make it impossible. Friendship, moving on. Anything."

"*I* make it impossible?" Charlotte shot back. "*You're* the one who won't give me a goddamn second to breathe!"

She hit a tiny bump—a rock or twig under the snow—and one of her poles flew from her hand, lost behind her forever.

Brighton didn't seem to notice. "I'm not trying to smother you. I'm just trying to be real!"

"Real?" Charlotte said flatly. "Real? Like when you left me standing by myself on our wedding day? That kind of real?"

Brighton grunted in frustration.

Good, Charlotte thought.

"Real," Brighton said, "like not lying your ass off about how you actually feel."

Charlotte's mouth dropped open, but she didn't have time to register that Brighton clearly knew she was lying about what she remembered from last night. Her balance was all off—physically and now mentally, emotionally. The bottom of the hill loomed, the finish line, thank god, but with only one pole, she couldn't find her center. She wobbled this way and that until her skis finally crossed and she went down. Some limb—foot, leg, arm, she wasn't sure—caught on Brighton, and soon they were a cartoonish ball of chaos, tangled and tumbling until they finally came to rest at the bottom of the hill.

Charlotte was on her back, arms splayed, one leg crossed over her body and stuck under Brighton's torso. The snow fell so heavily that she could barely keep her eyes open, could barely figure out if she was dead, injured, or simply a total idiot.

A shadow appeared above her, vaguely Wes-shaped.

"Are you two okay?" he asked.

"I don't know yet," she said. "Brighton?"

"Alive," was all Brighton said from next to her.

"Here, let's get you up and assess the damage," Wes said. The rest of their group had hurried over as well, and Charlotte gritted her teeth against all the fussing as Wes pulled her up. Dorian helped untangle Brighton, and soon they were both on their feet. Snow fell even harder now, swirled by the wind.

"Anything hurt?" Sloane said.

Charlotte's left ankle twinged a bit, but it wasn't bad, and she'd be damned if she admitted it.

"No," she said.

"I'm all right," Brighton said. "Just winded."

"Yeah, well, you're lucky," Adele said, folding her arms. "Those kinds of collisions are how people die on the slopes."

Charlotte just nodded. She wanted a hot bath. And a drink. And a damn cabin free of one Brighton Fairbrook.

Still . . .

She turned around, shielded her eyes against the heavy snowfall, and looked up at the mountain she'd just come down.

She'd done it.

She'd made it down in one piece.

Granted, not very gracefully, but it still counted in her book. She took a deep breath and turned back around, then noticed everyone around them hurrying toward the ski lodge, the ski lift stationary and seemingly shut down.

"What's going on?" she asked.

"Blizzard warning," Adele said. "Slopes are closing, and everyone's being directed indoors."

"Blizzard warning?" Charlotte said, panic flaring. "Your dad said six inches."

Sloane laughed. "Classic Dad. During the Blizzard of 2003, he kept saying, 'Ten inches, tops! Nothing to worry about!'"

"Biggest blizzard to hit Colorado in a decade," Adele said, then looked at the sky, which was morphing from a fluffy, snowy white to an ominous storm gray. "We should get inside."

The group quickly scurried to the ski shop and returned their boots, skis, and poles—in the rush to beat the storm, the shopworker didn't even register Charlotte's missing pole—and then set off on the path toward their cabins.

"Are we getting snowed in?" Charlotte asked Sloane, hurrying as fast as she could without revealing her sore ankle.

"Who knows?" Sloane said casually. "If it gets bad, we'll all hunker down in the big house."

"*If?*" Charlotte said as they came to a stop in front of her cabin.

Sloane squinted at her. "You okay?"

Charlotte huffed a breath. "Will you please stop asking me that?"

Sloane's jaw clenched. "Yeah, maybe I would if you'd tell me anything just a little bit close to real, Charlotte."

And with that, she turned away, hurrying to her own cabin without another word.

Charlotte's throat went tight. She was getting damned tired of that word—*real*. What was she, fucking make-believe? A made-up person, invisible until she was wanted?

The thought made her suddenly tired for some reason. Standing there in the snow, thunder rumbling across the sky as her friends hurried for shelter, she felt completely exhausted.

Brighton finally arrived with their key, opening their cabin door wordlessly, snow already building up a little at the entrance. Charlotte watched her face, ruddy from the cold, a tiny scratch on her cheek that hadn't been there earlier. It was barely red, but still.

"Are you okay?" Charlotte heard herself ask softly, before she could tell herself she didn't care, didn't need to voice it even if she did.

"Fine," Brighton said flatly as she swung the door open.

Charlotte's cheeks burned, embarrassment over the past twenty-four hours—actually, every hour since she'd arrived in Winter River—finally catching up with her. She practically ran inside, her ankle screaming at her the whole way, and headed straight for her bedroom, closing herself safely behind the heavy oak door.

chapter 20

omething woke Brighton in the middle of the night.

Not a sound, more like an absence of one. She blinked into the darkness and rolled over, reaching for her phone on the rustic nightstand. Every bone and muscle in her body screamed at her, bringing back her tumble down the mountain.

She was also cold.

Like, *freezing*.

She sat up and tapped her phone's screen.

2:32 a.m.

It was plugged in, but she noticed it wasn't charging, which was exactly when she realized just how quiet it really was. A bone-deep silence. There was no hum from the heater, no gentle whir from the ceiling fan she'd turned on before slipping into bed a few hours ago.

Honestly, everything after skiing was a blur. Adele had created a group chat and texted that the snow was so bad her dad had ordered them all to stay in their cabins. He'd stocked all of their fridges with cheese and fruit. That, along with the crackers in the pantry, would have to suffice for dinner.

Manish: This is how horror movies start

Elle: I think you mean end-of-days movies

Manish: No, horror! Serial killer in the woods, comes out in the blizzard and slaughters us all

Sloane: Cheery, Manny

Manish: Cheery and Queery!

Dorian: Sounds like a Hallmark movie

Manish: The slaughtering? What kind of Hallmark movies are you watching??

Dorian: 😂 I meant the Cheery and Queery thing

MANISH RENAMED THE CHAT **CHEERY AND QUEERY**.

Dorian: As long as I get to play the dashing love interest

Manish: Who else?

Wes: Get a room

Manish: WE'RE SNOWED IN WESLEY

And on and on it went, Brighton's phone dinging every few seconds with Manish and Dorian's banter. It would've been kind of cute if she weren't in such a foul mood. With Charlotte closed in her room, Brighton had turned off her notifications and did the same, watching a queer teen show on Netflix that only made her cry with love for baby queers everywhere before finally going to bed around ten.

Charlotte had never emerged, never said anything in the group chat.

Now it was the middle of the night, and it was slowly dawning on Brighton's sleep-muddled brain that the power was out. Which meant the heat was out. Which meant she was fucking freezing.

She slipped out of bed and sifted through her bag, putting on every spare piece of clothing she had. As this was just an overnight trip, there wasn't much—one extra sweater, a pair of socks. She found her only sweatpants on the floor next to the bed, as she'd shucked them off when she was ready to go to sleep because she hated sleeping in pants. Still, needs must. She found her knit hat as well, stuffed it on her head before going to the window. She peeked through the wooden blinds, and . . .

All she could see was white.

White swirling, white in the distance, white . . .

Wait.

She squinted harder, hoping she hadn't actually seen the snow landing just above where the window's glass started, but she had. It was piling higher and higher and higher . . .

"Shit," she whispered to no one, but honestly, she was too cold and sore to worry about it too much at that moment.

Brighton scurried back to her bed, burrowed under the covers, and tried to sleep, but she couldn't get warm. Her toes were like ice, and she could never sleep when her feet were cold. But it wasn't just her extremities. Her *bones* were cold. She couldn't stop shivering, her teeth clacking together. She spent at least an hour like that, close to tears, envisioning losing her nose to frostbite. She knew she was catastrophizing, but outside the snow still fell, accumulating around them like a cocoon, and she couldn't think straight with her blood slowly solidifying.

She threw the covers back, the need for warmth overriding everything else. She flung open her door and hurried to the other side of the cabin to Charlotte's room. She didn't knock. Didn't slowly creak the door open. She just barged in and tapped a sleeping Charlotte on the shoulder.

"Hmm," Charlotte said, unmoving.

"Charlotte," Brighton whisper-yelled, the name barely understandable through her shivers.

"M'sleeping," Charlotte mumbled.

"I know, I'm sorry. I just . . ." Brighton hopped from one foot to the other. "I'm freezing."

Charlotte slowly rolled over, cracked one eye open. "What?"

"The power's out. There's no heat."

Charlotte lifted her brows. "Seriously?"

Brighton nodded. "Can I . . . ?" She nodded to the bed. It was a queen, large enough that they wouldn't have to touch, but the concept of body heat was the only thing keeping Brighton going at the moment. She waited for Charlotte to laugh, to tell her to get lost, but Charlotte just stared at her for a second before flipping the thick green-and-red plaid comforter back. She scooted over a little to make room for Brighton—Charlotte's default was sleeping in the middle of the bed, which meant that when they were together, Brighton had woken up most mornings with some part of her girlfriend draped over or wrapped around her.

Brighton didn't hesitate. She practically dove into the warm spot created by Charlotte's sleeping body. Charlotte didn't falter either—she flung the covers back over them, locking them in. Brighton sighed in relief, tucked her hands to her chest, and waited for Charlotte to situate herself a few inches away, but then . . .

More warmth.

Arms wrapping around Brighton, pulling her close.

Brighton held her breath, nodded when Charlotte asked if it was okay, her words still slurred with sleep. Charlotte might not have been thinking clearly, might never have done this in the light of day, but Brighton couldn't bring herself to care at the moment.

Right now, the only person she'd ever loved was holding her, a chilly nose pressed to the back of Brighton's neck. Right now, there were no drunken confessions or abandoned altars or misunderstandings. There wasn't a New York or a Nashville. There was only *this*.

Two childhood best friends turned lovers, holding on to each other in a storm.

chapter 21

Charlotte flung off her covers, wondering why the hell she was so damn *hot*.

It was morning, but the light coming in through the blinds on her window looked odd, as though it were muffled in some way. She was sweating, her flannel pajamas damp, and when she moved her ankle a bit to see how it was faring, she ran into another leg.

Not her own.

"What the hell?" she said, scooting out of bed so fast she nearly tripped on a part of the comforter that was draping onto the floor.

Brighton stirred, rubbing her eyes as she sat up.

"What's—"

"Exactly," Charlotte said. "What's going on? Why are you in my bed?"

But even as she asked, foggy memories came back to her.

The power's out.

Can I . . . ?

Then there were absurd flashes of arms wrapped around bodies and nuzzling, but surely, *surely*, that wasn't Brighton.

She curled her hands into fists.

She knew it was.

Charlotte could feel the ghost of Brighton against her chest. She had always been a heavy sleeper and had never made good decisions when she was woken up mid-REM cycle.

"The power is back on," she said curtly.

"Oh," Brighton said, tucking her hair behind her ears. "Thanks for letting me . . ." She trailed off, waved toward the bed.

"It's fine." Charlotte grabbed her phone. "What time are we leaving?"

"I'm not sure. I think—"

"Oh, fuck," Charlotte said, staring at her phone.

"What?" Brighton pushed her share of the covers back. "What is it?"

Charlotte didn't answer, just left the room, her ankle still smarting enough to make her limp a little, and hurried to the big picture window in the living room. This window didn't have any blinds, only plaid curtains framing the glass.

Framing the snow.

"Oh, *fuck*," she said again.

All she could see was snow. At least halfway up the window. It shut out the sun, the clouds, the sky. She looked back down at her phone, at the group chat someone had created yesterday. Her notifications kept dinging and dinging.

Sloane: Well . . . we're snowed in, friends. Hang tight

Manish: HANG TIGHT????

Elle: Are we going to starve? Manish ate all the cheese
last night

Manish: HOW DARE

Wes: I'd hide if I were you, Elle

Dorian: Hallmark Horror Movie: A Cannibalistic Christmas!

Adele: You're all such idiots

Sloane: Dad said a crew is en route to dig us out

Manish: DIG US OUT????

Adele: Cool it with the all caps. It's giving me a headache

Manish: Speaking of headaches, Charlotte and Brighton
are strangely silent. Are they dead? Or making out? I'm
taking bets

Charlotte huffed and clicked her phone dark before tossing it
onto the couch. Brighton was now standing in her own bedroom's doorway, staring down at her phone, an amused expression on her face.

"This isn't funny," Charlotte said, heading to the front door.

"It's a little funny."

"We're *trapped*." She flung open the front door to find tiny
mountains of snow covering the porch, even jutting up against
the door like a wall. She could see over it but certainly couldn't

get through it. A bit of snow toppled into the cabin, and Charlotte slammed the door closed.

"Not for long," Brighton said, heading into the kitchen. "Coffee?"

Charlotte glared at her, hating Brighton's calm, hating everything that had led them to this point. "I suppose this is what you wanted."

Brighton's hand stilled on a K-Cup. "What I *wanted*?"

"Ever since we got to Winter River, you've been after me," Charlotte said. "Wanting to *talk*, to make it right. But you can never make it right, okay? There, I said it. What you did to me will never be okay, Brighton."

Brighton stared at her, then flung the K-Cup onto the butcher-block counter. She rounded the peninsula, looking ridiculous in her two sweaters and baggy sweatpants and hat.

"You know what?" she said, getting right in Charlotte's face. Charlotte backed up, but Brighton kept moving until Charlotte's back hit the wall. "You're right. I did want this. I do want to talk, want to make it right, because yes, god, I'm so fucking *sorry*." She flung off her hat, her dark eyes filling. "I'm sorry I hurt you. I'm sorry I destroyed us. I'm sorry I left you. I didn't want to leave *you*, but I didn't know what else to do. You were so happy in New York. It was where you belonged, and I wanted you to have that. I wanted you to . . . I don't know. Be *you*."

"You could've just talked to me," Charlotte said, her voice now a whisper, her anger snuffed out, replaced with . . . she wasn't even sure what it was. A tightness in her chest, a tug around her heart as Brighton's apology spilled out, tears escaping down her cheeks. "You could've just said."

"I *tried*. So many times, Lola."

Charlotte closed her eyes at that name. Opened them again.

"I told you that morning I was unsure about New York," Brighton said.

"Unsure doesn't mean miserable," Charlotte said. "It takes time to figure out your place in a new town, to settle in . . ." But even as she said all of this, the same things she'd said to herself and Brighton so many times after they'd moved to New York, she knew they were just that—words.

Because she'd known Brighton was unhappy in New York.

Fine.

There.

She could admit it now. Nothing else to do. No other excuses worked anymore.

She'd known.

And she'd ignored it. All the signs. The way Brighton went quiet when Charlotte talked about how much she loved New York. How Brighton talked to her mother more and more often as the weeks went by, sometimes multiple times a day, her voice quiet like a child's. How she seemed lost on the streets, overwhelmed and small. How she cried in the shower, thinking Charlotte didn't know.

But Charlotte had known.

Known and done nothing more than hold Brighton tighter at night, bring her flowers after a day of teaching or rehearsing. She'd convinced herself Brighton just needed time.

But *time* turned into six months, and then it was December, and they were heading to Michigan to get married, and still, Brighton's light had dimmed. Still, neither of them had talked about it. Neither of them had said anything explicit, the truth.

Until right now.

"I know I handled everything wrong," Brighton said. "The wrongest thing I've ever done. But you—"

"I didn't see you."

Charlotte's confession hung between them, thick and real. Brighton tilted her head, pain washing over her expression.

"But I did," Charlotte said, her own tears swelling. "I did see, Brighton. I just didn't know what to do. I didn't know how to fix it. And I . . ."

She closed her eyes, tears spilling over. This next part was hard to say. Hard to admit. Hard to let be true.

"I was so scared to lose you," she said, "because you were all I had. You were all I'd ever had."

"Lola," Brighton said, stepping even closer and framing Charlotte's face in her hands. "You never lost me. Never. I'm still—"

But Charlotte didn't let her finish. Couldn't. Didn't want any more words, any more explanations, not right now. She wanted Brighton, her only love, and she was so goddamn tired of pretending like she didn't. So tired of pretending at all—so many things she kept in, kept hidden and secret, scared to let anyone see her.

But Brighton had seen her.

All of her.

Always had.

Charlotte pushed through the space between them, their mouths colliding. Brighton let out a surprised gasp but opened to Charlotte, and it was like the sun breaking through a thick layer of clouds. They grabbed at each other, hands in hair, under sweaters and tops, yanking at waistbands. It was fumbling and desperate and messy. Charlotte felt like a teenager, just needing skin and friction and more. She pulled up Brighton's sweater, only to find another sweater, and they laughed when a button on the second one got caught in Brighton's hair.

"There you are," Charlotte said when Brighton was finally free. She took Brighton's face in her hands, Brighton's dark hair going everywhere, tangling between her fingers.

"Here I am," Brighton said against Charlotte's mouth, and then there were no more words, just low moans as their tongues touched, as Charlotte skimmed her hands down Brighton's neck to her chest, tracing her collarbones and lower. She cupped Brighton's breasts, thumbs swiping over her already hardened nipples.

"Fuck," Brighton gasped, tilting her head back. Then she laughed. "Boobs. They're nice."

Charlotte froze, her mouth on Brighton's neck, the memory of her drunken night coming back to her. "Oh my god. Did I—"

"Oh yeah," Brighton said. "You said it."

Charlotte laughed against Brighton's skin, then rolled one of Brighton's nipples between her thumb and forefinger. "Well. They *are* nice."

Brighton gasped again. "So damn nice."

"The nicest," Charlotte said, dipping down to take one in her mouth, sucking once before using her teeth.

"God," Brighton said, "I forgot how much I love your teeth."

Charlotte bit a little harder, pulling a moan from Brighton's throat, the sexiest sound in the world. Charlotte, for her part, hadn't forgotten a thing. How much she loved the taste of Brighton's skin, the sounds she made, the way she *did* love Charlotte's teeth, loved them on every part of her. Charlotte could do this forever, just spend hours on Brighton's perfect tits, but those sounds, they got her every time. Made her desperate for more.

She bit down again, then soothed the spot with her tongue

before she stepped back long enough to pull down Brighton's sweatpants.

"You too," Brighton said, pawing at Charlotte's flannel pajama pants, as well as her top. "Why the hell is your shirt still on?"

Charlotte's only answer was to pull off every piece of clothing she had on, including her underwear. Brighton flung hers off too, then yanked Charlotte against her, wrapping a thigh around Charlotte's hip.

"Oh my god," Charlotte said, the press of skin on skin almost too much. She hadn't done this in so long—not since the day of their wedding. She'd had a kiss or two, some pawing in some stranger's apartment, but she'd never made it this far, had never wanted to. She'd told herself she was busy. She was driven. She was satisfied with the luxury sex toys she'd spent a fortune on.

She told herself so many things, but there was nothing like this. Not just skin and someone else's breath and voice and hands, but *Brighton*.

The only person she'd ever slept with.

The only person she'd ever wanted to sleep with.

Maybe it was immature, unworldly, naive, but she didn't care. All she cared about was Brighton right here, right now, about making her come. Then making her come again.

She flipped them around so Brighton's back was to the wall, then slotted her knee between Brighton's legs, pressing her thigh right against Brighton's center.

"Fuck," Brighton said, her head knocking against the wall. "Lola, fuck."

Charlotte slid her hands down Brighton's waist to her ass, cupped her full cheeks, and rutted against her. "Like that?"

"Yes, oh my god," Brighton said, wrapping her arms around

Charlotte's neck. Charlotte could feel her, feel how wet she was, Charlotte's own wetness against Brighton's thigh. Then Brighton shifted a little, hitting Charlotte's cunt so perfectly that she cried out, nearly lost her concentration.

"Together," Brighton said, moving her hands to Charlotte's hips, pulling Charlotte up and then down, circling her hips here and there.

"Jesus," Charlotte said, moving with Brighton.

Brighton pressed her forehead to Charlotte's, her breathing intensifying, the air between them nothing but gasps, cries of *yes* and *yeah*, the smell of sex as they fucked against the wall. Their bodies were slick, their cunts sliding against thighs in a way that made Charlotte feel crazy. She grunted, pulling Brighton up on her thigh even higher, pumping her hips faster. Sweat broke out along her forehead, her chest, mixing with Brighton's own effort. It was perfect, everything.

"I want you to come," Charlotte said.

Brighton nodded, biting down on her lower lip.

Charlotte slapped her ass, just hard enough that Brighton cried out and started moving faster.

"Come for me," Charlotte said in her ear. "Come on my leg. Do it."

"Fuck, oh my god," Brighton said, her body jolting as her orgasm rushed through her. "Lola, fuck, yes, please."

Charlotte adjusted so her leg had more solid contact with Brighton's center, leaving her own needs unmet at the moment, but she didn't care. She wanted Brighton to come again, come like this, pinned against the wall, begging and perfect.

"Again," Charlotte said, loving how desperate Brighton sounded. "That's a good girl."

Brighton gasped, gripping Charlotte's shoulders. "Lola."

"That's right." Charlotte's muscles screamed at her, her ankle nearly giving way, but she found some superhuman strength watching Brighton ride her, perfect tits bouncing. God, it was the most beautiful thing Charlotte had ever seen. "Come for me. You can do it."

Brighton's nails dug into Charlotte's back, her hips grinding, her back arching to get that perfect friction. "Fuck," she said, moving faster. "Fuck, fuck."

"Good girl," Charlotte said, pulling at her hips faster too.

"Yeah, yeah," Brighton said, then broke, tossing her head back, dark hair everywhere, her chest flushed a gorgeous pink. Her movements jolted, then slowed. Charlotte dipped her head, pressing her mouth to Brighton's neck, breathing her in.

"Christ," Brighton said as Charlotte pulled her leg out from between her thighs. "That was . . ."

"It was," Charlotte said, still kissing Brighton, holding her close. She wasn't ready to let go. Not yet.

"You didn't come yet," Brighton said.

Charlotte smiled against her skin. "Worth it."

Brighton laughed but then pulled Charlotte's face up to look at her, hands framing Charlotte's cheeks. "You."

"Me?"

"You," Brighton said, then kissed her once before whispering against her mouth. "I think you need a shower."

Brighton's words shivered down Charlotte's neck and hips, settling between her legs, her need still desperate and pulsing. "Maybe I do."

"You definitely do."

Brighton took her hand, then led them both, still full-ass naked, to the en suite bathroom in her bedroom. The shower was large and modern, all glass and earth-toned tiles. Brighton swung open the glass door and turned the water on, not even waiting for it to get warm before she pulled Charlotte inside.

"Shit," Charlotte said, gasping as the cold water hit her heated skin, but then Brighton was kissing her, taking her breath, her thoughts, sliding hands down her ass, then drifting them to the front. The water gradually warmed, and the temperature play was . . . well, it was nice.

Charlotte laughed as Brighton squeezed the fronts of her thighs, whispered that she was dirty in her ear. Charlotte could only nod, then moan as Brighton's fingertip-light touch turned into nails on her skin. Charlotte was so wet, she knew she was, and had to grind her teeth to keep from moving Brighton's hands to her clit.

But Brighton was in charge now, and that was how they both liked it. They'd discovered throughout their sexual history that they each liked being the one in control sometimes . . . and sometimes they each liked being at the other's mercy.

There was a little tile seat in the shower, recessed into the wall, next to built-in shelves for shampoo and soap. Brighton eyed it, then sat down and pulled Charlotte onto her lap so that she faced outward. She kissed Charlotte's neck and spine, wrapped her hands around to her tits, playing with her nipples, rolling them between her thumbs and forefingers while she nipped at Charlotte's back with her teeth.

"God," Charlotte said, her pussy flooding and her legs parting instinctively.

"So impatient," Brighton said.

Charlotte laughed, spread her legs wider. "I think I've waited long enough." Her words had multiple meanings, but right now, all she wanted was for Brighton to touch her.

"I'll be the judge of that," Brighton said, trailing one hand up Charlotte's thigh while her other still played at Charlotte's nipples.

"Please," Charlotte said, a little whine to her voice. Brighton Fairbrook was the only person in the world who could make her beg, make her voice sound like that, desperate and pleading.

"Please what?" Her fingertips drifted north.

"Please touch me," Charlotte said.

"Where?" Brighton's touch rounded toward Charlotte's center.

"You know where."

"Tell me."

"My cunt," Charlotte said, a word she reserved only for sex, but god, she loved using it. "My cunt, please."

Brighton licked a stripe up Charlotte's neck, her fingers finally finding their mark, dragging gently up Charlotte's center.

Charlotte tilted her head back, cried out just from the initial contact.

"Like that?" Brighton said, even though she knew.

She knew how to touch Charlotte, where, how hard, perfectly every time after years of learning. And she hadn't forgotten. She hadn't forgotten a single thing.

"Yeah," Charlotte said, spreading her legs wider, as far as they'd go. The water cascaded down onto their thighs, the shower already humid and foggy. "More."

Brighton pressed harder, making Charlotte gasp, then slid her hand down, parting Charlotte with her fingers.

"So wet," Brighton said, and Charlotte could only nod, only beg again and again until Brighton finally showed mercy, slid two fingers inside her.

"God, yes, fuck," Charlotte said, her body locking up for a split second before softening around Brighton's fingers. Her body started moving, an instinct, a desperate need to undulate with Brighton inside of her. Brighton moved too, sliding in and out slowly, picking up speed as Charlotte grew more desperate.

"More," Charlotte said, and Brighton slid a third finger inside, making Charlotte whimper. When Brighton's palm pressed to her clit, she released a litany of swear words that made zero sense. Didn't care. It felt too good, felt too perfect. She gripped Brighton's wrist, her hips working to get as much friction as possible.

"Fuck," she said.

"That's right," Brighton said, biting down on her shoulder. "Fuck yourself on my fingers. Get what you need."

Charlotte groaned, her vision going fuzzy as Brighton did something—curled her fingers or twisted them or something, Charlotte didn't even care what, as long as Brighton never stopped.

"Please" was all she could say, one hand lifted and curled behind her, wrapping around Brighton's shoulder and pulling at her hair, the other on her own breast, tugging at her nipple. "Please."

Brighton fucked her faster, harder, palm pressing just where she needed it. Charlotte knew she was pulling at Brighton's hair harder and harder, but she didn't care, and she knew Brighton didn't care either. All that mattered was this, this shower and Brighton's fingers, Brighton herself.

Brighton.

Brighton.

Bright.

Charlotte said her name—Bright—as she came hard, so hard she nearly slipped off Brighton's lap, but Brighton held Charlotte tight, working her fingers in Charlotte's pussy until she came again, until she stopped convulsing around her, until she sagged against her, head on Brighton's shoulder, completely wiped out.

"Wow," Charlotte said, her lungs working hard for oxygen.

"I'll say," Brighton said, kissing Charlotte's neck, then sliding her fingers out and licking them clean.

"You're gonna get me started again," Charlotte said, lifting her head and turning to watch her.

Brighton just laughed. "I wouldn't complain."

Charlotte laughed too, but then the laughter faded, their smiles, as did the wild desperation they'd both felt for the last half hour. They just looked at each other, their eyes taking in features as if for the first time in years.

"Why did you get this?" Charlotte asked eventually, drifting her fingers along the tattoo on Brighton's upper arm. "I didn't know you were into tarot."

"I'm not, really. I pull a card every now and then," Brighton said, following Charlotte's fingers with her eyes. "It's the Moon card. I got it a few months after . . . after I moved to Nashville."

"What does it mean?" Charlotte asked softly, tracing the moon, the shaded trees around it, the little white pinpricks of stars.

Brighton sighed. "Well . . . it's kind of a dark card. It's about when things aren't what they seem. When you're sort of wandering in the dark forest, looking for your way, trying to find the right path, though it's hidden. But there's hope in this card too, because the sun, it always rises, doesn't it?"

Charlotte frowned, her throat suddenly aching.

"Have you found it, Bright?" she asked, lifting her eyes to meet Brighton's. "Have you found your path?"

"I . . ." Brighton swallowed, never looked away from Charlotte. "No. I don't think I have, Lola."

Charlotte's eyes stung, a sadness she couldn't parse spreading through her chest. Because in that moment, all her anger and resentment seemed so futile. Because she loved Brighton Fairbrook.

She wanted her to be happy, no matter what. She wanted her to find her path, her sun.

"Bright," she said, and that was all she needed to say, really. Charlotte turned enough so she could kiss her. Slowly, purposefully, with her full wits about her.

"Lola," Bright said against her mouth, and they stayed like that for what felt like hours, just kissing, whispering each other's names under the warm spray of water.

chapter 22

Brighton never thought she'd be happy about being trapped in a tiny cabin with only a single roll of Ritz crackers left to eat and exactly zero pairs of clean underwear left, but she was.

She was euphoric.

Charlotte—*Lola*—was in her bed. Laughing. Smiling. Kissing. Talking. She felt like they were seventeen again. Twenty. Even twenty-two during the good days in New York, the Saturdays when Lola didn't have to teach and Brighton convinced her to stay in bed half the day, having sex and watching shows on her laptop.

"So," Lola said, cracking open the roll of Ritz and popping one in her mouth, "we start in London, then go to Paris, Barcelona, Prague, and we end in Vienna."

She was sitting up in bed, naked and gorgeous, Brighton's plaid duvet wrapped around her but haphazardly, so Brighton could still see plenty of skin. Her silver hair was sex-tousled and perfect.

Everything was perfect.

"That sounds amazing, Lola," Brighton said, taking a cracker too. She lay on her stomach, feet in the air, a sheet barely covering her ass. "I've always wanted to go to Prague. All those places, really. How long will you be gone?"

"A month," Lola said, tapping another cracker against the plate. She didn't eat it, though, and silence spilled between them for the first time since they'd gotten out of the shower and fallen into bed. Brighton's mind flitted around a word, a terrifying word, and she assumed Lola's did too.

After.

Because despite everything they'd talked about in the last few hours—the Fairbrooks, Anna, Lola's music and how she'd met everyone in the quartet, all the wild things that had happened on this trip—they hadn't touched that topic.

They hadn't touched New York. Or Nashville. Or what would happen after Lola's tour.

And maybe that was okay. They'd only just reconciled, after all, and Brighton didn't want to ruin it by forcing them headfirst into the exact same problems they'd had five years ago.

She wanted to be happy.

She wanted Lola and Bright back, just for a little while.

Lola cleared her throat and took the tiniest bite of her cracker. Brighton was about to tease her for her rabbit eating, something she always did when she was pondering things, but then Lola looked at her.

"About the Katies," Lola said.

Brighton groaned and flopped her head into her arms, hiding in the dark cocoon they created. She didn't want to think about *after*, and she sure as shit didn't want to think about the Katies.

Not now, not ever.

"It's not even about them, Bright," Lola said. "It's about you."

Brighton didn't move.

"Brighton Katherine."

She arched her head up. "Pulling out the middle name."

"At least you have one."

Brighton cracked a smile, but sadness clouded her chest like it always did when she thought about how Lola didn't have a middle name because, well, Anna Donovan sucked.

"I'll give you a middle name," Brighton said, pushing up to her knees and shoving the plate of crackers to the side. She crawled toward Lola.

Lola's eyes widened, flicking down to Brighton's naked chest, breasts swaying as she came closer.

"Oh yeah?" Lola said, deftly peeling back the duvet to reveal her own full nakedness. She folded her arms. "Like what?"

Brighton had made it to her side of the bed now, and she slid her hands up Lola's shins, over her knees to her thighs. Stopped right at their tops, reveled in the goose bumps she felt under her fingers.

"Charlotte . . . Mildred Donovan."

"Over my dead body," Lola said.

Brighton laughed, curled her hands toward each other. Lola sucked in a breath.

"Charlotte . . . Millicent Donovan."

"What's with the *M* names?"

Brighton's hands stilled, and she straddled Lola's legs, pulling herself closer until their torsos met, Lola's hands going to her hips.

Brighton looked at her—at her Lola—pupils wide, swollen mouth open a little.

"Charlotte . . . Beautiful," she said, leaning down to kiss her.

"Now that's just silly," Lola said, but her voice was raspy and low.

"Charlotte . . . Sweet." Another kiss.

"Who'd believe that?"

"Charlotte . . . Brilliant."

"Obviously."

Brighton laughed, then grew serious. "Charlotte Rosalind."

Lola blinked for a second, her fingertips pressing into Brighton's waist. Rosalind, for her violin, her quartet, the Shakespeare heroine who made her own way, adapted, fought for what she wanted no matter what.

"Charlotte Rosalind," Brighton said again, a whisper against Lola's mouth.

Lola met her kiss, then another, and soon there were no more words, just breath and sweat, Brighton's body wrapped around Lola's, moving, seeking. Lola slipped her hand between them, curled her fingers, and Brighton was crying out in a matter of seconds, Lola's name on her lips.

When she recovered, Brighton climbed off and pushed Lola's legs apart, then settled between them, not wanting to wait another second to taste her, tease her, slide her tongue right where Lola wanted it. Lola grabbed Brighton's hair, tugging hard as she came, her cries so loud that Brighton felt a swell of pride, of pure elation that she could make this reserved woman sound so wild and frantic.

"You," Lola said as Brighton kissed her thigh, Lola's fingers still tangled in Brighton's hair. And that was all she said. Just *you*, but somehow those three tiny letters felt like the world, like five years evaporating.

"You," Brighton said back, pressing her cheek to Lola's leg, peering up at her.

She'd just decided she could stay like this forever, food and the outside world be damned, when both of their phones went off.

Brighton groaned. "Don't. Don't look."

Lola laughed and grabbed her phone off the nightstand, then sighed wearily at the screen. "Looks like we're free."

"I refuse to admit defeat," Brighton announced, sliding off the end of the bed, then walking to the nightstand to get her own phone.

Adele: Our front doors are clear, roads are plowed!

Manish: Thank god. I was about to eat my own leg

Sloane: Meet at the cars in ten?

Elle: Make it five, Manish is baring his fangs at my admittedly delicious-looking arms

Manish: Listen, I didn't ask for a snowpocalypse. We do what we must

Adele: We should hit up the lights tonight at Barstow Gardens. Mom said the storm didn't hit as hard in Winter River, so it should be open. I hear they're serving hot toddies this year

Manish: I'll endure a root canal for a hot toddy

Wes: I have to work. Gotta prep for that Two Turtledoves event at the restaurant on Thursday

Adele: Jesus, the Turtledoves. On Christmas Eve Eve?

Sloane: At least this one will be fun

Wes: Thanks, Sloane

Adele: Just one more after that, right?

Sloane: Yeah. Except it's the open mic where everyone confesses their love through bad poetry and even worse covers of Celine Dion songs

Wes: At least our hearts will go on with margaritas

Sloane: Ah yes, it's all coming back to me now

Wes: I know you're not disparaging the power of love

Sloane: I'd rather be all by myself, to be honest

Adele: I hate you both

Brighton chuckled at the banter but tilted her head, something from the day before tickling her brain. "So . . . are Sloane and Wes—"

"Totally in love?" Lola said, eyes on her phone.

"Um, I was gonna say flirting."

Lola blinked and glanced at Brighton wide-eyed. "Oops."

Brighton laughed. "Oh my god, really? Like *love* love?"

"He's in love with her, at least. They were high school sweethearts and everything until they broke up so she could go to New York."

Brighton felt a twinge somewhere near her heart. "How do you know all this?"

"He told me. The day of the horseback riding event."

Brighton shuddered. "Please, we do not speak of such things."

Lola laughed. "It's hush-hush, though. He's actually kind of cute about it."

"My lips are sealed," Bright said, miming zipping her mouth, then cleared her throat. "So . . . do you think she still likes him?" Somehow the answer felt monumental, personal.

Lola frowned, then opened her mouth only to close it again. "I don't know," she finally said.

Brighton nodded casually, but the silence that spilled between them felt heavy, like they weren't really talking about Wes and Sloane at all. Then Brighton put her hands on her hips, brows furrowed, mouth twisted dramatically like she was thinking really hard.

"So wait," she said, lifting a single finger into the air.

Lola groaned. "Yes, okay, yes. You were right. Wes and I were in cahoots."

"Cahoots."

"He's nice, okay? And I needed a distraction."

Brighton preened. "From me."

Lola just laughed, then smiled at her. "Turns out, you're hard not to notice."

Brighton smiled back, and they stayed like that, grinning like two sex-addled lovers for a few seconds. Soon enough, though, reality forced its way between them.

"Back to real life, I guess," Brighton said. Maybe they didn't have to deal with *after*, but they had to deal with *right now*.

"I don't want to go back," Lola said, sighing and rubbing her temples.

"Me neither."

Their phones buzzed again.

Manish: Don't think we haven't noticed the silence from cabin 1. Still accepting bets as to whether Brighton and Charlotte spent their time fucking or killing each other

Sloane: Manny, for god's sake

Manish: You're all thinking it!

"Well," Brighton said, tossing her phone on the bed. "Did we fuck or kill?"

Lola laughed, then groaned into her hands before glancing up at Brighton. "Fucking is much more fun."

Brighton grinned. "It is."

"So . . ."

"So . . ."

Lola took a deep breath. "So we fucked."

Brighton nodded. "Okay. We fucked."

"And . . . we might fuck again."

"Thank god for that."

They smiled at each other, their cheeks still flushed from all the, well, fucking they'd been doing for the last eight hours. Finally, though, Lola grew serious.

"I still don't want them to know," she said. "About our history."

Brighton frowned. "Why?"

"I just don't. Is that okay?"

Brighton swallowed, looked down, felt shame wash over her

for reasons she didn't quite understand. But if that's what Lola needed, she'd give it to her.

"All right," Brighton said. "We're fresh and new."

Lola nodded, then got to her knees and crawled to the side of the bed where Brighton was still standing, still naked. She put her hands on Brighton's hips. Kissed her on the mouth softly, and just once. "Fresh and new."

chapter 23

According to Sloane and Adele, Barstow Gardens was regionally famous. The Barstow family had run the homegrown, ten-acre botanical garden for generations, all of the design and care currently curated by Vivian Barstow herself, who, even at sixty-seven years old, was still rarely seen in town without dirt on her jeans.

And for the holidays, they covered every single tree, plant, and flowering shrub in lights.

"Holy shit," Manish said as the group stepped out of the car in the small parking lot. The space was already packed with cars, and plowed snow was piled on the sides like tiny white mountains.

Charlotte had to agree with Manish's assessment—the scene before her was like something out of a Hallmark movie, yes, but also Disney, Pixar, and DreamWorks all rolled into one. Honestly, she very nearly considered getting her sunglasses out of her bag—it was that bright.

The garden entrance was guarded by a pair of giant nutcrackers covered in red and blue and gold lights. A lit sign arched between the two soldiers, the words "Barstow Gardens" glittering in every color. Beyond that, a sort of sugar-shocked glow filtered over everything—flashes and blinks and sparkles, and happy holiday music echoed through the luminaria-lit pathways. Lights curled around every tree branch in sight, creating snakes of color against the black sky. There were more subtle signs of the snowstorm here, but the sidewalks were clear, and the fresh snow only added to the winter wonderland vibe, the lights glinting off the mounds of white.

Normally, Charlotte wouldn't step foot in a place like this. First, there was the saccharine nature of the entire gig, and second, she could absolutely imagine herself somehow getting tangled in a strand of lights, or knocking down a partridge in a pear tree and sending a disastrous domino effect through the entire "Twelve Days of Christmas" display.

But.

Brighton slipped her gloved fingers through Charlotte's, and somehow everything looked different. Felt different. Tasted, smelled, sounded different.

When they'd returned from Greenbriar Ridge, freshly released from their snow prison, a kind of shyness had overtaken Charlotte. In front of everyone, with Manish's sly smiles and Sloane's curious glances—particularly in light of Sloane's declaration the day of the storm about Charlotte and *realness*, which the two of them were apparently pretending hadn't happened— she wasn't sure she knew how to act or what to do. She'd never been with anyone in front of her quartet before, never held someone's hand, never smiled at someone the way she couldn't seem to help smiling at Brighton.

Hell, she probably didn't smile this much at all around her quartet, postcoital glow notwithstanding.

But then, Brighton had made it so easy. Taking her hand as they stood around the kitchen talking about the storm with Nina. Leaning her arm against Charlotte's at lunch. Lying her head on Charlotte's shoulder while they read on the couch. With those tiny movements, Brighton took them back years, like New York had never happened—no ruined wedding, no ruined future—and they were simply *them* again. Easy and natural and right.

Brighton had a knack for making overwhelming things— okay, *feelings*—seem manageable. Always had, from the very beginning. Whenever Anna skipped out on a parent-teacher conference, an end-of-year concert, a holiday, Brighton would simply take her hand, dance her around on the beach, like everything was made of light and air and water, even as she admitted things sucked.

That was just the way Brighton was.

She was light and air and water, while Charlotte was the solid earth.

Charlotte still couldn't believe the entire last twenty-four hours with Brighton had really happened. She had no idea what it meant, couldn't even really process that it was *her*, Charlotte Donovan, who was in bed with Brighton Fairbrook after all they'd been through, kissing her, touching her, gazing at her with actual stars in her eyes when Brighton wasn't looking. It was as though some foreign invader had taken over her body.

Or, rather . . . it was as though she'd come back to herself. A Charlotte she'd forgotten. A Charlotte she'd lost so long ago, she felt like a stranger to herself.

Lola.

Still, as Brighton stood next to her in the Barstow Gardens parking lot, that red plaid coat buttoned snug around her body, Charlotte couldn't help but want to be reintroduced, even if she couldn't quite see how Lola could function in the world Charlotte had built in New York. How she'd ever see over all the walls she'd constructed brick by brick.

After.

A terrifying word.

A word she knew Brighton must have been thinking about too, but neither of them wanted to bring it up. And maybe, right now, she didn't have to. Right now, she just wanted to be Lola.

"You okay?" Brighton asked her, shoulder pressed into hers.

Charlotte smiled and nodded, then kissed Brighton's forehead, her knit hat fuzzy and tickling Charlotte's lips. She breathed Brighton in, cold air and citrus from her face cream.

After they approached the nutcrackers and paid their fee to a pair of teenagers with matching lavender hair, they collected their hot toddies and started off down the path as a group.

But Charlotte didn't want a group. Selfishly, she wanted Brighton all to herself for as long as possible—for as long as they could keep *after* just a concept and not a reality looming on the snowy horizon. She wanted to kiss her between lit-up trees, get lost in the display of poinsettias, daydream about what this place looked like in the spring, brimming with real color and life.

"Come with me," she said, tugging Brighton off the main path and onto an almost cave-like walkway, illuminated by what seemed like a billion blue-white lights that looked like icicles dripping down from the trees above them.

"Wow," Brighton breathed, her face like a twilit evening as she gazed upward.

"Beautiful," Charlotte said, but she wasn't even looking at the lights.

Brighton caught her eye and laughed. "I forgot how romantic you can be."

"Did you?" Charlotte asked, pressing a kiss to the back of Brighton's hand.

Brighton laughed. "Okay, no. I haven't forgotten anything."

"Me neither." And god, she hadn't. She thought she had—selective memory loss as a type of self-preservation—but as they walked, sipping on the lemon and honey and whiskey mixture, holding hands, she realized she hadn't really forgotten anything. She'd just trained herself not to think about any of it, like she'd put every memory, every feeling, into a box and locked it tight.

But Brighton had the key.

"Tell me something," Charlotte said.

"Like what?"

"Something about you. About your life now."

It was unsteady ground, their lives for the last five years apart, but Charlotte couldn't help it—she just wanted to know Brighton like she used to. Know everything she could. Know what Brighton had been too unsure of five years ago to tell her.

Or what Charlotte had been too self-absorbed to see.

She swallowed around the knot in her throat, forced herself to focus on Brighton. Focus on right now.

"Well," Brighton said slowly, "I live in Nashville."

Charlotte laughed. "You don't say."

"I work at a bar. A great bar. Ampersand."

"Adele seems really great."

Brighton took a sip of her drink, then dropped her foam cup into the trash bin along the glowing path. Charlotte tossed her cup in as well. As it turned out, she didn't like hot toddies all that much. She'd have much preferred a boozy hot chocolate if they were going to get liquor involved.

"She is," Brighton said, taking Charlotte's hand again. They rounded a curve, the lights shifting from blue-white to golden, like in a fairyland. "The best. Has a real eye for talent too."

"Does she?"

Brighton nodded.

"So Ampersand has live music?" Charlotte asked.

Brighton's expression darkened, as though she realized the trap she'd just walked into.

"It does," she said coolly.

"Brighton, I really think—"

"You want to dance?"

Charlotte blinked as Brighton brought them to a halt, facing her and taking her other hand. Nat King Cole's "The Christmas Song" played through the garden, and the golden light, sparkling in Brighton's dark eyes, made everything feel soft and lovely. Charlotte squeezed Brighton's hand. She knew this was Brighton's way of begging her to drop the subject of music.

And Charlotte wanted to give Brighton everything she wanted.

She knew *after* would come soon enough. She wasn't stupid, wasn't naive. But she was . . . happy. Right now, Charlotte Donovan was happy, and she couldn't remember the last time she had truly felt like this, just a moment where everything in her life felt aligned.

Felt right.

And she wanted to take it and run.

Run as fast as she could before everything else caught up with them.

And maybe, probably, Brighton did too, and that included leaving the Katies behind for right now.

"Okay," Charlotte said, then lifted Brighton's hands and placed them around her neck before settling her own fingers on Brighton's waist, then pulling her close . . . closer . . . until their foreheads touched. They started swaying, the song moving them along. Others walking along the path smiled at them, angled around them, but Charlotte barely noticed anyone else.

"Everybody knows a turkey and some mistletoe . . . ," she sang softly. Her voice wasn't as magical as Brighton's, but she held her own. She leaned closer and sang into Brighton's ear. ". . . help to make the season bright."

Brighton laughed and tossed her head back, exposing her lovely neck before looking at Charlotte again. "It's my song."

"It is." Charlotte smiled. This classic Christmas song had always been Brighton's favorite for those lines alone.

Brighton wrapped her arms tighter around Charlotte's neck. "So."

"So."

"I have a fundamentalist Christian roommate named Leah."

Charlotte's eyes widened. "Do you now?"

"She sets me up with guys who wear boat shoes and tells me Jesus loves me even though I'm bi."

"Wow, how loving."

Brighton laughed. "Let's see . . . I want a cat, but Leah's allergic. I still have Carla."

"What?" Charlotte couldn't believe it. "You still have that old Corolla that Bonnie and Hank got you at sixteen?"

"Corollas last forever."

"They don't even sell them anymore."

"All the more reason to preserve Carla's vintage status."

Charlotte laughed and spun Brighton around in a circle once before slowing down again.

"What about you?" Brighton asked. "Tell me something."

Charlotte tilted her head, feeling like there was so much to catch Brighton up on and, at the same time, nothing at all.

And somehow she didn't want to say the words *New York*.

"I play violin" is what she settled on.

Brighton laughed. "I had no idea."

"And I . . ."

Her throat went a little thick. She played violin. She led the Rosalind Quartet. She taught at the Manhattan School of Music. She . . .

Charlotte looked down, took some surreptitious deep breaths. It wasn't like she was ashamed or that what she'd accomplished musically wasn't important. It was. She was impressive, and she knew it. She was proud of what she'd done, and in most ways, she wouldn't change any of it.

She loved her life.

She just . . .

Maybe . . .

Maybe there was more to life than just music. More than just work and practice and arranging and more practice. There was a time when she knew that. She'd forgotten, somehow, even when Brighton had been in her bed in their Manhattan apartment. Somewhere along the line, she'd forgotten . . .

"I missed you," she said. The words just slipped out. True and real and scary and right.

Brighton's smile dimmed, but her eyes went soft. Her chest swelled against Charlotte's, and she pulled them even closer together. "I missed you too."

Then they simply danced, turning in slow circles under the lights, the dreamy music shifting from Nat singing about chestnuts to Judy making promises about next year's troubles.

"Lola?" Brighton said after a while, lifting her chin from

Charlotte's shoulder to look at her, eyes searching Charlotte's. "I . . . I need to know something."

"What is it?"

Brighton blinked a bit, her mouth opening and closing before her question finally made it out. "Do you forgive me?"

Charlotte's own mouth dropped open. Closed. She hadn't been prepared for that question.

The question, really.

She'd spent the last five years being angry at Brighton, not to mention the last several days, letting that anger keep every other feeling at bay. It was a cleansing fire, keeping her moving, keeping her upright.

And god, she just wanted to lie down.

Because the truth was, she didn't think she'd ever get over what had happened with Brighton five years ago. She wasn't sure if that was healthy or not, but she did know this—she shared in their ruining.

She'd been tunnel-visioned and selfish and scared. She'd been career obsessed, and she'd taken Brighton for granted. Brighton had crushed her when she left their wedding . . . but she'd crushed Brighton too. By simply not seeing her for months and months. Or, rather, choosing not to see her, which was even worse.

Forgiveness wasn't forgetting. But it was just as real. Just as healing.

"Yeah," she said softly, framing Brighton's face in her gloved hands. The truth. "I do. Do you forgive me?"

Brighton's eyes filled, and she was nodding before the question was even fully free. "Yes."

"Good."

Brighton laughed. "Yeah. Good."

And then they kissed, opened to each other, and it felt like the end of something, the start of something, every kind of something that Charlotte couldn't name, couldn't understand, and for now, under the canopy of lights in Colorado, that was enough.

chapter 24

"I've never seen you smile this much," Sloane said to Charlotte as she attempted to roll a piece of slimy bacon around a fig. "I'm not sure how to handle it."

They were at Elements the next evening, Wes and Dorian's restaurant in downtown Winter River, with the rest of the Two Turtledoves crew. The space was gorgeous—rustic and elegant all at once—with round wooden tables, brushed-nickel light fixtures casting an amber glow over the room, wooden beams crossing the ceiling, and shots of forest green and navy worked in through local artwork on the walls. The restaurant had shut down for the night—Wes and Dorian's donation for Two Turtledoves—and Wes was giving them all a cooking lesson.

"A romantic cooking lesson," he'd said at the start of the evening. "A sure way to impress any first date, tenth date, or the love of your life."

Everyone had chuckled at that, but Charlotte hadn't missed the way his eyes had found Sloane.

And the way Sloane's eyes had found him.

Charlotte's eyes had very carefully and purposefully not found Brighton at that moment, but she'd also been watching Sloane and Wes all evening, wondering at Sloane's body language, her expressions, even her tone. She'd never seen Sloane in love before, and something about that fact left her unsettled, as though she'd forgotten something but couldn't remember what.

Still, that didn't keep her heart from picking up its pace at Sloane's comment, her mind working back through her and Brighton's time at Greenbriar Ridge and the gardens, as well as most of this past afternoon, which Charlotte and Brighton had spent entwined on the couch in the basement while everyone else watched *Scrooged* upstairs.

Charlotte didn't think she'd stopped smiling since they'd left the ski lodge, to be honest. And right now, working next to Sloane, she smiled again—her facial muscles were legit a little sore—and finished up adding a dollop of goat cheese to her figs. "I don't know," she said. "I'm just . . ." She shrugged, glanced at Brighton at the next table, where Brighton had paused her work on her own figs and was deep in conversation with Wes.

She was so gorgeous, Charlotte literally lost her breath for a second.

"Jesus, okay," Sloane said, laughing. "So you're in love."

Charlotte froze, goose bumps erupting over her whole body, and not in a pleasant way.

In love.

"I'm not," she said, looking down as she started to wrap her figs. "I'm just . . ."

But she wasn't sure how to finish that sentence.

In lust?

In like?

Nothing fit when it came to Brighton, including Charlotte's denial to Sloane, but she didn't know how to explain that without getting into their whole messy, ugly, humiliating history. So she just shrugged and changed the subject.

"What about you?" she asked.

Sloane snorted. "Me?"

Charlotte stayed silent. She suddenly realized she had no idea how to really do this—inquire about Sloane's innermost feelings. That was usually Sloane's role, asking questions or offering stories. Charlotte usually just listened.

When Sloane said nothing else, Charlotte took a deep breath and tried to imagine what Brighton would say. Or, even better, what Bonnie Fairbrook would say.

"I just think Wes is really nice," she finally said.

Sloane laughed. "You too, huh?"

"What do you mean?"

"I mean my entire family thinks I fucked that one up," Sloane said.

"Did you?"

Right away, Charlotte knew it was the wrong thing to say. Sloane stilled, blinked down at her plate of bacon and figs, her jaw tight.

Charlotte pressed her eyes closed for a second. "Sloane, I—"

"No, no, I get it. You're Team Wes."

"I'm not," Charlotte said. "I can just see he cares for you, and—"

"You can *see* it?" Sloane said, starting to slap her appetizer together, goat cheese leaking from her rolls. "Charlotte, you don't see anything but your own—"

Sloane closed her mouth, but Charlotte heard the end of her sentence anyway. Charlotte's face flushed with shame, with something deeper than any emotion she could name. Her chest tightened, thinking back through her entire relationship with Sloane, how one-sided it had all been.

Sloane asked all the questions.

She offered the stories.

And Charlotte just . . .

What? Nodded. Shrugged. Smiled even when she didn't feel like it. Moved them on to work, work, and more work.

God, she was so bad at love.

Bad at people in general.

And what was worse, she knew she could fix it, or at least start to mend this huge gap in their two-year friendship by sharing something, anything, about herself. But everything about herself—from her relationship with her mother to her failed engagement—felt unlovable. Leavable and forgettable, the real heart of Charlotte Donovan.

She didn't want Sloane to see how completely inconsequential she was.

She wanted to be seen as strong, as immovable, untouchable. Because if that's how people saw her, that's what she'd be. And she'd never have to feel inadequate again, never have to feel that innate *something* that was missing inside her, that *something* that made people leave her and forget her so goddamn easily.

Even though she knew that what had happened between her and Brighton wasn't that simple, that she shared blame—what of Anna? What of her own mother, who barely looked at her, barely talked to her, even when she was a child?

She should say all of that now. She wanted to, she did, but she couldn't get the words to form on her tongue, all those ugly truths about herself.

"I'm sorry" was all she managed to say.

She couldn't wait for what Sloane would say back either. Instead, she simply turned and hurried to the back of the restaurant, through the kitchen, where Dorian and Manish had stolen away to talk with their heads bent close. Manish frowned when he saw her.

"Hey, Char, you okay?"

"I'm fine," she said, an instinct. She kept moving and burst out the back door, the cold like a slap in the face but welcome.

She breathed and breathed and breathed, desperate for air, for something, anything, to soothe this ache in her chest, but all she got was dizziness. She leaned against the brick, put her head between her legs.

Breathe.

You're okay.

You're Charlotte Donovan.

Charlotte . . . Rosalind . . . Donovan.

"Hey," a voice said, the heavy metal door opening next to her and slamming shut.

Brighton. Of course it was Brighton.

"Oh my god, it's freezing out here," she said.

Charlotte felt a coat—her own, by the scent of it—slide over her shoulders.

"Put this on," Brighton said, tugging her to standing.

Charlotte complied, her breathing still a little fast, her body trembling. Brighton helped Charlotte get her arms into her coat, then buttoned her up and slid her own hands into Charlotte's hair.

"Hey," she said again, her voice so soft. "What's wrong?"

Charlotte shook her head, but "Nothing" felt like the wrong answer. She couldn't stop thinking about Sloane, about the last two years, about how she'd done everything wrong. Sloane had so easily summed it all up in a sentence she hadn't even finished. But Charlotte didn't know if she was brave enough to fix it. Didn't even know how to stand here with Brighton without a million questions and doubts and geographical issues crowding into her mind.

She didn't want her mind right now.

She just wanted her heart.

She just wanted *fresh and new*. With everyone.

"Kiss me," she said to Brighton. "Please."

And Brighton did.

chapter 25

Brighton slipped in her earbuds and pressed "Play" on her phone.

For the millionth time in the last few days, "December Light" filtered into her ears. The first notes hit like a punch, her heart rate climbing, then settled into her blood like an old lover, wistful and achy and lost.

It was Christmas Eve, and they'd all just finished the Berrys' traditional holiday meal of chicken saltimbocca—prosciutto-wrapped chicken—with homemade mashed potatoes, green beans, and peppermint chocolate cake. The house was warmly lit, snow fell outside, and Lola was nestled next to Brighton on the sectional in the living area, her feet tucked under her as she perused some emails on her phone. Everyone else sat around, sipping spiked hot chocolate and talking about Christmas Eve traditions—opening one gift or saving them all for the morning, reading "'Twas the Night Before Christmas," watching *It's a Wonderful Life*, sleeping under the Christmas tree.

It all made Brighton miss her mother, miss her home at Christmas. She leaned her head against Lola's and started the song over again, turning up the volume a bit more to drown out the hum of conversation.

Winter lake, December light,
tears on your face, but I'll make it right.
An empty house that I want to fill,
ten years later this is still what's real.

She closed her eyes, reliving those ten years, and before she knew it or could stop it, her mind was on *after*. She tried to picture New York, their apartment, which she knew Lola didn't live in anymore. She tried to see herself on the streets—maybe Brooklyn was a better fit for her. Soon her fingers were moving in her lap, creating the chords she'd written for "December Light," and she saw herself on a dimly lit stage, a crowd in front of her, small but rapt.

Listening.

To her.

To her stories, her words, the way she saw the world.

But she was in Nashville. At the 5 Spot or the iconic Bluebird Cafe. She tried to force her performance into New York, but it just wouldn't fit, like a puzzle piece being shoved into the wrong place. She'd been doing this more and more lately—daydreaming about shows, about stages. New York. Nashville. Chicago. She couldn't seem to stop them, the images behind her eyes, all that she still wanted for herself swirling in her mind with Lola, with *after*, with her nearly crippling fear about trying it all again.

But daydreams were safe, watercolor pictures, fading as soon as she—

"Brighton."

Her eyes flipped open, the daydream vanishing once again, to find Lola standing over her, bent slightly to shake her shoulder. Adele was staring at Brighton too, that old guitar of hers sitting between her legs. Brighton frowned at Adele, but then Elle, Manish, and Sloane came up from the basement, their instruments in their hands. Manish carried Rosalind in her case, set her gently on the coffee table.

"Sorry," Brighton said, "I was lost in thought. What's going on?"

"Nina wants us to play some Christmas music," Lola said.

"Oh, that's a good idea," Brighton said, taking out her earbuds and slipping them into a pocket of her jeans along with her phone.

Lola nodded, squeezed her shoulder. "I want you to play with us."

Brighton froze, her eyes going to Adele's guitar. Adele held it out, and Brighton felt herself shrinking into the couch.

"What? Lo—" She stopped, swallowing as she remembered that Lola didn't want anyone to know about their past. "Charlotte, I . . . I can't. You all know how to play together. I'll just mess it up."

"You won't," Lola said, her voice gentle.

Brighton knew that Lola wouldn't make her play. They'd been extra soft with each other since last night, since Brighton had found Lola outside Elements practically hyperventilating. Sloane had wordlessly given up her bedroom, moving in with Adele so that Lola and Brighton could share a room during the time they had left, and Brighton had never been so grateful. Just falling asleep with Lola. Waking up with her. The slow, quiet sex they'd had last night . . . then again this morning. It all felt like medicine in Brighton's veins. But a medicine that woke her up too. She'd felt restless all day, her fingers drumming on countertops, her thumbs running over the calluses that were very nearly gone.

She figured it was all because of *after*, because she and Lola still hadn't talked about it, hadn't talked about what had upset Lola at Elements, and every time Brighton thought about New York, she felt just like she had five years ago—trapped, giving away some part of herself . . . but that part of herself was gone anyway.

Wasn't it?

The Katies had destroyed her hopes of playing music. And yeah, she'd let them, but all those daydreams, they were just that. Dreams. As much as might want to, she wasn't sure she could make it alone.

She closed her eyes, saw herself again on a dimly lit stage. Just her . . . but then there was Lola, the two of them, just like they'd been at Java Blues and that tiny bar in Boston when they'd been at Berklee.

She shook her head, opened her eyes.

Impossible dreams. That was all those images were.

Still, when Adele stood up and handed the guitar to her, her heart rate picked up, her stomach fluttering, as though she'd just caught sight of an old lover after years and years apart.

Brighton stared at the instrument for a second—the shiny lacquered surface, the worn strings in need of changing.

"Take your time," Lola said, then kissed her on the forehead and turned away from her, opening Rosalind's case and lifting the violin out with a reverence Brighton remembered. Her chest tightened, then loosened, a dizzying dance that she couldn't seem to stop.

"Baby girl," Adele said, still holding out the guitar.

Brighton took it, her fingers tingling as she touched the wood.

Adele sat next to her while she watched the quartet tune and warm up, laughter on their lips, a camaraderie that Brighton missed so much she could cry. Nina sat on the other side of the sectional, her mug in her hands and Snickerdoodle's head lying in her lap, her eyes a little glossy as she watched Sloane at her craft.

The guitar felt hot in Brighton's lap, her hands barely holding on to it, like it might actually burn her. It was facing the wrong way. She flipped it, carefully, her left hand settling on the neck, her right draping over the body. Still, she let her hands hang there, barely pressing on anything.

"'The Holly and the Ivy'?" Elle asked, their fingers ready on their cello. They'd pulled in dining chairs, now situated in a semi-circle in front of the Christmas tree.

"Must we start with the Jesus stuff?" Manish asked, scooting to the edge of his chair, holding up his viola with his chin alone.

"It's festive and not *that* Jesus-y," Elle said. "And it's instrumental. Make up some words in your head about Dorian's long-ass eyelashes."

Manish sighed happily. "God, I could write a tome."

Lola laughed. "I don't doubt it. Does that song sound good to you, Sloane?"

Sloane just nodded. Didn't look at Lola. In fact, there'd been a lot of not looking between the two of them all day, Brighton had noticed.

Lola swallowed, then glanced at Brighton. She winked so surreptitiously that Brighton nearly missed it. But god, her wink was devastating. Sexy and badass and comforting all at once. Lola counted them off, and soon the most glorious sounds Brighton had ever heard filled the space. Even the quartet's movements were like a dance, their bodies bending and working to coax their instruments into singing.

Brighton felt herself moving with them, her fingertips full-on buzzing now with energy. She hugged the guitar closer to her, hearing where she could fit this particular stringed sound into what the quartet was playing. Her heart rate was wild, pulsing in her throat, her temples, her toes.

She bent her head close to the guitar and plucked a single string, the bottom E. It was horribly out of tune, just like she had expected it to be, and before she could overthink it, muscle memory took over, her ears pressed close to the sound hole, her fingers on the tuning pegs, turning and plucking until the guitar was as it should be, each string singing like it was meant to.

She didn't look at Lola. Didn't look at anyone. She just listened for a second. The key was in A, she could hear that much. She formed her fingers where they needed to be, just working through the chords first. She felt dizzy, her breathing heavy, but as the quartet played on, crescendoing and then coming back down for a quiet third verse, she started playing.

Her fingers plucked at the strings, playing along with the melody at first, then creating a sort of echo to what the violins were doing. As the song curled into the fourth verse, the violins fell away.

Everything fell away except for Elle, who kept up a low rhythm on their cello, and . . . Brighton.

Her notes unfurled over everything else, the melody now twisting through the room, the violins and viola joining as a soft pulse underneath her. Her fingertips burned, unused to the press of the strings, but she didn't care. Her hands flew like birds released from a cage, the motions so natural as she wove a story about love and family and friends, a story about the fucking joy of telling stories like this. She laughed out loud, even as she played on, winding her melody down softly, then joining everyone in a symphony of strings for the last chorus.

Brighton watched Lola, whose head moved to slow everyone down, then made a circular motion to cut them off.

The final notes rang through the room for a second. Brighton's right hand hovered in the air after her last strum, her chest heaving up and down as though she'd just run a race.

"Now that," Manish said, "was the ode to Dorian's lashes they deserve." He beamed at Brighton.

In fact, everyone was smiling at her. Adele reached over and squeezed the back of her neck. Brighton's eyes stung, just a little, and she couldn't get the smile off her face. Lola's eyes looked a little shiny too. Brighton's blood felt heated, like water coming to a boil—music always made her feel wild, feral, like something set loose that was always meant to be free.

Right now, she just wanted to play.

"Another?" she said, and strummed out a strong E, the chord reverberating through the room.

The next morning, Christmas morning, Brighton woke up cold. She blinked at the bright white light, remembering that she was in Sloane's bedroom. Remembering that she'd stayed up so late, playing with the Rosalind Quartet.

She pressed her thumb to the fingertips of her left hand. They were sore, red from the strings, grown tender from so many months of not playing. She smiled at them, knowing it would take a few months to build her calluses back up. But . . .

She wanted to.

She actually wanted to.

She had no clue what that meant or how it would all come together, what being a solo artist even entailed or if she wanted to look for other people to play with. Then there were the Katies,

"December Light," and she knew she had to deal with that some-how too.

The thought overwhelmed her, immediately making her feel small, incapable. Like it wasn't worth the trouble if she'd just fail anyway . . .

She moved her arm to the other side of the bed, searching for Lola's warmth.

But Lola wasn't there, her side of the bed cold, like she hadn't been there in a while. Brighton sat up quickly, eyes scanning the room, but she was alone.

She could hear voices downstairs, could smell coffee and cinnamon, along with the salty bacon of the breakfast casserole Nina said she made every Christmas morning since the girls were born.

Just like Brighton's own mother did every year.

Her throat went tight at the thought of finding herself in this strange bedroom, in a stranger's house, for Christmas. She flung her covers back, needing Lola's familiar face, needing her arms, her smile. She put on sweatpants and a long-sleeved tee before heading into the hall, ready to tromp downstairs to find Lola, but a sound coming from the bathroom stopped her.

A soft sob.

She changed course, tiptoed to the bathroom door. Laughter filtered up from downstairs, "I'll Be Home for Christmas" playing softly from Nina's Bluetooth speaker. At the door, Brighton closed her hand around the knob but didn't turn it. She pressed her ear to the white-painted wood.

They were faint, but she heard sniffles. A sigh. Some soft muttering she couldn't make out, but she knew those sounds.

Lola.

Brighton swallowed hard, wondering what she should do.

Five years ago, she would've knocked. She would've gone inside without even waiting for a response, taken Lola in her arms, wiped her tears away.

And god, she wanted to do that now.

But here she was, in the Berrys' hallway, the love of her life crying in the bathroom, and Brighton didn't know what to do.

Because Lola wasn't just crying in the bathroom—she was hiding. Whatever this was, she didn't want Brighton to see it, didn't want Brighton to try and fix it. If she had, she would've woken Brighton up, curled into her, asked to be held, like she'd sometimes done when they were together. Lola didn't always have the words, but she knew Brighton was her safe place—she knew she could just ask for a kiss, a hug, and Brighton would give it, no questions asked, that Brighton would take her out to the beach, twirl her around.

But that's not who they were anymore.

But you can never make it right . . .

What you did to me will never be okay, Brighton.

A helplessness spilled into Brighton's chest as Lola's words from the morning they were snowed in came back to her, sand pouring through an hourglass, unstoppable.

She shook her head. No. No, she hadn't ruined it. The last couple of days, she'd made Lola happy. She had, she knew she had. They'd forgiven each other. But Lola was leaving in three days. Leaving for a whole month. They hadn't talked at all about what they would do after the holidays, and as Brighton stood there listening to Lola cry, she knew she had to be the one to bring it up. She had to be the one to go after Lola, because she was the one who had left.

Inside the bathroom, the water turned on, and Lola cleared her throat. Brighton could almost see her washing her face, wiping at her eyes, pulling her hair back, then putting on that red lipstick that Brighton both loved and hated—loved because Lola was always beautiful, hated because she knew Lola wore it as a shield, a sort of armor against the world.

The water turned off, and Brighton hurried back to their room and sat on the edge of the bed. Her blood felt fizzy, carbonated, and she took a few deep breaths. Five minutes later, Lola came back into the bedroom, looking fresh and lovely, red lipstick firmly in place.

"Hey," she said, not looking at Brighton as she rifled through her suitcase, then sat next to Brighton on the bed and pulled on a pair of socks, tucking them under her sleek black jeans. "Merry Christmas."

"Merry Christmas," Brighton said, leaning her shoulder against Lola's. "Sleep okay?"

Lola nodded, but her smile was small.

"Lola," Brighton said, taking a deep breath. She could do this. She *had* to do this. "I wanted to—"

"Oh, hey, I got you a present," Lola said, shooting up from the bed.

Brighton frowned. "You did?"

Lola nodded and went back to her suitcase, her dark wardrobe perfectly folded in its place, of course. She lifted a pile of sweaters and pulled out a brown box hidden underneath, tied with a red-and-green-striped ribbon.

"For you," Lola said, setting it in her lap.

"Lola," Brighton breathed. "You didn't have to. I didn't—"

"I know," Lola said, waving her hand. "But I saw this the other day when I went to get some coffee downtown before the event at Elements. I just thought of you."

Brighton untied the ribbon, slowly, reverently, then lifted the box's lid and set it next to her. Inside, red tissue paper covered the contents. She peeled it back, and there, sitting on a bed of red and green crinkle confetti, was a leather guitar strap.

Brighton's mouth fell open. It was the color of maple syrup, the material buttery and perfect, so high-quality it was already worn in—she knew it would fit over her shoulder perfectly. She lifted it out, her fingers trailing over the embossed design pressed into the leather.

A sun.

Several suns, actually, spreading over the strap, rays curling outward, bold and bright and sure.

"For when you find your path," Lola said, but her voice sounded sad, far away. She leaned over and kissed Brighton on her temple, then whispered against her skin. "Because I know you will."

"It's beautiful," Brighton said, tears swelling. "Lola, I—"

But before Brighton could even say thank you, Lola stood up again, made her way to the door. "I'll see you downstairs," she said, and then she was gone, leaving Brighton holding her gift, those tears just starting to trail down her cheeks. She smoothed her hands over the leather and let herself cry for a few minutes.

But after she was done, she slipped the strap onto Adele's guitar, which she'd carried upstairs with her last night. She'd been hesitant to let it go. As though the entire evening of music, of *playing*, would vanish if she let the instrument out of her sight.

She stood, settling the guitar over her body, then looked at herself in Sloane's full-length mirror. Her sweatpants and tee notwithstanding, she didn't feel like an impostor, didn't feel like a stranger was looking back at her from the glass. She looked . . . good.

Natural.

She picked out the first few notes of a too-familiar song, an ache settling around her heart. But with that ache, there was a rightness too.

A realness.

And suddenly she knew exactly how to tell Lola what she was feeling—everything she wanted *after*.

chapter 26

Over the years, Charlotte had perfected the fake smile.

Not too broad.

Not too small.

Show some teeth.

Make sure her eyes crinkled in the corners.

In fact, she'd had so much practice with disingenuous smiles, she'd nearly forgotten what a real one felt like—the ache in her cheeks, the effortlessness to it. These past couple of days with Brighton, short as they had been, had reminded her how easy it could be, how easy it was to just be happy.

But *easy* and *happy* were fleeting, practically mythical concepts in her life, a fact made all the more real the second she realized, right there in the middle of Watered Down with a cheap Manhattan in her hand, that her perfect Charlotte Donovan Smile™ had once again settled on her face.

"I think I'm about to do something totally insane," Wes said, plopping into the chair next to her. The room was almost overly warm and loud. The small stage was brightly lit, everything else dim and moody, a single microphone and stool ready and waiting for the Two Turtledoves attendees to profess their love, lust, or like.

"Oh?" Charlotte said, sipping on her drink. She was not touching the pitcher of Mistletoe Margaritas at their table, nor was she planning on consuming more than one Manhattan. Her mind was already whirling with thoughts about Brighton and music and New York and Europe and whatever came after that—she needed every single wit she had in place.

Wes nodded. "Like, real, real dumb."

"It's not dumb," Dorian said, sitting down on Wes's other side. "It's necessary."

Charlotte tilted her head. "What is this real, real dumb yet necessary thing you're about to do?"

Wes blew out a breath, his eyes drifting to where Sloane sat a few chairs away, chatting with Elle.

"Oh," Charlotte said. "Really?"

Wes covered his face with his hands. "I don't know."

"Yes, really," Dorian said, clapping Wes on the back.

Charlotte assumed Wes had finally taken Dorian into his confidence regarding his feelings for Sloane. "What's your plan?" she asked. Her own eyes scanned the room, looking for Brighton, who had ridden to Watered Down separately with Adele, claiming she was running late when the rest of their group was ready to leave Nina's for the bar. This wasn't unusual—Brighton had never been the most punctual person, but Charlotte had yet to see her, a fact that made Charlotte's already anxious mind feel even more on edge.

"Well, I can't sing," Wes said.

"He's awful," Dorian said.

"I can't act or write poems," Wes said.

Charlotte circled her free hand. "So . . . ?"

"So . . . I convinced Manish to let me use his viola."

Charlotte nearly choked on her drink. "His viola?"

"I know," Wes said. "But remember how I joined orchestra for Sloane back in high school?" His eyes were so wide, and he was so totally gone on Sloane Berry, even Charlotte's cold heart melted a little.

But only a little.

"Wes, his viola is expensive," she said. "And we have a tour coming up."

"I know, I know, I'll be gentle, I promise. Just a few horrible notes."

"Enough to make a total fool of himself," Dorian said.

"What are you going to play?" Charlotte asked.

Wes laughed. "'Play' is a stretch."

"Just be careful, please," she said. "That instrument is at least fifty years old."

"No pressure," Wes said, then tilted his head at her. "What about you?"

"Me?" she asked.

"Yeah. Any love songs for Brighton?"

"It's not like that," she said. An instinct. The first thing that popped into her head, which meant it must be true . . . didn't it? But even as she thought this, her chest tightened, fingertips tingling the way they did when she was nervous.

"It's not?" Wes asked, his tone flat.

She just shook her head, took another sip to keep herself quiet. Because the truth was, she still didn't know *what* it actually was, this thing with Brighton.

Great sex.

A relief.

Perfect.

. . . a mistake?

As her tour loomed—the quartet's departure just two days away—she was having a harder and harder time parsing what she was feeling. Christmas Eve had been magical, seeing Brighton come alive like that again, a guitar in her hands, just where it belonged. She could tell that night—from the second Brighton finally took the leap and played the first note—that Brighton was born to play, to create.

And how could she do that in New York, a city she hated?

That was the question Charlotte kept rolling over and over and over again in her mind, the question without an easy answer, the question that had sent her into the bathroom on Christmas morning to cry, just to get some relief. Charlotte couldn't remember Brighton writing a single song while they lived in Manhattan, and that was before the entire Katies ordeal.

She wanted Brighton to thrive.

She knew this much, and that alone was such a monumental change from all her bitterness and resentment, it nearly felt like enough.

To simply let Brighton go.

Let her live.

But every time she readied herself to tell Brighton as much, she couldn't get the words off her tongue. They tangled there, mottling into nonsense, into a kiss, a tumble into bed. She knew Brighton wanted to talk about their future too, but she couldn't seem to let Brighton get the words out either.

She was scared of both options—letting go and trying again—and the only response was to stand still.

But she knew she couldn't stay in that space forever.

"Okay, lovebirds, we're about to start!" Eli, Watered Down's host for events, said as he hopped onto the stage.

Cheers went up around the room. Next to Charlotte, Wes sunk down low in his seat.

"I might throw up," he said.

"You don't have to do it, you know," she said.

He frowned at her, tilted his head. "You're not much of a romantic, are you?"

She laughed. "An understatement."

But even as she said it, she knew it wasn't true. She used to love romance. She would bring Brighton flowers and write her actual physical notes in high school before they even got together, because even then Charlotte had loved her.

She sighed, glanced at Sloane. "But you're right—you should do it," she said to Wes.

"Yeah?" he said, brows lifted.

Charlotte smiled at him, and this one was real. "Yeah."

He grinned like a little kid, and it was so cute that Charlotte couldn't help but laugh and pat him on the leg.

"Hey," Brighton said, walking up to Charlotte's other side, bringing a wash of cold air with her. "What'd I miss?"

"Oh, just my impending humiliation," Wes said.

Brighton frowned, but he turned to say something to Dorian.

"Where've you been?" Charlotte asked, both relief and panic surging as Brighton settled into a chair.

"Just running late," Brighton said, but she didn't make eye contact. Charlotte studied her as she took off her red coat, revealing a lacy black blouse with a black bra underneath, dark jeans, and hunter-green boots. Light-pink gloss sparkled on her lips, and her eyes were rimmed dark, lashes as long as a day.

"You look nice," Charlotte said, another understatement. Brighton looked ethereal, magical.

Brighton smiled before she leaned in, pressed a kiss under Charlotte's ear, and whispered, "Thank you."

"All right, all right," Eli called into the mic. "First up is Jameson with an ode for . . . well, we'll let him tell you!"

The crowd cheered, and Brighton pulled away, still smiling softly at Charlotte.

Charlotte smiled back, but her brain snagged on how crinkly her eyes were, and then she was overthinking her smile, overthinking why it was fake, overthinking every thump of her heart.

Jameson hopped onstage and proceeded to perform a truly horrific rendition of John Mayer's "Your Body Is a Wonderland" for someone named Rita, who beamed at him from the audience with her hands clasped to her chest.

"If he starts hip thrusting," Wes said, "I'm going to—oh, oh god, there he goes."

Charlotte tried to laugh, tried to get her stomach to relax. "Isn't he the glue eater?"

"The very same," Wes said, "though I hope, for Rita's sake, that he's moved on to more mature delicacies."

"Hey, there's someone for everyone," Dorian said.

"Yeah, like viola-playing South Asian men from London," Wes said.

Dorian just smirked as Jameson finished and proceeded to make out with Rita right there in the front row, tongue and all. A few more acts passed, even fewer of them decent, including Gemma performing original slam poetry for a person named Ash, whom Charlotte remembered seeing at the events. It was pretty incredible, actually, and Charlotte couldn't help but genuinely smile as the two of them kissed at the end to a chorus of snaps.

"Cute," Brighton said, sliding her hand into Charlotte's.

"Very," Charlotte said, her fingers closing around Brighton's and squeezing.

"And now, a song for a songstress by a songstress," Eli said. "Please welcome to the stage Brighton Fairbrook!"

Charlotte blinked, Eli's words falling into place slowly. "Wait, what?"

But Brighton just smiled at her, pulled her hand to her lips, and kissed her knuckles. Then she let her go and wove through the tables to the stage. She grabbed a guitar that was sitting on a stand to the side—Adele's guitar, now outfitted with the strap Charlotte had given her—and slid it over her shoulder.

Adele wolf-whistled as Brighton settled on the stool, and Charlotte could feel Manish's and Elle's eyes on her. She could only stare at Brighton, though, the girl she'd met at twelve, kissed at seventeen, and promised to marry at twenty-two.

Loved always.

Her heart sprinted under her ribs. God, Brighton looked amazing up there, under the lights, on a stage. But this, now, knowing what Brighton had been through with the Katies, how long it had been since she'd taken this kind of leap . . .

She was luminous.

"Hi, everyone," Brighton said, and more cheers and whistles erupted. She smiled. "This is a song I . . . well, yeah, I wrote. You may have heard it already, but that's another story."

Charlotte stopped breathing.

Brighton laughed, looked down for a second. "Anyway, I wrote this song a long time ago for the girl I loved then." She met Charlotte's eyes. "The same girl I love now. Lola, this is for you. This has always been for you."

Charlotte felt rather than heard whispers undulate through

her quartet, felt Wes turn to look at her, felt Sloane's eyes boring into her. She couldn't process any of it, because Brighton.

Because the first notes to "December Light" were starting to unfurl under Brighton's fingers, more whispers moving through the audience at the now-familiar tune. Brighton didn't seem to care, though. She kept playing, her eyes on Charlotte, and then . . .

She started singing.

Charlotte hadn't heard her voice in five years.

Not like this, not with their song on her lips.

It was breathtaking, pure magic, sultry and soft, her tone like a swirl of dark chocolate.

Winter lake, December light,
tears on your face, but I'll make it right.

The song wrapped around her, around all of them. Charlotte couldn't tell if her heart was breaking or mending.

That Tiffany lamp, a rainbow on the floor,
pieces of glass holding your whole world.

Whatever was going on in her chest right now felt like both life and death, a becoming and an undoing. Onstage, Brighton slowed down, quieted, her eyes closed as she sang softly, sang words Charlotte had never heard before.

December light, here we are again
standing together, come snow, come sand . . .

Her eyes opened. Looked at Charlotte. The entire room held its breath, waiting for what came next.

December light, it's you and it's me,
dressed all in white, the start of a new story.

Breaking. Charlotte's heart was definitely breaking. Because Brighton was magnificent. A true storyteller, weaving simple words with magic, captivating her audience, casting a spell. Everything felt soft, languid, everyone moving closer to one another, their eyes softly blinking at this love story unfurling from the stage.

Charlotte's love story.

And she knew.

She knew all she had to do was ask.

That's all it would take, and Brighton would come back to New York. She'd try again. Not at the expense of her own music—Charlotte could see the passion there, the drive sparkling in her eyes again—but she'd do it all in New York.

She'd do it for Charlotte.

She'd try and try, and hell, maybe it would actually work. Maybe Brighton would find a community of other singer-songwriters, find places that loved having her onstage.

But it wouldn't be for herself.

It'd be for Charlotte.

And she couldn't let Brighton do it. She couldn't watch them fall apart again, couldn't let Brighton choose Charlotte over herself again. Because that's what Brighton had always done, wasn't it? Berklee, New York—she'd always put Charlotte first, because she was the only person in Charlotte's life who *would*, and they both knew it.

And where had all of that gotten them? Brighton had been miserable, pushed so far to the edge of her own needs that she'd literally snapped and done the thing neither of them ever imagined she'd do.

And Charlotte couldn't do it again.

As Brighton finished the song, as the crowd leaped to its feet, shouting and clapping, Charlotte knew it was the right decision.

To let go.

She stood too, tears swelling for only a second before she wiped them away and a cool calm settled over her, like floating in deep, dark water. Peaceful. She slid her coat off the back of her chair and slipped it on, buttoning it slowly, methodically. She met Sloane's eyes for a split second. Sloane wasn't clapping and stood with her arms folded, a look that could only be described as hurt settling on her face, a million questions in her gaze.

Charlotte pulled her eyes away, then turned and started for the side entrance, slipping through the patrons like a ghost, everyone so enchanted with Brighton, they forgot all about her subject.

All the better, Charlotte thought.

She was nearly to the door, her phone ready to call a Lyft back to Nina's, when a hand grabbed her elbow.

"Lola."

Charlotte pressed her eyes closed, took one deep breath before turning to face Brighton.

"Hi," Charlotte said.

Brighton frowned. "*Hi*? Where are you going?"

Charlotte managed a smile, a small, barely adequate bend to her lips. "That was lovely, Brighton. Really."

Brighton shook her head. "Okay, what the hell are you doing? I thought—"

"This is over, Brighton."

The words were soft, barely audible inside the bar, but they fell like a guillotine's blade. Brighton said nothing.

"I'm glad we reconciled," Charlotte said, releasing her words slowly, carefully, thinking on them before setting them free. "I am. But we both know this won't work."

"The hell we do," Brighton said, her voice a whisper.

Charlotte forged ahead. "I'm in New York. And you belong in Nashville. We have different lives now. We're not seventeen anymore. We're not even twenty-three."

"Lola. Don't."

"This was good, really," Charlotte said, knotting her hands together so they didn't shake. "So good. We've forgiven each other, and we can move forward, maybe even be friends. But I'm leaving for a month, and you—" She cut herself off. She couldn't say any more. The more she talked, the more her emotions threatened to surge, and they both needed her to be strong right now. Logical.

Practical.

"Goodbye, Brighton," she said. "And good luck."

And with that, she turned and shoved the door open, then ran a block south before she even called for a Lyft, just in case Brighton—or even Sloane or Wes—tried to come after her.

But no one did.

And when Charlotte stopped under a streetlight, Winter Berry Bakery's windows dark, the bookstore just closing up shop, she was alone. Just like she'd always been.

Charlotte sat on Sloane's bed, Snickerdoodle lying at her feet and her closed suitcase next to her. She'd come back to a dark house—even Nina had gone to the Two Turtledoves event with her friend Marisol—and slowly packed up her things. Only Snickerdoodle had been there to greet her, his unbridled adoration of Charlotte nearly making her cry. Sweet, naive Snick. Still, with every noise, every creak of the tree branches in the winter wind, she expected the group's return.

Or at least Brighton's.

No one came, though. Not for another two hours, which was a good thing. She had enough time to stop expecting anyone—she would *not* be that person who demanded to be left alone, then pouted when people did as she asked.

Plus, she was used to this—the silence. The solitude. Her own mother hadn't even called or responded to her text on Christmas Day, had never called or texted on any Christmas Day, really, not even the year Brighton left Charlotte at the altar.

By the time Sloane opened the door to her bedroom, Charlotte had arranged an earlier flight to London, leaving near dawn from the Colorado Springs Airport. It was exactly what she needed—a couple of days to roam London by herself and get her head on straight for the tour.

Sloane stopped short when she saw Charlotte on the bed, her own dog still cuddled at Charlotte's feet. She closed the door without a word, took off her coat, and opened the closet with her back to Charlotte. Charlotte didn't say anything but worked on what she could say.

What she *should* say.

"Did Wes play you a song?" is what she settled on, and she could tell by the way Sloane's shoulders tightened that it was the wrong thing.

"You've got to be kidding me," Sloane said.

Charlotte sighed, pressed her fingers into her eyes until she saw bursts of color. "Sloane, I—"

"So you've been lying this whole time?" Sloane said. She didn't turn around.

Charlotte stayed silent.

"This whole fucking time," Sloane said, "you knew Brighton. No, no, wait. Not only *knew* but nearly *married*." She whirled around then, her coral-colored scarf in her hands, her dark eyes shiny and flashing. "And Adele knew. Fuck, *Wes* knew."

Charlotte just shook her head, her mouth open, words tangling on her tongue.

"For two years, I've been trying," Sloane said. "I've been trying to know you. Trying to be there for you."

"Sloane."

"Because god knows you're the saddest person I've ever met."

Charlotte frowned, her heart cramping under her ribs.

"You think you've convinced everyone around you that you're this self-sufficient stalwart of work and creativity, unemotional, don't need friends, don't need love, but that's bullshit," Sloane said. "And everyone knows it, Charlotte. Everyone but you."

Charlotte looked down at her lap.

"And I tried," Sloane said. "Because you're brilliant at what you do. Because I actually fucking liked you. I cared about you. And I thought, *Hey, if I can just crack that shell, just give her a little, she'll give something back*. But that's bullshit too, isn't it?"

"Sloane, I . . ." Charlotte took a deep breath, forced herself to look at her friend. "I'm sorry. I kept all this from you because I . . . I just—"

"You know what?" Sloane said, putting up a hand. "I can't do this right now. I've got to go deal with Wes, and since we both know you don't really give a shit about a reciprocal friendship, I'll leave you to your thoughts. Come on, Snick."

Sloane went to her dresser, grabbed a sweater and a pair of plaid pajama pants from a drawer, and was gone—Snickerdoodle trotting behind her—before Charlotte could even think of what to say next.

chapter 27

Three people in a queen-size bed wasn't the most comfortable way to spend a night, but it didn't really matter, as Brighton barely slept anyway.

Mostly, she tossed and turned on the edge of the mattress, both Adele and Sloane sleeping like the dead, Adele's limbs spread like a starfish in the middle. The woman was definitely used to sleeping alone. Still, sleep played a never-ending game of hide-and-seek with Brighton while the last week and a half—well, really, the last fifteen years—played through her mind.

She kept getting stuck on the transitions—following Lola to Berklee, agreeing to move to New York, and even letting Lola leave Watered Down last night. In the moment, Brighton had been too shocked to follow her, Lola's words processing and taking on meaning too slowly in her mind. And then, once everything had clicked, Adele had refused to let her leave the bar, instead guiding her back to their table and putting a glass of bourbon into her hands.

"Let her chill out," Adele had said, threading her arm through Brighton's. "You can't keep running after her all the time, baby girl."

"I'm the one who left her, Adele," Brighton had said.

Adele had only tilted her head, her eyes softly narrowed. "Are you?"

Brighton had opened her mouth, closed it. It was true, of course, that Brighton had done the physical leaving five years ago in Grand Haven, but maybe Adele was right too—Brighton had spent her entire life chasing Charlotte Donovan.

Who the hell was chasing her?

Brighton released a soft groan and sat up in bed. The room was quiet but for the soft sound of ambient rain emanating from Adele's phone. A full moon silvered through the curtains, making the space glow. After checking her phone—4:43 a.m.—Brighton gently lifted Adele's leg off her own and pushed the covers back. She put on her cardigan, then slipped out the door.

She walked down the hall, stopping in front of Sloane's closed door. There wasn't a sound, no movement, but Lola was a heavy sleeper. Brighton closed her hand around the doorknob, weighing her options. The last time she had invaded Lola's room in the middle of the night . . . well, good things had followed. Still, this was different.

Brighton had put everything on the line for Lola.

She'd gotten on a stage, played Lola a song—*their* song. And Lola had simply . . . gotten up and walked away.

Anger surged through Brighton's veins, sudden and cleansing. It felt good to feel rage instead of guilt and pain and longing. She was so fucking tired of this—the ways she bent herself for others, the ways no one, *no one*, seemed to really see her.

She gritted her teeth, ready to tell Lola all of this, to finally lay it all out instead of constantly racking her brain over Lola's needs, years of guilt driving her every action and thought.

She gripped the doorknob and twisted, then flung the door open, not giving two shits if she woke Lola up with the noise. *She* needed to talk, so that's what they were going to do.

Brighton stepped into the room, opened her mouth to say Lola's name—she even planned on using *Charlotte*—but everything died on her tongue at the scene in front of her.

A too-still silence.

A perfectly made bed.

A completely empty room.

No suitcase other than Sloane's, no violin, no black clothes hanging in the open closet.

Brighton felt her shoulders drop, realization settling over her like a heavy winter coat—Lola was gone.

The next couple of days were a blur of everyone treating Brighton like she was going to break, feeling like she might actually break, and wanting to punch a hole through Nina's wall.

Several holes, in fact. Several walls.

She couldn't really settle on an emotion—anger, sadness, heartbreak, disappointment, sheer white-hot rage. Adele tried to get her to talk about it, but Brighton didn't want to talk. The day after Lola left, Brighton's parents finally arrived back in the States, and Brighton spent two hours on the phone with them recounting the shit show of the past week of her life. Her mother wanted her to come home, to take some *time*.

But she was so goddamn tired of taking time. She was tired of thinking and wondering and regretting. Plus, if she went home to Grand Haven, she'd land on the living-room couch, watch every Pixar movie ever made while guzzling her mother's extensive supply of French wine, and quite possibly never leave the house again.

No.

She wasn't going to wallow, and she wasn't going to *talk* about how she wasn't going to wallow. There was nothing to talk about, really. Lola was right—they'd reconciled and had fun, but they had different lives.

Now Brighton wanted to live hers.

Unfortunately, living her life meant dealing with her Katies problem, as well as once again jumping on the Nash-Vegas hamster wheel of finding gigs and, you know, putting her entire heart and soul in the hands of strangers and booking agents.

"I don't know if I can do this," she said to Adele a few days after they'd gotten back to Nashville. It was New Year's Eve, and she was sitting at the bar with her laptop in Ampersand after her afternoon shift, clicking on one venue after another, reading up on their booking processes.

"You can," Adele said as she sifted through receipts. "You have to."

"I don't *have* to."

Adele lifted a brow. "You do if you don't want to be a sad sack nursing gin and tonics by yourself on New Year's Eve, mourning your dashed hopes and forsaken dreams."

"Jesus, dramatic much?"

Adele grinned. "Just putting it all into perspective, baby girl." She arranged the receipts in her hand, tapped their edges against the bar. "You talked to her yet?"

Brighton laughed through the tightness in her throat. "You clearly don't know Charlotte Donovan very well."

Adele shrugged. "I don't, you're right. But I do know what running scared shitless looks like, and Charlotte is—"

"Adele, stop." Brighton held up her hand, sighed. "Look, I know you're trying to help, but just . . . don't. Okay? I'm fine."

Adele sniffed. "Sloane hasn't mentioned her much, though I know they all reunited in London a few days ago. In case you were wondering."

"I wasn't." Brighton kept her eyes on her computer screen, her vision blurring on the Station Inn's booking page. She was lying, of course—every single day she had to stop herself from asking Adele if Sloane had said anything about Charlotte. She knew Sloane had been pretty pissed at Charlotte too, and part of Brighton really did just want to know if they'd worked it out.

The other part was hungry—dying of starvation, really—for any indication that Charlotte wondered about her too.

A bad habit.

And like any bad habit, she needed to wean herself off Charlotte Donovan. Eventually, she'd stop wondering. Eventually, her mind would stop wandering back to their time in Winter River, to their time as kids, as teenagers, even to their time in New York. Eventually, she'd stop feeling that thrum between her legs at the mere thought of Charlotte's mouth. Eventually, her chest would stop feeling like she'd been punched when she heard a violin play.

Eventually, she'd stop thinking about everything she would've done differently.

She shook her head, needing to focus on something else. She clicked over to the Katies' website, just like she'd been doing at least a dozen times a day since she'd gotten back, wondering what the hell to do about "December Light." She really didn't want to get lawyers involved. She had dated proof in her notebook that she had written the song, not to mention the track she and Lola had laid down at a studio in Grand Rapids, which she knew meant she owned the copyright automatically. Still, it all seemed so messy and involved. But she also knew she couldn't just let it go. "December Light," while bittersweet, was her song.

Their song.

And no matter how much Brighton was determined to finally move on, Charlotte was a huge part of her history, her story. And that song . . . it meant something.

Hell if she was going to let the Katies simply take it.

She clicked on their schedule page, her eyes snagging on today's date in a very long list of upcoming concert dates. She leaned closer, made sure she was reading the information correctly.

"Hey," Adele said, leaning on her forearms, the sleeves of her checkered button-up rolled to her elbows. "Idea."

Brighton looked up. "Oh?"

"I think you should play here."

"Here?"

"At Ampersand. You're comfortable here. I've got some slots open in January. It'd be a great way to get your feet wet again. This could be your home base."

Brighton sat back, folded her arms. It wasn't a bad idea. Ampersand was small but reputable. Already, a few bigger names had come through here, up-and-comers who went on to make real names for themselves beyond the Nashville bubble. And god, Brighton wanted to play. She'd already written two new songs since being back in town—as everyone knew, romantic misery was excellent fodder for art—and she was starting to feel restless, that artist's need to not only create but also put that creation out into the world.

"Okay," she said before she talked herself out of it. "You sure you don't mind?"

Adele frowned. "Mind? Are you kidding? Baby girl, you're *good*. You'll bring in business, I have no doubt. Deal with it."

She slapped a bar towel at Brighton's arm. Brighton laughed and grabbed it, pulling on the end. "Okay, but first . . . I need you to do something with me. Tonight."

Adele tilted her head, a mischievous grin already settling on her face.

chapter 28

Brighton could barely breathe in this crowd, but she kept ahold of Adele's hand and wove them through the bodies, the dim lights casting everyone into shadow.

She was determined to be front and center for this show.

3rd and Lindsley was a popular music venue and bar, but it was small, the audience space just a freestanding area in front of a raised stage. The Katies used to play here right after they booted Brighton from their midst—they were never even big enough to get into this place when Brighton was at the mic—and soon after, their popularity exploded. So it was no surprise they still played here, the origin of their more humble beginnings.

And it was no surprise the place was absolutely packed.

Brighton finally worked her way to the front, Adele cool and calm beside her.

"We're gonna get a neckache this close up," Adele said. Her eyes scanned the empty stage, mics, and guitars that Brighton recognized, a teal-and-navy paisley rug spread out on the floor.

Brighton just smiled. "I want them to see me."

Adele nudged her shoulder. "Look who's the badass now."

"I'm not," Brighton said, shaking out her hands, which felt tingly with adrenaline. "I'm just ready, you know?"

Adele hooked her arm through Brighton's. "I know, baby girl. Proud of you."

Brighton pulled her friend closer, and they stood like that for a while, the crowd wild and queer and beautiful around them. Brighton let herself feel it all, feel the jealousy, the bitterness, the rage.

The sadness.

For all her hurt and anger, she missed Emily and Alice as her friends. They'd been her first touchstone in Nashville, her first everything after she blew up her life with Charlotte. She didn't think she'd ever not miss them. And she didn't think it would ever not hurt, the way they'd cast her aside so easily. The way they'd taken her words, her music, her heart without even a phone call, a fuck-you, anything.

And what was worse, what hurt the most, was that they clearly just expected her to accept it. They didn't expect any recourse, any consequences. It was like they had seen some sort of smallness in Brighton that made them unafraid.

The same kind of smallness she'd let rule her for the last nine months.

Well, for the last five years, really. She'd been carrying what she'd done to Charlotte for so long, letting it nearly crush her, letting it rule how she felt about herself. But as she stood there, people surrounding her on all sides, ready to hear the band she'd fucking founded, she knew she wasn't that person anymore. She wasn't sure when it had happened, the change. Maybe it was simply being with Lola again, talking through what had happened, knowing Lola *saw* her.

Or maybe it was Lola's leaving. The crushing blow of it, the realization that she wanted Lola. She wanted Lola so much. For all their messy history, the pain they'd inflicted on each other, Brighton would always love Lola. Always miss her. Always want her, maybe. But she wanted herself too. She wanted her music and a career. She wanted stages and lights and applause and that hushed awe that settled over a crowd when a song really landed. She wanted love and sex and passion, and maybe it'd take a while to find that with someone else, but she had to believe it was possible.

She took in a deep breath, straightened her shoulders as the lights went a little dimmer. A man with a beard and a Panama-style hat came onstage, and the crowd erupted. He held out his hands, then gripped the microphone as the audience quieted.

"We've got a real treat for your New Year's Eve," he said. "Your local faves, the national sensation, the one, the only, the Katies!"

Then there was nothing but noise—and whistles and claps—but Brighton felt a silence settle around her, like she was in the eye of a hurricane. Emily, Alice, and Sylvie stepped onto the stage, gorgeous and confident and powerful. Emily went to her keyboards, Alice settled behind the drums, and Sylvie took the center with her guitar, her red hair flowing like lava. Brighton was standing to the left of her, right in front of Emily. She stared up at her old friend, her old *best* friend, tears clogging her throat.

Emily was luminous, her dark curls like a halo around her face, striped crop top and charcoal-gray high-waisted pants, makeup subtle and perfect.

"You good?" Adele said, tightening her arm, still hooked through Brighton's.

Brighton could only nod.

She was okay.

And she was a mess.

"Hey, Nashville!" Sylvie said into the mic, and the room roared in greeting as the Katies launched into their first song. It was fast and energetic, one they'd written with Sylvie, and Brighton could only stare as they performed, mesmerized by their energy, their magnetic charm onstage.

Would she have been able to do that?

Would she have been like Sylvie, moving around on the stage, head tossed back, hair flying?

The Katies' style was certainly different from her own, she knew that. And as she watched them, each song high-octane, pulsing drums and roaring keys, she realized they'd made the right choice.

The Katies, as they were now, weren't Brighton Fairbrook.

And she wasn't them.

"Okay, we're going to slow it down now," Sylvie said after a few songs, mouth pressed to the mic, sweat shining on her neck and collarbones. "Take a breath, tell you a love story. You all like love, don't you?"

The crowd cheered.

Brighton's stomach tightened.

"Here we go," Adele said.

Brighton tried to breathe as the first notes of "December Light" started up. The audience cheered, then quieted as Emily played the opening on keys. Brighton stared right at her. She didn't think Emily had seen her yet, but god, she needed it to happen.

Needed it to happen now.

The song was quiet, mellow, and the audience had quieted with it. Just before she knew Sylvie would come in with the lyrics, Brighton clapped.

Three times, and that was it.

But the venue was small, the crowd hushed in anticipation, so the sound of her clapping echoed enough that Emily's eyes sought the source.

And found it.

Brighton watched the color drain from Emily's face, watched her mouth drop open slightly. Her fingers even faltered on the notes a little, drawing a look from Sylvie as she started to sing.

Winter lake, December light,
tears on your face, but I'll make it right.

"You got this," Adele said quietly, and Brighton just nodded, kept staring. She'd never looked at anyone so hard in her life. It might've been slightly comical, the way Emily seemed to start sweating more, her expression one of pure panic as she struggled through the notes. Brighton didn't necessarily want her to choke during a performance. That wasn't her goal here. But she had to admit, this was a little satisfying, if only as evidence that Emily knew what she had done, and knew it was fucking wrong.

As hard as it was, Brighton maintained her serene expression as she continued to watch Emily. She watched her sing harmonies and get the words wrong, watched her blow a curl off her forehead, watched her swallow so hard Brighton could see her throat moving with the effort.

Three and a half minutes, the longest two hundred and ten seconds of Brighton's life, and it was over. The Katies moved on to "Cherry Lipstick," getting the crowd hyped again, but the damage was done. For the rest of the show, Brighton stood in front of Emily, and Emily kept glancing at her, a worried expression filtering up through her smile every time she did.

When it was finished, the last note sung, Emily took a bow, waved, and scuttled offstage before the other two, but Brighton was ready. She tugged Adele along, heading for the door to the side that led to the backstage area. There was a guy there—a bouncer for all intents and purposes, a barrier to the artists Brighton hadn't considered.

"Shit," she said, stopping a few feet from him while the crowd demanded an encore. "I need to get past this guy."

Adele waved a hand. "I've got this." Then she walked up to the man, hands in her pockets, completely chill. "Jack, is that you?"

He frowned at her. "I'm Sam."

Adele clapped, then shot a pair of finger guns at him that would make any bisexual proud. "Sam, that's right. God, it's been a while, hasn't it?"

Sam tilted his head, studying Adele to place her, totally oblivious to Brighton scooting past him in the dim light. Adele was a literal goddess, and Brighton couldn't help but smile as she hurried down a small hallway, searching for the greenroom.

It wasn't hard.

On the left was a small room with a leather couch and an armchair, a coffee table covered in magazines, and a stainless-steel mini-fridge.

And right there, sitting on the couch and packing her bag, was Emily.

"They're calling for an encore," Brighton said, leaning against the doorframe.

Emily's head shot up, her eyes wide.

"Brighton."

Brighton just smiled, no teeth. She felt wild inside, her pulse in her throat, emotions just at the surface. Adrenaline kept her moving, kept her focused on her goal.

"It's been a while," she said.

Emily nodded, stood up. "It has."

"Things are going well for you."

Emily just nodded again, stuck her hands into her back pockets. "Brighton, I—"

"Emily, what the hell are you doing?" Sylvie called, and Brighton turned to see the redhead barreling down the hall, hair licking at the air behind her like flames. "We've got to get back out there."

She stopped short at the door, eyes narrowing on Brighton.

"Brighton?" she said.

"Hi, Sylvie."

"Brighton, oh my god, hey," Alice said, appearing from behind Sylvie and angling around their front woman to wrap her arms around Brighton's neck.

Brighton patted Alice's back but released her quickly.

"Good to see you," Sylvie said, her voice tight.

Brighton didn't respond to that. "Listen, I'll get to the point." She had to do this fast, rip off the proverbial Band-Aid before she lost her nerve. "I need you to stop playing my song."

Sylvie frowned, her mouth pursing. "I'm sorry, what?"

"Ask Emily," Brighton said, nodding toward Emily. "Or Alice. They know."

Sylvie folded her arms as Emily sighed and looked down at the poured-concrete floor. Alice shifted on her feet, her eyes focused on Emily.

"I thought you said she gave you permission to use it," Alice said.

Emily opened her mouth, closed it.

"What?" Sylvie said. "Gave who permission for what?"

Before the open mic at Watered Down, Brighton had only

ever played "December Light" for three people—Lola, Emily, and Alice. The song had been like a bruise during Brighton's first days in Nashville, and she'd played it for Emily and Alice as a sort of exposure therapy, a way to tell her story without telling them everything. Emily had convinced Brighton to upload it to the cloud where they kept all their lyrics and charts, but then they'd all forgotten about it.

Or, rather, Brighton had made sure they forgot about it.

"Emily, what is going on?" Alice asked.

"What song?" Sylvie asked. "Someone tell me right the fuck now."

Emily just sent her hands through her hair.

"'December Light' is mine," Brighton said finally. "And no, Alice, Emily never asked my permission to use it."

"Wait a second, what?" Sylvie asked. "You told me you wrote that song." She jabbed a finger in Emily's direction.

"Emily, Jesus," Alice said, dropping her face into her hands.

"Look, we needed a ballad," Emily said. "It's a good song, and I—"

"Stole it," Brighton said.

"You left it with us," Emily said. "It was the Katies' property."

"That's not how copyright law works," Sylvie said, lifting her hands and letting them drop with a slap. "Goddammit."

Brighton was ready to get the hell out of there. She didn't want to get into this with Emily, didn't want to rehash the levels of betrayal, didn't want to end up soothing Alice and Sylvie in their outrage either.

Her hands shook as she readied to say what had to be said— her threat, as it were—so she stuffed them into her coat pockets, squared her jaw.

"Look, I've got dated notebooks and a recording done in a

studio to prove I wrote it before I met any of you," she said. "Stop playing my song, and remove it from your discography on all platforms, or I'm getting lawyers involved."

She let her words settle for one . . . two . . . three . . .

Let Emily's eyes meet hers.

Let Sylvie whisper a quiet *fuck*.

Let Alice say her name, which she ignored.

Then she turned and walked away and didn't look back until she found Adele, still chatting it up with her new friend Sam.

chapter 29

It was truly amazing how much a string quartet could accomplish without ever really speaking to one another.

Charlotte attributed the successful London leg of their tour—sold-out performances at the Royal Albert Hall, packed lectures at the Royal College of Music—to the fact that the four of them had been playing together for long enough that they instinctively read one another's body language, moods, cues. That, and they were stellar musicians.

Still, by the time a week had passed and they'd settled into their hotel in Paris, Charlotte had grown weary of Sloane's silent treatment. Mirian, their manager, had been able to procure sponsors for a lot of their trip, so they each had their own room, which Charlotte normally would have appreciated.

Now, though, as she rolled her bag into the crisp modernity of her room at La Belle Ville, the silence felt oppressive. Granted, she hadn't really tried to talk to Sloane about all that had happened in Winter River. She wasn't sure how to broach the subject, and she kept hoping things would naturally smooth themselves over.

After all, Charlotte was . . . Charlotte. She was reserved, stoic, even a bit prickly at times, and the entire quartet knew this. She rarely shared intimate details about her life, and that had always seemed to work just fine. But as Charlotte unpacked, trying to focus on their performance at the Paris Philharmonic the next day, she knew this time was different.

Sloane was hurt, and it was about more than Charlotte keeping things to herself. It was about Charlotte shutting Sloane out on purpose, when Sloane had done nothing but invite Charlotte in.

She set her toiletry bag on the bathroom sink, stared at herself in the mirror. The woman staring back at her was strong. Self-sufficient. She didn't need anyone's approval or help. She didn't need anyone's love or kindness, didn't need permission or forgiveness.

This was the Charlotte Donovan she'd become over the last five years—over the last twenty-eight years, really. A fortress. Impenetrable. Unflappable.

And she was miserable.

True, there were things in her life she loved—her work, her music, the beauty of creating, then hearing that creation unfurl with her quartet. She loved New York, loved Manhattan in the spring, the fall.

But she could love so many places.

She could love so much more than work.

She could love so many more people than just herself.

And what was more, she *wanted* to. God, she was so fucking tired of herself, of always and only keeping her own company, of swallowing feelings and fears and convincing herself that by doing so she was *strong*.

She wasn't strong.

She was a fucking coward.

With Brighton. With Sloane. With her mother, even. Desperate for love but convinced no one would ever fully give it, an insecurity that had only magnified after Brighton left her. Still, she knew it wasn't Brighton's fault—or not just her fault, at least.

Brighton had wanted to make Charlotte happy by staying in New York.

She'd always wanted to make Charlotte happy, and Charlotte had let her, over and over again, let her soothe Charlotte, let her make Charlotte feel secure, feel stable, feel loved, to the detriment of her own needs.

Charlotte braced her hands on the cool quartz sink, closed her eyes, and breathed, her forehead breaking out in a sweat.

Because she missed Brighton.

Fuck, she missed her so much. She'd told herself leaving was the right thing to do, a way to love Brighton when she'd failed at doing so before. Brighton was free to follow her own dream, without having to worry about Charlotte and New York and the past.

But, really, Charlotte was running scared.

Running away.

She knew it.

Everyone knew it.

She turned on the faucet, splashed some cold water on her face. Then she opened up her makeup bag and pulled out her red lipstick. Popped the cap off, twisted up the waxy tube. She stared at the fire-engine color, her eyes blurring on the bold crimson.

She twisted it back down, put the cap back on.

Covered her mouth with a clear gloss.

Let her hair down, silver-and-brown strands curling over her shoulder.

She straightened her black sweater, smoothed her hands down her black jeans, and left the room, turning to knock on the door right next to hers.

"Sancerre, s'il vous plâit," Sloane said to the woman tending the hotel bar.

"Moi aussi," Charlotte said.

Silence spilled in between them. Charlotte told herself she was waiting until there were two perfectly pale glasses of white wine in front of them, and then she was waiting until they both took a sip.

Really, she was gathering courage. Forming words and sentences in her mind.

"Jesus," Sloane said, holding her glass up to the light. "Everything is better in Paris."

Charlotte laughed nervously, nodded, and sipped again. The wine *was* fantastic, but she had to force herself to even notice it. Sloane sat next to Charlotte on a stool, her forearms on the lacquered bar top, her eyes forward, as though she were completely content to let Charlotte buy her alcohol and never say another word.

And at this point, she just might be.

But Charlotte wasn't.

And knowing that, knowing that she actually *wanted* to connect, was a pretty huge thing for Charlotte Donovan. Best to dive in, start simple.

"Sloane, I'm sorry," she said.

Sloane angled her chin toward Charlotte, looking at her askance.

"I messed up," Charlotte went on. "I've been messing up for two years now."

Sloane turned on her stool, her body now facing Charlotte. Still, she didn't say anything. She waited, sipped her wine.

Charlotte took another drink herself, thinking through her next words. She didn't want to make excuses, but there were certain truths about her life—about her past, the effect it'd had on her present life and relationships—that she needed to explain.

That she needed to face herself.

"I'm not good at love," she said. "At any of it. Believing in it. Accepting it. Giving it."

Sloane tilted her head.

Charlotte's fingers pressed into the condensation on her glass. "My mother is . . . well, she's not a great mom. She had me as a sort of, I don't know, experiment? Then she didn't like motherhood all that much, I guess, and that's pretty much how my childhood went. She clothed me, fed me, but that was it. We didn't have any other family."

Sloane's eyes narrowed slightly, her chest rising with a deep breath.

"And then Brighton Fairbrook moved in next door," she said. And even saying her name, recounting that monumental moment in her life, on the beach at twelve, the most beautiful girl she'd ever seen calling her Lola, Charlotte couldn't help but smile.

She told Sloane their whole history, every important moment from then on, the way the Fairbrooks had taken her in as their own, how she and Brighton had played music together. She told Sloane about how her friendship with Brighton had turned into something more—kissing for the first time on the paintball field, prom, deciding to go to Berklee together, New York.

The wedding.

"She really just left you there?" Sloane asked. Her voice was soft, her expression the same, and they were both on their second glasses of wine.

Charlotte nodded. "But it wasn't all her fault. I didn't . . . I didn't know how to love her the right way back then. I was too scared."

"Of?"

Charlotte sighed. "Being alone? Losing the only person who ever really loved me?" It sounded so pathetic when she said it out loud, but it was still true. But with that truth came a freedom. A cleansing. Her chest felt more open, breathing became easier. "And then I lost her anyway."

Sloane laid a hand on her arm, said nothing.

"I'm not telling you any of this to garner sympathy," Charlotte said.

Sloane laughed. "Only you would use the word *garner* at a time like this."

Charlotte smiled. "It's still true. I just . . . I do want you to know me, Sloane. And yeah, that wasn't always the case. But it wasn't because of *you.*"

"It's not you, it's me?"

Charlotte laughed. "But it *was* me. I was embarrassed. My own mother doesn't really love me. And then the one person who I never thought would leave me . . . did. What does that say about me?"

Sloane sighed, set her glass on the bar, and took both of Charlotte's hands in hers. "It says you got a raw deal. It says your mom sucks, and you and Brighton are complicated. It says it might be harder for you to trust people, and that's understandable. But it doesn't say anything about *you* and what you're worth, Charlotte."

Charlotte's eyes filled. She shook her head, looked down. She was starting to believe that, a glimmer of truth, but after twenty-eight years, it wasn't just a flipped switch.

And maybe that was okay.

"And it says you probably need a really good therapist," Sloane added.

Charlotte laughed through her tears. "Oh, there's no probably about it. Another thing I've been terrified to try."

"Everyone needs a therapist," Sloane said, squeezing her hands. "Literally everyone. And I'll help you find one when we get back to New York."

Charlotte nodded, squeezed back. "You're a good friend."

"Damn right I am."

They both got fresh glasses of wine and ordered some brown bread with honeyed butter that they both spent at least ten minutes lauding. Charlotte felt like she could fly, a weight she'd been carrying for days—maybe years—finally lifted. Still, even with all this new lightness, there was still a part of her that felt unsettled.

Restless.

"Can I ask you a question?" Sloane asked. They'd been talking about the tour, the music, what they wanted to see during their day off in Paris in a couple of days. "As a good friend?"

"Of course," Charlotte said, but she steeled herself. Nothing that needed permission to be asked was going to have an easy answer.

"What do you want?" Sloane asked.

Charlotte frowned. "What do you mean?"

"You know what I mean," Sloane said, then ripped off a piece of bread, popped it into her mouth. "Is this it?" She waved at the hotel lobby, the dim lights, the low conversations in French happening all around them.

"Europe has always been a goal of mine," Charlotte said, and even to her own ears, she sounded like a kid reciting a memorized line for a play.

Sloane just looked at her.

Charlotte sighed, let her eyes blur on her glass of wine. She *did* want this. She wanted a life full of music, interesting cities, performance, and art. And she had all of that. She'd spent her entire adult life chasing exactly what she had right now, at this moment.

So she should feel satisfied.

Happy.

Accomplished.

And she did . . . but there was something in the very corner of her chest, a hungry fragment of her heart that wouldn't rest. Wouldn't stop wanting. A piece of her claimed by a girl with wild dark hair she'd met on the shores of Lake Michigan sixteen years ago.

Charlotte's eyes stung. "Shit," she said, looking away from Sloane, her instinct still to hide.

"Hey," Sloane said, leaning close to her. "It's okay to want that. To want *her*. It is. And it's okay to go after her. Anyone can see you love her, Charlotte. In Winter River for those few days? You were happy."

Tears finally spilled, and Charlotte didn't even bother to wipe them away. "It couldn't work. I'm in New York, and—"

"Yeah, yeah, so am I. And Wes is in Colorado."

Charlotte stopped, her mouth dropping open. "Wes?"

Sloane fought a smile, but it won over her lovely face anyway.

"What can I say? I'm a slut for people who make complete fools of themselves for me."

Charlotte laughed, clapped her hands. "Did he really play Manish's viola that night? I've wanted to ask you so many times."

"He did. And horribly. It was truly abysmal."

"And that won you over?"

Sloane sighed, her expression growing serious. "I've always loved him. I was just . . ."

"Scared."

Sloane nodded.

"And you're not anymore?" Charlotte asked, her heartbeat picking up speed.

"No, I still am." Sloane shrugged. "I'm just ready for something more than just *not* being scared, you know? Something more than safe. More than okay."

Charlotte blinked, Sloane's words settling around her. She felt herself nodding, her blood already racing with *how* and *when* and *where*.

She picked up her glass, held it up between them. "To something more than okay."

Sloane clinked her wine against Charlotte's, and they both drained their glasses to the very last drop.

chapter 30

February in Nashville was usually pretty chilly—or chilly for the South, at least—but this week before Valentine's Day was frigid, icy winds blowing through the streets, made all the colder by a crystalline blue sky and a weak winter sun.

The weather was good for the bar business, though, sending patrons indoors, making them desperate for a little warmth via the company they kept or three fingers of bourbon. Either way, Brighton leaned against Ampersand's bar, looking out at a packed house. Energy sizzled down her arms to her fingertips, heat from all the adrenaline pumping through her keeping her more than insulated against the cold air that blasted into the room every time the door opened.

This never got old.

She'd been performing at Ampersand for a little over a month now, at least twice a week, and she loved every second of every show. The audience response was good too, and she even had plans to record a performance in a few weeks, use it as a demo for other venues. She was still in the hole with her roommate, Leah—she'd been to two potluck dinners since the new year—and couldn't quite afford a studio session yet.

Still, she was *playing*.

She was creating too. Five new songs in the last month, most of them about heartbreak and trying to move on and achy memories, but that was sort of her brand. At least, it was right now, and she was just fine with that.

"Hey, hey, Ampersand!" Adele said into the mic on the small stage. "Freezing your asses off?"

Cheers went up, hands in the air clutching liquor-filled glasses.

Adele laughed. "Well, we've got a local fave here to warm you the hell up with her tales of betrayal and woe."

"Excuse me," Brighton said, even though Adele couldn't hear her.

"Give it up for Brighton Fairbrook!"

Applause rippled through the bar, along with a few whistles from regulars who knew Brighton pretty well by now. She wove through the crowd, then hopped onstage and hugged Adele before sliding her guitar over her shoulder and launching into her first song, a tune called "Good At Falling" that made her feel like a badass. She always played something energetic first, then greeted the crowd after she had hooked them. It was a strategy left over from her Katies days, one of many.

As she played, the stage lights bright and warm in her face, she couldn't help but think about the Katies, about Emily and Alice. She always did, at least once a show, but it was just that—a thought.

There was no anger anymore.

No bitterness.

Last she checked—and she checked at least once a week—the Katies had removed "December Light" from their discography. There was a lot of speculation online as to why the song had vanished, but Brighton didn't care about that. She just cared that it was gone.

That it was hers again.

Still, she hadn't played it onstage. She was doing well, but she wasn't made of steel, and that song . . . it was just too much.

Too close.

She strummed the last chord of "Good At Falling," smiling as applause broke out.

"Thank you and hello, Nashville!" she said. More hoots and hollers, the best sound other than actual good music. She talked with the audience for a few seconds, then started another song. She went on like this for a good thirty minutes before she decided to slow it down. At this point, she usually employed the stool that lived onstage, loving the more intimate feel of just sitting around with friends. She turned, reached out to pull the stool toward her, and froze.

There was something set atop the cognac pleather of the stool.

She blinked, stepped closer.

It was a stone.

No . . . beach glass.

Turquoise and in the shape of a heart.

No, silly, you need a special name. A secret name. Brighton could feel the wet sand between her fingers, smell the mineral scent of the lake. *A name just for us.*

The stone was the most perfect piece of beach glass she'd ever found. Smooth and vibrant, that heart shape unmistakable, non-replicable.

I've got it. She set the stone in Charlotte's palm. *Lola.*

Now, with the audience quiet behind her, she picked up the glass, held it in her own palm. It was the same one. She was sure of it. She whipped her head toward the crowd, eyes searching, but everyone was in shadow, their faces dark.

"Um," she said, pocketing the glass and managing to get her ass on the stool without falling off. "I'm going to slow it down a bit."

But her mind was blank, the song she was going to play just a blur of words in her brain. Her eyes still searched, darting through the room for a glimpse of silver hair, a black turtleneck.

She clutched her guitar, trying to focus on what the hell she was doing, trying to get her heart to slow down.

A song . . . a song . . .

"How about 'December Light'?"

Brighton's head turned in the direction of the voice from the audience, near the left wall.

A familiar voice.

Brighton held up her hand to shade her eyes and could just make out her form.

Lola.

Leaning against the exposed brick wall, the dim lights just catching the silver in her hair, which was loose and long, waves tumbling over her shoulders.

And there, dangling casually in her hands, as though she carried violin cases everywhere she went, was Rosalind.

"Only if you join me," Brighton said quietly into the mic. Heads turned, murmurs rippling through the room, but Brighton couldn't play this off, get the audience laughing about a surprise guest. She could barely breathe as Lola stood still for one . . . two . . . three . . .

Then Lola pushed off the wall and made her way to the stage.

Breathing didn't get any easier as she got closer, black turtle-neck and all, soft-pink lipstick instead of red. A million questions burgeoned in Brighton's mind about why Lola was here, why she'd brought her violin along, why she'd placed the glass on Brighton's stool. But there was only one plausible explanation.

Lola was here for her.

"Hi," Brighton said as Lola stepped onto the stage.

"Hi," Lola said back, smiling softly.

She was so gorgeous. Brighton still struggled to breathe prop-erly as Lola set her case down at the back of the small stage, flipped the buckles, placed her violin on her shoulder. She zipped her bow over the strings, tuning.

It had been so long since they'd played together, just the two of them. Brighton felt an elation she'd only ever felt in such moments—Lola and Bright on a stage or in her bedroom or sit-ting around the living room. Anywhere, everywhere, as long as it was them, their instruments, their music.

Lola grinned at Brighton, nodding that she was ready, and the fact that they were onstage in front of at least a hundred people came flooding back into Brighton's consciousness.

"Um, hey, you're still here," she said to the crowd. They laughed. "Sorry for the delay. This"—she held out an arm to Lola—"is Charlotte Donovan of the Rosalind Quartet."

The audience clapped, and Charlotte bowed her head, ever the picture of elegance. Brighton didn't know how she did it—inside, Brighton was crying, screaming, throwing up.

"You're all in for a real treat," she said. "And this song . . ." She looked at Lola. Lola looked at her. Smiled so softly that Brighton's throat went a little thick. "This song is called 'December Light.'"

♪

They didn't talk much at all in the car on the way to Lola's hotel.

But they did hold hands.

Right over the gearshift, fingers tangled, Brighton doing her level best to steer one-handed, as though if she let go, this whole night would end up being a dream.

She was still buzzing from the performance—after the awkward pause caused by shock and elation at Lola's presence, it was the best show she'd ever put on.

Lola stayed onstage for the rest of Brighton's set, adding her inimitable talent to her songs, even those she'd never heard, as well as playing a couple of her own pieces, violin solos that had left the crowd in hushed awe.

She was fire.

And she was water and air and earth.

She was everything as a musician.

Everything to Brighton.

Now, after talking a bit with Adele and a few enthusiastic audience members, Brighton tried to process what the hell had just happened. The whole night felt both crystal clear and like an emotional blur. She wasn't even sure how they'd ended up in her car, Lola's hotel on her navigation app. She wasn't clear on how they'd entered the lobby of the Graduate Nashville on Twentieth Avenue North, a colorful splash of pink and white and red, a giant portrait of Minnie Pearl behind the retro wooden desk.

"Wow," Brighton said.

"Yeah," Lola said, the only words they'd spoken since leaving Ampersand.

Still, Lola kept hold of Brighton's hand, and Brighton let her.

Lola's room was just as wild—pink-and-white-striped walls, a four-poster king bed with a mint-green chintz canopy, and a smiling portrait of Dolly Parton over the padded purple headboard.

Brighton had heard this hotel was kitschy, a truly unique Nashville experience, and the reality did not disappoint. Honestly, though, Brighton couldn't give two shits about this room.

She sat on the edge of the bed, watched as Lola slipped off her red heels.

Watched as Lola walked closer to her.

Watched, neck arching upward, as Lola came close enough to touch.

"Hi," Lola said.

"Hi," Brighton said back.

Lola smiled.

"You're here," Brighton said.

Lola nodded. "I'm here."

"I'm scared to ask why, but I guess I really need to know."

Lola sighed, set her hands on Brighton's shoulders, lightly, fingers twirling Brighton's hair.

"The simple answer?" she asked.

"Sure," Brighton said. "Let's start there."

"The simple answer is that I love you," Lola said softly, thumb swiping along Brighton's neck. "I always have. I always will. And I guess when you think about it, love isn't actually all that simple, but right now, I think it is. It's the best reason I've got. All the other complexities, our past, and New York, and the *how* of everything . . . I don't know those things, Bright. I don't know anything right now except that one thing."

Brighton curled her hands around the backs of Lola's thighs, her heart suddenly wild and free and young.

"You love me," she said.

Lola smiled, her eyes shiny. "I love you." She cupped Brighton's face in her palms. "And, actually, there's one more thing I know."

Brighton tilted her head. "What's that?"

"Love . . . it's a lot. It's powerful, but I'd love you whether I came here tonight or not. I'd love you in New York, and I'd love you in Paris, and I'd love you in Grand Haven."

Brighton stood so they were face-to-face, wrapped her arms around Lola's waist, pressed her forehead to Lola's.

"So the second thing I know," Lola said, "is that I want you."

Brighton lifted her head, stared into Lola's usually fathomless eyes, but right now, they were clear and bright and shining with tears.

"I want you, Brighton," Lola said, her lower lip trembling. "I'm so tired of pretending like I don't. *Lying* that I don't. I just want to be real and have . . . have something more than just okay. We've hurt each other. You left, and I left, and I didn't see you, and I know we have different lives, and we have a lot to work through, but I don't care about any of that right now. I just want you in my life. I want you as my partner. I want you as . . . as my wife. Someday. I never stopped wanting that. And if that's what you want too, I—"

But Brighton didn't let her finish. Couldn't. Because she had to kiss Lola right then, a seal, a promise.

Yes.

Kiss.

Yes.

Kiss.

"Yes," she said against Lola's mouth.

Lola smiled, then dragged in a shaky breath and kissed

Brighton harder, opening to her, sliding her tongue against Brighton's, igniting her entire body.

"I missed you," Lola said, sneaking a hand under Brighton's denim button-up.

"God, me too," Brighton said, arching her neck to give Lola's mouth better access. Her breathing was so fast, she was nearly dizzy. "How . . . how was tour?"

"Later," Lola said, pushing Brighton onto the bed, fingers going straight for the buttons on her gray jeans. "Can I?"

Brighton laughed. "Please."

Lola didn't waste any time. Brighton's pants were off in a few seconds, her purple undies removed just as fast.

"Jesus," Lola said, pushing Brighton's legs apart. "You're gorgeous."

Brighton smiled, her hips already pressing upward, her need building. Lola grinned at her squirming, then slid onto the bed between Brighton's legs until they were face-to-face. They kissed like that for what felt like forever, perfect, entwined. Finally, though, their kisses turned more heated, and Charlotte moved south. She kissed Brighton's ankles first, sliding that mouth up Brighton's shins, tonguing her calves, making Brighton groan in pleasure and frustration.

When Lola reached her thighs, she bared her teeth, biting down on the soft flesh, gently at first, then hard enough to make Brighton gasp.

"God," Brighton said.

"Too much?"

Brighton shook her head.

"Good girl," Lola said, then bit her again, nibbling along one thigh, then the other, hard enough that Brighton was sure she was leaving teeth marks.

Good.

Brighton wanted marks.

Wanted the world to know she was Lola's and Lola was hers.

"Baby, please," Brighton said as Lola's teeth worked the tendon where her leg met her hip. It made Brighton feel wild, her pussy throbbing almost painfully.

"Please what?"

"I need you inside me," Brighton said, tugging at Lola's hair. "Please. Now. I need you."

Lola slid up quickly so they were face-to-face, her still-clothed hips pressing between Brighton's legs.

"You've got me," she said, kissing Brighton sweetly once, then twice, before the kiss turned less than sweet, teeth and moans, and then she inched down Brighton's body. She unbuttoned Brighton's shirt, sucking at her nipples through her cotton bra, making Brighton swear at the ceiling.

Finally, dear god, fucking finally, Lola's fingers settled on Brighton's cunt.

"Fuck yes," Brighton said. There was nothing like that first touch, the relief of it. She bucked into Lola's hand, but Lola would not be hurried. She never could be, and Brighton loved it.

Loved her.

Lola parted Brighton, fingers slipping between her folds, so wet that Brighton could hear her arousal.

"Please," Brighton whispered. "Please."

Lola smiled, kissed her way down Brighton's body to settle on her stomach between Brighton's legs.

"Beautiful," she said almost reverently, right before she slipped two fingers inside.

"Fuck," Brighton said, her hips lifting before settling again.

"Like that?" Lola asked.

Brighton could only nod, moan.

"Or like this?" Lola asked, sliding in a third finger.

"Oh my god, yeah. Like that."

"How about this?" Lola asked, then closed her mouth around Brighton's clit, sucking and licking, teeth grazing her skin.

"Jesus, fuck, yes," Brighton said, slapping the mattress with her hand. "Lola."

Lola hummed against her, her mouth too busy to ask questions now. Her fingers pumped in and out of Brighton's pussy, twisting every now and then, her tongue working Brighton's clit, building a scream in Brighton's chest. Brighton tried to be quiet, but she'd never been good at holding back with Lola, never wanted to be. She wanted to be consumed, decimated, ruined by this feeling, the love of her life, this woman who knew her inside and out, this person who'd been everything to her for sixteen years.

This person she'd lost.

This person she'd found again.

Nothing and no one would ever compare to Charlotte Rosalind Donovan, with all her talent and intelligence and flaws and her shy heart. Lola was *love*.

And Brighton had never felt so lucky.

To know her.

To get to love her.

"Lola," she said, because just that name made her heart feel as though it were made of fairy dust, all light and brightness. Lola hummed again, setting fire to Brighton's blood, her fingers still working inside her like magic.

This was one of those moments when Brighton was sure she was the only one in the world to ever feel like this, because if everyone felt like this, the world would simply implode from happiness.

"Baby," she said, getting closer, her whole body racing toward that peak. She dug her hands into Lola's hair but then pulled at her shoulders.

Lola looked up at her.

"Up here," Brighton said, her voice raspy with need and want. "I want to see you. Feel you."

Lola slid her fingers out, then undressed silently before crawling back onto the bed, settling alongside Brighton. They kissed, her hand back at Brighton's center, three fingers sliding inside again so easily. Brighton gasped, nearly coming right then, but she held herself off, wanting to feel this desperate as she touched Lola too. She pulled one of Lola's legs over her hip, exposing her perfect cunt, so wet and pretty. Brighton's fingers didn't waste any time, sliding between Lola's folds, circling her clit. Lola tilted her head back, moaning, and Brighton pressed her mouth to Lola's neck as she slipped her fingers inside.

Lola's free hand gripped her shoulder, and she nodded, whispering *yes, yes, yes*. They moved together, fingers fucking, mouths pressed together, breathing each other's air, murmuring words to urge each other on, both sweet and wild.

"Fuck," Brighton said, her orgasm building again. "Lola."

"Don't stop," Lola said, her own hips working with Brighton's fingers, her palm pressing against Brighton's clit.

"Oh my god," Brighton said, and Lola pressed hard, her face buried in Brighton's neck, Brighton's free hand tangled in her hair, pulling until she burst, body lighting up like stars, like a supernova. Lola followed her, tensing and then crying out against Brighton's skin.

They stayed like that for a few seconds, catching their breath, fingers still inside each other, joined and content and exhausted.

Happy.

Together.

Lola and Bright.

♪

Later, after they'd taken a slow shower together, just kissing and sliding soap over each other's skin, they lay in bed, Dolly Parton big-haired and smiling above them.

Brighton's eyes felt heavy, drifting closed to the rhythm of Lola's breath on her neck as the big spoon. Still, every time she nearly fell asleep, she jerked awake, Lola's arms tightening around her.

She couldn't stop thinking about when the sun would filter in through the cherry-patterned curtains. About when they'd wake up, when their feet would hit the colorful plush carpet and they'd talk about what to order for breakfast, but *after* would be hovering in the air between them, her rooming with Leah and Lola's inevitable retreat to New York.

A question haunted her mind, one she knew she had to ask, even as she kept swallowing it down.

When the clock rolled over to 2:00 a.m. and Brighton stuttered awake for at least the fourth time, Lola sighed, pressed her mouth to Brighton's neck.

"What's going on, love?" Lola asked.

Brighton turned in her arms to face her. She could barely see her features in the dark, but it was enough. She traced Lola's cheekbones, her perfectly thick eyebrows, gathering courage.

Finally, she jumped.

"What happens next?" she asked.

Lola was quiet for a few seconds, long enough to make

Brighton feel as though Lola were just trying to find a way to fight for New York. And it wasn't like Brighton was opposed to it—she just needed to be part of the conversation.

Needed to be seen.

She and Lola had a lot of things to work through—Lola surely had her own fears and insecurities about their relationship, about Brighton's ability to be frank, to stay, just as Brighton had hangups about standing on equal footing with their careers, with their dreams, and with what fit for both of them.

And Brighton also realized that was okay.

It was okay to have things to work through. They weren't perfect, no matter how fairy-tale-esque their story of childhood best friends turned lovers might be.

She just wanted to do that work together.

"Lola?" she asked, her voice a whisper.

Lola pressed her forehead to Brighton's, kissed the tip of her nose. "Whatever we want, my love. Whatever we want. It's you and me."

Brighton breathed out. Such simple words, and certainly not a plan at all, but right now, in the middle of the night, it was enough.

It was a start.

She kissed Lola once, whispered "I love you" against her mouth, and fell asleep.

chapter 31

Charlotte Donovan used to think she was cursed. And maybe, in some small way, she had been. Cursed by her own hyper-awareness on the streets of New York. Cursed with an indifferent mother. Cursed with a heartbreak the size of the Grand Canyon.

But as she stood in her small kitchen, an apron covered in rainbow candy canes around her waist as Bonnie Fairbrook taught her how to make a flourless chocolate torte for Christmas Eve dinner, she felt anything but cursed.

"And then we pour it into the molds and we're done!" Bonnie announced. "Why don't you do that, dear?"

Charlotte nodded, taking control of the ceramic bowl and eyeing a rubber muffin pan full of half circles. As she scooped her first spoonful of batter, her eye caught on her girlfriend.

No.

Her fiancée.

As of last night, in fact.

Brighton stood by the Christmas tree in their living room—the same tree Charlotte had knelt beside when she'd asked Brighton to marry her, while their labradoodle puppy, Pistachio, had watched with curiosity—and adjusted some ornaments with her dad with one hand, sipping on a glass of wine with the other. The aquamarine ring Charlotte had given her glinted in the sparkling lights.

Charlotte smiled.

Not cursed at all.

Lucky.

The luckiest.

Back in February, after a few days of barely leaving her hotel room, after several discussions about how they'd manage long-distance, after a lot of teary snuggles in bed, Charlotte had gone back to New York. She'd found a therapist she didn't hate. She'd taught her classes, wrote and arranged her music. Things were very much the same, and they were completely different.

For one, Elle had left the quartet. Mimi, Elle's grandmother, had decided to sell her apartment at the Elora and wasn't doing all that well by herself in LA. Elle wanted to go out West to be with her. No one blamed them—the quartet knew Mimi was everything to Elle, though Manish took the break especially hard.

Charlotte kept waiting for panic to overcome her—finding another cellist of Elle's caliber was going to be tricky, and Charlotte was, of course, famously picky—but it never happened. She didn't even really feel an urgency to search for a fourth. Manish was officially dating Dorian and was in Colorado half the time anyway. And Sloane . . . well, Sloane and Wes had been reunited for all of three months before they got engaged. Wes was moving to New York to open a restaurant in Brooklyn, and musically, Sloane had been doing more and more solo work lately.

The fate of the Rosalind Quartet was uncertain.

And Charlotte was okay with that.

She was shocked by this development, having built the group herself and poured her entire soul into it for the last two and a half years. She sat with her therapist, Talia, and discussed it over several sessions.

"I don't know what's happening to me," Charlotte had said. "The Rosalind Quartet is all I've ever wanted."

"Is it?" Talia had asked, resting her iPad stylus against her orange-framed glasses. She loved turning one of Charlotte's statements into a question. "Or do you want a musical career?"

"Of course I do."

"Does it *have* to be a quartet? Or even *this* quartet?"

Charlotte had sighed. Slumped back in Talia's leather armchair. She'd thought back to playing with Brighton on Ampersand's stage in Nashville. She'd felt electric. Wild in a way she'd never felt with the quartet. She loved the quartet, of course. Loved symphony halls, the quiet and awed audience.

But she loved the singer-songwriter stage too.

And she loved directing the small ensemble she'd been asked to conduct this last semester at the Manhattan School of Music. She loved arranging and writing, performing Rachmaninoff and Charlotte Donovan originals. Brighton Fairbrook originals. She loved so many things about music, about violin.

Talia was right—her career didn't have to be Rosalind. It could be anything she wanted.

And as winter shifted into spring, more and more she wanted Brighton.

Of course she wanted her career—that would never change—but the distance between her and Brighton felt like it was tugging at her more and more every day. Brighton never pressured her, and Charlotte never considered asking Brighton to move to New York. Sure, compromise was a part of any relationship, and she knew Brighton would try it if she asked. Which, honestly, was all the more reason for Charlotte to keep New York off the table. She loved New York, but she loved Brighton Fairbrook more.

When she started looking into possible openings in the music faculty at Vanderbilt University—she knew one of the viola professors there from Berklee—she didn't tell Brighton at first. Moving to Nashville was something she realized she really wanted—not only for Brighton but also for herself. But she knew she had to have her own life in place before she made it a reality.

She wanted to do it right this time.

So when the director of the Blair School of Music at Vanderbilt offered her a violin professorship off a phone interview alone, based on Charlotte's already impressive accomplishments and reputation in the classical-music community, she took it as a sign.

It was time to say goodbye to New York.

Brighton was thrilled—though a bit adorably pouty that Charlotte had kept her plans a secret—and Charlotte moved to Nashville during a blistering July. They rented a small house in East Nashville, and Charlotte started at Vanderbilt in August. Since then, the two of them had played at least fifteen shows at Ampersand, to a growing crowd each time.

They'd named their duo Beach Glass.

And Charlotte . . . Charlotte was happy.

"I think that one's full, dear," Bonnie said.

"What?" Charlotte said, pulling her eyes away from Brighton

and looking down at a half circle overflowing with cake batter. "Oh, shoot, sorry."

Bonnie laughed, then glanced at her daughter as she slipped an arm around Charlotte's waist, squeezing her tight. "No harm done."

Charlotte laughed too, cleaned up the mess. She'd just slipped the rubber pan into the fridge to set when the doorbell rang. Pistachio erupted into a series of adorable barks, and Brighton quieted her firmly, just like the dog trainer had shown them.

"They're here!" Brighton yelled once Pistachio was calm and settled with Hank. She flew to the front door, but she paused before opening it and turned to Charlotte in the kitchen. She held out her hand. "Babe?"

Charlotte nodded, then took off her apron and hurried to join her fiancée so they could open the door to their home together. It was a small thing, even a cheesy thing, and it made Charlotte's heart feel as big as a snowy Colorado mountain.

She laced her fingers with Brighton's, kissed her knuckles, then her mouth. Brighton beamed, took a deep breath, and opened the door, letting in a burst of cold December air and a chorus of greetings as Adele, Sloane, Wes, Dorian, and Manish spilled into the house.

For a few minutes, it was a flurry of noise and hugs and introductions to Brighton's parents, but Charlotte and Brighton finally found their way to a quieter moment with Sloane and Adele by the tree.

"Okay, let me see this rock," Adele said, grabbing Brighton's left hand, where a pale aquamarine stone sat on a thick silver band, filigreed gold branches and leaves curling over the surface.

Charlotte smiled every time she saw it. So did Brighton, which was the whole point. When Charlotte had decided she wanted to ask Brighton to marry her—well, she'd always wanted to ask Brighton to marry her, from the second she decided in that hotel bar in Paris that she wanted Brighton for herself—she knew she didn't want to use their rings from their first engagement.

This was a different time.

A different Charlotte and a different Brighton.

She'd started looking for rings pretty soon after she moved to Nashville, hunting the corners of the internet for something unique and handmade. Finally, she found a queer metalworker in Seattle with an Etsy shop whose style felt exactly right for Brighton Fairbrook. After several emails, the ring on Brighton's finger was born, as one of a kind as Brighton herself.

"Wow, gorgeous," Sloane said, peering closer, her own ring glinting on her finger.

"It's perfect, baby girl," Adele said, her eyes shining as she pulled Brighton in for a hug.

"Yeah, Lola did good," Brighton said, holding her friend close and winking at Charlotte over her shoulder. "We're thinking summer."

"Not December?" Sloane asked, nudging Charlotte's shoulder.

Charlotte laughed. "Going to try something a little different."

"Good plan," Adele said. "Plus, I want to swim in Lake Michigan. I've never even seen it."

"Summer for sure, then," Charlotte said.

"You'll be my best mate?" Brighton asked Adele.

Adele tilted her head. "Like . . . ?"

"Like maid of honor," Brighton said. "But Adele, my darling, you are anything but a maiden."

Adele roared at that, then pulled Brighton into her arms again. "Hell yes. To all of that."

Charlotte and Sloane smiled at each other. Charlotte had

already asked Sloane to be her own best mate last night, when she'd texted Sloane with the engagement news. The Berry sisters were the only people they planned to have in the wedding party, and Charlotte wanted Manish to officiate. She couldn't think of anyone more perfect for the job, and she hoped Elle would be able to come east to play their cello as Brighton and Charlotte walked down the aisle.

To a new song.

One they planned to write together.

"Okay, okay, enough of that," Adele said, but she wiped under her eyes a bit as she pulled back from Brighton. "I need a drink."

"Hear, hear!" Manish said as Wes handed Sloane a glass of wine and Dorian did the same for Adele. Manish lifted his own glass. "A toast!"

Bonnie slipped glasses into Charlotte's and Brighton's hands, and they all waited while Manish grinned.

Charlotte felt like she might burst—the soft lights of their Christmas decorations, Brighton at her side, the Fairbrooks, her friends.

Her family.

She'd invited Anna . . . who had declined.

And while it hurt—her mother's indifference would never stop hurting, as Talia had helped her realize and accept— Charlotte also knew, *believed*, that Anna was the one missing out. Anna's lack of care for her daughter was just that—*Anna's*.

"To the newly engaged Charlotte and Brighton," Manish said, eyes glinting. "I never thought I'd live to see Charlotte Donovan so decidedly ungrumpy."

"Easy," Charlotte said, but she was smiling.

Manish laughed, but then he grew more serious. "And to friends. To family. To love." He winked at Dorian, who grinned back.

"To love," everyone echoed, then drank.

"All right, enough sappy sh—" Manish cut himself off, smiling wide-eyed at the Fairbrooks.

Bonnie laughed. "You can say *shit*, Manish."

"Okay, then, enough sappy shit!" Manish said. "What we all really want is a live performance by Beach Glass."

Charlotte feigned confusion. "Who are they? Sounds made-up."

But Brighton clapped and squealed, then hurried down the hall to their guest–slash–music room while everyone else settled on the turquoise sectional—a gift from Elle upon their move—and the squashy cream-colored armchairs Charlotte had brought from her own New York apartment. Wes pulled over two mismatched dining chairs from their small table and set them up in front of the tree.

"Et tu?" Charlotte asked him.

He laughed, then side-hugged her.

"How's the restaurant?" she asked.

"Great. Not quite breaking even yet, but we will. Soon. Dorian's holding down Elements in Winter River."

Charlotte smiled. "Good. And hey"—she squeezed his arm—"I never said thank you."

He frowned. "For what?"

She opened her mouth, then closed it, pausing to get the words right. "For listening to me last Christmas. For being a good friend. You didn't judge me. Didn't think less of me. You just let me spill my guts, and I think it made a big difference. In getting me to where I am now."

His expression softened. "Charlotte. You did the same for me, you know."

"Yeah, but I didn't do it on purpose."

He laughed. "Fair enough."

"But you did," she said. "You're the best guy, Wes."

He grinned. "I'm glad you think so."

She full-on hugged him then. "Take care of the best girl," she said into his shoulder, his wool sweater tickling her cheek.

"We'll take care of each other," he said.

"I know you will."

They pulled apart as Brighton came back down the hall with her guitar already strapped on, Charlotte's violin case in hand. Wes settled next to Sloane on the couch, his arm around her while she held a sleepy Pistachio in her lap, and everyone chatted while Charlotte sat down and tuned her instrument. When she finished, she didn't call everyone back together immediately. Not just yet.

"Hey," she said to Brighton, who was sitting next to her and lightly strumming her guitar.

"Hey yourself," Brighton said, tilting her head at her.

"Come here," Charlotte said, tilting her chin, an invitation for a kiss.

Their lips met, and Charlotte breathed in her love, her best friend.

"I'm gonna marry you," she said against Brighton's mouth.

"Bet your ass you are," Brighton said back.

They kissed a few more times, enough that Manish finally yelled at them to stop being so fucking cute. They pulled apart, laughing. Charlotte set her violin on her shoulder. Brighton nodded at her, fingers ready on her guitar.

And then they played.

acknowledgments

Thank you, dear readers, for coming with me on this romance journey. You are the reason I write, and I hope you have loved Brighton and Charlotte's journey as much s I have, seeing in their story your own worthiness to be lov d as you are.

Thank you, as always, to Becca Podos my agent of nearly eleven years. It's been a wild, exciting, sometimes appalling ride, and you have stuck with me, passionate and supportive, through it all.

Thank you, Angela Kim, my editor, whom I trust implicitly and who knows just how to make my overwritten stories hit the right notes. Thank you to my whole team at Berkley—Kristin Cipolla, Elisha Katz, and Tina Joell—for their tireless work and passion.

Thank you, Katie Anderson, for the incredible cover design.

Thank you, Leni Kauffman, for yet another breathtaking cover illustration. Your talent knows no bounds!

Thank you to my writing buddies—Meryl, Zabe, Emma, Mary, Christina, and Crash. You keep me laughing and believing.

Thank you, Christina Tucker, for your early read and thoughtful insight into these characters' identities and emotions. Thank you, Brooke, once again my first reader, but thank you even more for your friendship, support, and love. Thank you, Meryl, for your friendship, your love, your humor, and your tireless support. Stars and skies.

And thank you, Craig, Benjamin, and William, for cheering me on at every new turn, every new endeavor.

Ramona Riley pulled her wavy brown hair up into a high ponytail and fluffed her fringe. Her myriad freckles were glitter
free, her dark brown eyes clear of any mascara smears or extra
lashes. She had on a high-necked black-and-white top, abstract
patterns swirling over the fitted cotton. It was one of her own cre-
ations, designed years ago when she was still working on her portfolio on a daily basis. Also, she had such a hard time finding unique
pieces to fit her plus-sized figure—her boobs in particular—that
she designed most of her own clothes back then. Luckily, most of
them still fit. She smoothed her hands down her jeans just as
April smacked her on the butt.

"You look hot," April said. "In fact, let me get a shot for your
dating profile—"

"Oh, what's that, oops, can't hear you!" Ramona singsonged,
then swung open the café's door and let it fall closed in April's
face. She winked at her best friend through the glass and received
yet another middle finger.

Clover Moon Café was a diner, coffee shop, and winery all in one. The atmosphere was warm, all amber wood bars and tables, with mismatched chairs and Mason jar lights hanging down from the pine ceiling in various shades of blue and green. Ramona loved it here, and as she and April sat at the bar so Ramona could eat before her shift, she reminded herself just how lucky she was.

She loved her town.

She loved her café, even if she didn't always love the work.

And she had a best friend who loved her enough to be a pain in the ass about, well, everything.

Ramona Riley was just fine, thanks very much.

"Something's got our beloved locals ruffled," April said out of one side of her mouth.

Ramona flicked the corner of the plastic menu she knew by heart, taking in how at least three-fourths of the diners were staring at their phones and chattering a little louder than normal.

"Hey, dolls," Marion said from behind the bar, setting glasses of water down in front of them. "The usual?"

"Marion, what the hell is happening around here?" April asked.

Marion popped her gum, her eyes going wide. "You haven't heard?" She was in her fifties and had been working at Clover Moon since she was a teenager. Thus, she knew everything about everyone.

"Heard what?" Ramona asked.

Marion grinned. "You'll like this, Mona."

She took her phone out of her apron and clicked around, then handed it over to Ramona. April leaned in close to read what seemed to be a post from Penny Hampton's daily blog about the goings-on in town, aptly named *Penny for Your Thoughts*. Clover

Lake had a town newspaper, but if you wanted the gossip, the *true stories*, as Penny said, Clover Lake residents knew just where to find it.

"Holy shit," April said, always a speed reader. Ramona had barely made it past the first couple of sentences.

> For several months now, Clover Lake's mayor, Amira Gates, has been in secret—very tricky, Mayor Gates!—negotiations with Skylark Studios regarding the possibility of a feature film coming to Clover Lake's shores. Well, those negotiations are at an end, and Hollywood is indeed arriving in our beloved hamlet in three weeks' time.
>
> That's right, Cloverians, the full cast and crew for *As If You Didn't Know*, a romantic comedy based on the bestselling book, will arrive at the beginning of June. Prepare for celeb sightings and possible shutdowns for a few of our small businesses and a more-clogged-than-usual downtown. It might not be convenient, but it sure is exciting! Sources close to the mayor say the studio is paying handsomely for our cooperation, and we all know money makes the world go 'round. So buckle up for a summer like we've never had before!

"Is this for real?" Ramona asked. Penny didn't *lie* necessarily, but she'd been known to stretch the truth for the sake of drama. "This sounds—"

"Perfect," April said, already on her own phone and tapping away.

"Oh, it's true," Marion said. "The movie is one of those 'love is love' stories, so you two ought to like that."

Ramona and April—bisexual and pansexual, respectively—shared a look, though admittedly, Marion had a point. Plus, in a tiny town like Clover Lake, where minds could be a wee bit small, a queer movie taking over the streets for the summer was a pretty big deal.

"It's based on that book that Reese's Book Club picked a while back, and it hit all the bestseller lists," Marion said. "Can't remember the author's name, but—"

"Iris Kelly," April said, who had returned to typing furiously on her phone. "Queer romance author, total Leo, love her."

Marion shrugged. "Anyway, Owen confirmed it when I came in at noon. Apparently, one of the main characters is a waitress, so he's getting paid the whole hog to close down the café here and there for filming."

"Really?" Ramona said, wondering just how much the studio must be paying Clover Moon's owner. This place was Owen's whole life, had been in his family for three generations.

"Really," Marion said, taking a pen out from behind her ear and tapping it on her order pad.

"That'll be interesting," Ramona said.

"Sure will," Marion said, then sauntered away to put in Ramona's turkey sandwich order.

Ramona took a sip of water just as April grabbed her arm, nails digging into the soft flesh above her elbow.

"Ow," she said flatly, nearly choking on a swallow of water, but April didn't budge, her eyes glued to her phone.

"Noelle" was all she said.

"As in . . . Christmas?" Ramona asked.

April finally looked up. "As in Yang."

Ramona felt her breath go still in her lungs. She blinked, but couldn't seem to get her mouth to close, her brain to properly compute. Noelle Yang was a costume designer. A legend. Had studied at RISD as well, decades ago, moved out to LA and famously camped out in front of Emmeline Roth's trailer on the set of *When Skies Collide* until the iconic designer agreed to speak with her. Noelle was even escorted off the set in handcuffs a few times, though Emmeline never pressed charges. As the story went, Emmeline finally grew so fed up with seeing Noelle's face peering into her windows, she let the twenty-two-year-old present her portfolio just to get the girl out of her hair.

What Emmeline saw changed both of their lives. They started a mentorship that lasted five years until Noelle got the chance to lead a design team for *Better Off Dead* and promptly won an Oscar for the costume design. Since then, she'd dressed actors in rom-coms, science fiction adventures, indie films no one understood, and mythological fantasies. She *was* Hollywood costume design.

And Ramona's idol since she was nine and fell in love with the costumes in *Greatness*, a sexy romp of a movie about Catherine the Great that won Noelle her third Oscar.

Now, Ramona finally managed to swallow. "What about her?"

April couldn't keep the smile off her face. "You know what about her." She turned her phone so Ramona could see the *Variety* article she was reading about *As If You Didn't Know*, a paragraph that featured Noelle's name and the words *leading the design team for the queer rom-com* highlighted from April's cursor.

"This is it," April said, turning her phone back around and scrolling.

"This is what?" Ramona said.

"The *thing*," April said, waving a hand around. "The thing that's going to *shift your perspective and deepen your understanding of your life's purpose.*"

Ramona slow-blinked. "Are we really talking about my horoscope right now?"

"Of course we are," April said.

Ramona pressed her fingers into her eyes. Yes, of course they were. This was April, who pretty much based her days on Madame Andromeda's weekly astrology column.

"I thought *the thing* was supposed to happen this week," Ramona said. "Cast and crew don't show up for another three."

April just stuck out her tongue.

Ramona chuckled, but inside, her stomach was in knots. Noelle Yang. In Clover Lake. In this café even, getting coffee to get through her day. Or maybe a croissant. Clover Lake's famous honey whiskey pie, which Ramona had recently perfected baking.

Ramona's mind flashed to her portfolio, the designs filling her sketchbook, the myriad files on her digital program, the fully realized garments she'd sewn herself filling up the spare room in her father's house, no one to wear them, no one to flourish inside their seams.

Once upon a time, she dreamed about exactly this kind of opportunity. As a RISD student, walking the same halls as Noelle had years before, planning out her own destiny to get herself to LA, get herself noticed, refusing to take no for an answer. Dressing actors in ornate gowns, warrior garb, or even a simple pair of jeans and a cardigan—the clothes that made actors come alive, made stories feel *real*.

And then her dad got hurt, her family needed her, and all that just . . . faded.

And now it was too late.

Wasn't it?

"Who else is in the film?" she asked April, just to give herself something else to focus on. She hoped they were actually queer actors and not some popular hets playing at being gay.

April scrolled and paused, scrolled and paused. She smiled. "Aubrey Daniels. She's playing Mallory. God, I'm so excited this book is going to be a movie."

Ramona snapped in approval, as Aubrey was a vocal lesbian and recently started dating the singer Reneé Ramirez.

"Who's playing Eloise?" Ramona asked, laying her napkin in her lap. She'd read *As If You Didn't Know* last year, just like everyone else in the world once Reese picked it for the book club, but she'd been an Iris Kelly fan for a few years, since both she and April devoured any queer romance they could get their hands on.

April's eyes narrowed, scanning her screen, then widened. "Oh, shit."

"What? Who is it?" Ramona picked up her water and took a sip.

April looked up, mouth hanging open slightly. "It's Dylan," she said softly. "Dylan Monroe."

And with that, Ramona not only spit her beverage all over her lap, but also dropped her drink, sending ice and water and shattered glass all over the pine floors of Clover Moon Café.

Ashley Herring Blake is an award-winning author. She loves coffee, cats, melancholy songs, and happy books. She is the author of the adult romance novels *Delilah Green Doesn't Care*, *Astrid Parker Doesn't Fail*, and *Iris Kelly Doesn't Date*, the young adult novels *Suffer Love*, *How to Make a Wish*, and *Girl Made of Stars*, and the middle grade novels *Ivy Aberdeen's Letter to the World*, *The Mighty Heart of Sunny St. James*, and *Hazel Bly and the Deep Blue Sea*. She's also a coeditor of the young adult romance anthology *Fools in Love*. She lives on a very tiny island off the coast of Georgia with her family.

VISIT ASHLEY HERRING BLAKE ONLINE

AshleyHerringBlake.com

𝕏 ⓞ AshleyHBlake

ⓟ AEHBlake